Praise for Joshua Corin's debut novel
WHILE GALILEO PREYS

"I never understood what spine-tingling meant
until I read this book."
—*San Francisco Book Review*

"Joshua Corin is a new name to watch
in crime fiction. Fearless, inventive and intuitive,
his writing is incredibly self-assured."
—J.T. Ellison, bestselling author of *The Cold Room*

"Enjoyable thriller [with] faultless action scenes."
—*Publishers Weekly*

"Corin has created a quirky,
savvy profiler in Esme Stuart and
a first-rate antagonist in the sniper.
Readers are going to hope Corin has
a whole series of books planned for Esme."
—*RT Book Reviews*

"For suspense/thriller fans like me,
author Joshua Corin is a dream come true. The
intensity levels were insanely high throughout this
book from beginning to end. I couldn't get enough."
—*Manic Readers*

"An excellent, bone-chilling tale.
The plot is tightly woven, and the action doesn't
stop until the last page. I look forward to seeing
more of Mr. Corin's work. This is a must read."
—*Romance Reviews Today*

Also by Joshua Corin

WHILE GALILEO PREYS

JOSHUA CORIN

BEFORE CAIN STRIKES

MIRA®

Recycling programs for this product may not exist in your area.

ISBN-13: 978-0-7783-2933-6

BEFORE CAIN STRIKES

For questions and comments about the quality of this book please contact us at Customer_eCare@Harlequin.ca.

www.MIRABooks.com

Printed in U.S.A.

To my niece Abby
(for when she is much, much, much older)

Prologue

We are a nation of outlaws. It's in our history.
It's in our blood.

Our first colony in Massachusetts was settled as a sanctuary and refuge for those souls brave enough to defy the Anglican Church. These men and women were the first American heroes and they were rebels one and all. That their ancestors should rise up one hundred and fifty years later and throw off the shackles of British tyranny was inevitable. What was the Civil War, really, but a re-creation of the Revolution from a Southern point of view?

We are not a people who respond well to authority.

Is it any wonder, then, where our sympathies lie? *Of course* the chroniclers of the Wild West preferred Billy the Kid to Pat Garrett. *Of course* we all know the legend of Butch Cassidy and the Sundance Kid, but how many of us can mention—or even care about—the Pinkerton detectives who were on their trail?

Look at our literature. Look at our theater. Time and again, our fascination sides with the felon, the ne'er-do-well, the desperado.

By sales alone, who is the most popular American comic

book character of the twentieth century? Not that "over-grown Boy Scout" Superman. Not "guilt-ridden" Spider-Man. According to industry experts, the most popular comic book character of the twentieth century was the shadow-dwelling vigilante Batman. *Of course* he was.

It's no surprise that we as a nation have become so fascinated by serial killers. As an ever-growing government has euthanized our convictions and emasculated our passions, we recognize in the serial killer a figure of unabashed liberty, and we are attracted.

Let there be no misunderstanding: murder is reprehensible. The thesis of this text will be an analysis of the recent series of murders committed by Henry "Galileo" Booth in the context of the outlaw mystique. If you are looking for a championing of men such as him, look elsewhere. There is a vital line between attraction and acceptance.

John Dillinger is much more appealing from afar.

Nietzsche in *Beyond Good and Evil* wrote that when we gaze into the abyss, the abyss gazes back into us. Hold my hand. Take a breath. The abyss we are about to study in its dark geography is at the very core of America and its honesty cleanses with acid.

Are you ready?

Let's begin.[1]

---

[1] Kirk, Grover. *Galileo's Aim: The Murders That Fascinated a Nation.* New York: Barrow Press. 2012: ii–iv. Published posthumously.

1

Timothy's first pet was a yellow-haired hamster named Dwight. Dwight came with his own glass container and his own wheel and Timothy's parents placed it all on a folding table by a window in Timothy's bedroom. Timothy was six years old. Dwight was his birthday gift. The next morning, after he and his mother fed Dwight his breakfast (a lettuce leaf), Timothy's mother left her son alone in his room with the creature. Timothy sat cross-legged in the center of his mint-green carpet and held Dwight in his hands and ran his fingers along the rodent's spine. The vertebrae reminded Timothy of a pipe cleaner. In nursery school, he built a man and a woman out of pipe cleaners. Timothy bent the hamster's spine this way and that way. Through it all, the animal kicked and kicked, so Timothy held him firm with his left hand and ran the fingertips of his right hand along the thin yellow fur and the ridges of Dwight's spine, which, again like a pipe cleaner, was so bendable, but just how bendable was it? Timothy grabbed Dwight's hindquarters and twisted. Dwight's feet kicked and kicked and kicked and kicked and then stopped kicking altogether and Timothy had his answer.

He opened the window in his bedroom and tossed the corpse out and told his parents in between sobs that Dwight had fallen. They consoled him. His father, a travel agent, helped Dwight bury the animal and took his son out for ice cream. Three weeks later, his mother, a veterinarian, got him a tabby. Timothy named the cat Boots. Boots, to her credit, lasted many months longer than Dwight, until Timothy was able to finally reach his father's tools, which were kept on a wall in the garage. Dwight chose the claw hammer, which proved doubly useful because he was able to later use it as a shovel to bury Boots in their neighbor's yard.

So his parents bought him another cat.

Then another.

Then a puppy.

Then a parakeet.

Then a pair of goldfish in a sealed aquarium.

The goldfish he poisoned with Drano. By then he was nine years old. The goldfish were his last pets for a long, long time.

Until today.

And today was a very special day not only because he had a new pet on a new birthday but because he had acquired her all by himself. No one else knew about her, which was fine by him. Pets were personal. And she was his.

Her name was Lynette. She had yellow hair—much like Dwight, actually—and a pair of eyes so blue they reminded Timothy of wrist veins. His were prominent. He used to wonder if he had the same number of skin layers as everyone else, but a simple dissection with a straight razor (from his dad's shaving kit) and a microscope (from his old grammar school) solved that mystery.

Lynette's limbs were meaty. Her whole body was, really. Whoever had owned her before him had fed her well. Catching her had been easy but transporting her had been a challenge. Timothy ended up stuffing her in a heavy-duty duffel bag he bought at an army surplus store and dragging her. No one asked questions. Why would they? By the time he brought her down the wooden steps of the unfinished basement and deposited her in the corner, his heart was pounding a cocaine rhythm and his vision had become misty with exhaustion. He left her zipped in the bag, climbed the stairs to the kitchen and poured himself a tall glass of ice water. That did the trick.

Then he returned to the basement and unzipped the bag. Lynette was still unconscious. Her bare chest—as amorphously plump as the rest of her—languidly crested and troughed. He looked to see if there were any scorch marks on her neck where he had Tasered her. That was when he noticed the dime-size mole at the bend of her left clavicle. He fingered its spongy texture. Hmm. He might have to take her to see a doctor. The mole could be cancerous. He filed that thought in the back of his mind and secured the leather collar around her thick throat and gathered the almost-empty duffel bag from under her and brought it with him to the wooden stairs. He had made it halfway up when Lynette made a noise.

Was it a conscious moan? Timothy wasn't sure. He remained fixed on that middle step and watched her. She lay fifteen feet away and, yes, she was beginning to awaken. Good. Good. He gently placed the duffel bag on an upper step, all the while keeping his gaze firmly on her body. Forearms twitched. Legs stretched. Eyes opened. Those eyes as blue as wrist veins. They belonged to him now. She belonged to him now. It was time for introductions.

"Hi," he said. The timbre of his voice quavered. Was he nervous? Of course he was. Lynette was the first pet that was truly his. "I'm Timothy. Today is my birthday. Welcome to your new home."

Her blue eyes widened. She saw him, standing there. Her mouth formed words. Her brow formed confusion. Those eyes flickered from Timothy on the stairs to the cement walls around her, to the eleven feet of heavy chain attached from her collar to a rafter ten feet above her, and then to her own bare thighs and breasts and finally to her arms, which used to conclude with long lovely hands but now ended only with…

Well, he'd declawed her.

Oh, how she screamed. And screamed. And screamed.

"Poor thing," muttered Timothy. "You're going to need to be housebroken."

She rushed forward. The chain yanked her back. She rushed again. She bared her teeth. She cried out something like *"What have you done to me?"* but Timothy wasn't paying attention. By then he'd reached the top of the stairs and shut the basement door.

It was lunchtime.

If there was any surefire way to domesticate an animal, it was with food. Wasn't that how his parents had tried to domesticate him? Timothy removed the remaining items from the duffel bag and then tossed it aside. Most of the items were, of course, Lynette's clothes. Those might come in handy later, but for now, they were useless, so he folded them up, just as he'd been taught, and placed them on top of the discarded bag. He had never folded a bra before. That proved the trickiest. He ended up doubling it over, cup onto cup. That seemed to be the thing to do. Then he returned to the kitchen and picked up the other items from the bag and placed them on the counter.

This wasn't his house, so he had to search for a pan and utensils. He finally found what he needed and set the pan on top of the gas stove and almost activated the burner when he realized he was skipping a very important step. His mother would have been very angry with him. Before cooking the meat, he needed to debone it.

That took some time, not because he was inexpert at what he was doing but because there seemed to be so many tiny bones to take away. Gradually, the garbage bin underneath the sink filled up with inches and inches of slender joints and ligaments, and all the while, from below, Lynette screamed. A bread-box-size TV hung below one of the kitchen cabinets and Timothy clicked it on. Lynette's voice, which was quickly hoarsening, was drowned out by a rerun of *Law & Order*. By the time the court case had begun, he had vegetable oil and soy sauce sizzling in the frying pan. By the time the shocking verdict was reached, he had fried the sliced boneless meat to a handsome brown.

The kitchen smelled like summertime.

Excited, Timothy switched off the burner. He forked several slices onto a green ceramic plate, sprinkled on some herbs he'd found in the cabinet above the TV and carried the meal, along with some eating utensils, to the basement door. Lynette had to be hungry and the fried flesh had a savory aroma that even a vegan couldn't resist. Not that Lynette, by all appearances, was a vegan. Timothy opened the basement door and descended into her home.

She was crouched on the floor in the corner. Her long

blond hair was moist with sweat and clung to her face like fresh-spun silk. Through the silky yellow, though, peered those blue eyes. He saw hatred in those eyes. That would change.

"I've brought you lunch," he said. "Doesn't it smell good?"

"Let…me…go," she rasped. All that screaming had really done a number on her vocal cords. Timothy regretted not carrying down a glass of water to accompany the meal. So thoughtless! He promised to reprimand himself later.

"Don't you want some nice steak, Lynette? I made it all for you."

"How…do you know…my name?"

"Why wouldn't I know your name? You're mine." He smiled at her. "And I also went through your wallet."

Her eyes briefly went to the meat, then back to his face.

"Why are you…doing this?"

Timothy's smile turned upside down. Had he chosen poorly? When he first spotted her in the library, those blue eyes so intent on the words in that thick paperback, he'd assumed she was intelligent. The last thing he wanted was a dumb pet.

"Please," he said. "Have something to eat. The food's not poisoned, if that's what you're thinking." He speared a slice with the fork and slid the thin wet flesh into his mouth. It was gamey, but the soy sauce and the herbs really added flavor. He chewed, swallowed, smiled. "See?"

Did her throat swell with a bated gulp? With that leather leash bound so tight, it was so difficult to tell. Timothy took a step forward. He speared another slice and held it out to her, mere inches from her nostrils.

She stared at it.

Timothy was certain Lynette had an appetite. It had nothing to do with her size. She had been through an ordeal, and animals dealt with stress via sex and/or food. He was just trying to make her comfortable. He wanted this relationship to work. After Dwight and the puppy and—

She reached forward and with her teeth she sucked the meat off the fork. Timothy wanted to clap, but that would have meant putting down the plate. Instead, he took another step forward. Now maybe fourteen inches away from her.

"Thank you," she muttered. Her lips gleamed with steak blood. "What is it?"

"*You* should know, silly. It's *your* left hand. Silly, silly pet. Want some more?"

With his left hand, he loaded another slice onto the fork and brought it to her mouth. He almost made an airplane noise.

Briefly, their breaths intermingled. This, finally, was intimacy. Timothy felt warm inside. This was true love, an owner to his pet.

And then she forcefully chomped down on his left wrist. Timothy recoiled, but her jaw held fast. Her incisors pierced his paper-thin flesh and dug deep into his plump antebrachial vein. Blood squirted into her throat and almost made her gag but she held fast and squeezed tighter with her jaw. She wanted to hear his bones snap. She heard something shatter but that was just the ceramic plate with the pieces of her hand, her hand, her hand…

She opened her mouth briefly for air—she needed to breathe, she needed to throw up!—and that's when Timothy stabbed the fork into one of those blue eyes that had attracted him so, stabbed her all the way into the soft tissue of her frontal lobe. Blue ran red. Blue ran red.

Timothy took a step back. He held his gnawed wrist to his chest. He would need a tourniquet. But first he took one last, long, disappointed look at Lynette. What a bad, bad pet she had turned out to be.

He found a first aid kit upstairs, in a bathroom attached to the master bedroom, and after dousing his wrist in fiery iodine, wrapped it tightly in toilet paper and then Ace bandages. It was a temporary solution, but it would have to suffice. While upstairs, Timothy wandered the halls. This wasn't his house, but he knew the occupants wouldn't be back for another twelve days (according to the information he'd gleaned at his father's travel agency). He tested each of the three beds. The king-size in the master bedroom was the most comfortable—firm but not too stiff. Timothy wanted to take a nap. His left hand felt…well, felt nothing at all, and he knew that was not a good sign. Begrudgingly, he roused himself from the king-size bed and made his way back downstairs to the kitchen. It was time to go.

But first, the photographs.

He slid out an iPhone from his jeans pocket. Taking pictures was not his cup of tea, but Cain42 had posted strict requirements, and Timothy intended to meet them all. Of course, he hadn't intended to meet them today—he'd hoped to have a lot more time with his pet—but c'est la vie. He ambled down the wooden stairs into the basement and aimed his smartphone's camera at his expet. She lay crumpled in the corner. Her head lolled to the side like an infant's. Timothy quickly snapped off a series of pictures and reviewed them on the camera's

LCD screen. They weren't the most original photographs in the world—for one, the sixty-watt lighting in the basement dispersed in uneven patches and cast some unfortunate shadows across Lynette's corpse—but they would have to do. Timothy slid his iPhone back into his jeans pocket, waved goodbye with his good hand to the one-eyed blonde in the corner and returned to the kitchen. Now it was time to go.

He dialed the gas stove. It activated with a hiss. He then opened the nearby microwave door, snagged six cans of Campbell's soup from the pantry shelves and hefted them one by one onto the microwave's glass plate. The microwave door closed with an agreeable click. Hiss, click. Such pleasant sounds a kitchen made. He set the timer for thirty minutes and hightailed it for the back door. He had no idea how long the metal cans would take to spark and ignite, and he didn't want to take any chances.

As it turned out, he was able to make it all the way to the end of the residential block before the kitchen exploded. One of Cain42's cardinal rules: the cleanest crime scene is a destroyed crime scene. Glass splattered onto the front lawn. Flames licked through the open windows at the house's placid green exterior. Green became black. Soon everything on that plot of land— the master bedroom, the grass, the remains of Timothy's pet—would be black.

Fire always painted in monochrome.

Timothy inconspicuously joined the gathering crowd come to watch the fireworks. There weren't many people, really. Most of the suburban neighborhood's occupants were at work. But there were enough to blend in, at least until the M7 bus arrived and Timothy was whisked far away from the blaze. The bus left the curb as the first of the fire engines showed up. Timothy hoped none of the firefighters got injured. Good people, firefighters.

He unrolled his earbuds, plugged them into his iPhone and listened to an album of Brahms lullabies as the Sullivan County bus traveled into the next town over. Once there, he transferred to a Trailways bus, which deposited him a few dozen miles east to New Paltz. By then it was dusk, dusk on his birthday. From the New Paltz terminal, Timothy used some cash from Lynette's wallet, which he had in his other pocket, to pay for a cab home.

Another of Cain42's rules: always hunt far from where you sleep.

Timothy's house was not far from historic Huguenot Street, a minivillage of Colonial America located in the heart of New Paltz. When he was much younger, sometime between the cats and the goldfish, Timothy's parents took him to Huguenot Street to tour rustic Locust Lawn and the nearby spacious Ellis House, with its spooky Queen Anne interior. All the while, folks dressed up in colonial drapery mingled to and fro. Many of them were students at the local university looking to earn a few extra bucks. Even at that young age, Timothy found the whole affair to be delightfully weird. He longed to live in the Ellis House, and often wondered how difficult it would be to break in, and steal a nap on that small, square, starched bed.

Timothy apparently had a thing for other people's beds.

His own bed lay in a two-story American foursquare on a street lined with two-story American foursquares. All were squat, with faces made of brick and stucco. Most had cookie-cutter porticos bookending their front doors, which were various shades of white. Timothy only recognized his by rote. He offered the cabdriver a modest tip and hopped out onto the well-trimmed front lawn. Old, knee-high bushes bracketed the two short steps that led from lawn to landing. Timothy had several pets buried in the soil behind those bushes. He thought of them with fondness every time he opened his front door.

"There he is!" he heard his mother say, and this kept him from bounding up the stairs to his bedroom. Instead, he made his way into the den. Mother sat in her chair, predictably engrossed in her needlepoint. Today's project was embroidering the smiley face of Christ Jesus onto a mauve cushion. She donated all of her needlepoint to the local Salvation Army, where she volunteered every Saturday from ten to two.

He stood in the middle of the den. She didn't look up from her needlepoint. "Your father and I weren't sure if you were going to come home. And on your birthday, no less."

Timothy noted that she didn't ask him where he'd been or what he'd been doing. Both she and his father stopped asking him that a long time ago.

The Ace bandages swathing his left wrist were becoming caked with blood. "I got bit by a dog," he said.

At this she raised her eyes from her work. "Oh, Timothy, come here." There was no concern in her voice, only disappointment.

He approached. Carefully, Timothy's mother unwrapped his bandages and examined the wound.

"Did you disinfect it?" she asked.

"Yes, ma'am."

She sniffed the iodine and nodded. "Good boy. Nevertheless, you're going to need stitches."

"Yes, ma'am."

She peered at his face, trying to read it. What could

she see? What did she know? It didn't really matter, because at that moment the garage door roared open. Father was home.

Quickly, she brought Timothy to the first-floor bathroom, rinsed his wrist under the faucet and reached down for her emergency supplies below the sink. She had an ample stock: antiseptics, gauze, a suture kit, etc. She got a discount through her veterinary practice. Timothy had a habit of getting cut up.

"Hello!" bellowed Father. "I'm home!"

"One minute!" she replied. Although much of the skin on her son's thin forearm had darkened a nasty purple, the broken vein itself had already clotted nicely. The sutures could wait until after dinner. She rewrapped his wrist in gauze, sealed the bandages with a metal clip and brought Timothy back out to the den.

Father was holding a large box.

"Happy birthday!" he declared.

"Thank you, sir."

While the box was placed on the dining room table, Mother sifted into the sideboard for candles, and then quickly went upstairs for the matches. She kept them hidden.

"Did you have a good day, sport?"

"Yes, sir."

"Good, good."

Their gazes never met. If Timothy's father had noticed the bandages, he hadn't reacted. Timothy didn't expect him to.

As Mother returned with the matches, the rectangular cake was removed from its box. German chocolate cake with genuine coconut pecan frosting. His favorite. Mother haphazardly arranged the pinky-size birthday candles across the cake's surface, lit one and used it to light the others.

"Make a wish, sport."

Timothy closed his eyes. He thought about Lynette. He thought about what went wrong. He thought about her blue eyes. He thought about Cain42. He couldn't wait to send him the pictures.

He thought about his next pet.

There were so many possibilities.

With a deep breath, Timothy blew out his candles in one gust, all fourteen of them. Happy birthday to him.

2

"And that's my point, Esme," said Rafe Stuart. "That's what I've been getting at all this time. You're knowingly and willfully killing our family."

Before Esme could respond, Dr. Rosen—a teensy, wrinkly pink woman in a green corduroy dress—cleared her throat repeatedly and yanked on her left earlobe. Dr. Rosen did this often. She claimed it was a combination of congestion caused by seasonal allergies and, well, being seventy-eight years old. Nevertheless, as a marriage counselor, she had come highly recommended.

Esme patiently waited until Dr. Rosen's fit passed, all the while wanting to give the bite-size old woman something, anything, to ease her discomfort. But Esme had quickly learned during their first session so many weeks ago, when Dr. Rosen had vehemently pushed away an offered blister pack of Sudafed, that any assistance offered in this office was strictly one-way. This office, part of a three-story walk-up in downtown Syosset, twenty minutes from their home in Oyster Bay. Their home, which Esme was apparently, knowingly and willfully killing by, what, serving as a consultant for the FBI?

"Bullshit," Esme answered.

Dr. Rosen leaned forward in her black leather chair, which, given her diminutive size, nearly swallowed her whole. "I think that statement calls for elaboration, Esme."

Esme looked to her husband, who sat at the other end of the long divan. His arms were crossed. His jaw was clenched. If she'd had to paint a portrait of Rafe in the months since all this had begun, it would have to include this: arms crossed, jaw clenched. She supposed it was a posture of defense, but that implied she was the assailant here, and she wasn't, was she? There were no villains in this circumstance, right?

"What I mean to say," she added, after a calming hesitation, "is that, well, to call what I'm doing intentionally hurtful? That I would want to bring conflict into our household?"

"You brought Galileo into our household."

And there it was. The elephant in the room. He didn't resent her for going back to work. He wasn't that prehistoric. He resented her because of Henry Booth, a crazed sniper who called himself Galileo and eluded national authorities until Special Agent Tom Piper, who Rafe hated, brought Esme out of her early retirement to help track him down. But at what cost? Time on the case had meant time away from home, away from Rafe, away from their six-year-old daughter, Sophie. In the end, in a bit of caustic irony, Booth invaded Esme's home and took Rafe and Sophie captive. A bit of last-minute ingenuity ended Booth's menace, but her husband and daughter had come so close to becoming casualties.

These were her sins.

And yet—

"Should we move to Iceland?" she asked.

Rafe raised an eyebrow. "Iceland?"

"I mean, it's really just one city and the temperature does tend to drop into the negatives six months out of the year, but they've got practically no crime rate, so we should move to Iceland. We'll have to take Sophie out of school, of course, and away from her friends, but she'll be safer. In fact, why doesn't everyone move to Iceland?"

"Esme…"

"Or Yemen. The crime rate in Yemen is, if you can believe it, even lower than in Iceland! There's the whole Sunni thing, but I think I'd look good in a burka, don't you, Rafe?"

"There's a difference between overreacting and performing common due diligence."

"I *am* performing due diligence! Do you know how many lives the FBI has saved in the six months—six months!—since I rejoined as a consultant? Do you, Dr. Rosen? No, you don't, because if we do our job correctly, it doesn't make the headlines. Balancing all of this hasn't been easy, but it's been necessary. It's been the right thing to do. And you talk to me about due diligence. I love my family, and for you to even suggest otherwise, Rafe, makes me want to fucking clock you upside the head."

"Okay," interjected Dr. Rosen. "And that's our hour for this week."

She scooted out of her chair and held out her arms. Every session ended with a hug to each of them, and then the requisite hug between husband and wife. Dr. Rosen was a big fan of rituals. Esme and Rafe eyeballed each other. Who would stand first? It was an unspoken game of chicken that they played. But after the past five minutes, Esme was not in the mood for games.

She stood, and left Rafe in her shadow as she embraced

their tiny therapist, carefully patting her potato-chip bones. By the time Esme stepped aside, Rafe was on his feet, and it was his turn. His black beard, shaggier than usual, brushed against the top of Dr. Rosen's white scalp.

And then it was their turn.

So they wrapped their arms around each other and squeezed. It was awkward and emotionless and lasted all of three seconds. Then they turned to Dr. Rosen. Did they have her permission to leave?

Dr. Rosen sighed, sounding very much like a deflating balloon. "My mother, may she rest in peace, always taught me to be frugal. 'Never waste,' she said. She was a good woman."

Rafe and Esme exchanged a confused glance.

"She raised two daughters, myself and my sister, Betty. She raised us all by herself, and in a community where women just didn't raise two daughters alone. Our mother's solution to every problem was always the same—preemption. Keep the problem from happening in the first place. Frugal, you see, even when it came to making mistakes."

"Um?" said Rafe.

But Dr. Rosen continued unabated. "Betty and I developed different ideas about problem solving. Neither of us had the foresight of our mother, so our methods were more reactive. I came to believe that the best solutions were reached through compromise. Betty, on the other hand, has more of a, shall we say, scorched-earth philosophy. So I became a marriage counselor and what did Betty choose to become?"

"A lawyer," Esme whispered. "She handles divorces."

Sometimes she did not enjoy her gift for riddles.

"That's right." Dr. Rosen smiled. "Very good. And so here we are."

Rafe raised an eyebrow. "What are you getting at?"

"She thinks we went to the wrong Rosen sister," replied Esme. "Don't you?"

Dr. Rosen shrugged her itty-bitty shoulders.

"So, wait, you're giving up on us?"

"You tell me, Rafe. Why should I invest my time and energy when you and your wife are unwilling to invest yours?"

"Because we're paying you!"

"How can I with a clear conscience continue to accept your money when I know it's just being thrown away?"

"Is that how you feel?" asked Esme, her voice still mouselike. "We have no hope?"

Again, Dr. Rosen shrugged.

'This is bullshit," Rafe grumbled.

"So prove me wrong," replied the doctor. "I'll give you two weeks. Today is Wednesday, November 10. Come back here on Wednesday, November 24, and show me that I am wrong and I will gladly offer an apology. And if I'm right, I'll put you in touch with my sister and that will be that."

"You're giving us an ultimatum."

"I'm doing you a favor. Two weeks, boys and girls. Good luck. And drive home safe. It's supposed to drop below freezing tonight."

They drove home, predictably, in silence. Dr. Rosen had been right: the weather had taken a turn for the chilly. Rafe kept an eye out for black ice. This helped to keep his mind distracted. Esme had no such luck. The dying trees they passed on the highway offered little respite from her dark, dark thoughts.

Eight years of marriage. Love, a family, a life.

A beautiful child.

Esme knew they were having trouble, but were they really that close to the edge? Could six months put an end to eight years? The math alone didn't make sense, but very little of this did. Why couldn't Rafe just be supportive? She stood by him through his dissertation defense, his job search, his battle for tenure. She had never asked him to scale down his responsibilities. She would never have asked him to give up on his passions.

There he sat, less than an arm's length away. Had he looked at her once since they left the therapist's office? What was he thinking? She could ask him, but she already knew his answer would be "Nothing," and that would be that.

Despite it all, she still loved him.

His lenses on his glasses were dirty. He rarely cleaned them himself, not out of laziness but plain apathy. How could he see out of them? She wanted to reach for his glasses case, take out that cheap piece of microfiber cloth that came with it and wipe his lenses clean right now, while he was driving. Six months ago, she would have. He would have protested and then he would have pretended to be blind and he would have forced her to take the wheel and it would have been fun.

Only six months ago.

They drove home in silence and pulled into their affluent neighborhood. The digital clock on the Prius's dash read 9:22 p.m. Sophie should be in bed by now. During the Galileo incident, Rafe's ornery father, Lester, had come down from upstate to help out and, well, never left. On one hand, this meant they had a babysitter whenever she and Rafe wanted some alone time. On the other hand, this meant that every day she had to put up with the old man's judgmental mutterings. He did not like her, had never liked her, and made no apologies for it.

As they neared the driveway of their two-story colonial, they could tell something was wrong. There was a car already in the driveway, not Lester's old Cadillac, which was in the shop, but a fat, immaculate white Studebaker. It was blocking Rafe's spot in the garage. There were lights on in the house, but the curtains were drawn.

"Are we expecting guests?" asked Esme.

Rafe shook his head and pulled alongside the Studebaker.

They had a gun in their bedroom, locked in the bottom drawer of Esme's night table. But Esme shuffled that overreaction to the back of the line and got out of the car. They were safe here in Oyster Bay. Yes, their home had been violated once before, but that had been a special case. To panic only gave credence to her absurd suggestion about Iceland. She looked over at Rafe.

He remained in the car.

"It's okay," she told him.

"You don't know that," he replied.

This wasn't cowardice. This was textbook post-traumatic stress disorder. Henry Booth had almost killed him. She wanted to reach back into the car and give her husband a real hug, a protective hug, a hug to keep away all the demons. But she couldn't.

Instead, she walked toward the front door.

Who would be visiting them at nine-thirty on a Wednesday night? There was a Florida license plate on the back of the Studebaker, so whoever it was had driven a long way. And nobody traveled one thousand miles for a surprise visit, not even one of Lester's old buddies.

Esme reconsidered her overreaction.

She glanced back at the Prius. Rafe remained paralyzed. He probably wanted to move. He probably was willing his muscles to move. But they weren't responding. Esme assumed he was thinking about Sophie, about his father, inside the house, possibly in danger, about her perhaps even, unarmed, her hand now on the doorknob. But still, his hands remained on the steering wheel and his legs didn't budge an inch. No, she wasn't upset with him. She pitied him. The cold air misted the breath in front of her lips, and through the dissipating mist, she turned the unlocked doorknob and opened the front door.

There was a stranger in the den. He had a glass of wine in his hand. His head looked like a penis. It was bald, ruddy, oblong, and protruded from a brown turtleneck sweater that looked scratchy and lint-infested. He was a large man, easily six-four, and had the gut of a beer keg.

"Grover Kirk," said the stranger, by way of introduction. He reached out a sweaty-looking hand. "I've left you several messages."

Grover Kirk?

"I'm writing that book about the Galileo murders. I've been trying to get an interview with you and your family."

Ah, yes. Grover Kirk. Esme glanced again above his shoulders. Definitely a dickhead.

"Mr. Kirk, who invited you into my house?"

"Your father-in-law. Lovely fellow. Relayed to me some terrific anecdotes. He's in the bathroom at the moment. I'm afraid he might have had a bit too much red wine. I brought up a bottle from my vineyard in central Florida. Would you like some?"

He reached for a half-empty bottle on the coffee table. The bottle had stained a purple ring on the cover of one of Esme's Sudoku books.

She knew forty-four ways of rendering him unconscious in five seconds.

"Mr. Kirk," she said, "if you'll recall, I did respond to your first phone message. I told you that I wasn't interested in participating. I told you that my family wasn't interested in participating."

"Your father-in-law seemed very interested." He offered her the bottle. "How was marriage counseling?"

The front door opened. It was Rafe. Finally.

"I... Who's this?"

Grover again reached out with his hand and introduced himself.

"He's the one who's writing that book about Henry Booth."

"And all associated with what he did," added Grover. "My book would be incomplete without long passages about you and your wife. Just to be here, in this house, where it all went down, is an honor."

Esme gritted her teeth. "He wasn't Elvis Presley, Mr. Kirk. He was a psychopath and this family is trying to put all of that behind us."

"You can't escape the past, Mrs. Stuart. Surely you of all people know that."

She wanted to ask him what he meant, but she really, really wanted to clock him upside the head, and had taken a step forward when they all heard the downstairs toilet flush. There was nothing like that sound to eliminate the tension in a room.

"Leave," muttered Rafe. "Now."

Grover looked to him, then back to Esme, then finally to his bottle.

"All right," he said. "I know when to call it a night. My card's on the table. I'll be staying at the Days Inn over in Hicksville. Give my regards to your father-in-law. Lovely fellow."

He waited for them to move out of his way.

They moved out of the way.

"Be seeing you," he said, and winked, and left.

Rafe locked the door.

"What an ass," he said.

"I liked him," replied Lester, shuffling into the room. "Wait...where's the bottle of wine he brought?"

"He took it with him."

Lester frowned. "Took it with him? What an ass."

His reason for socializing gone, the old man continued on his way to his room. Esme counted the seconds until she heard his door slam shut.

Then she turned to her husband. He hadn't moved far from the door.

"Are you okay?" she asked him.

"I…"

She reached out to him.

But once again: an interruption. This time it was Rafe's cell phone, vibrating in his pants pocket.

"If it's a Florida area code," said Esme, "don't answer it."

Rafe examined the screen. "Five-one-eight."

"Upstate?" asked Esme.

Rafe nodded and pressed Talk. "Hello?"

Esme watched him as he listened. His parents, Lester and Eunice, had raised him in upstate New York. It was only luck that Rafe chose a graduate school in Washington, D.C. Otherwise, they would never have met.

Eight years.

"Who is it?" Esme whispered.

Rafe put up a hand to silence her. His face had gone pale. Whatever he was hearing was not good news.

She had accompanied him a few times to his old house. His childhood in upper-middle-class suburbia had been very different from hers on the streets of Boston. But opposites attracted, right?

Rafe spoke a bit to the person on the other line, thanked them and then hung up the phone. He looked even more rattled than he had in the car.

"Rafe, what is it?"

"Do you…remember that girl you met at my reunion…the one I took to the prom?"

Esme vaguely recalled the woman in question. She was a sales rep for a vacuum cleaner company. A bit heavy-set. Very pretty blue eyes.

"Lynette something, right?"

"Yes. Lynette Robinson. She… Anyway, that was my cousin Randy…on the phone. The police…they just identified the…remains of…Lynette's body…in the basement of a torched house."

3

The funeral was done in black and white.

The black, of course, was provided by the mourners. More than a hundred people came out to pay their respects. Half of them didn't even know the deceased, but had read about the tragedy in the *Sullivan County Democrat*. The national press was there, too, at the outskirts of the cemetery, and even they had the good sense to wear dark colors.

The priest wore black, naturally. The grave diggers, who stood a few feet from the crowd, wore long black coats. When the time was right, they would operate the pulleys, which were painted brown to camouflage with the sod, and lower the coffin into the four-by-eight-by-three hole they'd shoveled this morning.

The weather provided the white, covering the soil and the grass and the hundreds of gravestones scattered about the cemetery. Almost an inch of pale accumulation lay fixed above the cold earth, with more to come.

Even snowflakes were eager to attend Lynette Robinson's funeral.

As the priest, a youthful redheaded tenor, recited scripture, Esme's mind wandered (as it was wont to do when in the presence of recited scripture). She thought back over the past two days, from Grover Kirk (who had had the audacity to phone her Thursday morning) to Lester's long list of supplies he wanted them to get while upstate. She and Rafe had arrived at his old house in the early evening. Immediately, they opened all the windows to air out all the dust and mildew off forty-year-old linen upholstery. Lester had kept the kitchen faucet dripping so as to prevent his pipes from freezing, but Rafe descended into the cellar nonetheless to double-check.

Esme phoned Oyster Bay.

"Hello," grumbled Lester on the other end.

"Hi, Lester."

After exchanging hollow pleasantries, Esme asked if he could put Sophie on the line. And she waited. A breeze wafted in through one of the open windows in the bedroom and tickled at the back of Esme's neck.

Then, finally: "Hi, Mom!"

"Hey, baby. How was school?"

"Zack Portnoy wet his pants. There was a big puddle under his chair. The janitor had to come and clean it up and everything. It was gross."

Esme grimaced. "I'm sure it was, sweetie. Did you learn anything today in class?"

"To clean up pee, you need to use ammonia."

"Did you learn anything else?"

Silence.

"Sophie?"

"I'm thinking, I'm thinking! Oh, yeah—Mrs. Morrow wanted me to remind you that you're shap...shap... uh..."

"Chaperoning?"

"For the science museum trip on Monday."

"Are you excited to go see the science museum?"

"Uh-huh. Will I get to touch the electricity in the crystal ball?"

"That's up to Mrs. Morrow. She might have a lot of activities planned."

"Okay. Oh, Grandpa Les bought Chinese tonight and I bet him that I could put a whole egg roll in my mouth and I did."

"Sweetie, that's not a good idea," said Esme, caught between a giggle and a groan. "You could have choked."

"Nuh-uh, I had water and also, if I choked, I would just put my arms up and I'd be all better."

Rafe stepped into the room, a pair of his father's worn workman's gloves in his left hand.

"Just promise me not to do it again, all right, Sophie?"

She'd said their daughter's name to let Rafe know who she was talking to.

Rafe indicated, a little vehemently, that he wanted to talk to her, too.

"Okay, Sophie. I'm going to put Daddy on. I love you."

"I love you, too, Mommy."

As the priest genuflected and stepped away from the podium, Esme's thoughts returned to the present, and the funeral, and all around her, amid the light snow, a concerto of sobs. She glanced over at her husband. Like many there, he wore dark sunglasses. They'd stopped at a Walgreens on the way to the service to pick them up and had run into Rafe's cousin Randy, from the ne'er-do-well branch of the Stuart family tree. Randy walked with a cane—not to support any actual injury but to support his claim for disability. He used to work at the Pepsi factory on the outskirts of the city and a case had fallen near his foot, and near his foot became on his foot and there it was. At Walgreens he bought a pair of knock-off Ray-Bans and walked off with a box of M&M's.

It was Randy who'd called Rafe and Esme about Lynette. Randy was drinking buddies with one of the deputies in the county sheriff's office, and rumor, when lubricated with cheap Scotch, traveled easy and fast. Randy had never personally known Lynette, but he was there at the funeral nonetheless, standing a few feet behind Esme and Rafe. He would be at the reception, too, with his cane, and would probably attempt to parlay his "disability" and his "grief" into a one-night stand.

The two grave diggers winched the coffin into the ground. Lynette's immediate family was seated up front—both parents, two pairs of grandparents, three brothers and a sister. They had the best view. Not for the first time, Esme longed (in the event of her untimely death) to be cremated.

The coffin reached its resting place four feet below topsoil. This cued the crowd of mourners to slowly, quietly disperse. Esme followed Rafe back to his Prius. A thin coat of snow outlined the carlike shapes in the cemetery parking lot. Were it not for the chirp of Rafe's electronic fob, they might have had to go door to door.

Once inside, Rafe powered up the seat warmers. Esme loved the seat warmers. Esme believed that every chair, couch and bench needed a seat warmer. They idled in the parking lot for several minutes while the windows defrosted the snow. In the rearview they could see the bottleneck of vehicles fighting to be the first to leave. Esme looked away from the mirror and clicked on the radio.

Rafe clicked it off.

"Have a little respect," he said.

So Esme respectfully sat there in silence as the hybrid's engine idled and the heat breathed out of the dashboard vents and the melting snow drooled down her window. Only once the parking lot had emptied did Rafe shift into Reverse.

The GPS navigated them to Lynette's parents' cottage, located at the end of a lower-middle-class cul-de-sac just outside the Monticello town square. The street was cramped with cars, so Rafe had to back up and park by the county courthouse. By the time they got out of their car, the flurries had thickened in a snowstorm. If they'd had the radio on, mused Esme, maybe they could have found out how many inches were forecasted. In the meantime, it was trudge-trudge-trudge and hope-hope-hope.

Esme wanted to be more sympathetic. She really did. Her sense of detachment didn't have anything to do with the fact that Rafe went to the senior prom with this girl. Lynette had seemed pleasant enough, and what had happened to her was a horror. But ever since that session with Dr. Rosen, ever since she'd pronounced her ultimatum, Esme had felt as if she were a dispassionate spirit, floating outside of her body. The only moment in the past two days she'd felt anything close to actual emotion was that confrontation with Grover Kirk.

In other words, when it had to do with Galileo.

Had she become an adrenaline junkie? When she had been full-time with the FBI, she'd known her share of those. The type who only smiled under duress. The type who sought out increasing scenarios of danger (whether picking fights in a D.C. bar or parasailing in South America). The type who, whenever their heart rate dropped below the speed of a Keith Moon drum solo, became inordinately depressed. But, no, that wasn't her…was it?

As expected, the Robinson house was wall-to-wall with the same black-clad guests as the cemetery. Lynette's immediate family was among the last to arrive; the media had dogged them the moment they stepped off the holy ground of the cemetery. Fortunately, some neighbors had volunteered to stay at the house during the service and set everything up. A few faces looked vaguely familiar to Esme, but she was hard-pressed to put a name to any of them.

Many people knew Rafe. They shook his hand, patted him on the back, told him how glad they were to see him, asked how his father was doing. Each time, Rafe dutifully introduced (or reintroduced) Esme. She could tell that his heart wasn't in it. He seemed detached, too, but for very different reasons. For the right reasons.

The local police were in attendance, as well, in uniform and paying their respects. Esme spotted Randy chatting up a freckled deputy. That must have been the drinking buddy. Then Rafe escorted her to the sheriff, a stout man in his sixties standing by a card table with a punch bowl. He had the awkwardness of a wallflower at a junior high school prom, albeit a wallflower with salt-and-pepper hair and a sidearm clipped to his belt. His name tag read Michael Fallon.

"It's a pleasure, Sheriff," said Esme, and shook his hand, which was dry but warm.

"And how's your father, Rafe? Still kicking your ass, I assume?"

"Yes, sir."

"We all heard about that ugliness last spring." Sheriff Fallon shook his head in sadness. "I'm glad you all emerged in one piece. Are you okay, Rafe?"

Rafe offered Esme a quick glance, then answered, "As good as could be expected, Sheriff."

The man nodded, then took a sip from his punch.

But Rafe wasn't finished.

"So you're aware, then, of who my wife is? Of what she does?"

This time Esme shot him a quick glance. Where was he going with this...?

"Of course," Fallon replied.

"Be honest with me, Sheriff, for my father's sake. This case... How out of your league are you?"

If Fallon was insulted, he didn't show it. "We've got every man in the county working on it."

"I'm willing to bet they're all working hard, Sheriff, but I'm also willing to bet that none of them have my wife's mind or her experience."

Now Esme was the one who felt like the flower—a shrinking violet. Where was all of this praise coming from? Rafe had never even hinted that he thought about her like this. Even when they were dating, he disapproved of her job, and now this?

"If we need the FBI, Rafe, if it comes to that, we'll call them. I promise you."

"That's what I'm saying, sir. You don't need to call them. They're already here. Esme is already here. And you're going to use her, or I'll tell the media camped outside that you could have but you didn't. They know who she is. You're going to put your provincial pride in your back pocket and let her help you solve this case. Are we clear?"

"What the fuck was that!"

They had retreated to one of the rooms in the cottage. Rafe motioned for Esme to keep her voice down, and he closed the door behind him. It took Esme a second to realize their dumb luck. This had to be Lynette's room. An assortment of national flags decorated one of the walls. Esme recognized maybe half of them. From what she knew about Lynette, the woman had never even left New York State. The flags must have represented a dream of hers: to travel the world. On her vanity lay a jewelry box, open. Lynette trusted people. Esme wasn't a profiler, but some of these conclusions were obvious.

Lynette probably trusted her assailant, until things turned dark.

The bedsheets were white and recently laundered. The room smelled sweet. There were lilacs by the window. Esme almost approached them to inhale their scent but then remembered what brought her into this room in the first place. She wheeled toward her husband, who was staring at the contents of the jewelry box.

"Let's start simple," she said.

He looked at her. His eyes were sad. "Fine."

"First, I am not a prostitute and you are not my pimp. Don't ever, ever offer my services without consulting me."

"I thought you'd want to help."

"That's so beside the point!"

Rafe shrugged. That obnoxious dominance he'd displayed with Sheriff Fallon had been replaced by a mournful smallness. His gaze shifted back to the jewelry box.

"Second, since when have you given a damn about what I do? Since when have you done anything but criticize and ridicule my job? Eight years ago, you forced me to quit! Two days ago you accused me of 'knowingly and willfully killing our family'!"

"I know what I said."

"What's changed?"

"Lynette is dead."

"Were you close with her? Had you even spoken to her since the reunion?"

"No."

"Then what makes her so special that you're willing to upturn everything you've believed in and argued?"

"I would think you'd be happy," replied Rafe. "Your husband finally values what you do. I would think you'd be thrilled."

"Thrilled? I'm dumbfounded! I need you to explain this to me, Rafe. I need you to do it now and I need you to do it so I understand, because at this moment I have no idea who you are."

"Someone I knew has been murdered. I'm asking you to help find who did it. It's what you tell me you do, Esme. Why is anything else relevant?"

"Because it is!" She caught her own reflection in the vanity mirror. The tips of her ears, poking out from her shoulder-length brown hair, were scarlet. As sure a sign as any that she was pissed off. "How can you not see how this has to do with us?"

Rafe ran a hand over his face and let out a long sigh. Then he reached into the jewelry box and took out a pair of teal earrings.

"She wore these once," he said.

Esme's brow furrowed. "I don't understand."

"Please don't make me… It's not important.…"

"Jesus, Rafe! Were you in love with her?"

"No! No. I never was in love with her. That's the… Okay, fine. You want to know the whole truth? You want to know the story? You want to know why this is tearing me up inside?"

"All I've ever wanted is honesty."

He chuckled at her for a moment, then proceeded.

"Honesty. People say they want it, but when they get it, they get it all right. You're heuristic. You always have been. You trust your instincts. I trust my intellect. But with Lynette Robinson…no, I wasn't in love with her. But she was in love with me. God knows why. She never told me, of course, but she didn't make a secret of it, either. The way she looked at me in class. The way she smiled at me whenever I got up to make a presentation. Her face would light up, and her eyes—she had these great eyes. Blue like, I don't know, a calming swell of the ocean. I liked that she was in love with me. I wasn't especially popular and some days were pretty brutal, but no matter what, she'd be there with that look of love in those blue eyes and that…helped. And I wish I could have loved her back. But I didn't."

"We can't choose who we love," said Esme.

"But why?" He looked at her. "Human society is based on our ability to exert free will over ourselves and in our interactions with others. I'm a sociology professor, for Christ's sake, and I still don't know what makes love so exceptional. I know it is exceptional, and I know I love you, very much, but I also know it has very little to do with my brain, and that's a little scary. So, back in high school, I asked myself, Why can't I love her back? Why couldn't I choose to think about her the same way she thought about me? And I followed the course of thought to its logical conclusion and decided that it was because of her weight."

"You were a typical, superficial, pigheaded—excuse the expression—teenage boy."

"No, I wasn't. Typical teenage boys don't score 1600

on the PSATs. Typical teenage boys aren't beaten by their fathers when they score A-'s instead of A's. But that's getting off track, because I'd reached what I felt was a logical conclusion and that left me sort of…satisfied. So I went to school the next day determined to speak to Lynette and share with her my realization."

"Oh, Rafe, tell me you didn't."

"Oh, I did. I thought I owed it to her. I wanted her to understand that it wasn't her fault. I wanted her to understand that I was, in fact, superficial, and it was my problem and there was nothing she could do about it. Esme, I thought I was carrying out an errand of mercy. I wanted to stop leading her on."

"That poor girl."

Again, Rafe chuckled. "You obviously didn't know her very well. Because I told her this, between homeroom and first period, and she didn't slap me or cry or yell or do any of the things that in retrospect she had every right to do. She just smiled at me with those blue eyes and thanked me and that was that. And nothing changed."

"I'll bet she came home that night and cried herself to sleep." Esme looked around the room. This was her home. This was her bed. This was where Lynette had retreated that night.

"The next day, tickets for the senior prom went on sale. I had no one to ask. There were a few girls I had crushes on—don't give me that look—but they were either unavailable or very much out of my league. But as silly as it sounds, I really wanted to go to the prom. It was a rite of passage. I was a sociologist even then. The senior prom was something I needed to experience. But I sure as hell wasn't going to go stag."

"So you asked Lynette."

"Yes. I made it clear to her that we were just going as friends—which must have been just another stab in the gut—but she acted cool about it and asked me the color of my cummerbund so she could get a matching dress and I didn't even know what a cummerbund was, but I learned. And on the night of the prom, I wore a black tuxedo with a teal cummerbund and I showed up at that front door and there she was, beautiful, wearing these earrings. They matched her dress so perfectly. And we left.

"We went to the prom. We had a good time. We ate, we danced. We laughed. We always got along okay. And it was obvious she was still into me. And you'd think that maybe, just maybe, with the dress and these earrings and the magical occasion, that I'd fall for her, and I knew that's what Lynette hoped. I could see it in her blue eyes. But I felt…nothing. And as the night wore on, I knew that this was not going to be a happy ending, but there was nothing I could do short of faking an illness, and that's more my cousin Randy's thing, anyway.

"So I ate and danced and laughed and then it was time to go home. And I drove her home. I walked her to the front door. This was the moment. It would have been so easy to just lean in and kiss her good-night. Even if it were just on the cheek, it would have been the right thing to do. But I knew how she felt and I didn't want to lead her on. We stood on her front stoop and she looked up at me with those blue eyes and I…shook her hand. And then I left."

"Oh, Rafe…"

He wiped his eyes. "We saw each other in class the next day, and the day after that, and we said hi to each other in the hallway, but that spark I used to see in her was gone. I'd extinguished it. I'd killed it. And now another monster has come along and I need you to find him and I need you to put him down because, you see, maybe if I do this for her, maybe…I don't know…she'll forgive me. And if she can forgive me…maybe someday you can, too."

4

After the reception, Lynette's boyfriend, Charlie Weyngold, was brought to the county sheriff's office for questioning. He came willingly. Rafe and Esme, with the sheriff's reluctant permission, accompanied them on the trek through the snow, almost three inches now and rising by the hour. On their way out the door at the Robinson cottage, Esme overheard two women mention one to two feet. She hoped they were talking about the size of their toddlers.

The interview was conducted not in a windowless cell with a dangling lightbulb but in the sheriff's cozy corner office. This was where Sheriff Fallon had interviewed Lynette's parents and siblings the day before. He passed the file to Esme as soon as she took her seat on a couch in the office. Sheriff Fallon sat behind his desk. The boyfriend, Charlie, took the room's other chair, a low-back folding number that couldn't have been comfortable even in the best of circumstances.

Rafe was to wait outside, kept company by those deputies and officers not out on the streets earning double-time behind the wheel of a county snowplow. He sipped herbal tea. He thought about high school.

Charlie Weyngold thought about his necktie. He didn't like it. It felt constricting around his collar, around his throat. He wanted to loosen it, but didn't. That would have been disrespectful to Lynette. For her, he kept his necktie tight. For her, he would have done anything, and so he thought about his necktie to keep from thinking about her, to keep from bawling like an infant right there in the sheriff's office. He had, however, taken off his suit coat. The button-down he wore underneath had short sleeves, which displayed the artful manga tattoos scrawling up and down each arm. He and Lynette were going to go to Tokyo next year. He and Lynette had plans. He and Lynette—

"You need a Kleenex, Charlie?"

Charlie looked up at the sheriff and shook his head.

Sheriff Fallon made a noncommittal grunt and glanced over at Esme Stuart, sitting there on his couch, perusing his case file. Some people in his position could be territorial, and loathed the FBI and any other intrusion from the federal government. Mike Fallon wasn't territorial. He welcomed assistance. He could stop and ask for directions without feeling the slightest bit less masculine. His wife, Vicky, had trained him well. No, Mike Fallon appreciated help when offered. But nobody appreciated having it stuffed down their throat, no matter how necessary it was. So a small part of him—the very small, selfish, spiteful part that sometimes kept him company late at night after a few too many Coors—hoped Esme Stuart found nothing, hoped this case made her stumble and fall, and publicly. Meanwhile, it was time to question the boyfriend, Charlie Weyngold, who probably had nothing new to add, and who probably was minutes away from a grief-induced nervous breakdown, but sometimes this was the job.

"Charlie, this is the timeline we have so far regarding Tuesday. Correct me if any of this sounds false to you, okay, son?"

"Yes, sir."

The sheriff peeked at his notepad, and then proceeded. "We've got the victim arriving at her office around nine in the morning. She took a coffee break at ten-thirty with a coworker of hers by the name of Lois Feinstein. Around ten forty-five, she left the office to make her daily rounds about town. Her first—and only—stop that day was the public library."

"She always stopped there right before lunch," said Charlie. "Sometimes I'd meet her there and we'd hop on to the internet and look at the websites for countries. She especially liked the ones that were untranslated. She'd try to figure out what it said, and then she'd use this program to translate the website to English and see how well she did. She…"

"Are you all right, son?"

"Yes, sir."

"Charlie, why don't you tell me about your relationship with the victim?"

Esme looked up from the file. The sheriff had twice now deliberately avoided using Lynette's name. Good. Keep it impersonal. Keep it objective. High emotion often obscured important truths, as with her and Rafe…

But that was for later. Now: the case. She returned to the file.

Sheriff Fallon's notes were comprehensive, informative and almost entirely unhelpful. The general facts were these.

11/09, 4:12 p.m.: Members of the Monticello fire department responded to reports of a fire at 18 Value Street.

They were able to extinguish the blaze, but the fire had destroyed most of the furniture and a considerable portion of the superstructure. Sections of the second floor had caved into the first, and sections of the first floor had caved into the basement.

11/10, 9:32 p.m.: Careful investigation by the arson team, coordinating with both the local police and the Sullivan County sheriff's department, determined the source of the fire was the first-floor kitchen and that the origin was electrical in nature. It was at this point, approximately 9:00 p.m., that volunteer fireman Bradley Langer uncovered human remains in the basement of the house. A leather collar attached to a length of industrial chain was found around the neck and—

Esme blinked. Leather collar? Was this some S and M game gone awry? She read on.

11/10, 10:55 p.m.: Forensics finished their documentation of the crime scene and the remains were delivered to the county coroner's office for determination of cause of death.

11/10, 11:13 p.m.: Sheriff Michael Fallon reached Todd and Louise Weiner, the owners of the Value Street property, by telephone. They are on a two-week vacation in Bermuda with their four children. All accounted for. The Weiners promptly agreed to return home.

11/11, 9:00 a.m.: First reports filed from canvassing. Neighbors are unable to identify anyone entering or exiting the house. The Weiner family is described as "friendly."

11/11, 11:16 a.m.: Dental records identify human remains as Lynette Robinson. Cause of death impossible to determine due to the deterioration of the body. Note: the hands of the deceased are missing.

Esme frowned. The hands of the deceased are missing? That pretty much nixed the S and M idea, unless dismemberment was a subfetish that she (gratefully) didn't know about. But she rather doubted it. Unless the hands got misplaced in the transfer from the crime scene to the lab, which was nigh unlikely, they almost definitely had to have been removed from the body by the unsub (unknown subject of the investigation, henceforth known as Sick Son of a Bitch).

"Was there a relationship between Lynette Robinson and the Weiners?" she asked the sheriff.

Sheriff Fallon answered with a red-hot glare.

Ah, right. He was interviewing the boyfriend. She had forgotten. When she fell into investigation mode, the outside world sometimes became an afterthought. This was a necessary part of the routine, although it did little to ingratiate herself with, well, most anybody else. And she usually amplified this distance even further with the aid of her iPod and some kickass British rock, but her iPod was back at her father-in-law's house. She made a mental note to retrieve it.

"I never heard of them," replied the boyfriend to her question. "I don't think Lynette knew them, either. I mean, I knew most everybody she knew. Maybe she sold them a vacuum. That's what she did. That's how we met. She sold me a vacuum. She… Excuse me, I need to get some air.…"

Charlie got up from his seat and left the room.

Sheriff Fallon's glare became incendiary.

"Sorry," said Esme. "Sorry."

"Are you through with the file? The Weiners should be arriving at the airport in about a half hour and I'd like to meet them there, if you don't mind."

"You really think they'll be able to land in this weather?"

Fallon glanced out his window. His already-caustic mood soured.

Esme considered how to play this. The man was a hornet's nest. She decided on a little reverse psychology. "It's not a big deal. They probably won't have any information that can help you. They're almost definitely incidental to the crime.…"

"Is that so? A couple hundred thousand dollars in property damage begs to differ."

"The neighbors said they didn't see anyone enter or exit the house," Esme explained, "but they weren't really watching the house until it started burning. So we know the arsonist left before the fire and we know that Lynette Robinson was already in the house by then, as well. She was brought there. Why?"

"With all due respect, ma'am, that's what I plan on finding out from the Weiners."

"Who knew they were going to be out of town?"

"Friends, family, coworkers. The usual assortment, I'd assume."

"That's who you need to interview."

"Is that an order?"

"It's a suggestion.…" Her harmless little exercise in reverse psychology complete, Esme handed him back the file. "Do you have a snack machine in this building?"

One to two feet proved accurate. Rafe and Esme wrangled a deputy to help them dig out the Prius, and they drove back to Lester's house at a steady, safe three miles per hour. The windshield wipers did little to keep the fist-size snowflakes from clotting up the front view. God was emptying his vat of Wite-Out over upstate New York.

If there was a God, thought Esme.

Henry Booth—her erstwhile Galileo—didn't think so. Henry Booth's atheism—and his anger at religion in general—had helped fuel his murder spree. Henry Booth had forced Esme to reconsider her own faith. She and Rafe never attended church, aside from the secular functions held there. She owned a copy of the King James Bible, but it was a relic from a lit course she took as an undergrad.

Henry Booth had targeted policemen, firemen, teachers. Mothers, fathers. Good people. In one of his notes, he wrote that if there were in fact a God, these violent crimes would not have been allowed to occur. If there were a God, divine intervention would have ended his massacre.

But God didn't stop him. Esme did.

And now someone had gone and chained Lynette Robinson, by all accounts a nice woman, in the basement of a house and cut off her hands. Where was God's hand in that?

More questions, no answers. She looked to her husband. His eyes seemed busy, full of concentration.

Rafe.

Talk about questions without answers.

"What do you want for dinner?" she asked him.

"Whatever Dad's got in the house. Probably canned soup."

"I'm sure there's a restaurant between here and there."

Rafe squeezed the steering wheel. "We stop, we get out, and an hour later we have to shovel out the car. Again. And by then it'll be nighttime. Unless it's already nighttime. I can't see a goddamn thing."

"You can see me," she said.

His busy eyes zipped in her direction. She crossed her eyes, wiggled her ears, pulled back her lips with her fingers and stuck out her tongue.

Rafe grinned. He couldn't help it. He wanted to remain serious, stoic, but when his wife whipped out the funny face, all hope was lost.

He murmured, "My beautiful bride."

"You better believe it."

They held hands the rest of the ride home.

By the time they pulled into the carport, it was indeed nighttime. The lights on the street gave each of the falling snowflakes an angelic aura. Esme was reminded of fairies, and then her mind went to Lynette Robinson's hands, and then each of the snowflakes became a woman's severed hand, falling, falling.

"Awful early in the season for a blizzard," noted Rafe as they entered the house.

Esme just nodded and tried to rid her imagination of dark thoughts. What she needed was her music. She quickly grabbed her iPod from her suitcase and searched around for a pair of speakers to plug it in. Surely Lester had something in this house that was compatible...

Rafe emptied two cans of chili into a pot and set it to boil.

"What are you looking for?" he asked.

"The twenty-first century," she replied, checking inside handmade cabinets and hutches.

"You're not going to find that here."

She returned to the kitchen, an exaggerated pout on

her lips. Rafe shrugged and started to stir the chili. Esme joined him at the gas stove, hip-checking him to make room, and cooked the contents of a box of white rice on an adjacent burner.

Apropos of absolutely nothing, Rafe turned to her and said, "So do you think it was the boyfriend?"

She lowered the temperature on Rafe's burner.

"He had an alibi at the time of the fire."

"Alibis can be falsified."

She smirked at him. "Since when did you become a criminologist?"

"Everyone who watches prime-time TV is an amateur criminologist." He grabbed some basil off the spice rack and sprinkled a few dashes into the chili. "I just want to make sure no stone goes unturned."

There was that melancholy again, quavering the timbre of his voice. Esme noticed the steam from the pots was misting up his glasses. He did nothing to remedy the situation. She waited. He continued to stir, his vision undoubtedly getting foggier and foggier. Christ, the man could be stubborn.

She handed him a dishrag.

"What's this for?"

"Just give me your glasses."

He did. She wiped them. He poured the boiled rice into the chili and stirred them together.

"The man who killed her took her hands."

Esme regretted saying it the moment the words came out. In fact, she had no honest idea why she'd shared with him this information, which was both grisly and confidential. He had no need to know. He had no need to ever know.

But now he knew.

He stared at her, his turquoise eyes so small, so

vulnerable, without his glasses on. At that moment he didn't look like a sociology professor or the father of a seven-year-old girl. He looked like a boy, a broken-hearted little boy.

"I'm sorry…" said Esme. "I—"

He began to pace the kitchen, thinking, thinking. Then he wheeled on her, fists clenched. "Why would someone do that?"

Esme shrugged. "Any number of reasons. What's important is—"

"There are *reasons?* There is more than one *reason* why someone would…?"

"Rafe—"

"This is your world, isn't it? This is what you deal with, willfully."

Willfully. That word harkened back to their argument in Dr. Rosen's office. How he'd accused her of knowingly and willfully killing their family with her selfish behavior. Goddamn it, couldn't they have made it through one day without this shit coming back up between them?

She handed him his clean glasses.

"I'm sorry," she whispered. "Really, I am."

He accepted the glasses from her hands, peered through the lenses and donned them.

"Thank you," he said.

"You're welcome."

They ate dinner.

They talked about the weather.

And then, while washing the pots and dishes, it all began again.…

"What are these number of reasons?"

"Rafe, it's not important—"

"You know that's bullshit. The reason someone does a thing is an essential ingredient in… I mean, come on.

What causes a person to decide, 'Oh, you know what? I think I need to lop off a person's hands'?"

"What you're talking about is profiling," replied Esme. She was avoiding his stare, but could still feel it. "That's not really my area."

"Then how do you expect to catch this guy when a major aspect of the work is not really your area?"

"I'm not the only person working this case, Rafe. I'm not even officially working this case at all. I'm consulting, off the books, as per your whatever. I'm sure the police have their own experts who can—"

"We're talking about a woman's life here!"

"Please stop yelling at me."

"You want me to stop yelling at you? Okay. Here's me not yelling."

That's when Rafe threw the pot against the wall. A stain of dirty dishwater, dotted with bits of chili, drooled down the white paint and to the linoleum floor below, where the pot had loudly clanged to its resting place, but not before soaking both of them in sodden crap.

They both stared at the mess on the wall. Then at themselves. Then back at the wall.

A minute passed.

"Did I mention," muttered Rafe, "that everybody who watches prime-time TV is also an amateur melodramatist?"

"That would explain the crescendo of violins I just heard."

Rafe nodded.

They continued to stare at the mess.

"I'll clean this up," he finally said. "Why don't you go take a shower?"

Esme nodded and walked to the bathroom. She could feel rice in her hair. Oh, how nuptial. She quickly got undressed and turned on the shower. The water would take a minute or two to heat up.

The funny thing was, she knew Rafe was right. This case was bigger than her. There was a sinister psychology at play, and she lacked the skills to analyze it. She needed an expert, but this wasn't an official FBI case....

Turning off the water, she wrapped herself in an oversize towel, and reached for her cell phone to call Tom Piper.

5

When the phone call came, Tom didn't hear it. He was too busy quite literally rolling in the hay with the farmer's daughter. To be sure, the farmer in question was ninety-two years old, half-deaf and asleep at the time, but life had taught Tom Piper that sometimes it was best to ignore the salient details in favor of sauciness. He (age fifty-eight) and Penelope Sue Fuller (age sixty-one) groped, fondled, licked, lapped, nuzzled, squeezed, bucked, sucked and thrust against each other in the pine loft of the Fullers' stables, several hay bales acting as their makeshift mattress. The hay was itchy, and poked a bit, but that just caused Tom and Penelope Sue to act upon each other with increased, well, assertiveness.

Through it all, Tom's heart maintained a steady, calm rhythm. Th-thump. Th-thump. Th-thump. Damn pacemaker. It really took some of the fun out of primal, no-holds-barred sex. The pacemaker was his souvenir from Galileo. The fucker had shot him in the chest. Only emergency surgery on Long Island—and the installation of his very own personal timekeeper—saved Tom's life. Now, six months later, his doctors here in Kentucky were impressed with his recovery. Tom was less than impressed. It was moments like this, moments with Penelope Sue, that he was reminded just how comprehensively Galileo had robbed him, because here, with a beautiful redhead and in an idyllic setting straight out of a dirty limerick, as they went at each other like a pair of id-addled bunny rabbits, Tom was having trouble maintaining his erection.

He tried everything. He concentrated on Penelope Sue, her full breasts, her perfume (peaches…oh, my!), how much she wanted him, how much he desired her. When that didn't work, he flipped through the Rolodex of memories. Other women he'd been with, other women he'd craved, high school sweethearts, coworkers, that bubbly clerk he once chatted with in Toronto and the way he wanted to bury himself in her dimples. He had more than four decades of memories to choose from, and yet he could feel himself deflate, deflate, deflate.…

Finally, between gasps, Penelope Sue asked him if everything was okay, and the sound of honest concern in her voice, of pity, was like a bucket of ice. He sighed, lay beside her and gazed up through the roof slats at the plump, indifferent moon.

She ran a hand across his long gray ponytail. "It's all right," she said. "We can just lie here," she said. "This is nice, too," she said.

"Mmm-hmm," he replied, not meaning a syllable of it.

Soon, though, the night air made them chilly, and it was time to get dressed. They did so in heavy silence and walked back to her farmhouse, shivering. Penelope Sue made some tea.

Tom envisioned their upcoming conversation. He'd seen variations of it in every Viagra, Cialis and Levitra commercial. She'd pull out a brochure. They'd go to the doctor. Next shot: they'd be walking hand in hand on the beach and grinning ear to ear as the waves cascaded in the background. Except he couldn't go the medicinal route even if he wanted to, not with his bad heart.

Which left them where and with what? He wanted to grow old with this woman, but he wanted her to be happy, and her sexual appetite was as gleefully voracious as his. As his was until six months ago.

She handed him his tea. Spice orange. Herbal. No caffeine for him. Hers was a special blend she bought at the farmer's market. She cuddled beside him on the living room couch.

Commercial time, he thought. Cue the music.

"Tom," she said, "this is why the good Lord invented vibrators."

She winked at him lasciviously and sipped her hot tea.

God, he loved this woman.

That's when he noticed his cell phone, which he'd left on her star-shaped coffee table, glowing on and off. He had a message.

"I should check on Mama in a bit," said Penelope Sue. "See if she needs her sheets changed."

"I'll go with you."

"I'd like that. Mama wouldn't, but that's her problem now, isn't it?"

She spoke with that sugary Kentucky accent that lent itself so sweetly to bourbon and bluegrass. Tom knew it well. He grew up not fifty miles from here. Hearing her speak was like hearing his past call him home. When Tom returned to Kentucky to recuperate, the hospital assigned him a certain physical therapist with long red hair that smelled of peaches and, well, here he was, in puppy love at age fifty-eight.

"It's past time to turn the farm over for the winter," said Penelope Sue. "Got to recaulk the windows and get the pumps double-checked."

"I can do that this weekend."

Penelope Sue nodded. Weekends were her busiest times at the hospital. Tom worked a desk at the FBI's Louisville division, but not on Saturdays and Sundays. His nine-to-five, Monday-to-Friday life couldn't have been more different from his schedule on the national task force, but that just made it all the better. Tom Piper had turned a corner. The pilgrim had finally settled down.

Was it the change in his health? Was it the influence of Penelope Sue? Maybe. But the greater cause, Tom knew, belonged to Galileo. Near-death experiences put life in perspective. It was a simple truism, almost trite, but accurate as a bull's-eye. And Tom wouldn't have it any other way.

"Ready for more?" she asked.

Tom knew she wasn't referring to the tea or (mercifully) sex. She was referring to the room's thirty-six-inch plasma TV and to the DVD player attached to it and the disc inside. He acquiesced, and she giddily reached for the remote control.

Two minutes later: "Space…the final frontier…"

Yes, oh, yes, the love of his life was a Trekkie.

They were in the middle of an original-series marathon, her adorable attempt to convert him to the cult of Trek. She had a uniform hanging in a bag in her closet. Her bedroom contained signed photographs. And when she'd revealed this part of herself to him, there hadn't been one ounce of hesitation. There never was, with Penelope Sue. And so he snuggled with her and watched hour after hour, and maybe through her infectious enjoyment he actually began to like this thing. Science fiction was far removed from his own interests, but Penelope Sue simply had a way about her that opened doors.

Around 10:00 p.m., he collected their mugs and washed them out in the ceramic sink. They had three more episodes to go, and it was time for a break. Besides, by now her mother upstairs was undoubtedly in need of a visit.

"It was Esme," said Penelope Sue, trotting into the kitchen. Tom put the mugs down. "She's the one who called."

Penelope Sue handed him his phone.

Tom clicked on the voice mail. He put it on speaker phone.

They listened to Esme's message.

"I'll go take care of Mama," said Penelope Sue, and without waiting for him to object, she walked away. So be it.

He dialed the number. He knew it by rote.

"Hello, Esmeralda," he said. He was the only one who called her by her full name. He'd done so for almost fifteen years. It was a sign of affection, and they never, ever talked about it. "It sounds like you've got yourself a case."

"I'd love to hear your take on it."

He sat down at the kitchen table. "I'd love to hear yours first." No matter how much his life had changed in the past six months, he would never stop being her Socratic mentor.

"The removal of the hands suggests a trophy. The fire could be some kind of funeral pyre."

"Or you could be giving more meaning to his actions than he is," he said.

"Everything has meaning, whether it's intended or not. All accidents have explanations. We can't help ourselves."

Tom glanced out the window at the barn in the distance. "No. We can't."

"I'm missing something important, aren't I?"

"We're all missing something important." He looked away from the window. "We can't help ourselves there, either."

"He didn't burn her, though. He torched the whole house. That's significant."

"Everything has meaning."

"You know the answer, don't you?"

He had a notion. It was rudimentary, of course, and without seeing the report and visiting the crime scene it was purely speculative, but yes, he had a notion. He often did.

"I think you need to trust yourself," he told her.

"I'm off the books up here, Tom. I could use your help."

The ceiling boards above him creaked. That would be Mama, stubbornly fighting off Penelope Sue's attempts to deliver her nightly shot. Talk about rituals…

"I have faith in you," he said to Esme. He stood. His knees were a bit stiff from the cold. "You can do this."

"Don't make me beg, Tom."

He could tell by the tone of her voice that she was teasing him. She knew he'd fly up there. He was reliable. He was ever her instructor. He was Tom Piper. Together they'd solve this case, and another in a long line of deranged scumbags would be in custody.

But that wasn't him anymore, right?

He looked out again at the barn, bathed in cold moonlight.

"Come on," she replied, still playful. "What'll it take? A tantalizing email?"

That was how, last winter, he'd coaxed her out of her early retirement. She'd already been intrigued by the Galileo case, still in its infancy, and he'd sent her a note that Henry Booth had left at a crime scene, and soon she was saying goodbye to her family and boarding a plane for Texas to meet up with Tom's task force. He'd pushed her buttons and she'd allowed them to be pushed and how was this, now, any different? Surely he owed it to her, if not to that poor girl Lynette. The Galileo case had nearly gotten Esme killed, and he knew the effect it had had on her marriage.

But what about the effect it had had on him?

Penelope Sue padded into the room, a look of curiosity on her brow. He held out his hand to her and she clasped it.

"I'm sorry," he told Esme. "I'm already home. Best of luck, Esmeralda. I know you'll do just fine."

Click.

Esme wasn't angry.

She expected to be angry. She expected to feel wounded and betrayed. But she didn't. She wasn't relieved or happy. She wasn't quite sure what she felt about Tom's refusal.

So she compartmentalized it, stepped into the shower to wash off the chili and rice and ruminated about other matters.

More specifically: why did the unsub burn down the whole house?

By all accounts, the fire started with a bang. Electrical fires often did. Some appliance shorts out, goes kablooey, and it's time to call your insurance provider.

The unsub undoubtedly set the fire on purpose, which meant he rigged an appliance to blow, which meant he knew there was going to be a bang, which meant he knew it was going to draw attention to the house—and to him, making a rapid and hopefully burn-free getaway. So he wanted the body to be found. And given that there were no signs of accelerant on or near the remains, he wasn't particular about the body being identified or not.

Esme moved on from body wash to shampoo, and thought about the victim herself. Maybe Rafe and the sheriff and most everyone else working the case were right. Maybe Lynette was the gateway. It made sense. It was the obvious choice. She rarely favored the obvious choice, true, but that didn't make it any less valid.

So: Who would want to cause Lynette harm?

No. Better question: What was significant enough about Lynette for someone to go through all this trouble?

Esme didn't mean to imply that it was difficult to believe that someone found Lynette significant. Her tattooed boyfriend was obviously enamored. And then there was the matter of Rafe's overcomplicated emotional relationship to her....

Rafe!

Christ, how long had she been in the shower while he waited, soggy foodstuffs still splattered over his hair and cheeks and neck? Granted, he'd done the splattering, but still. Esme hastened her ablutions and hustled out of the shower. She opened the door for Rafe while she was drying her hair. The door wasn't locked, and he could have come in at any time, and he *would* have come in during the first year of their marriage, joined her in the shower even, but that was a long time ago.

As her husband soaped and soaked, Esme climbed into a nightgown, rolled her iPod to Roxy Music and snuggled under the covers. Her mind drifted back to the case, back to Lynette Robinson and those teal earrings and her unfortunate fate. How differently people would live their lives if they knew how and when their lives would end. Esme wondered what she would do differently, if she knew, and by the time Rafe had toweled himself off, those musings had carried her off to sleep, at least until the pounding began at 6:16 a.m.

Thump, thump, thump, thump, thump.

Esme bolted awake. So did Rafe. A minute passed. Silence. They looked at each other. Had they dreamed that thunderous—

Thump, thump, thump, thump, thump.

Apparently not.

"Is it the pipes?" she asked. He'd grown up in this house.

Thump, thump, thump, thump, thump.

"No," he replied. "That's not the pipes."

Their eyes scanned the room for something to use as a weapon. But how did one defend against a sound?

Thump, thump, thump, thump, thump.

"Maybe it's the front door," said Rafe.

"At six in the morning?"

Rafe shrugged. Did she have a better idea?

Thump, thump, thump, thump, thump.

"Goddamn it," she mumbled, and swung her legs out of bed and onto the thin mauve carpet. Her robes were at home. Her slippers were at home. So she slid her bare feet into her sneakers, tugged a navy blue sweater over her nightgown and headed downstairs to probe out the invasive racket.

Thump, thump, thump, thump, thump.

As she neared the front door, she knew Rafe's conclusion had been accurate. Someone was on the other side, knocking. The door shook with each pound. Whoever it was at their door at 6:21 a.m. on this cold, cold Saturday morning, they were both large and insistent.

Maybe it was that dickhead pseudo-journalist Grover Kirk. He had the size and the lack of common decency to track them down to a funeral and pay them a visit. Either way, Esme vowed to use her resources at the Bureau to learn more about Mr. Kirk, maybe pull his IRS records.

She poked her head to one of the windows. Two sheriff's deputies, each the size of a Dumpster, stood there on the front stoop. They appeared cold and they appeared antsy.

She opened the front door.

"Morning, officers. What seems to be the trouble?"

"The sheriff told us to come get you, ma'am."

Of course he did.

"Give me a few minutes. Would you like to come in?"

The deputies exchanged glances. "No, ma'am. We're just fine out here."

Sure they were.

She closed the door in their frost-tipped faces and made her way back to the bedroom.

"Was it the front door?" Rafe asked.

Ten minutes later, both she and Rafe were back downstairs, fully dressed. She half expected to find two ice statues on the stoop where the deputies had been, but no, the two men remained flesh and blood. When she opened the door, one of them was doing a little dance to keep warm.

"Okay," she said. "Let's go."

"Just you, ma'am," replied the dancer. "Sheriff's orders."

Uh-huh.

Esme kissed her husband goodbye and joined the deputies in their brown squad car. She noticed that the streets were almost all clear of snow and that the sidewalks had already been salted. Impressed, she reclined in the stiff backseat as they drove downtown—and then past the county station and kept on going.

"Um," she said.

They took a left toward the interstate.

"Excuse me…" she said.

"Sit tight, ma'am. We'll be there in a jiffy."

"That's fine and all but, well, where's there?"

There turned out to be Stewart International Airport some forty-five minutes later. They pulled up to the terminal. The dancer got out and escorted Esme to the curb while the other deputy remained behind the wheel.

Behind a door marked Official Use Only, Sheriff Fallon was waiting for them, a cup of coffee in his hand. His grin left little doubt in Esme's mind; this, finally, was the cat that ate the canary.

"Good morning!" he said.

In an adjacent room, he went on to say, sat the Weiner family. A member of airport security was keeping them company. Their plane had finally touched down about two hours ago and he knew, just knew, that she'd want to be there when he questioned them.

"Thanks," she replied, and added Sheriff Fallon to her list of IRS record pulls.

They began with the father, Todd, who could have carried the sheriff's deputies in the bags hanging under his eyes. His hands couldn't keep still, either twitching and fumbling with the zipper on his L.L. Bean ski jacket or fixing the part on his thinning brown hair. This was not a calm man—but then again, how often did one's house get burned to the ground with a body left in the basement? Perhaps he was worried they suspected him. Perhaps he was worried they thought he put the body there.

"I didn't know her," he insisted. "We all looked at those photos and none of us had ever seen her before in our lives. I swear."

The interview lasted about an hour. Most of it consisted of Todd Weiner repeating that he didn't know her, or anything, or anyone, and asking several times if this would be covered by his homeowners' insurance. Esme believed more and more that her hunch—about the house being the key—had been way off.

And then Todd said something odd.

"I knew it was too good to be true."

Sheriff Fallon nodded at Esme, allowing her to take the bait.

"You knew what was too good to be true, Mr. Weiner?"

"This contest. I told Louise I didn't remember signing up on their website."

"What contest?"

Todd Weiner looked up at them like they'd just claimed two plus two equaled an apple. "Hammond Travel Agency. That's how we went on this trip. We won it in a contest from Hammond Travel Agency out in New Paltz."

6

Finally—finally!—Timothy had found the perfect pet. Like all true heroes of myth (the Norse legends of the Viking civilization being his favorite), he just needed to recognize his own hubris before achieving success. He had been so quick to blame his previous pet, Lynette, for everything that went wrong when, in fact, some of the finger pointing belonged in his own direction. Had it really been wise to capture an adult? Don't most pet owners start with puppies and kittens rather than dogs and cats? How foolish he had been to think he could improve on centuries of domestication.

In short, Timothy needed to think younger, and he found his ideal in, of all places, his mother's veterinary clinic. As the first snow fell Friday morning, he walked the familiar two miles from their house to her clinic, which was in the same strip mall as his father's travel agency. He enjoyed the taste of the snowflakes, and made sure to catch as many as he could with his tongue.

On his way to the clinic he passed the middle school, where the rest of his peers (and that was the right word— as loath as the old Timothy had been to admit it, these were his peers; he was not a young god) were crowded inside. Timothy hadn't stepped foot in that building in more than a year, ever since that incident in the cafeteria with Mr. Monroe's earlobe. His parents had filed the appropriate papers for him to be homeschooled and that was that. Still, as Timothy passed by it, his heart filled with a sense of longing. He was, after all, the new Timothy, person of the world, no different from anyone else. Well, hardly different.

The purpose for his snowbound stroll to Mother's clinic was to get his wrist reexamined. It had been three days since Lynette had bit him, and although his wound had been properly mended and treated, a bite mark was a bite mark. Perhaps Mother was going to give him a rabies shot.

The other businesses in the strip mall, besides the vet clinic and the travel agency, were a take-out Chinese restaurant, a discount shoe store and a nail salon. The nail salon always had its front door open and emitted such an overpowering reek of ethyl acetate that one whiff of it made Timothy gag. He had tried in the past to circle around and approach the strip mall from the back, but somehow that stench waited for him there. Lynette's fingernails hadn't smelled like that. He'd made sure to check each one before removing her hands.

As it happened, he still had the Taser C2 in the left pocket of his coat. He carried it around with him now wherever he went. It was soothing to hold and squeeze. He'd bought it with his father's credit card from a website in Hong Kong that Cain42 had recommended. The soldering iron, which he'd used to cauterize Lynette's stumps, had just been a purchase at the local Home Depot. He'd left it in the Weiner house. The soldering iron hadn't been nearly as soothing to hold and squeeze as the Taser C2, which actually resembled the electric razor he used to trim his peach fuzz. Timothy had once used Father's manual razor to shave, and had ended up slicing open his chin. He still remembered the blood droplets plunking into the sink—drip...drip...drip— like from a runny faucet. He had a tiny scar there now, a pale white hash mark, and late at night he sometimes ran his fingertips across it. That was soothing, too. He wondered what restful archaeology would be left by the teeth marks on his wrist.

These were Timothy's aimless thoughts as he crossed First Street at the light and ambled into the parking lot. He held his breath but it did no good. The nail salon's pungency attacked him, anyway, nauseated his stomach, sent acid up into his throat. He would be safe once he entered the vet clinic. The animals had a safe smell. He would be safe once he—

And then he saw her. Lying there alone in the backseat of a brown station wagon. The station wagon's engine was still running. Its owner undoubtedly had some kind of pet emergency; otherwise, why leave the engine running? Why leave such perfection alone in the backseat? She was sleeping there, so peaceful, her oversize head listing a bit to the left. A few tufts of blond hair covered what was otherwise a bare scalp. A soft scalp. Because the human skull took a while to completely harden, and this beauty, this wonder, this perfect pet of his, couldn't have been older than three weeks.

Timothy swooned. Love at first sight.

He had to be swift and very, very careful. He had two options: try to steal her out of her car seat or simply slip behind the wheel himself and drive off to a more secluded location. Given the complexity of buckles and belts and snaps he beheld crisscrossing his new pet's little body (most of which was swathed in a blue onesie that depicted a name—Marcy—outlined in red sailboats), he decided to pursue the latter course of action. His gaze danced to the clinic door, and then he moved, swiftly, carefully, to the driver's door. This he knew would be unlocked; the keys, after all, were still in the ignition. He slid into the front seat. It didn't need much adjusting. The infant's mother must have been around his own five foot five. The old Timothy may have scoffed at such pedestrian concepts as coincidence, but this new Timothy offered up a thanks to the Powers That Be for his height and for giving him this perfect pet and for his uncle teaching him how to drive when he was twelve. He shifted the brown station wagon into Reverse.

He drove off to his secret place, his special place. His new pet, Marcy, slept through the entire trip. Every ten seconds Timothy would peek at her face in the rearview. The eyes were closed, but Timothy knew what color they would be. Blue.

He parked near his secret place. By now an inch had accumulated on the ground, and his sneakers crunched powder with every step. That was fine. The time for stealth was almost over. He went around to the side of the car, studied those buckles and belts and straps for a good five minutes and then went to work unfastening them, which took another fifteen.

Behind him, traffic passed. No one paid much attention to what they saw. They were too eager to return home before the snowstorm really hit.

Then Marcy awoke. Her eyes were more green than blue, and they searched Timothy's face for the semi-familiar features of her mother or father. Her eyesight could discern shapes and colors, but details would be a mystery for another few weeks. This wasn't her mother, she concluded. So it must be her father.

She wanted her mother.

She cried.

Timothy picked her up out of the car seat. Marcy's face scrunched up and she cried some more. "Shh," he told her. She ignored him. He held her at arm's length. Snowflakes dissolved on her round reddening face. "Please stop," he said. But she didn't. They were not far from downtown, and although everyone was hurrying home, a crying baby would still draw attention. Had he chosen poorly? Was she maybe not his perfect pet?

"Please," he begged her.

Silencing Marcy would actually have been relatively easy. All he had to do was cradle her head with one hand and then smash that head, forehead first, into the roof of the station wagon. Her soft skull probably would explode like a piece of citrus, all pulp and juice and ripped ripe peel.

But that was the old Timothy. He was fourteen now. He was a man. He was more patient. The new Timothy held Marcy against his shoulder and bounced at the knee. He'd seen people do this in the mall. It seemed to work.

It had to work.

It worked. Marcy's face and body relaxed. Her cries stopped. Her eyes recommenced their exploration of the world around her. The sky seemed to be falling. How pretty.

Timothy didn't waste any time. He hurried her, still on his shoulder, to his secret place. Nobody would find her here. Nobody would hear her. She would be safe and warm and his. He settled her into her new home, made sure she was secure and then rushed back to the brown station wagon. Its engine was still running. He thought about Marcy's mother. By now she must have returned to the parking lot. By now she must have realized her child was no longer hers. He drove up to the university campus and parked in one of the more populated lots. He unrolled all of the car's windows, tossed the keys into a sewer drain and caught the next bus back to town.

He bought his new pet some supplies: formula, a pink blanket, diapers, a plush smiling antelope. The stores were beginning to shutter their doors for the day. People in line were talking accumulation. They were talking one to two feet. They paid no mind to a fourteen-year-old boy running an errand for his baby sister.

Once he had returned to his secret place, once he fed his new pet and played with her little hands and watched her close her green eyes—how big they were!—he knew he'd best get on his way. Blizzards inconvenienced the best of intentions, even for the new Timothy.

That night, Mother made lamb. The three of them ate quietly. No mention was made of the baby-napping that had occurred right outside her clinic. Their household was as soundless as the falling snow. Once he was finished, Timothy excused himself and went to his room. It was time to share his great good news with Cain42.

Later that night, around 3:00 a.m., he borrowed his parents' car, drove out through the snow to his secret place and spent some more time with Marcy. He wasn't surprised to find her crying, so he fed her some formula and changed her diaper and rocked her in his arms. He was genuinely surprised how much that seemed to quiet her down and deeply regretted having to leave, but he needed to return home before sunup, if only because of the borrowed car.

Timothy awoke late the next morning with rare verve. His thoughts immediately went to Marcy. He couldn't wait to see her again and play with her. Both of his parents had already gone to work. Mother had left him a note, reminding him to stop by the clinic, since he hadn't done so yesterday. That would have to be his first destination.

The outside air was crisp. Timothy tucked his hands into his heavy coat. His left hand closed around his Taser C2. He walked slower than usual along the road, cognizant of slippery patches. Such was the price he paid for always wearing sneakers. It was almost noon by the time he first spotted the strip mall and—

There was a squad car parked in front of the travel agency.

Timothy's mind whirred. Along the side of the squad car were the words *Sullivan County Sheriff's Department*. This wasn't about Marcy. This was about Lynette. Somehow they had made the connection between the house and the free trip. What had he done wrong? He had been meticulous! He had followed all of Cain42's rules to the letter, hadn't he? What would Father tell them? What was Father already telling them? If they had come this far, surely they would be able to piece together the missing child. After all, he had taken her from right in front of his mother's own clinic. Stupid! The old Timothy had been right all along.

He needed to contact Cain42. Cain42 would know how to proceed. Timothy headed back to the house, quickly, his breath sending smoke signals into the sky.

On the walls of Hammond Travel Agency were posters, dozens and dozens of posters, all depicting a Wonder of the World or a Work of Art or Great Sight to See Before You Die. They weren't arranged by country or even continent. Here was the Parthenon next to the Sydney Opera House next to an ad for a safari in Zaire.

It reminded Esme of a bedroom and a jewelry box and her heart sank a bit. How Lynette Robinson would have loved this place.

The proprietor of the travel agency was a pleasant-faced fellow named Patrick Hammond. "Call me P.J.," he told them. "Everyone does."

Esme and Sheriff Fallon sat down by P.J. at his geography lesson of a desk. Two globes occupied opposite corners of the desk. Esme spun one. She couldn't resist. Her finger landed on the Canary Islands.

"We actually have a package," said P.J., "that includes the Canary Islands and Casablanca, all expenses paid, for well under three thousand."

She smiled at him. This man wasn't one for the soft sell. He exuded confidence and calmness. It was only when she sat back in her seat that she wondered how much of it was an act. If Tom were here, Esme was certain that he would have been able to figure out Patrick "Call Me P.J." Hammond in half a second…if there were anything to figure out. But that's why she and Sheriff Fallon were here.

"So tell us about this contest," the sheriff said.

"Well, that's our pride and joy!" P.J. flashed them a grin that spanned from wall to wall. "It's a sales promotion, really, but you'd never know it. Once a year we offer a raffle. All you've got to do to enter is fill out a form on our website. That adds you to our emailing list, but it also makes you eligible for the annual contest. In the past, we've sent families on cruises to, oh, Bermuda, Cancún, Nova Scotia, the western Mediterranean. We have over a thousand subscribers to our weekly newsletter from all across the state and even a few in

Massachusetts and Vermont. Sheriff Fallon, have you ever been to Tahiti?"

"Sir, as I said on the phone, this is a murder investigation."

"Yes. You're absolutely right, and trust me, Sheriff, when I read about what happened in the newspaper, I was horrified. What is this world coming to, right? I can't imagine some of the truly terrible things you must encounter on a daily basis. Our jobs couldn't be more different. I have tremendous respect for law enforcement. I couldn't do it. Wouldn't that be funny, though, if instead of offering vacations to exotic places, we could take trips into other people's lives? Now that would be some travel agency."

Sheriff Fallon shifted in his seat. He was not charmed.

Esme, on the other hand, was enjoying P. J. Hammond very much. He was either a genuinely nice, optimistic human being or he was a fantastic performer putting out all the stops to conceal a bottomless darkness. Either way, it made for a great show.

However, Rafe was still stuck at the house, undoubtedly going stir crazy. "P.J.," she said. "Could you walk us through exactly how you came to choose the Weiners to win the contest?"

"You bet, although it really wasn't me who chose them."

"Then who did?" asked Sheriff Fallon.

Because whoever had selected them was their prime suspect.

P.J. pointed a finger at his laptop computer, which was plugged into a cable modem. "It did."

Sheriff Fallon blinked. "Excuse me?"

"It would take me too much time to sift through

everyone who's a subscriber. Like I said, we're talking over a thousand people. They don't make a hat that big, do they? Can you imagine a hat that big? Can you imagine a head big enough to wear a hat that big?"

"So you use a computer program," said Esme.

"Computers run the world these days," P.J. replied. "We just turn them on and off."

"Can you demonstrate this program for us?"

P.J. shrugged and double-clicked an icon. A small window appeared. It listed a number—1,024—and next to that number was a radio button that read Select.

"All I do is press this button," he said. "Except the name and contact information it's going to select now won't be the Weiners. It chooses at random from the 1,024 names in the system. I mean, the odds of it choosing the Weiners again—ever—would be…"

"One in 1,024?"

P.J. nodded. "Not astronomical, but high."

"Click the button," said Esme.

He did.

Another window popped up with a name and contact information.

Todd Weiner, 18 Value Street.

"Huh," murmured P.J. "Well, like I said, the odds weren't astronomical. That's kind of cool, actually. Todd Weiner must be one lucky guy. Except for, you know, that whole house-burning-down thing."

"Click it again, P.J.," Esme said, so P.J. did.

Todd Weiner, 18 Value Street.

This time, P.J.'s sunny composure dimmed a bit. He stared in confusion at his laptop screen. Then he clicked the radio button again, and again, and again.

"Where did you get this software from, sir?"

"I downloaded it from this business website. Lots of

people use it." His confidence was mushing into a stammer. "I've been using it for years and have never had a problem!"

Which left, as Esme saw it, two options: someone had tampered with his software *or* P. J. Hammond was a lying sack of shit.

Sheriff Fallon rose to his feet. "Sir, I think you're going to need to come with us."

The shop door jangled open. All heads turned and saw two men and one woman, all in police browns, saunter in. The woman had a sheriff's badge and a name tag that read Shuster.

"Afternoon, Mike," she said.

"Hey, there, Betsy. I know I had one of my guys call your office to give you the heads-up that we were going to be in your neck of the woods. I hope they didn't tell you we needed an escort."

"Mike, can I talk to you for a minute?"

"Sure."

He stepped away from the desk and followed Betsy Shuster outside. Her two deputies remained inside, appearing uncomfortable. Something was very wrong. Esme glanced over at P.J., who had become even grayer.

Sheriff Fallon returned.

"Let's go," he said to Esme.

"What's going on?"

He looked past her at P.J. "Thank you for your time."

By the looks of it, P.J. was as befuddled as Esme. She wanted to shout out, *Wait, wait,* but Fallon was reaching for her. He was eager to leave right now. And since she was only here at all as a courtesy, she really didn't have a choice.

That said, once they returned to his car…

"What the fuck was that!"

He exhaled a weighty sigh and stared out the windshield at Betsy Shuster and her deputies, who were making their way to the vet clinic several doors down.

"Yesterday a child was abducted here. About ten minutes ago, the police received an anonymous email from the abductor. He said that if the Lynette Robinson investigation didn't stop immediately, he was going to kill the child. To prove his veracity, he attached a very, very recent photograph of the baby's face. So get comfortable. We're heading home."

7

When Esme relayed the news to Rafe, she was certain he was going to slam another pot against a wall. She wouldn't have blamed him if he had. She felt like smashing a few pieces of cookware herself.

Sheriff Fallon had notified the state police in Albany of the situation. They were conferring about the matter. But Esme wasn't sure what they felt they could do. She wasn't sure what anyone could do. In one move, this psychopath had checkmated them.

If they'd had a stronger case, if they'd had more information, they might have been able to flank him, avenging Lynette Robinson's murder while simultaneously keeping him from harming little Marcy Harper. But they'd failed. She had failed. Rafe had imbued all this trust in her—for the first time—and she had monumentally fallen on her face. If only she'd had more time…

P. J. Hammond obviously remained the prime suspect. In truth, he remained the only suspect. Had P.J. sent the anonymous email to the Ulster County police? It was possible. Sheriff Betsy Shuster was attempting to get a warrant to sift through his computer. Since the abduction had taken place so close to his place of business, and since time was so essential…

But Esme knew that no judge, not even a provincial saint, would sign such a warrant, not even in antiprivacy post-9/11 America. The FBI possibly could have pushed the warrant through, and she was tempted to call the local office, but until the crime crossed state lines, this remained out of their jurisdiction. She could plant a tip that Baby Marcy had been seen in Vermont…

No.

Tomorrow, Sheriff Fallon would have to break the news to Lynette's family. Better they find out from him than from a leak in the department. She felt sorry for him. This was his land and an invader had murdered one of the citizens he'd sworn to protect and now that bastard was going to get away with it. There would never be justice. There would never be closure.

Now it was Saturday night. Rafe lay beside her in his parents' bed. Even though his back was to her, she could tell he was awake. She wanted to say something. She wanted to make him feel better. But how could she, when she was in part to blame for his restlessness? And so she stared at the shape of her husband's back, barely visible in the darkness of the room, barely more than the shadow of a shadow.

She dreamed about Galileo.

She was in her house back in Oyster Bay, on the second floor, in the hallway. All of the doors—to her bedroom, to Sophie's bedroom, to the bathroom—were shut. Esme tried her daughter's door first, but there was no knob. The door was really just an indented part of the wall. Even the flowery wallpaper was beginning to seep across the doors, as if its decorated ivy were real. She raised a hand to touch the design and could feel the veiny texture of the ivy. The width of the curly green stalks was oscillating, almost as if…almost as if the ivy were breathing. Almost as if it were alive. And hungry. Then the green veins bent toward her face and slowly extended, wrapping around her wrists, her forearms, her biceps. She called out for Rafe. She called out for Sophie. She called out for Tom. Her bedroom door at the end of the hallway opened. Henry Booth—Galileo—stood there. He was naked. In the center of his hairless, muscular chest was a peephole. Esme could see through it to the other side. Rafe and Sophie were on that other side, cowering, so small. Panicking now, Esme looked back at the door to her daughter's room and her arms were no longer being held by veins of ivy but by a pair of hands, and Esme knew they were Lynette's hands and Esme knew they were angry and would never let her go, and Galileo took a step toward her now and his hands weren't hands at all but eels, eels with jaws and teeth, snapping jaws, and he held them out to her and the jaws snapped as they approached, snapped, snapped, and soon they would be at her left ear, snap, and soon they would be at her left eyeball, snap, and then her—

She awoke in her own sweat. The bedroom was ablaze with early-morning sunlight. She checked her iPod. It was 6:58 a.m. Apparently, this weekend she was destined to undersleep. Great. At least Rafe, from the sound of it, had finally achieved some semblance of shut-eye. She curled her body around his, careful not to disturb his rhythmic snoring, and forced herself back into dreamland, all the while fearful of what might come.

They woke up together around 10:00 a.m., all warm and toasty under the wool blanket. The mesh of their body-to-body heat didn't hurt, either. They snuggled.

At that moment both Esme and Rafe were thinking about the same thing, and both wondering what the other was thinking about. It hadn't always been this awkward, surely, but they hadn't had sex in more than half a year. They knew each other's bodies as well as any two people could but at that moment, in that bed, they might as well have been desperate strangers.

The first, obvious step was that they needed to face each other, and since Esme currently had her face nuzzled against Rafe's nape, that meant the pressure was on him. And he knew it. His eyes were open but he wasn't looking at anything but what the next few minutes could become. And all the while he heard the *tick-tick-tick* of Dr. Rosen's two weeks.

Her hands were near his paunch. How easy it would be to simply guide them a few inches south. He would enjoy that. She would enjoy that. She always said she enjoyed that. She had always been honest with him. She was a good person. He'd married a good person. Why did he always let all of this extraneous bullshit get in the way? Hell, why was he ruminating about his wife, who was lying there right beside him, instead of making love to her? Why not just—

"I'm going to put on some coffee," she said, and he heard her walk away.

Way to go, Hamlet, he mused. Overanalyzing has won you yet again. He rolled over and buried his face in her pillow. He was his own cold shower. Shortly thereafter, he roused himself out of bed and joined Esme in the kitchen for some Sunday morning joe. Had Lester subscribed to the newspaper, they could have at least spent those few minutes perusing the headlines, trading entertainment section for sports section, but the old man had, of course, since relocating to Oyster Bay, let his subscription lapse, and so the only news Rafe and Esme had to occupy them was their own.

So they sipped in silence.

When they were through, Esme called home. She spoke to Sophie for a few minutes, assured her they would be back soon, and yes, she would be there tomorrow to chaperone the trip to the science museum. Then she handed the phone to Rafe.

"Hi, cupcake."

"Hi, Daddy!"

Esme started packing.

"So what did you and Grandpa Les do yesterday?"

"We built a snowman and it was tall except he added two pieces of snow to the front so it became a snowwoman." Sophie giggled. Her father didn't. "I miss you, Daddy."

"I miss you, too, cupcake. Very much. Do you have any homework to do for tomorrow?"

"Just some math. But I'm waiting until you come home because I know you like to help me with my math."

He smiled. "I think you waited because you don't want to do it."

"I hate math. It's boring."

"I know. But sometimes we have to do things we don't like so we can do the things we like to do."

"Like watch TV after my bedtime?"

"Maybe," he replied. "We'll see. Put your grandpa on the phone, okay? I love you ten times infinity."

"I love *you* ten times one hundred plus infinity and twelve!"

Once Lester got on the phone, Rafe informed him when they expected to be home. Lester chided him about the condition of his old house and warned him to make sure everything was left in good working order and that the faucets were still dripping and the windows were all shut, etc. Finally, Rafe was able to get to the goodbyes.

It was shortly after eleven.

Both Rafe and Esme were hungry for brunch, so they stopped at a twenty-four-hour diner that was on the way to downtown. Rafe didn't need to look at a menu. As a teenager, he must have eaten at this place, well, ten times one hundred plus infinity and twelve. The food was cheap and the service was quick. This was a no-nonsense establishment and, even as a teen, Rafe had been a no-nonsense type of guy. The kind who's too indecisive to get laid by his own wife, he noted, and paid for the check with a credit card.

Their next stop was the Robinson house.

They were still receiving visitors, of course. Many relatives had arrived from out of town to pay their respects. Misery may have loved company, but it was company which kept misery at bay.

Lynette's mother hugged Rafe.

"She was always very fond of you," the woman said.

And Rafe shattered into a million pieces.

Once he'd regained his composure in the bathroom, which took some doing, he found Esme in the corner of the den, noshing on an Asiago bagel. She had never been one for mingling. Back in Oyster Bay, he had to push her to get involved in local civic activities. For all of her toughness and acumen, his wife could be astonishingly shy.

"Ready to go?" he asked.

She finished her bagel in two bites and they headed outside to the Prius. Around them trickled the sound of melting snow. It had to be in the low fifties already, and probably was going to climb half a dozen digits more by midday. The highway would be clear of ice and Rafe wondered if they might even get to spend some of the drive with the windows down.

He checked his mirrors and shifted into Drive. He was eager to get the hell out of here.

"Can we stop at the station before we go? I want to say goodbye to Sheriff Fallon."

So instead of taking a left, toward the interstate, they took a right and pulled into the now-familiar parking lot, crowded if only because of the church across the street.

"Want me to stay in the car?" he inquired.

"Don't be silly."

They locked the car and mounted the steps to the weather-beaten brick-and-cement building, and were halfway across the front hall, which also led to the county's many other offices, but neither of them spotted the man by the door until he called out her name.

"Hello, Esmeralda," said Tom.

"But I thought…" said Esme.

"So did I," Tom replied. "And then my girlfriend slapped me upside the head for being a fool and got me on the next flight here."

"I can't wait to meet her."

"She can't wait to meet you."

Rafe didn't want to meet any of them. He stood off to the side while his wife and her erstwhile Svengali reconnected. No, he was not a fan of Tom Piper, special agent extraordinaire, still wearing that ancient black leather jacket even though there was no way he rode a motorcycle here, not in his condition, and especially not since his motorcycle was, due to a swindle, busy collecting dust in their garage in Oyster Bay. It had been Rafe's small victory and it had done very little to diminish the personal disdain he felt for this ridiculous John Wayne wannabe.

"Too bad you came all this way for nothing," said Rafe.

Tom and Esme looked at him.

"Oh, didn't you tell him, Esme? The investigation's been closed."

Esme sighed. "The unsub sent an untraceable email demanding the investigation be closed or he would murder a kidnapped infant named Marcy Harper."

"Are we sure he can make good on his claim?" asked Tom. "And that the email is untraceable?"

"He attached a jpeg to the email. And the address it was sent from is a bunch of nonsense."

Tom frowned.

"Well, it was good seeing you, Tom!" Rafe held out his hand. "Have a safe trip back home."

"Excuse me," Esme said to Tom, and led her husband several yards away where the two of them, well, traded words.

"Esme, there's no reason to waste his time, is there?"

"What is it with you? Whenever Tom comes around, you suddenly turn into a two-year-old brat."

"Me? I'm just trying to do what's best for everyone."

"What about Lynette? What about what's best for her?"

"There is no best for her. Some unconscionable prick saw to that."

"And I'd think you'd want that prick brought to justice."

"Of course I do, Esme, but that ship's sailed and we both know that. You couldn't catch him in time."

"Fuck you."

"Am I wrong?"

"After the way you treated the poor girl, I'd think you'd put aside your pigheadedness and consider anyone's help, even Tom's, but I guess I underestimated how much of a horse's ass you really were!"

"Call it whatever you'd like, Esme. I call it disrespect."

"You're a quitter."

Rafe blinked. "Excuse me?"

"The going got tough here and so you're running back home. Our marriage got tough so you threw in the towel."

"I'm the one who suggested we see a counselor!"

"You'd made up your mind about us months ago. And once your mind was made up, the best marriage counselor in the world couldn't have put us back together. Apparently, you were like this back in high school so how could I expect you to be any different today?"

"What could I have done differently back then? Huh? I gave Lynette everything—"

"—that you were prepared to give. But sometimes, Rafe, sometimes you just got to go beyond that. Sometimes you have to push yourself, rather than other people."

"The investigation is closed!"

"Those are his rules, Rafe. I don't play by his rules."

He stared at her. She stared back at him.

Then he started for the front entrance.

"Where are you going?" she called.

"To get your stuff out of the car. If you're staying,

you're staying. Our daughter needs at least one of her parents at home. Remember her? Our daughter."

"Of course I do, Rafe. She's your favorite excuse."

Rafe's left hand tightened on his keys. The iron edges bit into the soft flesh of his palm.

It took all of two minutes for him to heft Esme's suitcase out of the trunk, carry it back into the county building and set it with exaggerated gentleness on the thick oak floor. Then he looked up at Tom, who was standing there, stoic as a stone, as always.

"Never a pleasure," said Rafe. And then, to his wife: "Use the spare key to Dad's house. You know where it is. Use the bed for all I care." That last statement was for the both of them.

He indeed had his window open on the drive back to Oyster Bay.

It was still light out by the time he pulled into his tony development. His shoulders and hands ached with tension. He made sure to wave at every one of his neighbors he saw as he drove by, keeping to the child-friendly five-miles-per-hour speed limit. Some were out with their kids, at play in the softening snow. Some were winterizing the outsides of their homes. Winter was coming. Only a fool stood in the way of inevitable change.

Only a fool.

Rafe's thoughts turned to lawyers. He knew enough of them. Half of the men and women he greeted just now were either associates in a Manhattan firm or junior partners in a firm out here on the Island. No, there was no shortage of litigation in this part of the country.

So many of the people he knew from his own college days were divorced. Even some of his graduate students—bright folks only in their midtwenties—had one or two divorces under their belts. The American divorce had become its own subfield of sociology. Rafe had always leaned more toward popular culture, and contemporary popular culture was infused with the idea of most marriages being temporary. After all, this was the twenty-first century. Everything was temporary: trends in the stock market, personal careers, diets, e-companies. For he and Esme to still be married after eight years was practically quaint.

Not that that was a reason to seek a divorce. But he had other reasons, better reasons, didn't he? The situation had become untenable. Dr. Rosen had given them two weeks, but that had really been nothing more than her kind way of offering two weeks' notice on their marriage. Only a fool stood in the way of inevitable change, and a practical man like Rafe needed to act before the curve. Procrastination was a simpleton's game. She had called him a quitter, but it was she who had quit this marriage, wasn't it?

Rafe pulled into his garage. There was Tom's motorcycle, draped in a leather shroud to protect it in case, God forbid, it ever rained inside their garage. So often he'd wanted to take a bat to that piece of machinery, but all this reflection about divorce had planted a better idea in his mind. He would sell the motorcycle on eBay.

He carried his suitcase into the house and was immediately besieged by Sophie, her arms wrapping around his legs like a love-struck boa constrictor. How he missed his little girl. Why couldn't all love be this simple? Maybe true love was.

"Where's Mommy?" she asked. She peered up at him with his own eyes. They searched his face with the curiosity of innocence. How exactly does one explain divorce to an angel?

Before he could answer, Lester padded into the room,

half a grilled-cheese sandwich in his hand. The football game was on mute, and that just went to show how interested the old man was in what Rafe was about to say.

"She had some business she had to finish upstate," Rafe replied, choosing his words carefully. "It might take a while."

Almost immediately, Sophie's curiosity drooped into a pout.

Lester's expression was much more positive.

"Will she be back in time for the science museum?"

"I don't think so, cupcake."

"But she promised."

Lester stepped in. He couldn't resist. "Guess whatever she's doing up there she thinks is more important."

"More important than the science museum…?" Sophie's eyes watered. "But she promised…"

Rafe hugged her close. He would take care of her. He had his priorities in order.

8

Tom and Esme were at the twenty-four-hour diner, sharing a breastplate full of nachos and perusing the Sunday paper. There were front-page articles about both Lynette Robinson's murder and Marcy Harper's kidnapping. The reporters hadn't linked the two, but it was just a matter of time before someone in the county sheriff departments, either Sullivan or Ulster, leaked.

"So what's the plan?" she asked.

His eyes scanned hers. "If you want to talk about it…"

"I want to talk about *this*," she replied.

Tom nodded. Far be it from him to step in the way of her compartmentalization. For now, at least.

"First, I need you to update me on everything I've missed."

So she did. It took about twenty minutes and most of the nachos. Through it all, Tom absorbed the information, sifted it, organized it. The picture was far from vivid, but it was getting there.

He paid for the nachos. "Now we go to the crime scene."

They took his rental, a black Mustang that had seen

better days, but so had they, hadn't they? Regardless, Value Street wasn't too far away. Nothing was too far away here. Tom parked across the street from the ruins that had once been the residence of the Weiner clan. The snow had weighed down the police tape so much that even with the thaw, the yellow plastic remained only inches from the ground, only a deterrent now for ants and spiders.

The fire had gutted most of the interior and shattered at least the front-facing windows, decomposing the house into a thirty-foot-tall eyeless, toothless corpse. The uniformity in structure, color and condition of 18 Value Street's neighbors made the contrast even more hideous and distasteful. Here was a half-acre of 1945 Dresden in the middle of 1955 Levittown.

Esme stepped through slush toward the rotted two-story box and its contents of ashes. The ashes themselves intermingled with snow, resulting in salt-and-pepper scatterings all across the lot, occasionally carried aloft by currents of wind. It all had a strange, hellish beauty.

"So our most likely suspect is an affable travel agent from New Paltz, huh?"

Just hearing the words spilling out of Tom's mouth underlined the doubt she had in her mind that P. J. Hammond was their guy. But it wasn't P.J.'s affability that had her worried. She had, in her time, met plenty of gregarious psychopaths, and had studied the Ted Bundy case at the academy. Outward personality rarely mirrored inward turmoil, even in the most sane of people. What had her worried, what raised her concern that P. J. Hammond wasn't their guy, was all the evidence indicating that he *was*.

"Our first question has to be, how did he find this location? New Paltz is an hour away, isn't it?"

They looked around at the neighborhood. They saw houses and lawns. Some doors still had their papier-mâché Halloween witches. Some had their Thanksgiving turkeys. Several doors down from the crime scene, Value Street was bisected by Turner Road. Esme and Tom walked the length and turned the corner. Turner Road was more of a thoroughfare. A public library sat at the intersection, with a sign and bench for public transportation at its front curb. About a quarter of a mile to the east was a modest-size church. About a quarter of a mile to the west was a cemetery.

"Maybe he has family in the area." Her questioning of the suspect had been interrupted well before she'd had a chance to ask many personal inquiries. "But according to the police report, that library's the last known location of Lynette Robinson before she went missing. And we also know that the victim frequented the library on a fairly regular schedule. So he chose the house because of its vicinity to the library and knew when to show up to grab her. But it still doesn't answer the basic question of how he found her in the first place, or here, or anything."

"That's not the half of it." He turned on his heel and started back toward the crime scene. "You're the unsub. You go through the trouble of making sure a house is going to be empty for almost two weeks. You buy a collar, some chains, and you kidnap Lynette Robinson and tie her up. You've got plenty of time to have your fun, but instead you burn down the house?"

"Maybe something happened. Maybe there was an accident. Except the evidence contradicts that theory. The fire started in the kitchen and it was an electrical explosion. So unless our unsub is incredibly incompetent with appliances, there's no accident. Which means he burned the house down on purpose even though he had ten days left of free rein in the place. Something Lynette did set him off and he overreacted."

"You overreact by killing the victim. You don't overreact by destroying the sanctuary, do you? But that's what he did. He intentionally destroyed his sanctuary, his special place. Now why would a man do that?"

"Guilt, perhaps, after committing the actual murder?"

"And then he kidnaps a child from a running car?" Tom shook his head. "The kind of guilt that causes a man to burn down a house doesn't fade in a few days, does it? This wasn't an act of guilt."

"Then what was it? Why did he destroy his sanctuary?"

They had returned to the ash heap. Tom stood by the mailbox, incongruously brand-new, freshly painted red and planted at the foot of the driveway.

"We need to have a sit-down with Mr. Hammond," he said, staring at the rubble. "We're trying to draw a cube with two dots and a crayon."

"He's seen me. He knows I'm with the Bureau. I step foot anywhere near him and Marcy Harper's life gets put in immediate jeopardy."

"Make no mistake," replied Tom. "Marcy Harper's life *is* in immediate jeopardy."

They trundled through the slush to his rented Mustang. Its white sidewalls were already splattered with wet dirt from the roads. Value Street itself was narrow and his car, parked in front of the wreckage, nearly took up half the width of the street.

Tom climbed into the driver's seat.

Esme paused.

And then she walked back up to Turner Road.

Tom got out of the car and followed her.

"What is it?" he asked. "What are you thinking?"

"I'm thinking, where did he park?"

They looked back at the Mustang.

"Not in the street," replied Tom.

"Not unless it was a timed explosion. Half the neighborhood would have seen him peel away from the crime scene."

"So he escapes out the back door and cuts behind these houses to here. There's no parking on the road, but it looks like both the library and the church have plenty of space in their lots."

Esme crossed the street to the library, but stopped at the bench. "The police report said that a city bus showed up about five minutes after the explosion was first called in. Interviews with the driver verify that timeline."

"So you're saying our guy escaped on the bus?"

Esme sat on the bench, and then very quickly stood, the seat of her pants now moist. "Damn it. No. I mean, yes. I mean, it's possible. Isn't it?"

"When you're working with a blank canvas," replied Tom, "anything's possible."

The streetlight by the bus stop blinked on. It would be dark soon, and cold. Tom and Esme walked back to the Mustang. She gave him directions to her father-in-law's house. As they left the neighborhood, she turned around in her seat and watched the bus stop fade into the distance, and Tom watched it in the rearview, both of them hoping that there was a straight line that led from that bus stop to Marcy Harper and justice.

The candlelight vigil was very well attended.

Ostensibly, it was a spontaneous event. Word of mouth inspired acts of solidarity, and by 8:00 p.m. a swarm had gathered in the parking lot of the strip mall where Baby Marcy Harper had been taken. Not many of the attendees actually knew the Harpers, but a missing child was the universal horror, and so everyone sympathized with the mother, razor-blade-thin Gladys, and the father, alcohol-dipped Harold. Candles were lit. Hymns were sung. Strangers were hugged and held.

The manager of the local Kinkos had made a blow-up poster of Marcy's photograph. It sat on an easel under the strip mall awning.

From the outskirts, the media affiliates filmed b-roll. This had been a busy week for them—first the scandalous murder and now a child abduction. And not just a child, but an infant. This kind of kismet birthed national careers. This kind of drama led to Pulitzers. The reporters and anchormen and bloggers shuffled their ambition to the backs of their minds, where it remained, well-behaved and grinning. Of course, these journalists had as much compassion as the other attendees at the vigil. The other attendees, though, had Sundays off. The journalists, as they jostled for the prime footage, the most heartwarming interview, the pithiest encapsulation, were on the clock.

The mother, Gladys, smoked like, well, smoked like a burning house. She smoked Newports. She'd gone through half a pack in half an hour. It was her last pack. Soon she'd have to hit up someone in the crowd for a cigarette, maybe one of those journalists who interviewed her earlier. The least they could do was spare a cigarette. That's why these people were here, anyway: support. Her child was missing and her box turtle had cancer. That was what she was doing here yesterday, why she'd panicked and driven to the vet and left her daughter in the car seat. She knew what the other mothers were saying about her, that she was irresponsible, that she deserved whatever misery she got, but Gladys had had that turtle since she was two years old. Growing up, her classmates had made fun of her because she had a reptile for a pet while they had their cute little kittens and loyal dependable puppies but those kittens and puppies died after fifteen years, and she'd had Rex now for almost twenty-five. So when she noticed the curlicues of blood floating in the shallow water of Rex's terrarium, yes, she packed up Marcy and drove straight to see Dr. Hammond.

Now Rex was at home, convalescing, and Marcy was gone, and at that moment Gladys Harper didn't know her left from her right and so she did the only thing in her life that had been reliable as Rex. She smoked her Newports. Harold was no help. Harold worked his factory job and came home and drank. Harold was her cliché of a husband. Could a cliché offer comfort? Could a cliché ease pain? Even now he stood off to the side in a twelve-pack daze. At least that meant he wouldn't be coming to bed and she wouldn't have to deal with his grabby hands.

Gladys searched the faces in the crowd for Dr. Hammond, but the veterinarian still hadn't shown up. Her husband, P.J., was here, enjoying a pleasant conversation with some black fellow she didn't know, not that Gladys knew many black fellows or black ladies or black anything. Her parents had raised her not to associate with that type, and so she didn't. They'd had the foresight to get her a turtle instead of a kitten or puppy, so their judgment had to be sound. They'd recently moved down to Virginia to escape the north's implacable winters.

She hadn't told them yet about their granddaughter's disappearance.

The cigarette between her fingers was dying, its powdery tip crawling back toward her skin. Gladys had two, three puffs left at the most. How much longer was she supposed to stay out here? She at least was glad those moron county cops hadn't shown up here, coming to her place of residence this afternoon with apologies and some bullshit about that dead girl in Monticello. Who was she to care about some dead girl in Monticello? Were they trying to make her feel guilty for leaving the car running? The police were untrustworthy. They planted evidence and pursued their own agenda. Her aunt spent ten years in Sing Sing on some bogus drug charge and she wasn't ever the same once she got out. Calling them pigs was an insult to—

Well, no more cigarette. Time to see how much good-will goes for these days.

She chose P. J. Hammond.

"Excuse me, P.J.," she said.

"Gladys, I am so sorry for what's happened." He hugged her. "I'm sure everything is going to work out."

She eyeballed the black fellow standing next to him. He got the hint and walked away.

"P.J., do you happen to have a cigarette?"

"Me? Oh, no. If I smoked, I'd give you my whole pack. But you know my Mary. She's a stickler for health."

"Is she coming tonight?"

P.J. scanned the group, as if his wife could have snuck into the mix without him knowing. "Yeah, I don't think so. She's a bit under the weather, to be honest. It happens like clockwork, every year, first time we get a big dump of snow, she starts sneezing and coughing."

"That's too bad," replied Gladys. She needed a cigarette.

"Timothy's here, though. You know our son, Timothy, right?"

He indicated a lanky boy shuffling his feet by one of the camera crews. His father probably dragged him down here.

"Timothy, come here and say hello to Mrs. Harper."

Timothy crossed toward them, his gait unmistakably teenage in its awkwardness. He bumped into a few people on his way. Poor shy kid, Gladys decided.

"Hi," the boy whispered. His eyes were dark and downcast.

"Hello, Timothy. Your mother's a very good veterinarian. I'll bet you're an animal lover. I have a pet turtle named Rex. He's twenty-six years old. Can you believe that?"

"You must take good care of him," replied the boy.

"Oh, turtles are easy." She leaned in confidentially. "It's people you've got to watch out for."

Timothy nodded at the sage advice. Then he seemed to be working up his courage to ask a question. His brow curled in concentration and his chin dimpled like a golf ball. Then, finally, the question came: "Does your daughter cry a lot?"

Gladys blinked. "Does she what?"

"When she gets upset, how do you make her stop crying?"

Wisdom out of the mouths of babes, and the defense mechanism her subconscious had built, fixating about cigarettes and her lazy husband, blinked away like the illusion it was. Her eyes went to the giant picture on the easel, which at first she'd found to be a tasteless display—none of these people even knew Marcy—but now, now it looked so much to Gladys like a headstone.

"God…" she muttered, and almost fell to her knees right there in the parking lot. The hot, raw emotions her brain had kept in illusory check these past few hours were flooding and flooding her being and it was too much, too much, but she had no protection against it, not anymore, and still the emotions came, this unceasing onslaught of grief, yes, but *grief* was such a small word to describe this hellish deluge drowning her very soul. "God..."

The boy, apparently unaware of her change, continued his line of inquiry. "Does she have a favorite toy? Do you sing her a song?"

"Timothy..." said P.J.

"A song..." Gladys echoed, and angled her body toward Marcy's photograph.

P.J. grabbed his son by the arm. "It's time to go."

But then she began to softly sing.

Only Timothy and P.J. could hear her at first, especially with the hubbub of the crowd. They stood at her side, almost like sentries.

She took a step toward her daughter's photograph. Her voice raised itself, in volume, in emotion.

My God, she was singing Patsy Cline's "Crazy."

Now some in the crowd were hearing and seeing. They parted, made room for her to pass, on her way to the easel with her serenade.

Even Harold now perked up, the familiar song piercing through his sudsy stupor. It was Harold, after all, who'd wanted to name the child Patsy.

She was almost at the easel, only three feet away, almost close enough to touch. Her hands reached out, ready to embrace.

P.J. looked away from the scene. He couldn't watch it anymore. He turned to take his son away with him, back up the hill, back to the house, but Timothy was gone.

9

Monday morning and, with it, Tom and Esme drove out to New Paltz in his black Mustang to catch a killer. It was a handsome day to do so. The sun, perhaps to make up for his absence over the weekend, had climbed high into the attic of the heavens and was splashing his warmth and cheer across upstate New York. It was the kind of November weather that reinforced one's reluctance to pack away the short sleeves and flannels of autumn.

Esme thought about her daughter. She'd called Oyster Bay last night, after a grease-soggy meal at McDonald's with Tom, and it was obvious that Sophie was still upset. And who could blame her? A promise had been made and a promise had been broken. From Sophie's reductive point of view, the facts were that simple. Even from Esme's more adult perspective, even though she knew she had made the responsible choice, she couldn't help but feel tremendous guilt. Sophie was the heart of her heart. Someday she would understand what Rafe never could: it wasn't a choice of work over family; it was acting, changing, fixing, rather than remaining on the sidelines. If she could make the world a better place, then certainly—

"Here we are," said Tom as they exited the rusty Wallkill Bridge. The state road became Main Street, as all state roads eventually did. Esme tried to recall the directions from Saturday, but everything looked so different under sunshine than it had in the previous post-blizzard gloom. They took a left and passed by what looked like a historical district, and it was those familiar antique landmarks that Esme used to fix their location. The strip mall wasn't far from here.

The Science Museum of Long Island, which occupied an old mansion not unlike the ones in downtown New Paltz, had, that day, a special exhibit on magnets. Sophie Stuart stood with the other first-grade classes as a man with comically large blue glasses explained how magnetic fields worked through a demonstration involving a huge metal U and a collection of Matchbox cars.

Sophie tuned him out. She wanted to play with the crystal ball with the lightning inside, but it seemed that the teachers, including Mrs. Morrow, had their own agenda and so far it hadn't included crystal balls with lightning inside.

So she discreetly snuck away.

She didn't feel bad for doing it. She had every right to go exploring. And if she got in trouble, what could her parents do? After all, her mother had broken her word. If she'd been here, then Sophie would have had no reason to go off on her own, would she?

It made perfect sense to Sophie.

She passed by a display about atoms, which looked a lot like a map of the solar system that Mrs. Morrow had on their classroom wall. What an unusual coincidence. She then entered another room full of fossils. She was on the second floor, and was sure the lightning ball was on the second floor. Her parents had taken her here last

summer, after that bad man broke into their house. She
didn't remember too much about him. But she vividly
recalled the crystal ball of lightning and all the bolts of
electricity shooting harmlessly at her hand like she was
Storm from the *X-Men* and her father had even taken a
photograph of it with his digital camera so it must have
been true—

And here it was. The labyrinth of the second floor led
here, to a room dedicated to electricity. There was the
crystal ball of lightning on a short pedestal, but in the
room there was also a kite with a key at the end of its tail
and a series of lightbulbs attached to a series of levers
and buttons. Sophie didn't remember the lightbulbs from
before and was tempted to try them out, but she knew
she had limited time. Eventually, Mrs. Morrow would
realize a student of hers was missing and that would be
the end of her adventure. Unless Mrs. Morrow never realized it and they got on the bus and left her here. That
wouldn't be so fun.

So Sophie hesitated, pivoting between decisions.
Should she rejoin the group to keep from being abandoned or should she do what she came here to do, what
she had every right to do, what she was supposed to do
with her mother? When she put it like that, the decision
was simple.

She approached the crystal ball of lightning with an
eager grin and a pair of outstretched arms.

"Careful there," said Grover Kirk, who had been
watching her, arms crossed, from the exhibit hall entryway. "You might get shocked."

Esme and Tom had a plan to outsmart the killer and
nullify his threat. Their plan was easy to both implement
and execute. They were going to blitz him.

And so, once they'd made sure the strip mall was clear of any suspicious witnesses, they charged together into the travel agency, and before P. J. Hammond could even look up from his paperwork, Tom had locked the door behind them.

"Hi, there," said Esme.

P.J. cocked his head, confused. "Uh, do we have an appointment?"

He started to stand.

"Please remain seated," answered Tom, "if you don't mind."

Esme didn't lower the window blinds. She and Tom needed to make this seem, to any outside observers, as a casual conversation. It was unlikely that she would be recognized, especially without the police escort.

Still, they had no time to waste.

"I'm Special Agent Piper. You already know Mrs. Stuart. Now, if you could be so kind," Tom said, "please explain your connection to the murder of Lynette Robinson and the disappearance of Marcy Harper."

Nope, no time to waste at all.

"I'm not sure..."

Esme leaned forward and looked the man in the eye. "Yes, you are."

She couldn't read him. He still seemed the affable, if flustered, gentleman she'd met on Saturday. But the preponderance of evidence was undeniable. P.J. was either their guy or was being framed by their guy. Either way, he was the key.

"Who else has regular access to your computer?" she asked him.

"Just me. I run a small business. One-man operation. Look, I'm just a travel agent, and—"

"I like your wedding ring," Tom interjected. "Silver. Simple. What's your wife's name?"

"Mary. Why do you—"

Now Esme: "How's her computer skills?"

"Okay, I suppose. She doesn't work here, though, so you can cross her off whatever list you're compiling. She runs the vet clinic a few doors down and, trust me, that's a full-time…"

Tom and Esme exchanged glances.

Then Tom took the lead. "Do you and Mary have any children, P.J.?"

"That's none of your business."

"Mmm-hmm." Tom leaned forward. "See, P.J., that's what, in our business, we'd refer to as an unusual response. You answered every one of our other questions truthfully and with full disclosure, but when it comes to your children, you go the other way. Now that's either because you don't have any kids and you don't want us to know about it because it's a sore subject—or it's because you do have kids and you don't want us to know about it because…well, you tell me, P.J."

P.J. squirmed in his seat. He was scratching at his thumbnails with his index fingers. What an odd nervous habit, thought Esme.

"Please leave," he said quietly. "I'm begging you."

"Look at me, P.J."

To which P.J. responded by looking everywhere but at Tom. So Tom slammed the flat of his palm against the man's desk. The hollow thump captured P.J.'s attention—he had no choice, it was instinctual—and Tom caught his gaze and held it.

"Now listen. A little girl is in danger. You have the power to save her, but you're trying to protect someone else, someone whose well-being means a great deal more to you than that of an innocent child. It's obvious we're talking about one of your own kids. They've either been taken themselves and you don't want to risk harm coming to them…"

"…or they're the ones causing the harm," finished Esme. "So which is it?"

Sophie took a step away from the tall bald man. "I'm not supposed to talk to strangers."

"That's where you and I are different." He smiled. His teeth were perfect. "I go out of my way, every day, to talk to someone I don't know. I love people. But that's actually beside the point, Sophie, because I'm not really a stranger. I'm an acquaintance of your Grandpa Lester. How else would I know your name?"

Sophie thought about it for a minute. He had a point.

"My name's Grover. Like on *Sesame Street*. Do you like *Sesame Street*, Sophie?"

Sophie replied, "When I was little. Now I watch different stuff."

"I'm curious…" He took a step toward her. "Why did you sneak away from your class?"

"I…"

"I'll bet I know."

She watched as he took another step toward her, and another. He was within jumping distance, then reaching distance, then breathing distance. She could smell his cologne. It smelled like almonds.

He outstretched his hand…and touched the crystal ball of lightning. Immediately, all the forks of electricity inside the ball zapped harmlessly against the glass near his hand. It was so cool. And he was right. That's what Sophie had wanted to do.

He smiled at her again, those teeth of his like carved snowflakes.

"It's okay," he said. "I won't tell."

He removed his hand from the crystal ball and motioned for her to touch it. She did, and watched the electrical forks storm at her hand. The glass was warm, but the blue-white rips of energy didn't hurt her at all. They were at her command. She was Storm from the *X-Men,* just like on the TV, mistress of lightning.

"You're like me," said Grover. "You're curious. That's a wonderful thing to be."

He gently placed his hand over hers. His hand was quite large and covered hers completely. It was almost as if she had no hand at all. She immediately felt uncomfortable and tried to slip her hand away, but couldn't. His hand pressed hers against the glass like a lead weight, and all the while the lightning zapped and zipped.

He leaned down to her level.

Her breathing sped up. If she screamed, people would come, right?

But at that moment she couldn't scream. She couldn't say a word.

"Sophie," he said, "I need you to give your mother a message."

P.J.'s gaze never left Tom's face.

"You don't have any kids," P.J. said.

Tom frowned. "Sir, I—"

P.J.'s eyes briefly flickered to Esme. "But you do, don't you?"

Esme nodded.

"What's her name?"

Tom sighed. "This isn't really—"

"What's the matter? You can ask questions but you can't answer them? That makes you a bully, Special Agent Piper."

Tom sat back in his seat. He looked to Esme. The decision was hers to make.

"Her name is Sophie," she replied. "She's seven."

P.J. nodded. "Seven's a good age. My boy just turned fourteen."

"What's his name?" Tom asked.

But P.J.'s attention had shifted to Esme. "Your Sophie...is she well-behaved?"

"Yes. She is."

"I always wondered what it would be like to have a daughter. Sugar and spice and everything nice, right? But God gave us a boy. He works in mysterious ways. Tell me, Mrs. Stuart, would you sacrifice your life for your child?"

Esme answered without hesitation. "Yes, I would."

"Because that's our obligation. As parents. No matter what, the child's security and happiness comes first."

"P.J.," said Tom, "tell us what he's done."

But P.J. was lost in the valley of his own thoughts.

So Esme took a stab at it. "It's our job to protect them, but it's also our job to teach them right from wrong. It's our job to rein them in when they misbehave. And punish them."

"But whose fault is it, in the end, when they do the things they do?" His voice was so distant, so emotionally faraway. "It can't be theirs. They're children. Somewhere along the line, we did something that made them this way. Maybe it's the way they were raised. Maybe it's the genes we gave them. Either way, every horrible, horrible thing they do...it all tracks back to us."

* * *

Sophie was unusually quiet during the bus ride back to school. Her friends Robyn and Holly attributed it to the tongue-lashing Mrs. Morrow had given her for running off. Robyn gave Sophie a butterfly sticker. Sophie thanked her softly and put it in her pocket.

The north shore of Long Island trundled by. Factories, homesteads, shopping malls. The waters of the Sound sparkled like a field of blue diamonds.

Robyn and Holly were talking about earrings. Holly had just gotten her ears pierced and wanted to know anything and everything there was to know, and Robyn knew anything and everything there was to know, or at least pretended as if she did.

Sophie wanted to take a nap.

They arrived back at school right before lunch. Because of the field trip, though, the first-grade classes were receiving early dismissal, so Sophie halfheartedly waved goodbye to Robyn and Holly and walked over to her grandfather's blue Cadillac, parked with all the other cars in front of the school. He was listening to talk radio and didn't notice her approach.

"Hey there, pun'kin," he said, and lowered the radio's volume. "Have fun at the museum?"

Sophie shrugged her shoulders.

"Well put," replied Grandpa Les, and he shifted into Drive.

The house wasn't far, but he drove slowly. Sophie was desperate to find out if he actually knew that man, Grover. Part of her hoped he did. Part of her hoped he didn't. She leaned back in her seat and clutched tightly on the strap of her seat belt.

When they arrived home, Grandpa Les, perhaps noticing her downcast mood, offered to make her a peanut-butter-and-Fluff sandwich. Even on her worst of days, she couldn't turn down peanut butter and Fluff. But first she asked him to leave the kitchen.

"I want to call Mom."

"So?"

"So it's *private*."

Grandpa Les chuckled at her precociousness and wandered over to the desktop computer in the living room. He could use the time to finish his online search for a good divorce lawyer for his son.

Once she was sure he was out of earshot, Sophie picked up the kitchen phone and dialed her mother's cell number. Whatever her mother was doing, she wouldn't be too busy for a call from home.

And Sophie really needed to speak with her.

But the call went to voice mail, and Sophie was left relaying Grover's message—and emptying her heart— to a machine.

P.J. scratched again at his thumbnails, absently, habitually. Esme knew that the past fourteen years of his life was flashing before this poor man's eyes. She'd made it sound as if she'd empathized with him, but what parent could? Could she really know what it was like to be, say, the father of Jack the Ripper or the mother of Ed Gein? That someone you brought into this world got pleasure out of murder...

And then P.J. smiled. He beamed, really, that effervescent charm suddenly glowing off him like stardust. He stood, smoothed out his crisp white button-down shirt and held out his hand.

He might as well have been offering them a dead fish, for all the enthusiasm Tom and Esme demonstrated. P.J.

noted their confusion, so he just opened his smile even wider and elaborated.

"You are both absolutely right. I've been a passive observer and I required an intervention. I want to express my gratitude, to both of you, for providing it."

"Um?" said Esme.

"The world moves on whether we shut our eyes or not, and if our eyes are shut, we may be able to block out all the negativity, but look at all the wonder we'll be missing, as well!"

He illustrated his point with a flourish of his hands at the walls of his office and the dozens of exotic destinations promised by dozens of colorful posters. The pyramids, the Great Wall of China, the Kremlin. The moai statues of Easter Island. Not to mention Atlantic City, now for only ninety-nine dollars each way.

"There are so many places to see. Mary and I make an effort to travel at least once a year to a different country. The next one on our list is South Africa. Have either of you been to South Africa? I hear they make the best barbecue in the world. Well, I've been to Rio during Carnival, so we'll see."

He passed them both and headed for the door.

"I'm pretty sure Timothy's at home, but I'm also pretty sure I know where he's keeping Marcy Harper. There is a place he's been going to the past few days. He thinks I don't know about it, but the fact of the matter is I've known everything all along. He is my son, after all. I was too busy trying to protect him from the world that I didn't bother trying to protect the world from him. Anyway, come on. The child's almost certainly there now."

P.J. unlocked the door and stepped out into the sunshine.

Esme looked at Tom. Tom looked at Esme.

Then they followed the man out the door.

10

P.J. wanted to drive, but Tom insisted they take his Mustang. Before he joined them in the car, though, he suddenly stopped, turned and walked along the strip mall parking lot toward the Chinese restaurant.

"P.J.," said Esme.

"I just want to give a heads-up to my wife."

He passed the Chinese restaurant and reached for the door to the veterinary clinic. Esme and Tom quickly caught up with him and followed him inside.

The small lobby was full of chairs, and the chairs were full of people, and the people were full of pets. Esme recognized half the dog breeds and maybe a quarter of the cat breeds. One rail-thin gentleman hugged a cage to his chest; inside the cage were a pair of chatty parakeets. The dogs were barking at the cats. The cats were hissing at the dogs. Several fish in a bowl held by a four-year-old boy were ignoring them all and casually swimming away in their water-filtrated universe. The whole place smelled like wet fur. P.J. waved hello to the people he knew—which numbered about fifty percent—and approached a window cut into a wall, behind which the frog-faced receptionist, Bonnie Twitter, sat and typed.

"Hey, there, P.J. What's the buzz?"

"Is Mary busy?"

"For you, doll? Please."

Bonnie tapped a buzzer and the door to her side loudly unlocked. P.J. grasped the knob, turned to the two special agents and said, "I'll be just a minute."

"Are you kidding me?" replied Esme. "We're coming with you."

P.J. shrugged—no big deal, apparently—and opened the door to let them through. Though exasperated at his suddenly cavalier attitude—when Marcy Harper was somewhere in God knows what condition—Esme and Tom knew they had little choice at the moment but to placate the man. Tom was wearing his shoulder holster, and it did have his 9 mm Glock snugly tucked into its leather pocket, but he knew from experience that P. J. Hammond, especially in his current mental state, would probably shut down entirely at the first suggestion of violence.

So, for now, they played along.

"Hello, Mary, my buttercup!" P.J. opened his arms in a Y and rounded his wife in an O. She was standing beside her examination table, its surface covered with wax paper, its wax paper covered with a large and lazy schnauzer. The schnauzer's owner, a delicate coed swathed in an oversize SUNY New Paltz sweatshirt, sat off to the side, chewing a pen.

"Dr. Hammond, should I leave?" she asked.

"No, no," replied Mary.

P.J. gave her shoulder a subtle squeeze.

"Well, maybe just a minute, if you don't mind."

The coed nodded, cooed a fond farewell to her half-asleep dog and exited back into the waiting room.

"What's wrong with him?" asked P.J., indicating the animal.

"Heartworm," his wife answered. "Not too bad, though."

Mary Hammond then waited for her husband to introduce her to the two strangers currently in her examination room. P.J. abashedly picked up on her cue and did so.

"Mary, may I introduce Special Agent Piper and Mrs. Stuart of the FBI."

Mary's reaction was understandable. She didn't smile. She didn't offer her hand in welcome. She just nodded. She knew.

"They're here to help us fix things, Mary. Isn't that terrific of them? And it's about time, too. I'm sure you agree."

In a glance, a thousand words passed between husband and wife. Esme and Tom had little way of deciphering their meaning, but they hoped for the best. This was, to say the least, a very delicate situation for everyone involved.

Esme checked the time on the wall clock. Every second they spent here, little Marcy Harper was alone—or worse, not alone.

Her mind went to Lynette Robinson's hands.

"P.J.," she said, "we really need to…"

"Yes, of course," he replied. "Mary, do you have any suggestions for our guests?"

But the good doctor just shook her head. Her expression remained fixed, and filled with countless conflicting emotions. Again, Esme tried to imagine what it could be like to be this woman, to know that your child was responsible for such ugly acts of depravity and violence. Again, Esme failed. It was beyond her considerable powers of comprehension—and she was grateful for that. She didn't take Sophie for granted...but just the same, her daughter would be receiving a very long hug from her mother, hopefully very soon.

"All right," said P.J. "I guess we'll be off. I'll call you when we're through, Mary."

He hugged her again and briefly whispered something into her left ear and petted the schnauzer goodbye and headed for the door.

"Goddamn it," muttered Tom.

Esme picked up on his line of thought. "P.J., wait."

P.J. stopped, but he couldn't help adding, with his usual cheer, "I thought we were in a hurry."

Tom let out a long sigh. "Dr. Hammond, we're going to need you to close up for the afternoon."

Mary seemed to be expecting this news.

P.J. wasn't. "What? Why?"

"Because now we need to keep track of both of you," Tom explained.

"I'm sure Mary's not going to interfere with a federal investigation."

"Why not?" quipped Esme. "You did."

P.J. replied with a grimace, but didn't protest the argument.

"Let me just finish up in here," said Mary.

While Mary administered some medicine to the schnauzer, who by then was fast asleep, Tom took Esme off to a corner of the room. Before Tom even opened his mouth, Esme knew what he was going to say and said it herself. "We're going to have to split up."

"Yeah."

"This is getting suckier by the second."

"Mmm-hmm."

"Maybe we should call the county sheriff."

Tom shook his head. "Too many cooks in the kitchen."

Esme wasn't sure if she agreed with him. Reinforcements might actually be ideal here, especially when the locals knew the area far better than two visiting FBI agents. Because what if Marcy Harper wasn't where P.J. led them? What if P.J. were deliberately obfuscating the investigation? But Tom was Tom, and that meant going it alone.

Which made her, what, his sidekick? She preferred to think of him as her partner, but knew their relationship would never be like that. Nor did she really truly want it to be, come to think of it. Tom had the experience. Tom taught her everything she knew. To consider him an equal—or for him to consider Esme an equal—that just felt wrong to her. So maybe she *was* his sidekick. That meant the most perceptive criminal investigator she had ever met trusted her implicitly. And who could complain about that?

But the question remained: Who would go with whom?

In the end, they decided to cross along gender lines. Esme would go with P.J. to the probable location of Marcy Harper, and Tom would accompany Mary back to her house and confront Timothy himself. This made sense if only because Tom was armed and Esme was not, although they both hoped it didn't come to that.

Mary Hammond rushed her patients (and their owners) out the door and closed up shop. She and Tom would take his Mustang. Esme slid behind the driver's seat of P.J.'s bulky RAV4. And they were off.

* * *

The drive to the house took mere minutes, but Tom made sure to park the Mustang a block away so as not to put the boy on alert. He got out of the car, but Mary remained in the passenger seat. So Tom returned to his. He could have proceeded without her but he preferred to have her cooperation, if only to defuse a potentially violent confrontation.

He watched her eyes peek at his shoulder holster.

"Are you ready?" he asked.

She nodded.

They started toward the house.

The day couldn't have been more beautiful. As they strolled toward their destination, they even heard, from the emaciating branches of this tree and that, a flock of birds carrying on a musical conversation. What did they care about justice or Monday or even November? They were probably gabbing about their favorite places to dine, perhaps partial to the Dumpster behind Bouton Hall at the SUNY New Paltz campus or the Mohonk Preserve, just a short wing-flap away from their current perch here on Parliament Drive.

Mary led Tom to a house quite like its neighbors—a square two-story with whitewashed wooden porticos—only distinguishable really by its yellow door and the healthiness of the bushes that lined its forefront. According to her, Timothy was at that moment almost definitely in his bedroom. Tom considered instructing her to return to her car and to pull it into the garage—so the boy wouldn't be alarmed by the sound of the opening door not being preceded by the sound of the opening garage—but by the time the thought had occurred to him, she had already inserted her key into the knob and twisted it. The die was cast, and they crossed the threshold into the Hammond home.

On the drive over, Tom had also asked Mary if the boy had, in his bedroom, anything sharp. Tom offered himself as an example, recollecting to her about the BB rifle he used to store underneath his bed when he was ten years old. His father hid the BBs themselves in his toolshed, which had encouraged Tom, at ten, to learn how to dismantle a toolshed lock. There was whimsy in Tom's voice as he shared this tale, but they both knew that, today, this wasn't simply a question of BBs or even boys and their toys. If Timothy came at him with a blade, he would do his best to disarm the boy defensively, but if matters escalated…

"Timothy!" she called. "I'm home!"

There were no scampering footsteps from the bedroom to the top of the stairs. Tom hadn't expected any. From what little he had learned about the boy, and this hadn't even included Timothy's checkered history with pets, Tom had postulated, not surprisingly, a diagnosis of psychopathic personality disorder, and antisocial behavior was a tenet of this categorization.

In short, he wouldn't come to them. He would force them to come to him.

So Tom mounted the first of the softly carpeted steps. He casually reached for the railing. His pacemaker maintained a steady mechanic rhythm, but Tom still felt a bit off. He hadn't been back in the field since his confrontation with Galileo. He wasn't nervous per se, but he did feel a growing sense of uneasiness, as if there were a precaution, something utterly obvious, that he had overlooked.

He took the steps slowly. Ten, eleven, twelve, thirteen.

Mary stood at the foot of the staircase. At any moment, her maternal instincts could get the better of her and she could cry out a warning to her son. *Run, run!* But where would he run to? If he escaped out his bedroom window, he had nowhere to go but down, and it would be difficult to dodge the law with a pair of broken legs. No, if she alerted him, Timothy wouldn't run. He would arm himself. She had told Tom that she didn't know what weapons he might have in his bedroom. She had told Tom that she hadn't gone into her son's bedroom in more than a year, not since the time she'd opened the door to ask him if he needed anything from the store and…well, she refused to say what she saw. And that was fine by Tom.

Fourteen, fifteen, sixteen.

Seventeen.

Once Tom was out of Mary's eyesight, he drew his Glock. Better to be safe. He wouldn't fire unless he had no choice, and maybe the sight of the pistol would be enough to get the boy to surrender peacefully.

The bedroom lay at the end of the hall. The door was ajar, but only by a thumb-length.

Tom heard no sounds coming from the room. The boy could be asleep. The boy could be quietly reading a book. The boy could be lying in wait behind the door, breath held, a blade in his grip.

Tom swallowed his own breath and approached the bedroom door. The Glock remained in his left hand. With his right, he reached for the door and tapped it open. It creaked with every inch and revealed the sparse blue bedroom of a fourteen-year-old boy.

Minus the boy.

Tom checked behind the door.

Tom checked in the bedroom closet.

Tom hustled through each of the other rooms on the second floor, perusing each possible hiding spot for Timothy Hammond but finding no one. He made a mad dash down the stairs. Mary, still at the foot, stepped aside, confused. Tom whipped through the kitchen and dining room and living room and every room and Timothy wasn't there, and Tom realized—recognized—the something utterly obvious he had overlooked: What if the boy wasn't here at all?

What if he was at his special place?

By now Esme was there. And she was unarmed.

Tom reached for his cell phone, knowing even as he dialed her number that it was too late.

Timothy's special place was the Ellis House, a three-hundred-year-old mansion located off to the side of New Paltz's historic Huguenot Street. In truth, only the stonework first floor of the mansion dated back that far; the second story, as it stood now, was a wooden reconstruction built approximately one hundred years later by George Ellis, great-great-grandson and namesake of the house's first owner. The result was a surprisingly elegant marriage of colonial and Queen Anne architecture, the light green coloring of the house providing a pleasant complement to its acre of still-green grass and healthy brown pines. As Esme approached the place, she wondered what secret ingredients the groundskeepers used to keep the property in such healthy shape when everything else around them had begun to dull and decay as autumn began its lumbering slouch to winter.

"The rest of the houses are open to the public pretty much year-round," said P.J., "but the Ellis family only keeps this place open from May till October. It saves them money, I suppose. Nobody I know has even met an Ellis. Some people wonder if maybe the family's all gone and the house is being run now by some law firm out in Boston."

"Why would he bring the child here?" asked Esme.

"Well, for one, Timothy loves the place. He's crazy about it. Ever since he was a little kid, he's made sure we were here the first of May for its annual opening. Don't ask me what it is he loves so much."

P.J.'s sunny demeanor had once again begun to dim. Maybe the gravity of the situation had finally been too much for his facade to bear. When Esme ascended the house's slate landing, P.J. remained steadfast on the lawn.

Just as well, she thought. She didn't want to have to wrangle both him and the baby, anyway. She climbed up to the house's gray stone porch.

The door was locked, but that was to be expected. Somehow, Timothy had found a way in. P.J. didn't know what it was, but Esme, encouraged by the puzzle, intended to find out. Not to mention the fact that she refused to be outsmarted by a fourteen-year-old.

The house lacked a basement, so Esme could immediately rule that out. There were, as far as she could tell, two doorways on the first floor, the most obvious being the front entryway, which faced the street, and the other being a rear set of doors that opened out onto another foreshortened patio, and the back lawn. Those doors, too, were locked.

Also, the first floor had ten windows. These were much more difficult to access since they were quite high off the ground. But Esme figured that if she couldn't reach them, neither could Timothy. Unless he were freakishly tall. Or employed a ladder…

There was a tall strip of shrubbery off to the side,

separating this property from the next. Esme didn't find a ladder, but she did find where Timothy had stashed his bicycle. If Timothy carried it back to the house and locked its wheels, it could function as a handy-dandy, if somewhat wobbly, stepstool. And a quick examination of the earth around the house's foundation revealed the impression of tire tracks underneath one window in particular. She set the bicycle wheels in their own earthen grooves, placed her left foot on the leather seat, and hefted herself up to the height of the window, making sure to catch the sill with her fingers to keep from toppling back down. Keeping a precarious grip on the sill, with her feet crowding the small bicycle seat, she used her free hand to nudge the window open. It squeaked, but complied, and within a minute she had the window lifted high enough for her to climb through into a tiny room.

Esme had been to enough minimansions in Oyster Bay to recognize this cramped space as the butler's pantry. The walls in here weren't papered, but the shelves still held an assortment of Victorian cleaning products and household tools, all utterly useless and simply for show. There were two swinging doors on either side of the pantry. Esme chose one and found herself in a sizable dining room. There were fourteen place settings, complete with soupspoons, soup bowls, salad forks, salad plates, dinner forks, dinner plates, dessert forks, knives and embroidered napkins. The china appeared genuine.

For a moment, she was tempted to steal some of it.

But then she heard an unusual sound. It came from upstairs—and it sounded like singing. The acoustics in the house being what they were, she couldn't decipher the words, but the melody seemed so very familiar and the voice was undoubtedly male.

Timothy was here.

Esme had been aware of the possibility. She had hoped otherwise, but, ah, well. At least his presence confirmed P.J.'s suspicions—and hopefully confirmed that Baby Marcy was here, as well. And that he hadn't heard the squeaking window. She turned to her right and stepped into the foyer.

Now she could hear the song lyrics. Now she could identify the words sung from upstairs in a boy's soft tenor voice.

My God, he was singing Patsy Cline's "Crazy."

The stairs leading up to the second level were narrow and wooden. Esme snatched an ornate carving knife from the dining table, removed her sneakers and with her feet encased in nothing but pink socks she took the stairs, two at a time, using the railing to help keep her balance. With each giant step, Timothy's tenor lullaby became clearer and louder.

She reached the landing, her footsteps quiet, her shoulders hunched, turned the corner to meet the second flight of stairs and her cell phone sounded, the jaunty synth-pop of Squeeze's "Pulling Mussels from the Shell" emanating from her pants pocket. The ring tone meant the call came from home, probably from her daughter to tell her about the museum trip, but not right now, Sophie, please, and Esme silenced her phone without answering it, and the ring tone hadn't been that loud, right? She gazed up at the second flight of stairs and prepared to take her next step but Timothy was already there, with his beloved Taser C2 aimed squarely at her face.

"Hello," he said, and from fourteen inches away sent fifty thousand volts of electricity straight into her body.

11

This is how an ordinary Taser works:

Inside the grip is a pair of batteries. The batteries power an internal circuit that generates an electrical charge, as internal circuits are wont to do. When the trigger on the grip is depressed, a compressed air cartridge within the apparatus is released. This propels forward a pair of electrodes, which are attached via wires to the internal circuit, which generates a considerable voltage, which travels the length of the wires, which zaps and thus briefly incapacitates anyone unfortunate enough to be struck by the two aforementioned electrodes. The End.

However, Timothy's was no ordinary Taser. Using instructions provided by Cain42, he'd juiced up his weapon from its legal limit of .05 amps to a rather scary .10 amps. This increased the likelihood of the victim suffering from prolonged loss of consciousness as well as heat burns and possible nerve death.

He dragged Esme's limp body up the remainder of the stairs, her feet in their pink socks thumping against each step they passed. Fortunately, the nursery wasn't far and the wood floor relatively smooth.

When Esme awoke, she felt as if she were filled with a thousand tuning forks, each of them vibrating against her organs and veins and tissues. A horrible relentless tingling reverberated throughout her brain, behind her eyes, beside her ears. As her vision cleared, she beheld a Victorian room, its walls papered with endless prints of chubby-cheeked cherubim. She tried to lift her hand, either hand, any hand, but her arm muscles refused to obey, as did her legs, as did her neck. Her mind was awake, but her body remained stunned and useless.

Then she noticed the shadow across the wallpaper and her eyes followed the shadow to the boy, Timothy, who stood beside a one-hundred-and-fifty-year-old cradle. Through the bars along its sides, Esme could see Baby Marcy in a blue onesie. She appeared asleep, mercifully asleep.

Next to the cradle was a toddler's cupboard, and on top of it was a bottle of formula and an assortment of disposable diapers, all neatly piled in a small white tower. On top of the tower of diapers was his Taser C2.

The carving knife was in his right hand.

He must have detected a change in Esme's breathing, because he turned his attention from the baby to his intruder. The sunlight that decorated his shadow on the wall originated from the room's small hexagonal window. By now it was probably noon. By now Sophie's museum trip was over. Esme's mind went to her daughter and thoughts of Sophie kept her grounded. Thoughts of Sophie kept her from screaming, because Timothy was approaching her now and her muscles remained as fixed and firm as the approaching long blade of the—

"Agent Stuart?" It was P.J. He was coming up the staircase, the floorboards creaking with his every step. "Agent Stuart, are you up here?"

Now she tried to scream, but it was too late, it was far too late, because P.J. was here, he was here in the nursery and his son was facing him, his shadow on the wall elongated now by the shape of the knife, almost as if it were, Christ, an eel, stretching out from Timothy's own flat belly toward his father.

"So," said P.J.

Timothy didn't move, not yet. He didn't have to move. He had the advantage. He had the knife.

Then P.J. grinned. "So here you are, after all! I could have sworn you'd be at home. I did swear you'd be at home, in fact. Is that little Marcy over there in the crib? Can I see her?"

"She's asleep," replied Timothy, softly.

"I can see that. That couldn't have been easy, calming a baby to sleep. She must have taken to you. You get that from me, you know? When you were a baby, you used to scream and scream bloody murder in the middle of the night and you didn't stop for your mother, not even when she offered to feed you. You only stopped for me. On one hand, it was a bit of a pain. I don't think I got a full night's rest for six months. On the other hand, though… it was lovely."

Esme remained immobile, propped up against the wall, but she could feel that maddening tightness in her muscles beginning to ooze away. Its replacement was soreness, but it was a soreness that might, maybe, allow mobility, and the cupboard with the diapers and the Taser were only a short crawl away. If P.J. kept distracting him, then perhaps…

But P.J. then pointed straight at her.

"What did you do to her?" he asked.

Now Timothy's attention returned to her, too.

Damn it.

eased the knife, blade first, into the boy's back. He felt Timothy's body tense up in his arms, so P.J. just held him tighter, with all the love in his heart, until the tension slipped away, like a shadow at dawn.

Over his son's shoulder, he saw Esme standing with wobbly balance by the cupboard, the Taser in her hands, the barrel aimed in their direction.

"You didn't have to do that," she muttered.

"Yes," P.J. replied, "I did."

It actually took Mary Hammond, in her addled state of mind, quite a while to figure out where Timothy might have gone to, so by the time Tom showed up at the Ellis House, with a good portion of the Ulster County sheriff's department in tow, Esme and P.J. were exiting onto the front porch. She had Baby Marcy in her arms. The child appeared malnourished, but alive. The Taser and the murder weapon she left upstairs, with Lynette's murderer.

With an eerie serenity, P.J. held his wrists out to the police to be cuffed and led away. He had almost made it to the cruiser before he broke, like a snapped marionette. Just fell to his knees. For a moment that was all, and then his mouth gradually opened, as if in slow motion, and P.J. let out a deep-throated guttural moan. It had hit him. He had murdered his own boy.

It took two uniformed officers to carry him into the back of the cruiser.

An ambulance came five minutes later and took Marcy Harper. One of the paramedics gave Esme a once-over, but she shrugged off his concern. She still felt jittery, but at that moment she wasn't sure if it was from what had happened to her or from what she had seen happen afterward or from the haunting sound of P.J.'s primal grief that, even though he was now long gone, refused to leave her ears.

She gave her statement to Sheriff Betsy Shuster back at the Ulster County Law Enforcement Center in Kingston. Sheriff Fallon and a pair of his deputies showed up halfway through the deposition. Esme spotted him and nodded in his direction. He nodded back. Enough was said.

Which left it to Tom to explain to the FBI special agent in charge of the region why two federal officers were operating without authority or notice or even proper jurisdiction in this investigation. Tom grinned through most of the phone call. Something about him just loved giving the bird to authority.

While Tom was on the horn with the demigods of the Justice Department, Esme turned her phone back on, ostensibly to call Rafe and, if he didn't hang up in the first five seconds, inform him that Lynette's death had been avenged, but she noticed she had two new messages, so before she called anyone, she listened to them.

As she expected, the first message was from home. She still remembered the Squeeze ring tone going off on the landing of the Ellis House. So sad that such a good song would now be associated with such a bad moment.

"Hi, Mom, it's Sophie."

Only four words, innocuous, uttered all the time, and Esme immediately felt a pit in her stomach. Something was wrong. Her daughter sounded…not upset, really, but rattled. She sat down on a pine bench outside the squad room and listened to the rest of Sophie's message.

"A man, he said his name was Grover, he came up to me today at the science museum and he touched my hand and his breath smelled like corned beef and he told me he was friends with Grandpa and then he said he had a message for you and I didn't write it down but I remember it so here it is. He said, 'Get in touch with me or I'll get in touch with Sophie Ellen.' Mommy, how did he know my middle name? Is he really a friend of Grandpa's? He scares me. Oh, I have to go. Grandpa is making me a peanut-butter-and-Fluff sandwich. I'm not very hungry, though. Can you come home now, please? Bye."

Click.

And Esme seethed. Oh, how she seethed! Grover Kirk had the audacity—no, the fucking impudence—to approach her daughter, to approach Sophie, and in a public place no less. And how did he even know she was going to be there? Was he stalking her?

Esme now understood Rafe's impetus the other night, tossing the pot against the wall. She suddenly wanted to throw every bench, chair and appliance in sight. She almost pitched her cell phone against the nearby stairwell.

That son of a bitch.

He dared to mess with her family? He dared to threaten her family? Well, Grover Kirk was in for the clusterfuck of the century. Esme bolted back into the sheriff's department and found Tom, sitting in an unused office, still on the phone.

"Is that Ziegler?" she asked. Karl Ziegler was the bureau chief of the New York field office. He also was a bit of a prick. "Are you on the phone with Ziegler?"

Tom covered the phone's speaker. "What's wrong?"

"Give me the phone."

To his credit, Tom didn't ask her any more questions. He just complied with her request.

"Karl? Hi, it's Esme."

"Mrs. Stuart?" Karl Ziegler's voice hovered somewhere between a grumble and a whine. And he emphasized her title as Mrs., as if to remind her she was now only a consultant—but that was a battle for another day. "Mrs. Stuart, I was in the middle of—"

"Yeah, yeah, and I'll give you back to Tom in a minute. My seven-year-old daughter was just confronted while she was on a goddamn field trip by this middle-age hack named Grover Kirk. He's been trying to get me to talk with him about this exploitative piece of garbage he's writing about the Galileo case and I've been noncooperative and so he confronted my daughter and told her to tell me to 'get in touch with him or he'd get in touch with her.' I want you to find him and I want you to detain him, and when I come down there I'm going to personally introduce him to some of our more controversial post-9/11 interrogation techniques. Okay?"

"Mrs. Stuart, you know full well that—"

"He crossed state lines to come here, Karl. That makes it a federal case. Are you going to tell me that a threat to my seven-year-old daughter doesn't constitute action? Are you that desperate to be reassigned to Juneau?"

"You don't have the pull you think you have, Mrs. Stuart."

"Are you kidding? Do you think Grover Kirk is the only person who knows who I am? Galileo turned me into a semicelebrity. I'm one of the highest-profile employees the Bureau's got. So tell me again that you're going to ignore this request. Please. I would love to send you your Christmas present via sled dog."

Silence, as Karl Ziegler mulled over her words. It made her sick just to speak them, to feign such unbridled arrogance. It just wasn't who she was. But bullies like

Karl Ziegler only responded to bullying, and so that was the tactic she had to take.

Nevertheless, Tom was sitting back in his chair and staring at her with a look of complete astonishment. Whether his reaction was to her news or to her behavior, she cringed for his benefit.

Ziegler's breathing returned to the phone. "Do you happen to know where this Grover Kirk may be at the moment?"

Shit. Where was he staying? He'd told her. He'd given her his card. Damn it. It was on the tip of her—

"The Days Inn in Hicksville," she blurted.

"Fine. I'll keep you posted. Now with your permission, Mrs. Stuart, may I continue to speak with Special Agent Piper?"

Esme grinned and handed the phone back to Tom.

"You're my hero," he muttered, and resumed his after-action report.

Feeling much better, she gave Tom some privacy and wandered back out through the sheriff's department, which remained abuzz with the Timothy Hammond case. At this moment, forensics would be combing through his bedroom. Detectives would be interviewing his peers, his teachers, everyone who might have ever known him. The case wouldn't really be closed until they had accumulated everything they might—and answered every question they could—about this very troubled fourteen-year-old.

By now, Lynette's family must have been told. Esme hoped it was Sheriff Fallon who had imparted the news. She had seen him here, briefly, but he must have trucked on back to his home territory to the west. He was a good man, and she felt bad about the way Rafe had pushed him into letting her work the case, although had that been any different at all from the way she had just pushed Ziegler into nabbing Grover Kirk…?

She needed to give her husband a call.

He picked up on the second ring.

"Professor Stuart."

"Rafe," she said, "it's over."

There was a pause, and Esme instantly realized why.

Her statement could refer to so many things right now in their life.

So she elaborated, and one thing led to another, and soon she and Rafe were actually having a chat. It was so easy to fall back into the old rhythms. Once they'd finished discussing the case, their conversation didn't really consist of anything substantial, but it was peaceful. No hidden accusations. No verbal sparring. They just talked.

And that made it all the more painful, because Esme knew it was fleeting. By the time Esme said her goodbyes and their peaceful conversation had reached its peaceful end (due in part to her convenient omission of Sophie's encounter with Grover Kirk), she was near tears. It wasn't fair. They had been so happy once. It was obvious they could be happy again. If only…

If only what? If only she quit her job as a consultant with the Bureau? That was not an option. And why should the onus be on her, anyway, to make the sacrifices? Because she was the woman? Just thinking about that notion made her tense up again—and such began, she realized with a sigh, the cycle anew. Hell, even Dr. Rosen had all but given up on them. They had nine days to repair their marriage, and she was going to spend most of it on a train from New Paltz to Oyster Bay—Christ, if such a train even existed. If not, she was in for the most expensive cab ride of her life.

Tom trundled out of the empty office. Esme met him by the water cooler and filled up a cup for him. He accepted it graciously and cleansed the bureaucracy from his palate.

"Listen," she began.

He held up a hand. "Thank Penelope Sue. She's the one who kicked me in the ass to come up here."

"So you wouldn't do it for me, but you'd do it for Penelope Sue."

"Damn straight." He grinned, crunched up his paper cup and tossed it into the receptacle. "You'd really like her."

"Maybe I'll come down for Thanksgiving."

She forced a teary grin.

Tom stared at her for a moment, then sighed, then embraced her tightly, paternally.

"It'll work out," he whispered. "Rafe may be a jackass, but he's not a moron. He'll come to his senses, realize how lucky he is."

Esme wiped at her face. They both started toward the door.

"So how are you getting home?" he asked.

"I think I'm going to end up hitching. If you were driving an eighteen-wheeler and you saw me on the side of the road, would you stop?"

"Hmm."

He gave her a scholarly once-over.

"Well?"

"I'm thinking, I'm thinking."

She punched him in the arm.

He chuckled and reached for the door.

If he had been a little quicker, maybe they could have

escaped what happened next. But he wasn't, and they didn't. At that moment, Sheriff Shuster hustled out of her office, a look of panic on her tired face. She spotted the two FBI agents and made a beeline for them.

"There's a problem at the Hammond house," she said.

12

Grover Kirk handed the long-haired clerk a twenty for his assortment of magazines (the latest issues of *Psychology Today, Newsweek* and *Barely Legal*), told her to keep the change and trundled out of the cigar shop to his vintage wonder: his angel-white 1954 Studebaker Champion Regal Starlight. God, how he loved this car! He was aware of the clichés of men with their automobile fetishes, but he didn't care what other people thought. He rarely cared about what other people thought. Other people weren't the proud owners of a white 1954 Studebaker Champion Regal Starlight.

This car was America.

He tossed his purchases into the backseat, its smooth vinyl causing the slick magazines to slide from one end of the seat to the other. Grover started up his beauty's eighty-five-horsepower engine and cruised out of the parking lot and back onto the tree-lined byroads of central Long Island. Although most of this weekend's snow had melted, he still couldn't get over how much of it had come down and stayed down. Back in Florida, where he lived, the precipitation didn't ordinarily solidify. He had been concerned on Saturday morning that the Studebaker

wouldn't start, that he would have to call for a jump—
or worse, a tow—but one turn of his key and, oh, how
she'd purred.

He was making good progress on his book.

On Saturday, he drove out to Nassau Firearms, site
of Galileo's most infamous crime—the assassination of
Bob Kellerman, the popular (and populist) governor of
Ohio and Democratic candidate for president. Kellerman, to his eventual detriment, had also been a bit of a
gun nut, and had stopped at Nassau Firearms on his way
from a function on the North Shore the previous night
to a meet-and-greet in New York City.

Esme Stuart had been at the North Shore function,
as well.

After the assassination, the township didn't know
quite what to do with Nassau Firearms. The owner and
his wife were dead, and the inconclusiveness of their will
turned the property back over to the government. Some
had wanted to turn it into a landmark. Others expanded
on that idea and saw it as a potential touristy cash cow.
Ultimately, though, the decision was made to table a decision, and the two-story structure that Grover found was
abandoned and in disrepair. Most of the windows and
all of the doors had been boarded over. Such a pathetic
testament to such a significant moment. Grover took out
his $2,500 Canon EOS and let it do its thing. The result-
ing photographs would look nice in the book beside a
set of "before" shots he had found on Nassau Firearms'
still-running (but hardly operational) website.

On Sunday Grover stayed in and watched TV in his
motel room and typed. He could have afforded a full-
featured suite in a four-star hotel, but he had deliberately

selected the Days Inn because so much of the Galileo story was blue-collar, and he wanted to stay true to its roots.

Although he had read countless true-crime books, he had never written one until now. There was just something about the Galileo story that had piqued his interest, ever since that first series of murders in Georgia. By the second series of murders in Texas, Grover was hooked. He had found himself a new hobby. The vineyard practically took care of itself, anyway. After all, wasn't that what his family paid the foremen for?

He really had expected the bottle of wine to win Esme over. All of the profiles he had about her, and he had collected and read them all, suggested that she had put the grassroots life of the FBI agent behind her and had become the model of an affluent suburban housewife. To Grover, this was code for alcoholism. But no, her reaction had been less than desirable. The indignant tone she'd displayed on the phone had been nothing compared to the outright rudeness she'd tossed in his face. Why couldn't she, of all people, appreciate the value of his project? He was single-handedly making sure that she didn't become like Nassau Firearms—undervalued and unappreciated. His book was going to solidify her well-deserved fame for as long as it was in print. Didn't she realize that she needed him as much as he needed her?

So, yes, if this morning he'd shaken up his tactics a bit and went with the hard sell, it was only because she'd left him no choice. Lester, God bless him, had already told him Esme was upstate, and the weather made it impossible for him to track her there, so he did what seemed to him to be the next best thing. He tracked Sophie to the museum, again thanks to Lester's information. The old man had been so set off by Esme ditching her chaperoning responsibilities that Grover had had trouble to get him to *stop* talking.

And now it was Monday afternoon, and he awaited Esme's call. In fact, as he pulled to a stoplight, on his way back to the Days Inn, he checked his phone to see if he'd missed anything. No, not yet. But that was okay. She probably had her hands full with that investigation. She would get in touch with him, one way or another. He would get his interview. And his opus would be complete.

Grover even had a title for it: *Galileo's Aim*. He loved the double meaning of the word *aim,* on one hand referring to the killer's modus operandi (a sniper rifle) and on the other hand referring to his motivation (to have religion in America publicly and permanently denounced). He could imagine the title on the nonfiction bestseller lists. He could see his book on shelves. He could see himself touring the country, sharing his fascination with other hobbyists like him. And he knew he wasn't alone. The bookstores were stuffed with shelves about Jack the Ripper and he'd been dead for more than a hundred years! Galileo was fresh in people's memories. Galileo was current events.

He could see himself on Fox News.

But he wasn't glamorizing what Galileo had done. He made sure to dedicate his book to the American men and women who had fallen victim to his spree. It was the first page he typed, and he'd included every single one of their names. It had filled up the whole page. And every time he loaded his word processing file, that first page and those names were what he saw. This book was a labor of labor not just for him, but for them.

Plus it would finally get his family off his case, and that was perhaps the biggest bonus of them all. All that nagging about getting an education and finding himself a wife and blah, blah, blah… He'd assumed it would have ceased by now—he was in his forties, for Christ's sake!—but no, his father and his mother and his sisters and his brothers persisted in their noise. But once this book hit it big, they would all finally, inexorably, be silenced.

He just had one more chapter to go, one vital ingredient left to add to the mix.

Esme Stuart.

He pulled the Studebaker into the rear parking lot of the Days Inn, grabbed his magazines from the back and headed for his room, making sure to first set the car's alarm. Although the vehicle was retro, the alarm system was pure twenty-first century. Onboard door and wheel lock relays, an eight-tone, eighty-decibel siren that also activated his high beams. No one was going to drive off with his baby.

As he neared his first-floor room, he heard two car doors slam behind him. People needed to treat their vehicles with more respect. He fished in his jacket pocket for his room key and an authoritarian male voice called out to him, "Grover Kirk!" and he turned around to face two lean men in the cheap brown suits.

"Do I know you?" he asked.

They each flashed federal badges.

"Would you come with us, Mr. Kirk?"

"I think there's been a mistake."

"There's no mistake, sir." One of the agents gently clasped Grover's biceps. "Let's go."

The other agent grabbed his other biceps. "I hear you like little girls," he murmured.

"Are you kidding me? Is this a joke? You can't just

grab people off the street. I'm an American citizen! I have rights!"

Grover searched the parking lot for somebody, anybody, to help him. He saw an elderly couple heading toward their coupe.

"My name is Grover Kirk!" he called to them. "I'm being taken against my will! My attorney's down in Florida. His number is—"

But they had him shoved into their unmarked sedan before he'd had a chance to say any more. All in all, an efficient snatch-and-grab.

The Hammond house was infested with cops. Sheriff Shuster must have called in every technician, investigator and volunteer deputy on the county payroll—and Ulster was not a small county. On one hand, Esme could understand the sheriff's desire for overkill. This had the potential to be one of the highest-profile cases the county had ever handled. On the other hand, though, the more people there were on-site, the more likelihood there would be for contamination of evidence.

One of her deputies, a mountain-man type labeled Carlyle, met them at the front door. His massive hands were encased in overstretched latex gloves. "It's up here, Sheriff."

Tom, Esme and Sheriff Shuster followed Deputy Carlyle up the stairs.

"Déjà vu," muttered Tom.

Unsurprisingly, their destination was Timothy's bedroom. Another deputy, labeled Nunez—as fresh-faced as Carlyle was furry—stood by the boy's bed, awaiting their arrival.

"Sheriff," he greeted them.

"What have we got, Nunez?"

Nunez shared an uneasy glance with Carlyle, and then reached down and lifted Timothy's mattress (which was rubber, nicely fitting into the serial killer equals bed wetter paradigm). Underneath it lay a manila folder. Sheriff Shuster pulled a pair of latex gloves on and slid the manila folder out from its hiding place.

Delicately, the sheriff opened the envelope's flap and reached inside and withdrew a small packet of eight-and-a-half-by-eleven-inch pages. She looked them over, expressionless, and then handed them to Tom and Esme.

They appeared to be screenshots of a website. The website was organized in a simple frame-and-content structure, with a menu bar at the top of the page listing the website's various pages: "Tips of the Trade," "History of the Trade," "Photographs of the Trade" and "Support Group." The website's URL—which between the "www." and the ".com" was just a long series of apparently random numbers—was visible both in the address bar at the top of each printed page and at the bottom, separate from the screenshot, with a date and time beside it.

At the top of the website, in clear sans serif type, was its name: "A Handbook for Serial Killers."

Esme blinked. "Is this a joke?"

The two deputies shrugged.

"Has anyone tried this website?" asked Tom.

This time, the two deputies deferred to their boss, who crossed to Timothy's small writing desk and opened up his laptop computer. It took a minute to boot up, and Esme used that time to look over in further detail some of the printed pages.

The screenshot from "Photographs of the Trade" depicted a collection of black-and-white thumbnails to be clicked on and enlarged. She turned the page. One of the thumbnails had, in fact, been clicked on and enlarged and here was Lynette Robinson, naked, limp, a collar around her neck. Her hands were gone and something metallic appeared to be jammed into her left eye.

She showed the picture to Tom.

"Give me one of those pages," said Sheriff Shuster, and she typed in the website address straight from the printout. A popup window appeared, asking for a username and password. "Damn it."

"He's, uh," rumbled mountain-man Carlyle, "probably still got the website, maybe, stored in his, you know, internet cache. I think."

They all stared at him, then stepped aside. Sheepishly, the mountain man shuffled up to the computer and started clicking keys.

Esme and Tom flipped their handheld pages back to the "Tips of the Trade" and read down the list with rising disgust.

"'Vary Your MO.' 'The Cleanest Crime Scene Is a Destroyed Crime Scene.' It's a how-to for the ambitious psychopath."

"That's why Timothy burned down the house," noted Tom. "He was just following these suggestions."

"This is not good...."

Deputy Carlyle called them over to the desk.

"It's not live," he explained. "And it won't be the whole site. His computer just stored bits and pieces of it so it wouldn't have to reload the whole thing."

"But it doesn't matter, right?" This from Deputy Nunez. "I mean, it's just something this crazy kid created when he was busy stealing little kids. It's not like anyone else has been on this website. Look at its address. It's a bunch of nonsense! No one could find it."

Esme, having spent more time than she cared to admit online, stepped forward. She had an idea—and needed to disprove it. "We don't have a printout of the "Support Group" page. Can you see if he's got it stored in his cache?"

Deputy Carlyle double-checked to make sure the laptop was still offline (yes, it was) and clicked the tab in the menu bar. As Esme had expected, the "Support Group" page was little more than a message board broken up into various categories and polls. Most of these links were inactive.

"Scroll down," she said.

Most message boards listed, if not the names, at least the number of its active members. The message board at this website was no different: 2,037 members.

"Fuck me," mumbled Esme.

"There's, okay, but there's still no proof he didn't create this website out of thin air and type all this up himself." Nunez ran a hand across his smooth chin. "He fixed that contest on his dad's computer. He's obviously got skills. And the mom, she said he was homeschooled, so he's got the time."

Esme thought about it. Maybe Nunez was right. What he said made sense, in a desperate, grabbing-at-straws sort of way. There had to be a quick and easy way to prove that not only was this toxic website legitimate but so were its members. That would be the first step.

The second step would then be to track down 2,036 lunatics.

The cybercrime boys and girls in D.C. were going to have a field day with this.

She reviewed the thumbnail photographs again. There had to be dozens of them, and according to the tiny

numbers near the top, this was just page one of four. If
Nunez was right and this website was simply a fabrication
for Timothy's own strange enjoyment, what were they to
make of these grotesque photos? Either the people depicted were real, which meant that the fourteen-year-old
boy was an astonishingly prolific and twisted murderer,
or the pictures themselves were fakes, which meant that
the fourteen-year-old boy was an astonishingly proficient
and twisted photo-manipulator.

Why couldn't there be a more palatable option C?

Meanwhile, Carlyle was entering some keywords
from the website into various search engines. So far
there weren't any hits. This was good news. It weighed
the argument in favor of fabrication.

But there had to be ways to hide websites from search
engines. When she had served on the task force, she had
been privy to any number of websites that must have
been hidden due to their confidentiality. Even the websites for ordinary companies had information online that
they needed to keep internal.

Deputy Carlyle must have been reading her mind.
"Just because it's, um, not showing up in these search
engines doesn't, you know, mean anything one way or
the other. All he, or whoever, would need to do is insert
some code in the server root and it will be like the website's invisible."

"Then no one could find it," replied Nunez. "Which
means this 2,037 number has to be fake."

Tom's frown deepened.

"What is it?" Esme asked him.

"Just because no one can find you," he said, "doesn't
mean you can't find them."

"How? How would this kid find all these people who
just happened to share his interests?"

Sheriff Shuster stepped in. "Nunez, you know how many fucked-up websites there are? We've seen them. These days, whatever your fetish, all it takes is a couple of clicks to find a comrade."

"And then you go from there," Esme added. "You sift through enough crime junkies and you eventually find some hard-core fans. There's a whole floor in the Keeney Building in D.C. dedicated to tracking this kind of crap."

"CCIPS. Cybercrime squad. See, Nunez. Big Brother is, in fact, watching you."

"Isn't that, you know, unconstitutional?"

"In a post-9/11 world, liberty takes a backseat to security. For better or worse."

"Usually worse," mumbled Tom.

Esme agreed…mostly. As with most Big Subjects, her feelings on the matter were complicated. But high debate would have to wait, because at that moment her phone rang. The ring tone was Bauhaus's macabre goth track "Bela Lugosi's Dead."

"Hello, Karl," she said.

"Mrs. Stuart, I just wanted to let you know that we have your guy Grover Kirk in custody. If you want to have a chat with him, you've got twelve hours. Then I'm releasing him."

Karl didn't seem impatient or upset or in any way put out, and that was what raised a red flag. He had done as she'd asked, but he was gunning for her now. And it wasn't a good idea to have the assistant director in charge of the New York regional office of the Federal Bureau of Investigation gunning for you.

But Grover Kirk shouldn't have gone after her daughter. It was that simple.

"Tom and I will be there in a little bit, Karl," she replied. "And round up some folks from CCIPS and tell them to drink their Red Bull, because we're bringing them a nightmare."

13

"Hello, Grover."

Esme sat on the table, cross-legged, and stared down this penis-headed exploitation artist. His wrists were chained to a metal chair. His brown cotton slacks were dark along the crotch and the inside of his thighs. The irony was lovely—this man who had intimidated her seven-year-old child had pissed himself. This otherwise antiseptic room now smelled like urine. Once Karl Ziegler, famously germaphobic, found out what Grover had done to one of his interview rooms, he would go apoplectic. Lovelier and lovelier.

"Want a glass of water?" she asked. "You look dehydrated."

He remained silent.

"Come on, Grover. A person really needs to replenish their fluids."

She reached out a hand to him and he instinctively flinched. She had him scared. Like Sophie had been scared. Good.

"Tell me, Grover, what did you think would happen? Did you expect that you could just walk up to my daughter and intimidate her and there wouldn't be repercussions? Did you think I wouldn't react?"

His bald head oozed perspiration. It ran in streams down his eyebrows, cheeks, jowls. Soon there would be enough to add another human odor to this room.

"What do you have to say for yourself, Grover? Huh? Now that you've seen what happens when you shove someone and they shove you back. Well? What do you have to say for yourself?"

His gaze lifted and matched hers. Then he answered her question in a soft, measured tone.

"Thank you."

Thank you? What the hell did that mean? Christ, had they already pushed him past his saturation point? Had Grover Kirk already lost his mind?

"What are you thanking me for, Grover? Is it the steel chair you're bolted to? How about the invasion of your privacy, the way you invaded my family's privacy? Huh? What are you thanking me for?"

To which his lips curled a bit, almost in a grin.

"For finally meeting with me."

Her fingernails scratched against the grain of the wooden table. It took all her willpower to keep from smacking the prick in the jaw.

He knew all along she was going to react like this, coming at him aggressively and, more important, personally. He'd planned on it, hoped for it. She'd been played, and had now given him exactly what he needed for his goddamn book: her.

The laptop was handed over to the care of Mineola Wu, a statuesque Amerasian who was one of the DOJ's top young experts on violent-crime websites. Mineola happened to be at the Javits Center in Manhattan, attending an exposition on Web 2.0, when she got the call from her superiors to pay a visit to the Federal Building in neighboring TriBeCa. She walked all thirtysomething blocks, experiencing the sun dipping below the city's skyscraped skyline. Mineola loved to walk.

"Yeah, this is bad," she said, after a ten-minute perusal of Timothy's C: drive. A silver cow dangled at the end of a necklace she wore, and it hopped up and down with her every syllable. She still wore her casual black dress and high heels from the exposition. Or maybe that was just her regular attire.

She had walked all thirtysomething blocks in those high heels.

"So it's a real website?" asked Tom. He sat in a chair by the empty cubicle she'd been temporarily assigned. Agents passing through this maze of tiny offices had to make an effort to avoid bumping into him. "It's not just something Timothy Hammond whipped up in his spare time?"

"No, it's real, and Hammond was one of its members."

She brought up his cache of saved emails. Many of them were from a Cain42 to a Mothman, both of whom had web addresses linked to the serial killer handbook domain name.

"Mothman," Tom echoed. As in the legendary monster that haunted Point Pleasant, West Virginia. Timothy "Mothman" Hammond. "So who's Cain42?"

"That is the million-dollar question."

She quickly brought up several violent-crime websites on Timothy's laptop, including an image-heavy shrine to mutilation.

"Most of these have message boards so the denizens can gab among themselves," explained Agent Wu.

"We've been infiltrating them for years now, posing as hobbyists, whatever. Over the years, the nicknames, especially the active contributors, become familiar. Notice anyone you recognize?"

For Tom's benefit, she scrolled through one of the message boards, which was mainly dedicated to rants against local police, state police, the FBI, the CIA, the NSA, the DEA, the Secret Service, the U.S. Marshals and the Department of Homeland Security. It didn't take Tom long to see her point. Some of the lengthier, more scholarly responses belonged to one poster.

"Cain42."

"So this is what you wanted, Grover?" Esme hopped off the table and eyeballed the winemaker/journalist/dickhead. "To be chained to a chair, sitting in a pool of your own urine?"

"All knowledge comes with a price. You should know that as well as anyone."

"And why's that?"

Grover shrugged, or did the best shrugging he could with his wrists fixed to the chair's arms. "You needed to return to the FBI where you belonged. The price you paid was Galileo."

"Funny. I seem to recall it was Henry Booth who paid the price with two bullets to his chest."

"You were there."

"Yes."

"And you must have been so happy to see him put down. I'll bet you even wish you'd been the one to pull the trigger."

Esme swallowed a breath. "Yes."

"Which is ironic, considering that of everyone else he encountered, he singled you out for mercy."

Again there it was—the shadow of a grin on his lips. As if Grover Kirk were so arrogant he didn't even have to smirk in order to smirk.

"You know what I'm talking about, of course," he continued. "He had you in his sights in Amarillo and he purposefully let you go. He killed everyone else he ran into, but he let you go. According to my sources, it's because he knew how good he was—and how bad he was—and he wanted to be stopped. He wanted there to be someone in the world to put an end to his crime spree, because he knew divine intervention was out of the question. So he chose you. And while bodies fell all around you, people you knew, people you'd known for years, you remained alive. He even shot your old boss, Tom Piper."

Esme didn't remember crossing toward him, but suddenly she had her hand around his throat. And was squeezing. Still, he stared at her, dispassionately.

What a perfectly circular ending to his book this would make.

She released his throat and stepped away. He was breathing hard now and coughing. She shook the tension of her hands. Damn this son of a bitch. The longer she stayed in here, the more she was playing his game. She had to leave this room.

She left the room.

Karl Ziegler stood there, clattering a breath mint against his teeth. He clicked the sound off on the speakers that allowed outsiders to eavesdrop on the interview room.

"Mrs. Stuart, you know you're not finished yet," he told her.

She knew.

She took a moment, exhaled her anxiety and reentered the room.

Karl Ziegler flicked the speakers back on and continued his observation through the one-way glass.

Mineola Wu studied the thumbnail photographs for a full five minutes. One of them in particular, near the bottom of the page, seemed to draw her attention. Finally, Tom couldn't take it anymore, and asked her what she recognized.

"About six months ago," she replied, "one of our deep covers received an email inviting him to join an 'exclusive website.' The email was sent by Cain42."

She switched over to the cubicle's desktop computer. She was soon on to the CCIPS's own database.

"So you've already infiltrated it," he said. "What I brought you today is old news."

"The email stipulated that, for security purposes, a background check needed to be performed in order for our cover to be allowed access. If those terms were agreeable, our cover was to email back with his name and his address. No social security number, no driver's license ID. Just his name and his address. So he provided the name and address that had been fabricated for his cover and waited."

Mineola punched a key and the dossier of a DOJ operative named Evan Muller appeared on the screen.

"One week later, while having dinner with his wife at their real address, Agent Muller responded to a knock at their front door. She opened the door. We assume this because her body was found by the door in a position that suggested she had opened it. Someone had punched a three-inch hole in her throat and let her bleed to death right there on the floor. Agent Muller's body was not found at all. The next morning, his cover finally received a response from Cain42."

She punched another key, and the email appeared.

Dear Sir:

We regret to inform you that the background check that you authorized raised several red flags with our organization and as a result your application for membership has been denied.

Sincerely,
Cain42

"How did Agent Muller get exposed?"

Mineola shook her head. "We don't know. But he wasn't our only active infiltration. Several weeks later, another one of our covers received the exact same invitation to join. She accepted. You see, we'd heard enough chatter about your serial killer website to know that it was real and that we needed someone on the inside, and if this was how people got in, so be it. While we waited for Cain42 to conduct his background check, we had our operative hide out in a safe house under protective duty. Her name was Heidi Osborne. The DOJ recruited the both of us out of MIT. I knew her. Anyway, a week passed. No response. Another week. So Heidi sent him an email, asking about the status of her application. The very next day, cockroaches began to appear in the safe house, coming out of the vents. Thousands and thousands of cockroaches."

"Someone had dumped a vat of roaches into the air ducts?"

"Apparently," she replied. "Well, they had to move. They didn't have a choice. The security detail booked a room at a nearby motel and they transferred Heidi there and…we don't know what happened next. We do know that the two gentlemen on her security detail were both found dead, shot at point-blank range by a .38 pistol."

Mineola clicked on the thumbnail that had so captured her attention. It displayed a bone-thin woman in her midtwenties, dangling from a noose made of barbed wire. Most of her white tank top was soaked in her own blood.

"That's Heidi Osborne. And I'll bet on another one of these pages of photographs, one of the ones we can't access offline, we'll find a picture of Agent Evan Muller."

Tom shook his head, disgusted.

"By the way," she added, "Agent Muller was living in Maryland at the time of his disappearance. Heidi was being secluded in a safe house in Oregon."

"He somehow traced her email and was able to get to her with an army of cockroaches the next day?"

"Our theory, Special Agent Piper, is that Cain42 didn't do it at all."

Tom frowned, and then he realized her implication. "He's got a pool of over two thousand psychopaths to draw from."

Esme leaned against the antiseptic wall of the interview room, crossed her arms and waited for Grover to open his mouth. But he just stared back at her. His whole point in all this, after all, was to get *her* to open up.

Maybe it was time to give him what he wanted.

"You're right. Henry Booth murdered many people, and I knew some of them. Some of them were friends of mine. And I miss them. But what you want to know is if I have survivor's guilt."

"Do you?"

Esme pushed herself off the wall and closer to the bald pseudo-journalist. She could see the hunger in his eyes.

"Yes, Grover, I do. But not in the way that you think. You see, I know that even though Henry Booth is dead, there's still a target on me, and maybe on my family. It's faded a bit, with time, but it's still there. And people like you are attracted to it. You think you can piggyback off it. You came at us with, what, with a pen? Someone else might come at me or my family with a knife. To take down the woman who took down Galileo."

She watched that hunger fade a bit, replaced by something else, something more vaguely human.

She persisted. "The FBI—you may not know this— the FBI recommended after Henry Booth's death that we go into protective custody. They knew that the infamy surrounding the case would attract crazies and they were concerned for our well-being. They wanted us to move, change our identities and start a new life. My husband considered it. We do, as you know, have the welfare of a daughter to consider. In the end, he decided it was a good idea. He was willing to sacrifice his tenure and his friendships for the safety of his family. But I wouldn't do it. I said no. I wouldn't be intimidated by some looming *what if.* I wouldn't let my family become the last casualties of Henry Booth's terrorism. I said no. And it's driven a rift between myself and my husband that probably can't ever be repaired. So you want to know, for your book, if I have survivor's guilt? Yes, I do. Every day. But not in the way that you think."

She sat down on the table and leaned forward, inches

from his face. He tried to flinch away, but she just angled her head to catch his gaze.

"You know what I'm talking about, don't you, Grover? You may be a hack of outrageous fucking proportions, but you've interviewed a lot of people for your book, haven't you? And not just witnesses and family members. You've interviewed people who view Henry Booth as some kind of a folk hero, am I right?"

"Yes," he replied, quietly, abashedly.

"How did you find them? Or did they hear about your project and come to you, to make sure you told the 'whole story'?"

Grover, visibly uncomfortable, tried to shift in his seat. It was futile. "A little bit of both."

"Online mostly?"

"Yes."

"You started posting on some message boards and newsgroups, telling people about your project, asking for their points of view, and you got them."

"Yes."

"Charismatic guy like yourself, I'll bet you have a pretty high profile right now in this community. Lots of fans of your own, championing your tell-all about their latest idol. After all is said and done and your book comes out, and maybe you say a few negative things about Henry Booth, did you ever stop to think that you're going to have a target on your head, too? That these new friends of yours are going to come after *you?*"

"I…"

Esme left the table and strolled toward the door. She reached for the knob and stopped, turned.

"Tell me, Grover. What nickname did you use when you posted on these killer-friendly message boards?"

He whispered his reply.

"What was that?"

He repeated it, louder now, though swathed in embarrassment and guilt. "Galileofan."

"Thank you, Grover."

She left the room.

Karl Ziegler stood there, loudly sucking on what had to be another breath mint.

Tom was there, as well, now, along with Mineola Wu, who was perusing her laptop. Esme had been on the phone with her family while Mineola had exposed Tom to the world of Cain42, and then received a summary of the case from Tom himself.

All this had happened *before* she went in to interview Grover Kirk.

"Well?" Esme asked Mineola. Had they gotten what they needed?

Mineola looked up from her computer. "It checks out."

Esme turned to Tom. It was Karl's decision, but she needed Tom's approval.

"Let's use him," he said.

Esme nodded and turned back to the one-way mirror and stared at Grover Kirk, looking so pathetic and small in that chair. Somehow, Cain42 had seen through the DOJ's cover identities, so to successfully infiltrate the website, they needed someone who didn't have a cover identity. They needed an actual civilian who already had a history on these various violent-crime message boards.

Grover "Galileofan" Kirk had just become their bait to catch Cain42.

14

"We sleep, we eat, we fuck, we kill. Everything else is decoration."

He had them both bolted to the chairs, not unlike how Esme had fastened Grover Kirk. Only Cain42 used duct tape. It was so much cheaper and leaps and bounds more reliable than handcuffs. He had their wrists duct-taped to the arms of the chairs and their ankles duct-taped to the legs of the chairs. It was a trite setup, used in countless B-movies, but it did the job.

He had the newlyweds, both stripped down to their underwear, facing each other. The wife's cheeks were stained with teary mascara. The husband had a small scar on his upper lip, perhaps from a chicken bone he'd accidentally bitten into as a child.

"Why do we sleep? We sleep to conquer exhaustion, one of two necessary by-products our active lives incur. Sleep is our fail-safe, our daily retreat to the womb of infancy. We curl up, hook our umbilical cords into the subconscious and sustain ourselves with dreams."

Cain42 was preening for them, and he knew it. It was the small excess and revelry he allowed himself in these moments at work. And he took his work very seriously.

"Why do we eat? We eat to conquer hunger, the other necessary by-product our active lives incur. With food, though, we seek more than replenishment. We seek sensation. We seek sweetness, bitterness, texture, pleasure. Too much pleasure and we gorge. Too little and we waste away until we wear our skeletons as our clothes."

They were in a spacious meat locker, not far from the loading dock where the meat trucks would come in the morning to pick up the slaughtered cattle. Hundreds of gutted cows dangled from thick steel hooks. Cain weaved among them as he spoke. The acoustics in here were wonderful. Maybe it was the high ceiling.

The newlyweds in their chairs were positioned near the center of the meat locker. Their lips had begun to turn blue. Their ears were red with blood. Every so often his walking path brought him back to them, audibly shivering in their restraints of duct tape.

Oh, the meat locker. Cain42 was nothing if not a traditionalist.

"Why do we fuck? We fuck to conquer the future. We create generations with our loins. As with food, it serves a practical purpose and yet we quest beyond the utilitarian for the hedonistic and, unlike with food, over-abundance is not a vice. A surfeit of food and we twaddle toward obesity. A surfeit of sex and we race toward athleticism and the physical ideal."

He wore a ski jacket and gloves to combat the cold. In all honesty, the temperature wasn't much warmer outside. He also wore a black wool hat, which warmed the top halves of his ears and concealed most of his hair. He was not fond of his hair. It never seemed to comb straight. On some days, he considered shaving it off, but he was scared of what he would find underneath, of what might be irrevocably exposed. So he wore hats.

"And, finally, why do we kill? If sleep and food conquer exhaustion and sex conquers time itself, what does murdering conquer other than the life force of other men? What value can be gained from the creation of corpses? And yet, although technologies exist which allow for better sleep and produce better food and enable more pleasurable sex, our scientific efforts as a species have undoubtedly been poured into the refinement of murder. Abortions. Capital punishment. War. Our priorities are obvious. One might say that when we kill, we are fulfilling our historical imperative."

He faced them now, his hands tucked into the pockets of his ski jacket.

"Who shall I kill first? I'll leave the choice to you."

Both the husband and the wife turned their heads to look at him. They waited for him to continue.

He didn't.

Instead, Cain42 grabbed another chair and sat down, a few feet from them, and waited for them to continue. He had all night. He was relatively warm. He had the music of his thoughts to keep him occupied and an inhaler in his pocket in case the dry air rattled his asthma.

The wife wore a pink silk negligee. It showcased her slim, dark figure. She probably bought it especially for their honeymoon. The husband wore a simple pair of cotton boxers, white with blue dots on them. His physique was solid. Cain42 could have traced the man's abdominals with the tip of his hunting knife.

Hmm. Perhaps he would.

Seconds passed. Minutes passed. Ten minutes passed. Thirty minutes passed. The husband and wife simply refused to play his game. He had a tremendous amount of patience, but the first shift at the slaughterhouse would be arriving in a few hours. So it was time to speed things up. He grabbed a nearby meat apron and donned it.

"Okay," he said, and drew out his hunting knife. "This is stainless steel. It can cut through a tin can as easily as it can cut through a tomato. Do you see the serrated edge? That means it's going to hurt going in, and it's going to hurt even more as it goes out. It's especially designed to cut through tissue. Let me give you an example."

He then proceeded to saw off one of the husband's nipples. He probably could have lopped it off, but sawing took longer and caused more pain. And, oh, how the husband screamed and screamed.

Cain42 flicked the nipple into the distance.

"In case you haven't yet figured it out, I'm a bit of a sadist. That means I want to cause you as much pain as possible. It's a psychosexual thing. You don't need me to get into it. But I'm going to put my offer on the table one last time, and now it comes with a twist. One of you I'm going to kill quick, and the other I'm going to kill slow. If you don't choose in the next two minutes, I'll make sure you both suffer. Now, are you sure you want your loved one to undergo that kind of torture? Choose, please."

That got them talking.

Him: "Baby, I love you!"

Her: "I love you, too, baby! Oh, God!"

Him: "It's going to be okay! As long as we're together!"

Her: "We'll be together forever!"

Him: "I don't want you to suffer, baby!"

Her: "I don't want *you* to suffer!"

Him: "I can take it!"

Her: "Let me do this for you!"

Him: "No!"

Etc., etc.

Cain42 watched the second hand tick past two minutes on his wristwatch and stepped in between the weeping lovebirds.

"Time's up," he said. "So, who gets to leave class early?"

"He does," the wife replied.

The husband opened his mouth to protest, so Cain42 thrust all six inches of his steel blade into that open gap. He tugged upward, and then pulled back, tracking bits of reddish palate along with it, and finally, with some effort, withdrew the knife through the man's nose. The husband gagged, twitched in the chair and died, just as promised.

The wife was sobbing.

"Don't cry for his fate," replied Cain42. "Cry for yours."

And he went to work.

Seventy-two minutes later, he was both exhilarated and exhausted. What remained in her chair more resembled one of the hook-laden cows than a human being. Cain42 photographed the crime scene, splashed both corpses with a gallon of refrigerant (the cleanest crime scene is a destroyed crime scene) and left them to be discovered by the morning crew.

It was one of his acolytes from the website who had provided the address of the slaughterhouse. They'd assured him that the nighttime security was lax, and so it was. He ambled back to his silver Camry (bought for its ubiquity) and drove off without one rent-a-cop asking for his ID.

The meat apron (which he'd left behind) had absorbed

most of the blood, but not all of it. He would need both a new coat and a new pair of jeans. Ah, well. Such were the sacrifices he made for a job he loved.

Sunrise was still an hour or so away. The poets called this the magic hour, when the demons of the night were still awake and the darlings of the day were stirring from their beds. A melting pot of good and evil for one blessed, cursed span of minutes. Cain42 didn't wonder which side of the spectrum he was on. As far as he was concerned, moral relativism was for patsies. He considered stopping for a late-night snack, maybe a doughnut or a cup of soup, but his exhaustion dictated otherwise, and he headed for his motel.

As he idled at a stoplight, he noticed a homeless woman trundle toward the sidewalk. She walked rigidly, as if the joints in her knees had fused solid, and kept her head down. Most of her face was concealed by her shaggy gray mane. Her body was concealed by a shaggy gray coat. She shuffled up to the curb. Cain42's light turned green. He didn't drive forward. She glanced up at him, one green eye peeking through that fuzzy amoeba she called hair. No one else was in sight. Just the woman, the man and the hour of magic. He waved her forward. She nodded to him and stepped into the crosswalk, clopping forward in that steely gait of hers. She passed in front of his Camry.

He floored the accelerator and collided with the woman at a steady clip of twenty miles per hour. Most car accident victims toppled up, and Cain42 had braced himself for her impact on his windshield, but this homeless woman toppled down. Maybe the stiff joints in her legs were to blame. Either way, she went down and under the carriage of the one-ton-plus vehicle. Cain42 felt his car roll over her body, as if it were a speed bump near a church, and continued on his way. A quick check in the rearview mirror—and her arms were still in motion, swatting at imaginary flies, the rest of her body impossibly twisted up under that shapeless gray coat she wore. Was she still alive or were those frantic arm motions simply the impulses of a dying nervous system?

Hmm. Maybe he could go for a cup of soup, after all.

He stopped at an all-night coffee shop conveniently located near his bed-and-breakfast, changed into his other pair of jeans, left his bloody coat in the car. He checked the front of his Camry for any victim debris, flirted with the waitress and spoon-fed on a pint of piping-hot chicken broth. A few errant vegetables floated in the yellow sea, but their presence seemed more a culinary afterthought than an essential ingredient. *Eh, it's 6:00 a.m., let's toss some leftover shit in the guy's soup.* Cain42 enjoyed his meal, flirted again with the waitress on the way out, regulated his breath with a hit from his asthma inhaler and left a sizable cash tip.

His B and B was called the Shellmont Inn and, as far as he could tell, its entire staff consisted of an old gay couple named Lou and Norm. The Shellmont Inn had seven rooms available, each named after a heavenly virtue. Cain42 stayed in Temperance. Above the headboard of his bed was a framed print of Luca Giordano's Baroque masterpiece *Temperantia*.

Cain42 loved B and Bs. He subscribed to "B and B USA," an online newsletter that highlighted the best inns, cottages and guest homes in the continental forty-eight states. Since he was always on the road, knowing the best local place to receive room and board with a personal touch came in quite handy.

Lou was already awake, rounding up the morning's eggs from the chicken coop. He and Cain42 shared a wave. He trudged up the steps to Temperance. He so desperately wanted to just fall into that lovely queen-size bed the Shellmont Inn provided, but first he had one final bit of business to attend.

His MacBook rested on his pillows like an oversize mint. Cain42 unlocked it and brought it out of sleep mode. He could have used the Shellmont's wi-fi, but preferred his own 802.11n modem, already plugged into a USB port. It offered both higher speeds and better security, and he needed both if he was going to properly maintain his website.

And he treasured his website.

Delightfully, the thread he'd introduced earlier in the day under "Announcements and News" had received even more responses. Members were openly sharing their grief—and anger—over the death of one of their own.

i'll light a black candle in his honor
—*Peterkurten*

mothman always made me laugh
—*new_world_order*

im gna gt myself cawt jus so i can kil that sombitch myself!
—*lambofsatan*

It was one of the bylaws of their brotherhood. Cain42 would hold their identities a secret—even from fellow members of his ersatz "killers labor union"—unless and until the event of their deaths. Then, in a heartfelt obituary, he would lift the veil of secrecy.

He had had to do it too many times as of late.

More often than not, a union member got himself killed by ignoring the valuable tips Cain42 himself offered right there on the home page of the website. They weren't difficult to follow, but some people just couldn't be relied on to follow any rules, and some people, at the end of the day, were just plain lazy.

Mothman had been neither. Mothman had been a child prodigy. He had only yet begun to actualize his potential. When Cain42 heard about the events in Ulster County—from another member, who had speculated openly whether Timothy Hammond had been one of them—he had been brought to tears. To be taken from the world at so young an age. So sad.

But it was a danger of the trade. This line of business had a history of unhappy endings. This labor union sought to diminish those odds, but nothing could stand in the way of human nature and human error. Steelworkers and coal miners still died, and so did his men and women (mostly men, but as a proponent of both women's rights and affirmative action, he was actively pursuing more female and minority recruits).

To get his mind off Mothman's tragic demise, Cain42 clicked on another thread on the message board and started up one of his silly polls.

What is your favorite murder weapon?

Knife
Ax
Gun
Blowtorch
Poison
Chainsaw
Hands
Candlestick
Wrench
Lead Pipe

The last three made him grin.

He sifted through his in-box, sorting the significant from the banal. Most of the private emails he received were complaints, one member sounding off about another's foolish and/or insensitive remarks in some thread. Some of the members, even though they didn't know one another's IRL, had developed grudges and rivalries. Publicly, Cain42 denounced such disputes as petty and unbecoming, but privately, he knew that anything that bolstered competitiveness had to be an asset.

The positive rate of growth in the "Photographs of the Trade" archive seemed to point in that direction. It was the most popular page on the website, and with good reason. Words were just words, especially online, but authentic photographs of actual union work boosted morale and fostered intelligent discussion. And ninety-nine percent of the photographs submitted were authentic. Cain42 fact-checked each and every one.

Although the most recent photograph wouldn't have to be fact-checked at all. He uploaded tonight's JPEGs from his camera to his laptop and added them to the "Photographs" archive. The thumbnail of the husband and wife now occupied the space in the top row recently held by Mothman's masterful kill of that woman in upstate New York, the space reserved for the newest and the freshest.

Time moved on.

The best way to honor Mothman—or any casualty—was to learn from their mistakes. What had the boy done wrong? He had fallen into that teenage pitfall of letting his parents get involved. That was really no fault of his own. The second best way to honor Mothman would be to replenish the union's membership. So Cain42 fought his cloying tiredness and opened his database of potentials. He had seven names on his list. Maybe it was time to be bold. Maybe it was time to contact them all. How wonderful would it be if all seven checked out?

His eyes scanned the list. Some of the nicknames these people came up with sure made him roll his eyes. *Jack_the_Ripperest?* Really? He stopped at the last name, though, and smiled. *Galileofan.*

Now there was a man after his own heart.

15

For his own protection, Grover Kirk had been placed under house arrest—and that house turned out to be Esme's. This was Grover's only request, and given the certain amount of danger he was putting himself in, it was not an unreasonable one. What made it worse, of course, was that it also made perfect sense. He had, after all, come to Long Island to interview her. If, in a fictional world, she had been copasetic with his interests and supportive of his book, she might have allowed the budding journalist to crash at her house for a few days while he did his research. This would clear Cain42's background check because, well, it contained a terrific amount of plausibility, and meanwhile, she could keep an eye on Grover in case Cain42 did come a-knocking. In this fictional world, Grover Kirk was apparently not a pathetic creep who had intimidated the little girl he was now living, temporarily, with under the same roof.

Convincing Rafe to acquiesce to it all had been a task and a half.

"First of all," he'd barked at her over the phone, "you didn't even tell me about what happened in the museum.

I had to find out from Sophie. Who's still a mess, by the way, thanks for asking."

Esme rubbed her forehead and sat back in the car. Was it still only Monday? God. When would this day end?

"What you should have done, wife of mine, is tell your boss to go fuck himself."

"Oh, yeah, Rafe? Is that what I should have done?" She glanced to her left, at the sallow companion with whom she was sharing the backseat. He was typing on his computer. The dickhead didn't even have the good sense to get carsick.

"Esme, I will not have that man in my house."

"One, it's not just your house. Two, it's not your choice. It's not mine, either. Do you think I want him within five hundred miles of Sophie?"

Grover glanced up from his laptop, opened his mouth to say something, changed his mind and returned to his writing. Up front, the rookie FBI agent driving them to Oyster Bay switched on the cruise control and leaned back in her seat.

Tom was asleep in the front passenger seat. Apparently, the day's events had taken its toll on him. Esme wondered, not for the first time, just how much Henry Booth's bullet had permanently emptied him of his vitality and spirit. Had she made a selfish mistake? He had been so content, living in semiretirement with Penelope Sue, working at a desk. And he could have returned to Kentucky on the next flight out of Newark, but he'd insisted on accompanying them to Long Island. In for a penny, in for a pound. That was Tom Piper.

"Well, Esme, I'd like to know how you plan on explaining all this to our daughter."

Esme sighed. So would she. And she also would have preferred her husband offer assistance rather than dumbheaded interference, but this was her life, and not the fictional utopia they hoped Cain42 would purchase (along with, perhaps, a bridge and a pair of unicorns).

"And where's he going to sleep, Esme? Have you thought about that?"

Where in the house would Grover sleep? Had the argument really reduced so fast to nitpicking? "He'll sleep on the sofa," she answered, and as the words tumbled out of her mouth, she realized why Rafe had posed the question. It wasn't a nitpick, really. If Grover slept on the couch, she and Rafe, no matter how much enmity currently flowed between them, would have to share the bed. There would be no middle-of-the-night retreat for either of them.

Esme made a vow to, the next time she was in Manhattan, locate Karl Ziegler's place of residence and leave a flaming pile of dog shit at his front door. Not that this was all his doing. He couldn't have been aware of their marital problems. He had inflicted Grover Kirk on her, not on them. And the plan was sound. No, no. Next time in Manhattan: place of residence, flaming pile of dog shit. Done deal.

The next exit off the Long Island Expressway was theirs. Soon they would be home. Esme massaged the bridge of her nose. If only home were home.

"Rafe," she said, "what's done is done. As much as I'd appreciate your support, this is happening whether you give or not."

"I still don't understand why he has to stay here, why the FBI can't just put him up in a motel room."

"Because he needs supervision and if the bad guys have him under surveillance and notice he's spending all his time indoors accompanied by two men carrying government-issue firearms, he's going to get a little suspicious."

"'The bad guys.' I hate it when you condescend to me like that."

"Yeah, Rafe? Well, I hate it when you're an asshole."

She hung up.

Not that it mattered much. In twenty minutes they'd be pulling into the driveway, and then she and Rafe could recommence their jolly squabble. Esme leaned back in her leather seat, closed her eyes and longed to live in a Calgon commercial rather than an Albee play. While she was at it, she also wished for world peace, an end to starvation and a pair of comfortable heels.

Rafe was standing outside when they arrived, a mug of hot coffee his only companion. The steam swirled up and smoke-screened his mouth and eyes. Esme frowned—where had she seen that image before? She and Tom, both sleepy-eyed, got out of the car. Grover sidled into the front seat. For the sake of verisimilitude, he had to pick up his own vehicle from the Days Inn and bring it here. He and the young FBI agent drove off to do just that.

"Rafe," said Tom.

"Tom," said Rafe.

Rafe went back inside. At least he had the courtesy not to slam the door behind him and in their faces.

"Your husband's as congenial as ever," murmured Tom.

Rafe was in the kitchen, washing out his mug. Esme expected to find her father-in-law splayed out on the sofa but the old man was nowhere to be found. Even the door to his room was wide-open. Just as well. She told Tom she would be right back, and headed up to her daughter's bedroom. Sophie would probably be asleep, but it felt like forever since she'd seen her beautiful face and Esme just wanted to hold her and squeeze her and—

Sophie wasn't in her room.

Esme frowned, checked the master bedroom. Maybe Sophie was in there, curled up under their sheets?

No.

Panicking now, Esme checked the bathroom, then bolted back downstairs.

"Where's Sophie?" she asked Rafe. No, not asked— *demanded.*

He clinked his mug into the dishwasher. "With my dad."

At this time of night? Past her bedtime? What the hell was Rafe—

And then she knew. She turned to Tom, who looked away. He must have figured it out even before she had.

"She wasn't too happy about spending the night in a hotel room," Rafe added, "but then again, you didn't really give me much time to get her prepared. She was really looking forward to seeing her mother."

On one hand, Esme wanted to knuckle-punch him in the spleen for what he'd done, and without telling her. On the other hand, though, he'd been absolutely right to do it. And she hated herself a little for not thinking of it.

Of course Sophie wouldn't be sleeping here tonight. She wouldn't be spending any time at home, not while Grover Kirk breathed its oxygen and occupied its furniture. It was in her best interest to keep the two of them as far apart as possible, even if it meant uprooting the little girl out of her own bed.

Esme took a calming breath and asked, "Where are they staying?"

"The Worths'."

Esme nodded. Their friends—well, his friends, really—Nolan and Halley Worth owned a towering lighthouse on the North Shore that they had ingeniously converted to a bed-and-breakfast. The Worths also had a grandson named Billy who was a year younger than Sophie, and whenever he came to visit, they always teased that one day everyone would be attending Billy and Sophie's wedding (a conversation topic that always inspired the two children to fake-retch).

"I'm going to make myself scarce," said Rafe. "I make it a rule not to be in the same room as the guy who accosted my daughter. At least, not when there's law enforcement present."

He shuffled to his office and made sure to slam the door shut behind him.

Twenty minutes later, Grover's Studebaker was parked in the driveway, and the other sedan idled by the front curb, waiting to carry Tom back to New York City. Before he left, though, he spent a few private minutes in the garage with his motorcycle. He left looking solemn and with dust on his fingertips.

Esme hugged him goodbye and stood outside until the car had disappeared from view and the sound of its motor had faded into the silence of the cool November night.

"I like your neighborhood," said Grover.

Esme did her best not to be startled by his sudden appearance behind her. "Thanks," she replied, then quickly passed him back into the house. He closed the door behind them.

"The last time I was here, Lester didn't really give

me a tour. Where is he, by the way? I still have some of that wine he enjoyed."

"He's not here." She surveyed the two bulky vinyl suitcases he'd hefted in with him from his car. They were currently leaving dents on the sofa cushions. His only other piece of luggage, apparently, was the cloth valise which hung off his shoulder strap. "May I please have your car keys and computer?"

"In a minute."

He strolled around the living room slowly, as if he were marking his territory.

"I have somewhere to be," said Esme. "May I have your car keys and your computer, please?"

"Relax, relax." He made his way to the bottom of the stairs and gazed upward. "Nice house. Roomy. Too big for just one child, though. Does Sophie get lonely?"

Grover's face belied innocence, but Esme didn't care. She curled her left hand into a fist, casually approached the dickhead standing in her home and popped him in the jaw. He staggered back and fell onto the bottom three steps. She reached toward him again and he reflexively raised his arms in defense, which allowed her to easily slip the valise off his shoulder with one hand and the car keys from his pocket with the other.

"Thank you," she said.

"You're the psycho, not me!" He rubbed at his jaw. "Not me."

"There's ice in the fridge." She slid the laptop out of its case, set it on the kitchen counter and booted it up. "Help yourself."

He didn't move.

Esme followed the instructions that Mineola had given her, and with a few keystrokes, she had locked Grover out of his own laptop. The only time it would be used was when she was present and supervising.

She shut the computer down and padded to Rafe's office. The door remained shut. She considered opening it, poking her head in, perhaps offering an olive branch, but decided now was not the time. Also, her knuckles were throbbing from the jab.

"I'll be at the Worths'," she called through the door.

Waited for a response.

Nothing.

So be it.

Back in the living room, Grover still hadn't moved from the bottom of the stairs. Let him sleep there for all she cared. She passed him by without even a glance, entered the garage, climbed inside the driver's seat of her Prius, plugged her iPod into the car stereo and started its engine. She needed to clean today's shit off her soul.

The Eurythmics would do the job quite nicely. By the time Esme was on the main road, she was singing along with Annie Lennox about sweet dreams and the seven seas. Sing it, Annie, sing it.

As she neared the lighthouse, the black expanse of the sea, always an unseen neighbor in Oyster Bay, came into view. Although the town had begun as a fishing village so many years ago, with most homes located close to the water, the only people who lived seaside now were the very rich. And so the shoreline became foreign. It belonged to other people. Esme and Rafe were upper middle class and that entitled them to frequent the public beaches, but the actual parcel of water adjoining Oyster Bay went untouched by them, aside from the occasional sojourn down to Barney's for the world's finest (and smallest portion of) grilled flounder. This was the playground of the tourists and the millionaires, and as she pulled into the gravel lot beside the Worths' B and B, Esme felt like a tourist, here to visit her daughter in a tower.

When the Worths had purchased the original lighthouse from the town, their first goal had been reconstructive renovation. After all, the structure was more than two hundred years old. They spent countless fortunes making it a place where people could live, and then countless more making it a place where people would want to live. The renovations had been successful, and it was now unimaginable that the lighthouse had served any other purpose but to host and cater to discerning guests.

"B and B USA" gave it five out of five stars.

The tall front door opened to the ground floor, which was a museum dedicated to Oyster Bay itself. Like all the floors, this was circular, and if one followed the wall in a clockwise rotation, one could trace the town history in vivid chronology, through a series of murals and backlit displays. But Esme had been here before, and so she continued up the winding stairwell that wound the core of the structure to the first floor, the main floor, where Halley Worth sat behind a shipwright's large desk, reading a library copy of *Typee*.

"What a pleasure," she lied, and placed her book facedown on the desk surface. She stood to give Esme an aristocratic hug (the kind which lasted half a second and served no purpose other than for the two huggers to see how close they could come, arms around each other, without their bodies actually touching, actual human contact being gauche).

The Worths were Rafe's friends. Most of the intelligentsia and glitterati of the town were Rafe's friends. He was, after all, a young and ambitious professor at the college. Esme's line of work was somewhat less respectable, if only because so much of what she did made for inappropriate dinner conversation. Even before she'd rejoined the FBI as a consultant, she'd always felt like an outsider in this world. She had grown up impoverished, and no matter how expensive a dress she wore, no matter how many galas she and Rafe attended or how many charities they supported, she always felt as if she were ostracized. Perhaps it was all in her head. Many of Oyster Bay's socialites were lovely people.

Though not Halley Worth.

Halley Worth, age sixty-two, was a genuine old-school snob-bitch. Her husband, Nolan, had made a killing in the stock market while she'd played house, and now it was her turn to run the show while he spent his days playing poker with his right-wing buddies. The Worths suffered fools gladly, if those fools shared the correct politics, and so Esme's father-in-law got along very well with them. In fact, as Esme and Halley broke their almost-embrace, a toilet flushed, and moments later Lester stepped out to join them.

"She's on the fourth floor," he said.

No *hello*. No *sorry about your situation*. Ah, Lester.

Esme bid farewell to the lovely pair and ascended the winding stairwell up, up, up to the fourth floor. There were two doors here, one of which led to the restroom and one of which led to the bedroom. Esme knocked on one, opened it, waved to the WC, closed the door, knocked on the other, opened it and beheld her beautiful daughter, asleep in bed, dreaming.

Sophie was safe here. What better setting than a lighthouse to protect her from the darkness of the world? And there was so much darkness in the world. Esme faced it daily. It was inevitable that some of that darkness would creep across the threshold of her own home, and so if this was the temporary solution they had, so be it, right? The child's welfare needed to be prioritized over lesser concerns like a mother's love.…

Esme thought about P. J. Hammond, and what he'd done for his flesh and blood, and what he'd ultimately done *to* him. So much darkness in the world to keep at bay, and if that darkness came from within, the responsibilities of the parent did not change. Protect the child. P.J. had protected Timothy for so long. Esme would protect Sophie, even if it would drive her daughter to despise her for her absence. Why couldn't she have a normal mother like everyone else?

She probably still resented Esme for not being there today at the museum, and rightfully so. If Esme had been there, Grover wouldn't have. If Esme had been there, there would be no nightmares for Sophie's fragile imagination to conjure. Because as she lay there on the fourth floor of the tower by the sea, it was obvious to Esme that Sophie was experiencing a nightmare. Her fists were curled up around her blanket, and her lips were twitching toward a frown. Loose strands of hair were beginning to stick to her wet forehead.

Not even the lighthouse could shield her from the darkness of her own making.

Esme crossed the threshold of her daughter's room, knelt down beside her borrowed bed and gently rocked her exposed shoulder until those perfect eyes of hers flickered open, already shiny with tears.

"Mommy…?"

"I'm right here, baby."

The girl's small arms rose up and wrapped themselves around her mother, tightly, tightly, because if they were tight enough, if she were strong enough, maybe she could keep her mother from ever, ever leaving.

16

The FBI put Tom up in a two-star hotel not far from the Federal Building. It was a prewar building, and the hotel's four elevators were still operating at their original speed. Tom waited ten minutes for one to open and lift him up to the twelfth floor. An assortment of giggling teenagers crowded in with him, and one of them, a spiky-haired girl with braces, felt the impulse to push all of the buttons on the brass panel. Tom felt the impulse to knock her unconscious with a carefully placed uppercut to the back of her right ear. Unlike the teen, he practiced self-control. But it was difficult.

Tom ached. He ached in his temples. He ached in his shoulder blades. He ached in his biceps and his triceps and his forearms and thighs and calves and especially, especially, the soles of his feet. He had managed to keep the ailments of age at arm's length for so long, but his convalescence over the past six months seemed to invite it all, every joint inflammation in the medical dictionary. They all ended in *-itis* and they all hurt like hell and he wasn't even sixty years old. So what if he'd pushed his body for decades, as if it belonged to one of these obnoxious teenagers rather than that of an aging man who'd survived not one but two motorcycle accidents, not to mention a long history of work-related injuries (stab wounds, bullet wounds, punctures from a staple gun, multiple gashes from multiple box cutters, just to name a few). But it was Galileo who had finally beaten him. Penelope Sue, bless her heart, had done her best to build him back together, but not all the pieces fit, not anymore. He was becoming a relic, just like that motorcycle in Esme's garage.

And he was kind of okay with that.

He slipped his electronic card key into the door, pushed his way into his room and willed himself to stay awake and mobile long enough to undress and step into the hot propulsive shower. God bless the water pressure in New York City. It didn't quite melt away the soreness in his muscles, but it did liquefy them a little, and returned some much-missed flexibility to his neck. By the time he'd toweled himself off, he was warmed, massaged and oh-so-ready for sleep.

His head had barely tapped the fluffed hotel pillow when his cell phone buzzed. He considered ignoring it, but his abject curiosity curtailed that option.

"Hello?" he murmured.

"Oh, shit, did I wake you?"

Tom smiled. "Not at all, Penelope Sue."

"You're such a liar."

"Then you're in love with a liar," he replied.

"So I am."

Tom spotted the digital clock. It was 12:32 a.m.

"Why aren't you asleep?" he asked her.

"Why aren't you?"

"Because you called me, you adorable lunatic."

"We haven't talked all day," she said. "I've missed you."

"We talked a couple hours ago."

"That was Monday. Today is Tuesday."

Tom checked the clock again: 12:33 a.m. Dear Lord, he was in love with a dork. In spite of himself, his smile widened. "Mmm-hmm."

"So are you in bed, Tom?"

"It's almost one o'clock in the morning, woman."

"Well, I'm not in bed."

"That's because you're a weirdo."

"No, it's because I'm walking in a hallway."

"Why are you walking in a hallway?"

"Because it's the only way to get from where I'm going to where I need to be, silly."

"And where is it you need to be at almost one o'clock in the morning?"

"I'm almost there, actually."

"The refrigerator?"

"Tom Piper, are you calling me fat?"

"No, love. I'm calling you insane."

"Insane for you, maybe."

Tom audibly groaned. "Mmm-hmm."

"Oh, I forgot to tell you about this wonderful client I had today. Well, yesterday. He was about your age and—"

There was a knock at his door.

"Excuse me a minute," he told Penelope Sue, and he wiped a hand over his face to clear away any nap-goo that may have accumulated, whipped the covers off his long body and ambled to the door, not even bothering to put on a T-shirt. The Big Apple bellhops had probably seen a lot worse than the late-night topless body of an over-the-hill gunslinger from Kentucky. The real question was, why would a bellhop be buzzing him at 12:34 in the morning?

Tom hesitated. The door didn't have a peephole.

The stab wounds, bullet wounds, punctures from a staple gun and the multiple gashes from multiple box cutters had made him a wee bit paranoid.

He still had his Glock. It was in his shoulder holster, hanging with his black leather jacket in the sliding-door closet to his right. He could have it in his hands and ready in seconds, and cause some hapless bellhop to wet himself. Because although the local clerks were undoubtedly used to all variations of undress, nobody, no matter how seasoned, reacted well to the sight of a gun.

"Tom?" called Penelope Sue's voice from the phone. "Is everything okay?"

"Yeah," he replied. "Just a second."

He held the Glock behind his back with his right hand and with his left hand, still holding the phone, he reached for the knob. The door was heavy, thick. Practically soundproof. Great.

He took a breath to steady himself.

"Okay, Tom," continued her voice, "in the meantime, let me tell you about this client. He's kind and sweet…"

He opened the door.

"…and as handsome as can be," she finished, staring him straight in the eye.

He blinked.

"Hello, sexy," she said, and leaned forward to kiss him full on the mouth. Her arms smoothly wrapped themselves around his body.

He remained awkwardly unresponsive.

She stepped away from him, confused. Was he not happy to see her?

"I…" he replied, and then, "One second."

He shut the door in her face and quickly returned the Glock to its holster. By the time he'd reopened the door, any semblance of seductiveness or gleeful surprise had vanished from her face. Penelope Sue appeared ticked off.

"Are you kidding me?" she asked.

"It's not like that. I didn't know it was you."

She raised an eyebrow. "Were you expecting someone else?"

"I didn't know who it could be! It's almost one o'clock in the morning!"

"I know. I've been on a plane for two hours."

"And that's wonderful! And I am so glad to see you! Come here."

He held out his arms.

She didn't budge.

"Please?"

She budged. And, finally, they embraced, both of them, chest against chest, lips against lips. They parted, but only an inch, and stared into each other's eyes.

"I'm sorry," she said.

"*I'm* sorry," he said. "With the day I had, and being back in New York for the first time since… I was just… jittery."

"I know." She held her hand against his heart. She could feel its rhythm echo into her palm, and let its music fill her. "That's why I'm here. Let Penelope Sue take care of you."

He nodded, and she led the way to the bed. The heavy door shut by itself.

The following morning, after a lengthy shared shower (which both of them required for a variety of reasons), Tom took Penelope Sue to a bagel shop he knew down the block from the hotel. In true New York fashion, though, the bagel shop had become a Starbucks. After a momentary grousing, Tom and Penelope Sue then did what any other New Yorker would have done if faced with this disappointment—they tossed away their plans and went inside the Starbucks for some coffee, pastries and Enya. Halfway through their scones, their conversation took its inevitable detour from idle to serious.

"I've got to head to the office soon," he said.

She nodded, sipping on her hot apple spice cider.

"I feel bad about it," he added, "leaving you alone after you came all this way."

"Tom Piper, will you please get over yourself? No woman with a charge card is alone in New York City."

"You're going to rent a male escort?"

That she didn't expect him to say. As the laughter spilled out of her body, the hot cider spilled out of her mouth and nose. She reached for a napkin to clean herself up, but for whatever reason, that just made her laugh harder and louder. This being New York City, nobody paid her much attention, except Tom, who nearly swooned at the sight. He was so head over heels in love with this goofy woman.

They made plans to meet up for lunch and went their separate ways, he to the bureaucracy of the Federal Building and she to the cash registers of Macy's. The line at the security checkpoint snaked all the way across most of the lobby floor, and Tom patiently waited his turn. Most of these people, he knew, were here for their visas. New York's USCIS was by far the busiest in the country. In many ways, it had become the new Ellis Island.

Once at the head of the long, multicultural line, Tom showed his credentials to one of the security guards, passed his firearm and wallet onto the conveyor belt and stepped through the metal detector. He then approached a second guard, showed his badge and was allowed to proceed to the elevator bank. His destination lay almost a hundred yards skyward, on the building's twenty-third floor.

Judging by the empties stacked in her borrowed workspace, Mineola Wu was already on her sixth can of Mountain Dew. She waved him over. Cain42's website, or at least the cached version they'd acquired off Timothy, lay open on her desktop computer.

"So I've been feeding the details from these photographs through VICAP, Google, whatever, hoping to get a hit...and I got a hit."

"Show me."

She showed him by blowing up one of the thumbnails off the "Photographs" page. It featured a storefront window with three mannequins, each draped in a froufrou autumnal sweater-pants ensemble. In place of their three plastic heads, though, were three human heads— three blondes, all with their eyes open in horror. A good amount of blood ran down from their open throats and over the froufrou autumnal sweater-pants ensembles.

Mineola clicked another button, which brought up an AP news article from October 31. An early-morning jogger named Marie McConnell, age twenty-six, spotted the display in the window of Hot Cotour, a local high-end clothing store for women. Police were called to the scene, and quickly cordoned off the area. The remains were identified as belonging to Summer Sholes, age nineteen; Lydia Patel, age twenty-two; and Rosalind Becker, age twenty-four. All three had been employees of the store. There were no suspects at this time. The location of the incident: Hoboken, New Jersey, just over the river from the island of Manhattan.

"Let's go," said Tom.

Mineola downed some Mountain Dew. "You have fun there, chief."

"We need to coordinate with the Hoboken P.D., maybe shed some light on their investigation."

"Maybe, but I'm staying planted right where I am."

"You don't want to come?"

"Do I look like a field agent to you?"

He gave her high heels and geek-chic attire a once-over.

"Have fun in Hoboken," she said. "Give my regards to Ol' Blue Eyes."

Tom opened his mouth to retort, perhaps convince her to come along, but changed his mind. He could have done it, too. He had a good idea which buttons he needed to push to get her out of that chair. Instead, he asked her to call ahead to Hoboken to give them a heads-up, and he headed back toward the elevators. Technically, he was supposed to clear this trip with Karl Ziegler, but in the half second Tom spent looking around, he just couldn't spot him. Oh, well.

New Jersey meant the PATH trains, and the PATH trains meant Penn Station, which was practically across the street from Macy's. He could pop into the department store and surprise Penelope Sue. It would take only a few minutes out of his already-flexible schedule.

No, he'd do it when he returned. Take care of Hoboken, get that out of the way and then spend as much time with Penelope Sue as they wanted, with nowhere they needed to be and nothing they needed to do.

Eight cities had a Pennsylvania Station, leftover hubs from nineteenth-century America's vital railroad network. There were three in Pennsylvania itself (Philadelphia, Harrisburg and Pittsburgh), one in Baltimore, one in Cleveland, one in Cincinnati, one in Newark, and the oldest, busiest of them all: New York's Penn Station, occupying more than ten acres of commercial real estate underneath the west side of Manhattan. Tom joined the steady mob as it flowed underground, purchased his ticket from one of the many electronic kiosks and boarded his train.

Fifteen minutes later, he was in Hoboken, New Jersey, birthplace of baseball, soft-serve ice cream and, yes, Ol' Blue Eyes himself, Francis Albert Sinatra. Tom had never been to Hoboken before, and wasn't quite sure what to expect. He also didn't know where the city's police departments were located, but he was sure one of the many uniformed cops patrolling this end of the PATH line could be of service.

Apparently, One Police Plaza was just a short walk west on Hudson Place and then a brief stroll north along Hudson Street. It was a much more scenic trip than Tom had anticipated. Years of old jokes at Hoboken's expense—not to mention endless reruns of *On the Waterfront*—had given him a lopsided and by all accounts incorrect opinion of the place. The view of Manhattan on this clear cool day was nothing short of majestic, and the shops he passed along the way to his destination possessed an ethnic charm he associated more with Brooklyn than New Jersey. He even spotted a red phone booth. He thought of Penelope Sue. In addition to *Star Trek,* she also loved *Doctor Who*.

Once he'd arrived at One Police Plaza, he produced his badge, explained his business and shortly thereafter was introduced to detectives Paolo Briggs and Antwone Vitucci, keepers of the murder book for a certain triplet of Halloween decapitations. They signed out an unmarked car (a Crown Victoria, to match the stereotype) and drove out to the crime scene.

"Yeah, we got the email from what's-her-name," said Briggs. He was behind the wheel, and alternating each sentence with a drag off a brown cigarette. "Don't know how it'll elucidate our dead end."

Vitucci made a show of fanning the smoke out of his face. "There was no sign of forced entry so we assumed it was an inside job. That narrowed it down to the owner and manager, a Mrs. Carolyn Harbinger; the assistant manager, her nephew Jefferson—"

"Fag," Briggs noted.

"You know, Briggs, you got a hateful streak in you that's almost as ugly as your face."

Briggs shrugged, ashed out the window and commenced a five-minute attempt at parallel parking.

"Anyway," Vitucci continued, "the only other employee was this girl Sandra Washington. She and the dead girls all went to school together at the technical college. She was the one who got them the jobs at the store."

"And the alibis?"

"All solid. Carolyn Harbinger and her nephew—"

"The fag."

"—were at some… Jesus Christ, Briggs, how many bumpers you trying to hit? They were at this swank family Halloween party at night, lots of guests, and Sandra Washington was palling around SoHo with some artist types, after which she crashed at a friend's place."

Briggs shifted into Park, apparently satisfied with being three feet from the curb. The three of them left the vehicle and walked half a block to the former location of Hot Cotour, now an empty pair of windows and a rolling security door with a For Lease sign taped to it. The contact information still listed Carolyn Harbinger as the owner. The other four shops and restaurants on the block were up and running as if nothing had happened here, as if the hideous deaths of three girls had been just one of those things.

"They had a camera running inside but the thing was conveniently switched off the night of the incident. Another indication of an inside job."

"Motives?" asked Tom.

"You tell us, Dixie," Briggs replied. "I mean, if this is the work of one of those website psychos, maybe we need to start interviewing the neighborhood dogs, see if one of them told our guy to do it."

"Okay, Briggs."

"You know, like the Son of Sam."

"We got it, Briggs. Anyway, to answer your question, Special Agent Piper, there were no motives we could find. I mean, one of the dead girls had an ex-boyfriend who was a little on the angry side, but his alibi checked out, too, and besides, it's a big leap to go from angry ex to Son of Sam."

Tom frowned. On one hand, the ritualistic element fit in with the website's glamorization of serial murder. On the other hand, as Vitucci noted, the evidence did suggest an inside job. The psychologist inside of him pondered the nature of the crime. Multiple beheadings were one thing, but putting those trophies on display, on top of mannequins, for all the world to see? Was the killer making a statement or was he just having a sick Halloween laugh?

"Were the bodies ever found?" he asked.

"No," answered Vitucci.

The three men stared in silence at the empty storefront window, and at the ghosts of three dead girls waiting to be avenged. For Tom Piper, Hoboken's charm had begun to wane a bit. And something about this case gnawed at him. If he could only get into a room with the man (or woman) responsible for these murders…

"Do you mind if I look over your case notes?" he asked.

"You can have the whole thing for all we care," replied Briggs. "You think we want an unsolved next to our names?"

"We'll talk to our L.T.," Vitucci added.

Briggs and Vitucci led Tom around an alleyway in back of the block and showed him Hot Cotour's rear door. The only other features of the narrow, filthy alley were the six rear doors, presumably to the block's other restaurants and stores, and an overfull Dumpster. The second, third, fourth and fifth stories were residential apartments. The Harbinger family owned the entire block.

Just for kicks, Tom tugged on Hot Cotour's alleyway door. It was locked, of course. He sighed and followed the two detectives back out to the street.

He needed Esme.

As he took out his cell phone to dial her number, it began to ring—and it was Esme calling him. Eerie.

"Hello, Esmeralda," he said. "I was just about to give you a call."

"Looks like I beat you to the punch, old man."

"Do you have news or just quips?"

"Can't I have both?"

Tom grinned. "Talk to me."

"Cain42 just responded to a thread that I had Grover post last night about the Lynette Robinson murder on a website called 'Blood Read.'"

"What did Cain42 have to say?"

"And I quote: 'Dear Galileofan, I completely agree

with your analysis here. What we need now is not a re-treat from authority but a call to arms. Open-minded and intuitive people like us exist in this country to provide leadership, and I look forward to our next discourse.' He's so hitting on him, right?"

"Sounds like our fish has begun to take the bait," said Tom.

"So what were you going to call me about?"

"Actually, it's a tangential case. I'd like your opinion. Here are the details…"

17

Cain42's invitation arrived on Wednesday at 12:55 p.m. Esme read it, showed it to Grover and then promptly forwarded it to Mineola (who immediately ran a back trace on it, which led absolutely nowhere), Tom (whose reply was "!"), Karl Ziegler (who immediately instructed her to accept the invitation, which she did), and even forwarded the invitation to herself. And then she read it again. And then she frowned.

This was all too easy. Here was a man (probably a man) who had not only outsmarted two government agents but had also managed to collect the uncollectible—society's loners, malcontents and crazies—into a working group. Cain42 was clever, and it would be foolish to believe they had so easily bested him.

Underestimating Henry Booth had cost many good people their lives.

Esme sighed. Why couldn't she get the dumb criminals? Most career felons, statistically, were of lesser-than-average intelligence. But no, the cases she got involved in always seem to revolve around some monomaniacal polymath. Then again, stupidity offered less of a puzzle to solve. Stupidity was stupidity. Had Cain42 been some run-of-the-mill whack job, her interest level in the case might have been, well, lower. Scary but true. Then again, had Cain42 been some run-of-the-mill whack job, he wouldn't have been able to supply Timothy Hammond and countless others with the tools and know-how to murder.

And the wheel spins around and around.

"You going to be on the computer for long?" Lester hovered over her shoulder, encroaching on her personal space and obviously attempting to spy on her activity. "I need to check my email."

Behind them, on the living room sofa, Grover Kirk was taking a midday nap. The man slept more than a newborn kitten, or at least pretended to sleep. Working with him on these message board posts had proven as thrilling as she'd expected. Every suggestion she offered him somehow got twisted around into a question about Henry Booth. Grover was relentless. He was also about to complete the first draft of his book, and wanted her to be the first to read it. It would be an honor, he said.

Part of her considered how easy it would be to "accidentally" delete the Word document containing his book. But no, as much as she loathed the man, that would have been vicious. This was America. He was entitled to write whatever he liked, and she was entitled to hate it. Free speech, of course, only went so far. The anarchic, potentially deadly advice Cain42 doled out on his website crossed the line.

"If you're just going to sit there, Esme, sit somewhere else. Some of us have work to do."

Esme sighed. Her father-in-law: as treasonous to the law and order of her marriage as Cain42 was to the law and order of this country. An exaggeration? Maybe, but not by much. And she could tell by the old man's recent boost of energy that his subversive behavior was winning.

Today was Wednesday, one week left on Dr. Rosen's deadline, and she and Rafe had barely spoken two words in two days. He spent Tuesday night at the lighthouse with Sophie, and didn't even come home to shower and change. For all she knew, he had taken their daughter and driven overnight to Williamsburg.

Damn it all to hell.

"Esme," grumbled Lester.

"Okay, fine." She exited the chair. "By the way, in the future, when you surf the web for divorce lawyers for my husband, you may want to refrain from bookmarking the websites."

He scowled at her, which was satisfaction enough. Or at least it would have to suffice. Savoring her tiny victory, she left Lester to his browsing and trotted outside to retrieve the mail. A cold wind scattered brown leaves across her worn-out sneakers. She reconsidered going back inside to grab a pullover, but concluded that a little chill out here was preferable to the emotional Antarctica currently settling inside.

As she approached the mailbox at the end of her driveway, she was reminded of the Weiners' mailbox, the only part of their property that had survived Timothy Hammond's arson. That poor family. More victims of a little boy's rampage. Forgotten victims. The Weiners, the Robinsons, the Hammonds. The community at large, really. Cain42 taught Timothy how to toss a pebble into a pond and these were the ripples.

This got her thinking about Tom, and the case in Hoboken.

If they nabbed whoever decapitated those women, and he had, in fact, uploaded that picture to the website, he was a member, and the more members they could compromise, the more access they could achieve, the better chance they would have at snagging Cain42.

No more ripples.

At least until the next psycho came along.

She removed several envelopes from the mailbox, sifted through them (bill, bill, junk mail, bill, *Pennysaver,* bill) and glanced around the neighborhood. The morning-session kindergarteners would be home by now, devouring their macaroni and cheese in the company of (in this neighborhood) their nanny or au pair. A few of her neighbors were work-at-home moms, but for the longest time, she was the only housewife. And now she wasn't even that…

Stop it. Christ. Back to the case in Hoboken.

Esme knew how dangerous and counterproductive rampant speculation would be, especially since she hadn't even visited the New Jersey crime scene, but something struck her as odd about the crime itself. It was her reflections on the Weiners that brought this thought to the fore. Since the bodies of the three women remained missing, where were they? If he'd committed the murder in the store, how had he smuggled the bodies out without being noticed? According to Tom, the shop lay on a busy street. Only the foolhardy and the stupid would risk transporting the bodies out the front door. This meant that if the murders had been committed in the store, he must have parked his vehicle by the alley entryway and transported them out the rear door. Still, though, that risked exposure, and it also would have left a tremendous amount of physical evidence—namely, blood, gore and skin—trailing from the shop and into the alley, and no such evidence was found. And October 30 had been a clear night, so no amount of rain had washed it all away.

Which indicated that he murdered the women else-where, disposed of the bodies beforehand and then ar-rived at the shop with their heads. The only flaw in that argument was the lack of trace evidence found on the heads themselves. With decapitation, the head either rolled off, in which case it gathered whatever fibers lay along its path, or, if the act were performed on a horizon-tal plane such as a bed, the head remained still, in which case at least the wound itself would sponge up whatever fibers lay at its base. And the fibers that Hoboken fo-rensics had identified at the women's necklines were consistent with the carpet of the store. Which indicated that he murdered the women there.

Argh.

Esme carried the mail, useless as it was, back to the house. She half expected Lester to lock her out, but the knob turned and the door opened. Sleepy-eyed Grover was now awake, and he and Lester were chuckling about something, probably a ribald joke. It seemed only natural to Esme that these two miserable human beings would enjoy each other's company so much.

As she shut the door, their smiles faded a bit.

"So, warden, my pal Lester and I were thinking…"

"Don't be shy," the old man encouraged. "Just say it."

"Since I've been a model prisoner, we were wonder-ing if I might be allowed a, what's it called, furlough."

Esme raised an eyebrow. "Excuse me?"

"It makes sense," Lester added. "If you're trying to make them think that everything's on the up-and-up, won't it be more suspicious if Grover here never leaves the house?"

Her lips curled southward. The old man had a point, and that in itself was unnerving. She asked where they were planning to go, even though she knew she would hate the answer.

And she did.

"Angel Eyes," said Lester.

The strip club he frequented. Of course.

"You want to go now? It's not even one in the afternoon."

"It'll just be for a few hours, boss," Grover added. "I've been very respectful of this situation. I haven't complained or tried to undermine you, and I'm the one who's taking the biggest risk here. I don't want to be in Cain42's crosshairs. All I ask in return is a few hours with my pal Lester. We'll be back before dark. What do you say?"

"I say…let's go."

Her eyes sparkled mischievously.

And Lester's eyes lost their sparkle altogether. "Us?"

Angel Eyes was surprisingly busy for one-thirty in the afternoon. Various customers of all ages, sizes and genders occupied the large room's assortment of booths, round tables and bar stools. The overall ambience lent itself more to a sports bar than a strip club, and Grover might have thought he was in T.G.I. Friday's were it not for naked (natural) blondes dangling upside down on the steel pole. Unlike most strip clubs he had attended—and he had attended many down in Florida—the stage here was in the center of the room. This made so much logical and practical sense to him that he wondered what all of the other owners were thinking.

Lester led them over to a large round table, where a group of retirees had already gathered. Green felt was being laid across the wooden surface, and poker chips were being distributed. Grover glanced over at Lester, who replied with a crafty wink. So this was the surprise he had promised. Grover was tempted to bear hug him then and there.

In truth, the past few days had driven Grover Kirk stir-crazy, and this excursion had been necessary. True, the home confinement had allowed him to finish his book, but he hadn't been allowed to celebrate the occasion… until now. He and Lester sat down in the two empty seats at the table.

"Boys, this is that winemaker I told you about," said Lester. "Grover Kirk, these are the boys. Keep one hand on your wallet at all times."

The boys—none of whom was less than sixty-five years old—all laughed and welcomed Grover with handshakes and waves.

Then Esme cleared her throat.

A few pairs of eyes glanced in her direction.

"The bitch hovering behind us is my daughter-in-law. On the count of three, let's give her the gentleman's salute, okay, boys?"

On the count of three, most of the men chivalrously displayed their middle fingers for her benefit.

"I'll be at the bar," she murmured, and wandered away.

"If that's all it took to get rid of her," said Grover, "I'd have flipped her off days ago."

This inspired the appropriate laughter around the table. Grover smiled, at peace with himself, and ordered a Seven and Seven from the scantily clad waitress. He, of course, hadn't wanted to get rid of Esme—in his mind, she was as much a celebrity as Galileo—but he knew the words would raise his likability with the men.

"Fifty dollars up front, no buy-ins," explained Lester, and Grover reached into his pocket for the easy cash.

The game was Texas Hold'em, as Grover expected it to be, and he quickly gauged the skills and personalities of the other seven players at the table. He also enjoyed the floor show, of course, but most of his energy was devoted to the woman at the bar. In the past few days, he felt that he had gotten to know Esme Stuart very well, and he was fascinated by her. Here was a woman who had survived repeated adversity, retired at the top of her game to start a family, put an end to one of the most vicious mass murderers in American history and had absolutely no idea of how special she was.

Or how beautiful she was. Because despite the obvious assets on display in the center of the room, Grover's libido remained fixated on Esme. His eyes traveled along the strands of her light brown hair as they ran down, down, down, past earlobes, past jawline and came so close to those kissable shoulder blades. He could glimpse her face in the mirror at the bar and even though he couldn't make out the faint freckles that dotted her nose and cheeks, he knew they were there, and adored each and every one. And even though she wore a bland sweatshirt and jeans, he was confident that underneath those clothes lay a shapely, athletic body perfect for—

"Hey, Grover, you in or out?"

He peeked at his hold cards. A pair of nines. He tossed in a one-dollar chip to match the big blind. The betting continued around the table.

"So, Grover, how long you up here for?"

"A little while longer," he replied.

"Lester here tells us you're working on a book about Galileo?"

Grover nonchalantly glanced at the three cards on the

flop—two of clubs, nine of clubs, king of hearts—and limped into the pot with another dollar. The flush draw scared him. "I just finished it, actually."

"That was one fucked-up son of a bitch."

"Yes, he was," Lester said with authority, as if to remind everyone that he had been a hostage when the fucked-up son of a bitch went down.

The table went quiet for a moment, each gentleman imagining what they would have done in that situation. Then Nolan Worth, the snow-haired proprietor of the lighthouse bed-and-breakfast and the card dealer for this round, broke the silence.

"So whereabouts you staying while you're up here, Grover?"

Lester chuckled. "Tell him."

"What's so funny?" asked Nolan.

Grover squirmed in his seat.

"Get this," Lester said. "My daughter-in-law has Grover here under house arrest."

"For writing a book?"

Lester elbowed Grover. "Tell him."

"Lester, maybe we shouldn't—"

"No, these guys know how the world works. How the government reaches into our lives and forces us all to dance."

"Here, here," said Nolan.

"Relax, Grover. You're among friends here. Why else would I hang out with these douche bags?"

The men at the table gave Lester the gentleman's salute, and then all laughed and laughed. A chesty waitress refilled their drinks.

"You're under house arrest because you wrote a book?"

"Well…"

"He's under house arrest because our government, including that Jodie Foster–Clarice Starling wannabe sitting at the bar, can't do their jobs. He's under house arrest—and I negotiated this little shore leave, I might add—he's under house arrest because the government are using him, an ordinary citizen, to help ensnare some Henry Booth–Galileo wannabe off the internet. You heard it right, boys and girls. They conscripted the poor SOB."

Grover opened his mouth to rebut, to defend Esme or at least declaim Lester for, well, *spouting out classified information,* but the looks of sympathy from the men at the table silenced all protest. These men—these strangers, really—actually cared about his plight. They were friends. And it wasn't as if Lester had lied. The FBI had, for lack of a better word, conscripted him. Only they didn't send him overseas to fight the Vietcong. They sent him to Long Island.

Nolan flipped the turn card. Nine of hearts. Grover now had four of a kind. The hand was his to win. He slow-played it at first, tossing in the minimum bet, but Lester swallowed down a finger of Scotch and raised him. The other three gentlemen at the table still in the hand matched the raise. The pot was getting sizable, and there was still another card to go, and no one at the table could possibly have a hand better than Grover's. Life was good.

It was time to step out of the shadows.

He added twenty dollars to Lester's raise, leaned back in his chair and let the four other players fight among themselves. By the time the river card—an ace of clubs—was revealed, only Lester remained in the hand with him.

Grover Kirk knocked.

Lester, perhaps sensing weakness, splashed all of his chips into the pot. Grover, sensing victory, casually moved his own stacks to the center of the table. Lester flipped over his ace-high flush. Grover flipped over his four of a kind. The gentlemen erupted in shock and applause. Grover leaned back in his chair, basking in their adoration. Had Esme spotted his act of glory? He hoped so. And if not, one of these comely waitresses must have…

Nolan Worth collected the cards and passed them clockwise to the man to his left. "Nice hand," he said, and flashed Grover a child-eating grin. But the writer was too busy trading verbal jabs with poor, humiliated Lester. Ah, well. Nolan excused himself from the table, shuffled off to the men's room to relieve himself of the quart of Guinness he'd consumed since arriving, and while at the urinal activated his BlackBerry to locate the email he needed. Cain42 had sent out a bulletin to all members in the New York City area to check out the veracity of a prospective member's application. Nolan, who first connected with Cain42 on, of all places, a bed-and-breakfast listserv, certainly hadn't expected Grover Kirk to fall into his lap so neatly, but when Lester had started gabbing the other night at the lighthouse about his new houseguest and how poor Sophie had been forced to spend the week before Thanksgiving at their bastion tower, well…was it possible this was the same Grover Kirk? Apparently, it was.

Nolan whistled as he washed his hands, and then emailed back with the news of his discovery. Cain42 was going to be so proud of him. Maybe he'd be selected to do the deed. What an honor that would be for his first kill. He'd do Grover, then that blowhard Lester and his bitch of a daughter-in-law, and then maybe spend some quality time with that cute brown-haired granddaughter of his, Sophie, before doing her, too. The thought of his claw hammer crashing into Sophie's wrinkle-free prepubescent forehead made him hard, and he tried to think about bunny rabbits and dandelions before he could return to the table, but decided the hell with it—they were at a strip club, for Christ's sake—and sauntered back to his friends, his cock, as always, leading his way.

18

What to do, what to do.

It's not that Cain42 was overly surprised by Nolan's information. The FBI had already tried to plant two moles into his organization. Perhaps they'd assumed the third time would be the charm.

Perhaps it would be.

The surest way to trump one's enemy was to give them what they wanted, and Cain42 had been so negligent of late in catering to the FBI's egos. No, it was time to boost their confidence. Instill the G-men with a little pride. Make them think they'd bested him. The closer they got, the easier it would be for him to cut out their overinquisitive brains.

Cain42 needed to think. So he went to the nearest hardware store.

Oh, how he loved hardware stores! Even as a little child, barely able to reach above the shelf, the sheer variety on display held him rapturous. He could spend hours simply peering into a plastic container of nails. Like people, they came in all shapes and sizes. Like people, they served a purpose. Like people, they could gouge and cut.

Cain42 preferred local hardware stores to the big box chains, and in this particular town, he found a dandy of a place right on the main street, nestled between a barber and a pharmacy. The barber even had the vertical-striped pole out in front of its screen door. These modern-day salons, the kind one often found inside cavernous malls, never displayed a barber's pole. This country was in danger of losing its history. The red stripe in the barber's pole symbolized blood. Up until quite recently, barbers used to perform surgeries. After all, they had the tools for the job.

How appropriate, then, to find a barber's shop next to a hardware store.

This hardware store was called Mitch's, but the punk-haired teenager behind the counter most certainly was not Mitch. She wore a red apron and little else, not that there was much else to see given her anorexic frame. Nevertheless, Cain42 flashed her an all-American how-do-you-do grin. She responded with an all-adolescent leave-me-alone glare.

So he made his way to Aisle 1 (of 5), momentarily distracted by the thought of crushing the glasslike bones of her clavicles with the balls of his thumbs. The sight and smell of fresh-cut lumber carried him back to reality. Here, arrayed by length and width, were long strips of pine and cherry and oak, each sanded as smooth as a human cheek. Cain42 ran his fingertips along these, the carved bones of forests, and his mind swooned in memory of porches built in backyards and of cages built in basements. Historians demarcated ancient civilization into ages of Stone and Bronze and Iron, but wood—wood was mankind's oldest earthborn friend. On his website, Cain42 posted instructions on how to manufacture a longbow and arrows out of hardwood ash. Longbows were excellent for long-range, silent kills. Cain42 preferred intimacy in murder, but he was aware that some of his online friends were shy, and so he did what he could to accommodate them—accommodate *all* types, really.

As webmaster, he did not tolerate discrimination.

Aisle 2 housed plumbing supplies. As Cain42 ogled the curlicues of pipes and a dangling assembly of toilet seats beside them, and a wall of faucets in every style from simple steel to stenciled gold, he reminded himself that he was here to ruminate on a problem. But it was so easy to become distracted! He marveled at the creativity of it all. So much in this aisle, once installed, became the stuff behind the walls, out of sight, ignored—and yet look at how much time and effort had been spent in making even these drains and traps and washers not only functional but beautiful. Indoor plumbing was taken for granted, but the era of chamber pots and bedpans was not too long ago. Cain42 once put an elderly woman's head in her own bedpan and then put the bedpan in the woman's gas oven. He didn't turn the oven on, of course. That would have been overkill.

Thinking about ovens reminded him of Timothy, and thus his obligations. Oh, yes, he had to best the FBI, not only out of spite but vengeance. But what was the solution? What was the plan?

Maybe the answer lay in Aisle 3.

Or maybe not. Aisle 3 was gardening supplies, and Cain42 loathed gardening so much that he'd never even buried a body, not one, not even for the experience. There probably was some psychological source for his aversion to gardening, but Cain42, for the life of him, couldn't pinpoint it. To be sure, Aisle 3 did have its gems. Lost among the noise of seed packets and miracle-grow sprays and aerosol insect repellants were a pair of un-boxed pruning snips that he just had to take off the shelf and hold in his hands. The snips were almost as dainty as sewing scissors but could just as easily cut through a stubborn twig or a human pinkie. And here, at the end of the aisle, were the long arms of gardening: the rakes and shovels and hoes. Cain42 once monitored a lively debate on the message board about the merits of a shovel versus the merits of a hoe. In the end, the two connoisseurs agreed to disagree. All the while, Cain42 had hoped someone would chime in a word or two in defense of a weeder or a rake, but, alas, no.

Would any of these tools be of use in his retaliation against the FBI? It didn't seem likely. Aside from the appropriate metaphor—the Feds were very much weeds in his garden—nothing here jumped out at him as being especially apropos, although he did keep the pruning snips in his hand as he turned the corner to Aisle 4.

Hunting supplies.

Here Cain42 pored over the usual assortment of jackets—all in bright colors so you don't accidentally get mistaken for a deer, ha-ha—and snares and traps. An old man, even more skeletal than the punk-haired clerk up front, stood planted in this aisle and appeared to be entranced by a packet of multicolored smoke bombs. A thin clear tube trailed down from his nostrils, snaked around his left arm, and found its destination in an oxygen tank, one of those small portable ones on wheels. For all his imagination, Cain42 couldn't guess what use this man might have for a packet of multicolored smoke bombs. Perhaps the old man had no idea what he was seeing. Perhaps dementia was pilfering his eyesight, just as whatever evil had so obviously stolen off with his lungs.

And yet euthanasia was verboten. Cain42 glanced

down at the pruning snips held tightly in his right hand and then shook his head in disgust. Would he end up someday in the aisle of a store, drooling whatever saliva he had left in his bony craw? Men like him, if they were lucky, if they managed to be tried during a left-leaning election year and capital punishment was kept off the table, were nearly guaranteed to spend their autumn years behind bars. But this was before the website. This was before he began teaching amateurs around the country—around the world, even—how to avoid capture. What kind of legacy would be left if he himself ended up in prison? No, better to be trapped inside the prison of one's own body, like this pitiful old man and his pet oxygen tank, than spend a day inside a cell. And if, in his old age, in his senility, Cain42 slipped up and revealed to some hospice nurse an example of his darker deeds, well, so what? The government wasn't about to lock up an octogenarian. The way Cain42 saw it, if he adhered to the rules of safety he had established, he had a good forty years left of healthy mayhem.

Just as soon as he took care of this niggling problem of the FBI.

He didn't even have to peer into Aisle 5 to know what it held. It had to be the miscellaneous tools, the hammers and handsaws and screwdrivers and chisels and drills and levels and rulers and knives and wrenches and mauls and perhaps even an ax or two. Well, look—a stack of single-bit axes balanced on a pair of nails, well above the reach of a child but easily within reach of Cain42's fingers. How he loved employing bladed death. His favorite weapon, his handy survival knife, was tucked into its leather sheath under the back of his shirt, but who could argue with the efficacy of an ax? So simple in design and yet so mighty in action! With the proper aim, he could

cleave that punk-haired bitch up front from scalp to hip
and then watch each half of her body part and then fall
its separate way. Or did that only happen in cartoons?
Hmm. Experimentation would be required.

But not right now. His priorities were fixed. He was
not here for fun. He was here to contemplate, to muse,
to…

Wait.

With a curious smirk, Cain42 stepped back into Aisle 4.
The old man hadn't budged. He and his oxygen tank
remained statuelike in front of the smoke bombs. And
thus the wheels in Cain42's mind began to whir…

As he headed toward the old man, Cain42 tried to remember the last time he'd been to New York. No matter.
He was sure the subways hadn't changed that much.

Oh, his friends were going to love this.

On Thursday, November 18, exactly one week before
Thanksgiving, Tom Piper cracked the Hoboken case.
Sort of. This came after a splendid night on the town
with his lady love. They shared a corned-beef-on-rye
sandwich that must have weighed more than a pound
and saw, at Penelope Sue's behest, *Mamma Mia,* which
Tom made fun of so effusively the rest of the evening
that it was clear he'd actually enjoyed it. They shared
a slice of chocolate cheesecake for dessert, which also
must have weighed more than a pound, and returned to
their hotel room for an enthusiastic round of midnight
nookie.

Before heading out to Hoboken that following morning to (unbeknownst to him at the time) crack the case
(sort of), he made his daily stop at the Federal Building
to check on the status of Mineola's hard work.

Including the shot of Lynette Robinson and the shot

of the three human-headed mannequins, there were forty thumbnails on that cached website page. The last time he'd called in, she'd identified twelve of them. On that Thursday morning, November 18, a good two hours before Tom cracked the Hoboken case (sort of), Mineola, bleary-eyed and caffeine-jittery, led him into a conference room, one wall of which had been converted to a gigantic blowout of the web page, with locations and dates and the names of victims scribbled beside now *nineteen* of the crime scene snapshots.

"Well done," he said.

"Google is a wonderful thing," she replied, and crushed her latest can of Mountain Dew in her right fist. "Ziegler's got teams tracking down every one of these leads."

"But not you."

"I'm a homegirl, Piper. I belong indoors and seated."

"Mmm-hmm."

They strolled back to her workstation.

"Mineola, what are you afraid is going to happen if you go out in the field?"

She crossed her arms and pouted. "You really want to get into this with me?"

"I'm curious."

"Can't you be satisfied with 'it's not my job'? I don't have some deep dark fear of the big bad world or anything. I'm just a fiber-optics kind of girl."

"That sounds so…"

"Twenty-first century?"

Tom shrugged.

"Hey, it's not a competition. You do your thing and I do my thing. I'm not looking to make you obsolete."

Tom frowned. Was that why he kept pushing the issue with her? Did he feel threatened? He didn't think so, but she had to be reacting to something. Maybe she *was* looking to make him obsolete and felt guilty about it. He mused the permutations as he headed up to Penn Station and across the river to Hoboken.

Briggs and Vitucci picked him up in their Crown Vic and together they drove back to Hot Cotour. The two detectives had, um, "encouraged" Mrs. Carolyn Harbinger, former owner of the boutique, to meet them there with her set of keys. As Briggs pulled up to the curb (leaving a good foot for breathing room), there she stood, staring with forlorn nostalgia at the emptiness of her former life. She wore a gray pea coat and a pair of black pumps that matched perfectly her short dark hair, which was topped with the only touch of color in her ensemble, a small kelly-green beret. Carolyn Harbinger was beautiful, and so beautifully sad.

"I bet she's a monster in bed," Briggs muttered, and tossed his brown cigarette toward the incoming traffic. The three men joined her in front of the vacant glass windows. The other four restaurants and shops were quiet. It was, after all, a weekday morning.

"Mrs. Harbinger," said Vitucci, "thanks for coming down. It's good to see you again."

Hands were shaken. Then Tom introduced himself.

"The FBI?" Her brow furrowed, but only slightly due to Botox. "I wasn't aware…"

"It could be related to another case, ma'am."

She nodded, and took out a large key ring from her pocketbook, which, like Tom's jacket, was stitched black leather (although hers came from a decidedly younger cow). She inserted the wrong key into the lock, and then the right one, and then lifted up the rolling security door. Vitucci assisted her in raising it above the level of the

Joshua Corin

front door, which she then proceeded to unlock. The three detectives followed her inside.

Why had she inserted the wrong key? Tom puzzled this quandary. This was her store. Unlocking the rolling security door should have been, at this point, muscle memory. Was she nervous? Did the presence of the FBI rattle her? Her demeanor remained calm, but actions always betrayed their facades.

"This is it," she said. "Help yourselves. I'm going to go back outside."

She handed her key ring to Tom and went outside.

Briggs and Vitucci walked the crime scene for the umpteenth time. The blond carpet was clean, save for some dust and a few paint chips. The store consisted of the main showroom and a smaller stockroom in the back, accessible through a door locked with a punch code. The stockroom, which had an exposed wooden floor, led to the rear door, and the rear door led, as Tom knew, to an alleyway. He strolled back out to the alley, accidentally scaring off a feral cat who had been napping in a shadow. It was as it had been before. Dumpster. Access from the street. Six doors leading back into the building.

Six doors...but only five storefronts...

Tom returned inside. Briggs and Vitucci were in the stockroom. If the women had been slain in there, perhaps the killer had covered the walls with plastic sheeting to contain the blood spatter. But, no, that still didn't explain the traces of carpet fibers at the bases of their necks.

Look for the bodies, Esme had suggested. And it made sense. What had the killer done with the three bodies? The men walked across the floorboards of the empty stockroom.

"I'll be right back," said Tom, and he joined Carolyn Harbinger outside. The day already had taken a nasty turn, with bruised clouds and a galloping wind moving in from the east. She stood erect on the sidewalk, a cigarette in one hand (suck, puff) and the other placidly resting on a hip. She looked like a 1970s ad for Virginia Slims.

"I'm sorry," he said to her.

"Thank you." Suck, puff. "I appreciate your sympathy."

"Were you close with the three girls?"

"I liked to think of my employees as an extension of my family, so, yes, I was close with them."

"They were recommended to you by another of your employees, right? Sandra Washington."

"Yes." Suck, puff. "Sandy went to school with them. I trusted her judgment. They were good girls, all of them."

"If you don't mind my asking, Mrs. Harbinger, why did you suddenly need to hire three employees?"

Again, her brow attempted to furrow. She was trying to concoct a lie. Tom made another mental note and waited for that lie to come, which it did, a half second later.

"Business was booming. I needed to expand my sales force to keep my customers satisfied."

"And so by October your sales force included the three girls, Sandy Washington and your cousin Jefferson."

She nodded. Suck, puff. She ashed into the street, careful to leave the sidewalk in front of her store clean. Old habits died hard.

"And your family owns this block of shops and apartments?"

"Yes. We bought it before the downtown revitalization. Now the property's worth twenty times as much as we paid. Not that we're going to sell. I'd never let that happen. I owe it to Summer, Lydia and Rosalind, don't you think?"

Briggs and Vitucci sauntered out to meet them.

"I thought you wanted to check the place out," Briggs said to Tom.

"I did," Tom replied.

Suck, puff.

Briggs grunted and, perhaps inspired by Carolyn Harbinger, lit up another brown cigarette.

"Mrs. Harbinger," asked Tom, "would it be all right if we kept these keys for a few days and continued our investigation inside your store?"

She shrugged. "Whatever will help."

"Thank you."

Soon, they were escorting her back to her tiny Porsche (the same green hue as her beret) and, shortly after that, she was so much dust in the ever-chilling breeze.

Tom took out his cell phone to call Esme. Once again, as he started to dial her number, she called him.

"I was about to call you. Again."

"I just like to beat you to the punch."

"Mmm-hmm."

"I swing, you duck, I goose, you…"

"Mmm-hmm."

"You go first this time, Tom."

He stepped away from the cops, who had recommenced their Punch-and-Judy act. "I think I've solved the Hoboken case."

"Was it the bodies?"

"It was, in fact, the bodies, yes. What's your news?"

"Grover Kirk just got his acceptance letter from Cain42." Her voice brimmed with giddiness. "We're in."

19

As teams of agents, using Grover Kirk's newly acquired password, scoured and combed Cain42's robust website for information, as Mineola Wu converted the home page to HTML and perused the code as if it were some kind of poetry for programmers, as Tom Piper shuttled back to the Federal Building to lend his insight and expertise, Esme Stuart remained in suburban Long Island, trying to kick out a houseguest who had long-long-long since overstayed his welcome.

The previous night, after they'd all returned from the strip club and Lester had gone out to join his son and granddaughter at the lighthouse, Esme had retired to bed and closed her eyes and clicked her heels three times, muttering, "There's no place like home, there's no place like home, there's no place like home." Only she was home and it was her family who had been whisked away to Oz. She fell asleep before the tears on her pillow had dried... and was awoken at two o'clock in the morning by a shift in weight on the bed. Rafe had come home. Rafe had missed her. Rafe had left Sophie in the care of Grandpa Les and the twin fires of love and hope still flickered somewhere in the universe. She opened her eyes to stare into his, and Grover Kirk stared back at her.

"I'm lonely," he said.

The normal reaction would have been to scream, and perhaps retreat into the bathroom, but Esme was a graduate of Quantico. Esme had wrestled madmen and thieves. An oversize Floridian with a head shaped like a penis was not much of a threat.

She curled her fingers so that the knuckles of their joints formed a solid weapon, with her index finger knuckle as the tip, and she lashed out with snakelike speed at the hollow behind Grover's ear. The hard knuckle of her index finger flattened his auricular artery and, predictably, sent poor Grover rolling off the bed in agony and confusion. He paced around Rafe's side of the bedroom with the aimlessness of Frankenstein's monster, all the while rubbing and rubbing at his wounded ear.

"I can't hear!" he cried. *"I can't hear!"*

She sat up calmly. "What? What was that? You'll have to speak up."

"I can't hear! What did you do to me?"

"I used some rudimentary karate to knock out one of your mastoidal pressure points!" she replied, her volume raised, but her body still serene. Perhaps more serene than she had felt in days…

He opened and closed his jaw, with obvious pain, and stumbled into the wall.

"Yeah, you should probably go see a specialist about that!" she said. *"Common side effects include blurred vision, tinnitus and an unhinged jaw!"*

Grover stumbled again into a wall, bounced off it, lost his balance, fell on his ass and began to drool. Loss of consciousness soon followed. Esme considered calling 9-1-1, but a quick check of his pulse didn't indicate any cause for alarm. From the smell of it, though, Grover had soiled his Fruit of the Looms. Lovely.

So Esme spent the remainder of the evening in her daughter's bedroom, curled up with the few dolls Sophie hadn't brought with her to the lighthouse. They were the newer acquisitions, the Purple Princess and the Disney penguin in the top hat and posable raven-haired Amazon Queen (with her removable girdle of strength), and they just hadn't made it yet into Sophie's pantheon of required bedside companions and, God, how Esme missed her little girl! Meanwhile, she had to babysit that dickhead in the other room and therefore had to stay away from her daughter.

But providence arrived the very next morning, around the same time Tom Piper got off the train in Hoboken to meet Carolyn Harbinger. Esme woke up, peeked in on Grover (who hadn't moved from the bedroom floor) and then padded into the living room to check his laptop and, lo and behold, earlier that morning an email had arrived from Cain42.

Grover's application for membership had been accepted. A user ID and password were provided.

They were in.

Esme pumped her fists in joy. Success! She forwarded the missive, ran back to the bedroom to grab her cell phone, where it lay in its charger, and immediately dialed Karl Ziegler.

"Check your email," she said.

"Good morning, Mrs. Stuart."

"Check your email," she repeated.

He sighed. "One moment, please."

Silence, then: "Well."

"You sure as hell can say that again."

"This is quite encouraging. Thank you."

"So now I can kick him out, right? I mean, he doesn't need protection anymore."

"Mrs. Stuart, we just obtained inside access to what essentially is a major criminal organization. Are you telling me that your bigger concern is that your guest is using up all your clean sheets?"

Esme clenched her teeth to keep from yelling, took a breath and asked as tranquilly as she could, "Is Grover free to go or not?"

"Tell him to stay local."

"Yes, sir."

Click.

Esme sighed. Why did all the men in her life turn out to be utter jackasses? Well, not all. She dialed Tom and informed him of the good news, and he shared his, as well. They agreed to meet up this afternoon at the Federal Building and compare notes.

In the meantime, she had a houseguest to extricate.

Esme nudged him in the cheek with her big toe.

No response.

So she nudged him again, a little more forcefully.

Still nothing. And now she was beginning to smell the mess he'd left in his briefs. Ugh. Time for expediency.

She grabbed Grover's thick wrists and began the arduous task of dragging the large, limp man into the bathroom, all the while keeping an eye on the carpet to make sure nothing in his underwear left its mark. She was reminded of her college days, and her first roommate, Roberta, who often drank well beyond the tolerance level of her four-foot-eleven, ninety-two-pound frame. According to the alumni newsletter, Roberta was now a successful pediatrician in Cleveland. Esme made a mental note never to bring Sophie to Cleveland and tugged Grover onto the cold tiles of the bathroom floor.

With Roberta, the trick was to escort her into the shower and then blast her face with cold water. Well, by the time Esme reached the bathtub, she reconsidered that option for Grover Kirk. One, his body was a lot more cumbersome than Roberta's ever was. Two, the porcelain wall of the bathtub was a good two feet in height, and Esme just didn't feel like hefting Grover's body up and over that high a barrier.

So she did the next best thing.

She dunked his head in the toilet bowl.

In movies, the bullies and thugs who did this often punctuated their action with a flush, but the rush of water immersion awoke Grover almost immediately. His arms flailed blindly against her, so she just stepped away and watched as he launched his head out of the toilet bowl, spraying the wallpaper behind him with a swarm of droplets, and gazing around the bathroom in muddled unawareness.

Then he spotted Esme, and it all sunk in.

"How's your hearing?" she asked.

He reflexively put a hand to his ear. "Ringing."

"That could be from the water."

He scowled at her.

"I'll go get you a change of clothes," she added. "You dumped a load in your shorts."

At which his scowl dribbled into horror and embarrassment, and it was that look of stone-etched shame on his face, this man who had forcibly inserted himself in her family's life, that made it all worthwhile.

By noon, she kicked him to the curb, or at least to his Studebaker. He informed her that, per Ziegler's wishes, he would be returning to the Days Inn, and drove off. Esme took a long shower, scrubbing extrahard to remove all those Grover-cooties, and drove out to New York. On the way, she stopped at the college to visit her husband.

The department secretary, a wispy man named Hector, informed her that Rafe was currently teaching in Lecture Hall B. Esme thanked him, followed the signs to the lecture halls and snuck into the back of the five-hundred-seat indoor amphitheater. Her husband paced the stage, a microphone bud clipped to the lapel of his blue sports jacket. She bought him that jacket one year for Christmas. On the dry-erase board, in Rafe's semi-legible script, was a quote from Ovid: "Nature in her genius had imitated art."

"But who is to blame?" he said. Many of the four-hundred-plus freshmen and sophomores in the room's cheap plastic chairs were actively taking notes. Some weren't. A few were asleep. But it was their loss. Rafe had been nominated twice by the student body as Professor of the Year. "The easy target is the media. The first target is the media. The violence is their fault. Violence in movies and TV propagates violence in the streets. Life imitates art. But the cinema and television are inventions of the twentieth century, and violence surely existed before the twentieth century. So what does that leave us? Books? Who reads books? No, seriously, raise your hand if you've read a book, for pleasure, in the past two months."

About a third of the class raised their hands.

"If we as a society don't read, we can't very well blame our ills on literature. But we do. The Harry Potter novels are still banned in some American communities. So is *Huck Finn*. All out of fear of influence. And this is what we're talking about. Fear of influence. Art doesn't inspire bad behavior but it can shape it. It can point it in a certain direction. After the tragedy at Columbine, Stephen King had a novel he wrote about a school shooting taken out of print. In 1989, cinemas across the country refused to show Spike Lee's *Do the Right Thing,* because they believed it would incite violence. Fear of influence. D. H. Lawrence had to go to court to defend the publication of his novel *Lady Chatterley's Lover.* Critics were sure it would plant seeds of sin into the minds of children. Fear of influence. *A Clockwork Orange* was filmed in England but wasn't allowed to be shown there for thirty years. And I'm sure you all remember the anarchy and gang violence that ensued after that film's eventual London release. No? There was no anarchy, you say? Life didn't imitate art?

"Well, then, that puts us in a tough position, because if we can't blame art for our woes, we as a society have run out of scapegoats, and if history teaches us anything, it's that we react very poorly when the onus of blame falls on us."

Esme watched his eyes quickly dart to the clock on the wall—and they found her. He hesitated, but only for a moment, and only she, of all the people in the room, noticed.

"Okay, for Tuesday, please read the chapter on 'Hot and Cool Media.' There…*hint-hint*…may be a quiz… *hint-hint.* Have good weekends."

She remained in her seat while the students dispersed. A few lined up at Rafe's podium to discuss with him today's lecture or their grades or perhaps just to leave an impression with the prof. She waited out these stragglers, as well.

And then she and he were alone in the cavernous lecture hall.

"Where's your ward?" he asked, filing his notes back into his valise.

"I set him free." She remained in her seat in the back row. "Do you really believe what you said? That what we see or read has no effect on how we behave?"

"I didn't say that at all," he replied.

"What about *The Anarchist's Cookbook?*"

"Two kinds of people read *The Anarchist's Cookbook,*" said Rafe. "There are those who read it to satiate their own curiosity and there are those who read it to learn how to weaponize C-4. The former are not going to get inspired by the book to blow up city hall and the latter are already predisposed to violence before reading page one. Fear of influence, Esme. But my lecture was about the assignment of blame in a media-based global village. Maybe you should audit my course."

She bit her tongue. She hadn't come here to argue with him.

"I'm going to be in the city this afternoon," she said, "but I'll be home for dinner. We should eat out. As a family. Maybe Little Romeo's or Michelangelo's. What do you say?"

"I say that you're a funny woman."

Esme knew it wasn't going to be good, but she had to ask. "How so?"

"You'll make a special trip home so we can then immediately leave said home and go out. And where would that home even be, exactly? Because it sure as hell isn't the house you spent the past few nights sleeping in. That hasn't been a home ever since that monster violated it six months ago, and we've been fools pretending otherwise. I've said it before, Esme. The only way we're going to repair this family is through change. Change of venue or change of vocation. Either one. You want to go out to dinner tonight? That's fine. I'm sure Sophie would enjoy that. I know she misses you." He looked away. "I miss you."

"I miss you, too, Rafe." She wanted to stand. She wanted to run down the aisle and into his arms. She wanted there to be violins. She also wanted to be ten years younger and have firmer boobs, but she didn't move from her seat, not at all, paralyzed by her own insecurities.

A student walked in. Of course a student walked in. There was undoubtedly another class set to meet in the lecture hall. So now Esme rose from her seat, and now Rafe climbed the aisle steps to the wall of doors at the aft of the wood-and-plastic cavern. They walked out together, but nobody would have known from their disparate body language that they were emotionally close, much less husband and wife.

"The lighthouse?" he said. "Around seven?"

"Okay," she replied.

They parted. End of conversation.

Esme returned to her Prius, cranked up the melodic snarl-rock of the Jam, and shouted along with Paul Weller all the way across the George Washington Bridge, down into the Bronx and onto the many-fingered island of Manhattan. The Federal Building had its own parking garage, thank God, but it still took her a good half hour to navigate the avenues. The other cars didn't make her as nervous as all the pedestrians rushing from street corner to street corner or simply milling so inconsiderately in the crosswalk with their strollers and their dogs. But finally she arrived, and parked, and passed security checkpoint after security checkpoint until the elevator emptied her out onto the high-altitude level of the TriBeCa skyscraper.

The briefing had already begun in the conference room. Karl Ziegler himself was addressing the twenty or so underpaid federal agents who crowded the chairs and along the available wall space. Esme snuck in beside Tom, who conveniently stood near the door.

"Miss me?" she asked, sotto voce.

"Who are you again?" he whispered back.

Esme ran her gaze along the dozens of annotated photographs on the walls, recognizing some of them from the cached website, but not recognizing most. These must have been the older ones culled today from the live site, which they could access with Grover's password, which they had because of her. A little pride never hurt anyone.

"—and through examination of the message boards," Ziegler intoned, "we've been able to associate and verify the information you see here. We have the names of the victims. We have in many cases the locations where their bodies were discovered. We have detailed confessions from their murderers, identified here with their user names. And we are compiling profiles on each of these user names, based on the murders they committed and on any messages they may have posted."

Someone raised a hand. "Can you trace the user names to the computers they used to post the messages?"

Mineola Wu, who stood off to the side, answered that one. "No. The website is a closed system. What we need right now is to access its servers."

"And where's that?"

She hesitated. "Switzerland."

"We've already been in touch with the Swiss government," said Ziegler. "And we're coordinating with the Agency and the State Department in trying to seize the servers."

"Good luck with that," Esme murmured. The Swiss were notoriously unforthcoming when it came to access. Any assets stored within their ever-neutral borders were secure and private. Housing the servers there had been a stroke of genius.

Another hand went up. "Why don't we just shut the website down?"

"We could restrict it in the United States, but that would just alert Cain42 to burrow underground and any initiative we'd have gained here would be lost. We need to remember, our goal, ladies and gentlemen, is to track down the people who committed the vicious crimes you see on these walls. This has to proceed like any other undercover operation, and that means allowing them to continue what they're doing for a little while longer. Every minute that passes, every post that's made, we learn more information and we get closer to shutting down a national crime syndicate. This is progress, people. Now I have your individual assignments here. Let's do this thing."

The agents gathered around Ziegler.

"'Let's do this thing'?" echoed Esme.

Tom shrugged.

Mineola weaved through the crowd. "There's something I need to show you," she said, and led Tom and Esme to her workstation.

"This came right before the meeting." She went to the message-board page and clicked on the "News" header. "We're still trying to decide what to make of it."

It was a post from Cain42, dated an hour ago.

As Thanksgiving approaches, it occurs to me that we should celebrate this gluttonous day in our own lovably gluttonous way. So I propose a Great Hunt. The rules are simple. From 12:01 a.m. Saturday morning until 11:59 p.m. Sunday evening, I urge you all to do as our ancestors did in Plymouth and to hunt, only I imagine your quarry will be much more satisfying than theirs. Make sure to upload pictures of your kills. Whosoever has accumulated the most kills by 11:59 p.m. Sunday evening will be rewarded with the grand prize, and I will personally hand-deliver this prize to the winner before Thanksgiving Day. Remember: this contest is not an excuse for rushed or haphazard behavior. Stick to the Rules of the Trade. Be smart and be safe. And happy hunting.

20

"Well," said Esme, "this is the best bad news I think I've ever seen."

"Mmm-hmm."

"Best?" Mineola looked at them both in bewilderment. "He's riling two thousand people to go on a killing spree!"

"That's one way of looking at it."

The tall Asian threw up her hands. *"Are you both out of your minds?"*

"Should I explain?" Esme asked Tom.

"You explain," Tom told Esme.

Esme explained.

"He's forcing his followers to act under a deadline, which means, despite his warnings to the contrary, they'll get sloppy. They'll be easier to catch, and our rat-catchers are going to be on alert this weekend, you better believe it. Finally, we're on the proactive side of the game, rather than the reactive side."

"But that's not even the best part," added Tom.

"No, it's not. The best part is the grand prize. Personally delivered by Cain42. Which means when Grover Kirk wins the prize, we get to meet the man himself, and cart off his sorry ass to ADX Florence for the rest of his hopefully miserable life."

"So all we have to do is kill the most people by Sunday night."

Both Esme and Tom nodded.

"Allow me then to backtrack for a second to a previous question."

"All right."

"Are you both out of your minds?"

Both Esme and Tom smiled.

"We're not going to really kill anyone," said Tom.

"We're going to fake it," said Esme.

"How?"

"Why do you want to know?" Tom replied. "I thought fieldwork wasn't your thing."

"I'm not allowed to be curious?"

"Of course you are." Esme smiled at her. "That's what makes it a magic trick."

"Let's go talk to Ziegler," said Tom.

"Do we have to?"

They ambled back to the conference room, where Karl Ziegler was handing out the last of the assignments to the last of the agents. Tom and Esme waited until those agents left before they entered the room.

"Piper, what's the status of the Hoboken operation?"

"Our suspect will be back in town on Sunday. That's when we're bringing them in."

"Thank you." Karl collected his papers, then looked up quizzically at Esme. "Mrs. Stuart, why are you still here?"

So it was going to be like that. Okay.

"We know about the Great Hunt."

Karl Ziegler shrugged. "It's not your concern."

"It's not my...? Is that stick so far up your—"

"Karl," Tom interrupted, "I feel so sorry for you."

"Excuse me?" He raised an eyebrow. "And why's that?"

"Every G15 in the Bureau must be salivating over this case. I can't imagine the pressure you're under. I'll bet right now the director himself is angling to get this entire case moved to Washington."

Karl didn't reply.

"All these careers that hang in the balance...all these lives at stake...easy for the fat cats to lose sight of what's important, isn't it, Karl? But you and I know what matters, and it's got nothing to do with politics or ambition. Because that's what separates us from the bureaucrats, and you're not a bureaucrat, are you, Karl?"

"I happen to admire bureaucracy, Piper. It's the engine that powers the machine."

"You can admire an engine without having to become a mechanic."

Karl frowned.

Esme stepped in. "Look, we're not here to steal away any of your thunder. We're just here to help and fade back into the shadows. You want us to say the countermove was yours? We'll sign whatever you want."

"Which countermove would that be?"

They told him.

He ruminated.

Finally: "It'll work."

"Yes. It will."

"It's not going to be cheap," he added.

"Neither is the promotion you'll get for clearing a case like this, Karl."

Karl eyeballed the two of them, and then nodded. "Do it."

"Thank you," said Esme, and she and Tom headed for the door.

"Mrs. Stuart? May I have a moment with you, please?"

"Uh, sure."

Tom waited outside the conference room.

Karl closed the door.

"What's up?" she asked.

"You tell me."

"I…"

"You seem to have forgotten an essential fact."

"And what's that, Karl?"

"You're no longer in the Bureau. You're a consultant. You might think of yourself as some quasi-agent, but in reality, you belong on the sidelines and that's where you yourself chose to be. But if you regret that decision…if you want to play, then you need to be wearing a uniform again. Otherwise, go home."

"Is that an ultimatum?"

"No. Believe it or not, it's advice. And I've a feeling I'm not telling you anything you don't already know. Split priorities keep you from contributing all that you can. Trust me, I know."

"Why, Karl…are you opening up to me?"

"You're incorrigible." He shook his head and opened the door. "Go enact this countermove of yours."

He walked away.

"What was that about?" asked Tom.

Esme shrugged, implying ignorance, which was a lie. She knew exactly what that was about, and worse, she knew that Karl Ziegler was absolutely right. By having one foot at home and one foot in the Bureau, she didn't belong to both. She belonged to neither. In theory, consulting had sounded like the perfect compromise. In practice, it had eroded her family and diminished her capacity in the field. It was what Rafe had been saying all along.

She had to make a choice.

"So," said Tom, "how about some overpriced New York takeout?"

"I…can't," she replied. "I told Rafe I'd be home."

"So call him again."

She hesitated, then thought of Sophie, and shook her head. "I need to be there."

She could see the disappointment in Tom's face, and she knew there was no way she could make him understand. She had tried so many times in the past. That was one of the reasons she'd left the Bureau in the first place, so many years ago.

"Are you sure? I can call Penelope Sue. We could get a quick bite across the street. I know she'd love to meet you."

"I'm sorry, Tom. I can't. I'll be back tomorrow, and we'll put together what we need to do for this weekend."

"We can't wait until tomorrow."

She knew.

"We'll have to start without you."

She knew.

"Okay," he said. "Get home safe."

He touched her on her shoulder and walked away.

Oh, my God—Sophie *loved* eating out. Even though she never knew what to order, the food was always better. Now that she could read (and order for herself), she took her time. Her parents never seemed to mind. They always told her that she could order whatever she wanted (as long as it was off the children's menu).

Tonight, at Michelangelo's, she ordered spaghetti and meatballs. It was always a reliable choice, although it had taken her the better part of fifteen minutes to decide. Even after voicing her order to the waitress, a smiley redhead in a tuxedo who had a cool diamond stud in her right nostril, Sophie wanted to keep the menu and continue to read and read and read. Some of it was in Italian and some of it was in English, and if she studied it enough, she could maybe remember what the Italian meant…

…but she handed in the menu without complaint. She was a good girl. And besides, she didn't want to upset the peace. This was the first time they had all been together in days, and it was wonderful.

Too bad Grandpa Les couldn't come. Something about acid reflex. It probably was an old person's disease, like the ones they have on TV with the people on the beach. Poor Grandpa Les. Sophie hoped he felt better really soon so he could teach her some more card tricks.

"Sophie bear, do you want some bread?"

"Sure, Daddy."

He handed her the basket and she picked out one of the warm fresh-baked rolls. Why couldn't they find rolls like this at Stop & Shop? She'd eat them all day. But maybe if she had rolls like this every day, they wouldn't be as special. Life was complicated.

Michelangelo's was by the water, not too far from the lighthouse. Although the weather was too cold for them to eat out on the patio, one whole wall of the restaurant was made of glass so everyone could look out at the ocean, so dark underneath the moon, as if God tipped over a giant bottle of black ink and it ran, ran, ran.

"Mommy?"

"Yes, Sophie?"

"How do fish see in the dark?"

Her mom frowned and scratched at her chin. "I don't know. Maybe Daddy knows."

"Daddy, how do fish see in the dark?"

"Fish?" He chewed a hunk of his roll and washed it down with some ice water. "I think it has something to do with, uh…"

Sophie waited expectantly. Both of her parents were very smart.

While she waited, she looked around the restaurant. The dominant color was red, which was logical since this was an Italian restaurant and Italian restaurants used a lot of tomatoes and tomatoes were red (except in the South, where, according to her friend Holly, the tomatoes were green). If some of the tomato sauce stained the walls, no one would notice because they were already red. Very sensible. Each of the tables had a small white candle at their center that flickered inside a glass cylinder. Sophie wondered if the cylinder in the center of her table was hot from the flame, and was tempted to investigate with her fingertips. Everyone who worked here wore tuxedos, even the women, which was funny. Sophie tried to imagine herself in a tuxedo. How silly. The owners probably were too lazy to buy different outfits for the men and the women. Did the cooks in the back wear tuxedos, too? That would have been even sillier.

"I think, uh," her father said, "I think at night fish rely more on, uh, vibrations."

"Vibrations?" echoed Sophie.

"So they don't poke one another!" Esme explained, and then proceeded to poke-poke-poke Sophie in her ticklish spot to the left of her belly button. She laughed and laughed—she couldn't control herself! Being tickled made her lose complete control of her body. Her legs kicked up and her arms tried to push away her mother's single index finger but still that single finger jumped up and down Sophie's belly and still she laughed and laughed.

The arrival of the salads ended the torture. Sophie still felt giggly, but that soon passed as she gobbled down her lettuce and tomatoes and cucumbers and olives, all drenched in tangy Italian dressing. She didn't eat her radishes. She ostracized them to the side of her bowl. Not even tangy Italian dressing could make radishes taste good.

Next came the entrées. Her spaghetti and meatballs was steaming, and she waited a few minutes for it to cool down. It smelled perfect. There were two meatballs the size of Ping-Pong balls and a steep hill of spaghetti, all as drenched in tomato sauce as her salad was in dressing. Dressing and sauce were kind of like frosting, Sophie decided.

Both of her parents ordered the lasagna. They, too, waited a little bit before eating, but instead of sipping water, they sipped wine. Sophie tried wine once, on New Year's Eve. It tasted like grapes mixed with paint thinner, and the only reason she knew what paint thinner tasted like was because—

"Sophie?"

She looked up at her father. While she was daydreaming, he apparently had asked her a question. "Huh?"

"I said, are you excited about Thanksgiving break?"

She nodded. Thanksgiving break started next Wednesday and lasted all the way until Monday. On Tuesday, they were having a Thanksgiving parade at her school. She wasn't going to dress up—that was so kindergarten—but she was looking forward to the movie. Every year before Thanksgiving break, all the classes gathered in the auditorium and watched a movie projected on a big screen. Last year it had been *Pocahontas*. What would this year's movie be?

Her meal cooled to a nonpainful level, Sophie dug in, and vacuumed up her spaghetti. She knew she was supposed to wrap it around her fork and eat it like a lady, but that took too long. She didn't want it to get cold. The heat was part of what made it so good!

"Slow down, Sophie. You'll get heartburn like Grandpa."

"I thought he had acid reflex."

"Acid reflux," her father corrected. "And that's the same thing."

"So acid is burning his heart?"

"Kind of. But it just hurts for a little while."

Poor Grandpa.

After they were all finished, her mom asked if she had any room for dessert. Sophie very much wanted to try the ice cream—she'd seen another little girl eating it when they'd first arrived at the restaurant—but she was, tragically, too full. She didn't even finish her second meatball. Just looking at it made her throat taste all sour and gross.

So they walked back to Dad's car. Both her mom and her dad had the same type of car. It was a hybrid. That meant it ran on gas and electricity. But she'd learned in class that all cars needed gas and electricity. Some things, she noted, were just confusing on purpose.

A bigger mystery, though, was where they were headed. Would she be spending the night again at the lighthouse? She really loved it there. Going to sleep with the sound of the waves in the background was so peaceful. She imagined her blanket was a seashell and she was inside and she was being rocked gently by the currents. Plus Mr. and Mrs. Worth were very friendly. Mrs. Worth let her eat all the cookies she wanted, and Mr. Worth said he needed her help repairing the outdoor shingles. How could she go home when he needed her help? Someone had to hold the nails while he hammered those new shingles beside the lighthouse windows. And what if their grandson Billy came to visit? Thanksgiving was coming up, after all.

However, if they were going home, she could sleep again in her bed, and she missed some of the dolls she'd neglected to bring with her, and she knew at least some of them missed her, too. The Amazon Queen probably was doing okay, but the others were very sensitive. Staying at the lighthouse was like a vacation, and she knew all vacations came to an end.

Her father braked at the stoplight. If he continued straight, that meant the lighthouse. If he took a left, that meant home. Which would it be?

The stoplight turned green.

He continued straight.

The lighthouse it was!

"Where are you going?" Mom asked him.

"We're going to the lighthouse," explained Sophie.

"Rafe, why—"

"You want to discuss this now?" he asked, obviously indicating their backseat passenger. "Do you?"

"Were we going to discuss it ever?"

"We should have moved out of that house six months ago. After what happened there? We should have moved out of that house the next day. But we didn't. We pretended that we were above it all, that we weren't going to be affected, but we all know now that was crap."

Sophie's eyes widened. Dad said *crap!*

"If we're going to move forward," he said. "The first thing we need to do is move. I've already started looking at a few properties. I've been waiting for you to return from the city to show you and Sophie."

Wait. Move? What? Sophie leaned forward. This was a very important conversation.

"We can afford a nicer place," he said. "Maybe with a sunroom. A library for all our books in the basement. An office for you. A few more bedrooms for, you know, the future. Because that's what I'm talking about. The future. Our future. If you want to be a part of it, Esme."

They pulled up to the lighthouse.

He turned to her.

Sophie looked to her, as well.

They both waited for an answer, as if it were another entrée in their meal, as if it needed to cool down before it could be sampled. They waited and they waited and then Esme opened her mouth, and delivered.

21

The first step, Tom realized, was deciding who to kill.

But he couldn't decide.

He stared at the phone inside the cubicle Karl Ziegler had assigned him. Esme was just seven digits away. This was her kind of puzzle. He picked up the receiver...and put it down. No, Esme had been emphatic. He wasn't going to pester her. She wasn't a member of his task force anymore. There *wasn't* even a task force anymore. Galileo had seen to that.

When she and Rafe first became serious, Tom had pestered her. Sometimes he had been downright possessive. But at the time she had been on the task force. She was his employee. She was a valuable member of the team and everyone depended on her. Perhaps if she'd been with Rafe earlier, it would have been different, but they'd become accustomed to her being available 24/7 and when that flexibility, that status quo, suddenly changed...

Tom sometimes wondered if his aggressive behavior during those months had, in fact, pushed Esme even closer toward Rafe. It was classic, in a way. Here he was, her father figure, essentially telling her not to date, and so of course her instinct would be to run into her lover's arms. For all Tom knew, his stubborn resistance was the single greatest motivator for Esme marrying that schmuck. Rafe Stuart was the love of her life? Please. She could do so much better. She deserved so much better. But instead of helping her realize that, Tom just stood in her way.

But he was digressing. He needed to work this plan. He needed to figure out who Grover Kirk was going to "kill" for the Great Hunt. And with what weapon. And when. And where. It needed to be a viable scenario, something that fit in with who Grover was. Pretending that he suddenly went on a knifing spree wouldn't sell.

Tom glanced again at the phone, then at the clock: 9:24 p.m.

Fuck it. He'd tackle this tomorrow. If Esme came in, great. If not, so be it.

He phoned Penelope Sue and told her he was on his way home. She was, predictably, still out, exploring the Upper West Side. They agreed to meet up at a brightly lit diner on Broadway and Ninety-ninth—if only because that was a landmark in front of her while they were on the phone.

By 10:00 p.m., they were in a corner booth, sharing a six-dollar plate of nachos. Every now and then, the wind smacked against the windowpane beside them, shaking it slightly. Penelope Sue held her palm to the glass to feel the vibrations. She closed her eyes and imagined she was a fish and the wind was the waves in the sea.

"I love this city," she said.

"Want to live here?"

She opened her eyes. "Hell, no. I love nachos but I wouldn't want to eat them every day of the week."

"Mmm-hmm."

"Okay, man of a thousand grunts, why don't you like New York?"

"I never said I didn't like it." He picked at the nachos, dragging a line of cheese from one end of the plate to the other. "I just prefer where we're from."

"Even though you've been to all fifty states…"

"I've never been to Hawaii."

"You went to Alaska and you didn't go to Hawaii? What kind of a tourist are you?"

"Alaska wasn't a vacation," he replied, and left it at that.

Their main courses arrived—a pair of burgers. Penelope Sue dove into hers, but Tom barely lifted a finger. Finally, she asked him what was wrong.

"Nothing." He picked up his burger and took a bite. And put it back down.

"Tom Piper, look at me."

He looked at her.

"You tell me what's wrong or so help me you're sleeping on the floor tonight."

"It's my hotel room."

"You think that makes a difference to me?"

He knew it made no difference to her. This was a woman who ran her own physical therapy business, dealing every day with clients whose emotional states ranged from depressed to suicidal, not to mention the holier-than-thou doctors she had to put up with day in and day out. This was a woman who sometimes wore a Starfleet uniform to the grocery store. No, the fact that the hotel room was under his name made no difference to her.

And he couldn't help but grin.

She smiled back at him. "Okay, then. Now that your wall's down, tell me what's wrong. Is it this case?"

"No. Maybe."

"Are you afraid of change?"

His eyes found hers. What made her say that?

"When I get a new client, a car accident victim or someone recovering from a stroke, you know what the first thing I ask them is? Do you remember the first thing I asked you?"

He thought. Those first few weeks of recovery were such a blur. His only real memories of that time were of attending the funerals of Galileo's victims, and of being unable to breathe without the aid of a respirator. He had never felt so old, or so alone. And then she had come into his life.

"You asked me what scared me the most," he said.

"That's right. Do you remember what you answered?"

He didn't. "Do you?"

"You don't remember what you're most scared of?"

"Change?"

Once again, the wind shivered the glass. She didn't feel it with her palm this time. Her attention belonged to Tom.

"No," she replied. "Failure."

Ah, yes. Failure.

"But that's all fear of change is, anyway. Failing to prevent the inevitable. Failing to beat the clock. The clock always wins, Tom. The trick is to not be alone when it happens."

She clasped his hand in hers.

They finished their meal with innocuous chatter about the weather (she was praying for snow) and about the upcoming holiday (deep-fried turkey, ahoy!), and by the time it came to pay the bill, they both were a little sleepy. To keep themselves from dozing off on the train, they played a game of I Spy.

"I Spy with my little eye…"

"Your adorable little eye…"

Tom blushed. "Will you stop that?"

The train, sparsely populated on this Thursday evening, careered southward. At the Forty-second Street stop, the few passengers on the car with them got off. They were alone. The train recommenced its rickety journey.

"Did I ever tell you," said Penelope Sue, "that I knew who you were before we met?"

"No, you most definitely did not."

She replied with a smirk.

"How did you know who I was?"

"I do read the papers, Tom Piper. The Galileo case was on the front page for days. Your name, right there, lead investigator. But not your picture."

"I don't like having my picture taken."

"Who does? But I always wondered what you looked like."

"And now you know."

"Galileo was targeting you and you knew he was targeting you and you still went after him."

"It was my job," replied Tom, shifting in his seat.

They were nearing their station.

"And I wanted to meet the man who did that. He sounded like a good man to me."

Again, Tom blushed. Fortunately, at that moment, the train squeaked to a stop, and so did this topic of conversation (he hoped). He and Penelope Sue trundled out into the icebox that was their subway station.

"Do you ever worry about it?" she asked him.

"Worry about what?"

They approached the metal turnstiles.

"You know," she replied. "People reading all that

Galileo stuff in the papers and thinking, well, he's famous now, maybe I can be famous, too. Copycat killers. Does that happen in real life? Because it happens all the time in movies and—"

He stopped.

"Tom?"

He smiled.

"Tom?"

He knew exactly who he was going to kill.

Grover was in the shower when he heard the door to his hotel room open. He almost hadn't heard it—he was warbling Sinatra while soaping his privates—but thought he'd heard *something*. When the hotel room door shut with a loud thump, he knew he hadn't been mistaken and someone had, in fact, just illegally entered his room.

Panicking, he searched the shower for a possible weapon. The bar of soap in his hands had been reduced to a misshapen nickel. Since he was bald as an onion, he didn't shampoo. His razor was over on the bathroom sink, but it was electric, and its rotating blades were nothing more than slivers. The best he could do with it was give his intruder a close, personal shave. Damn it! Why had the FBI released him? Actual psychopaths knew who he was and where—because he'd told them! Psychopaths who were this very minute—

The shower curtain was slid to the side. The two lean FBI agents who had accosted him so many days ago in the parking lot stood there, wearing the same cheap brown suits.

"Your presence is requested downtown," said the taller. Was he the one who'd called Grover a pedophile and shoved him into the backseat of the car? "You should get dressed first."

The other G-man just stood nearby, arms crossed, staring unimpressed at Grover's dangling privates as the rapidly cooling shower water continued to jet, cascade and drool across the would-be journalist's paunchy body.

Having an audience inspired him. He dried off and dressed up in under five minutes. He failed to towel some of the soap off his testicles, though, and as he sat down in the backseat of the now-familiar unmarked sedan, he could feel his balls begin to itch. This was going to be a long day.

Since traffic transformed the Long Island Expressway at this early hour into a fifty-mile-long parking lot, Grover used the downtime to reflect on *Galileo's Aim*. Yesterday—Thursday, November 18—had been a very fruitful day in his literary life.

With the manuscript now complete, he phoned several of the publishers in New York to whom he had sent his proposal months ago to update them on its status. Most of the editors he wanted to reach were in meetings, but one of them gave him the name and phone number of an agent to contact. So he contacted the agent. The agent was in a meeting. So he left a voice mail, and searched online for more publishers. He wanted an answer *now*. Current-events stories like this lost their interest value with every day that passed. So he compiled a list of smaller publishers that accepted email submissions and sent out query letters to them, emphasizing the blockbuster potential of his exposé. His wasn't the first book to be written about Galileo, of course—the market had been flooded with trashy tomes that had obviously been scribbled by some hack in under a week—but *Galileo's Aim* was the only comprehensive examination of not only the many murders but also of the man himself.

The audience was there for this book. Heck, he'd just joined a website with more than two thousand people who would love to have a copy in their home. Perhaps not on display, true, but purchased. Ka-ching.

So far, no one had replied.

He hoped this new business with the FBI, whatever it was, didn't take too long. If he got out early enough, maybe he could stop by some of the smaller publishers. Person-to-person communication was always preferable, anyway. He had made sure to interview every person in his book face-to-face. He could have settled for a phone call, but no. He needed to see their expressions. He needed to feel the texture of their hands when they said hello. It made his book matter. The right publisher would see that, and together they would make a fortune. Together they would—

Goddamn it! There went his ear again. Ever since Esme had Vulcan nerve-pinched him, the quality of hearing in his left ear had been diminished, and sometimes plain went silent, as it did just now. Should he have climbed into her bed like that? Maybe not. But her violent reaction had far outweighed any invasion of privacy he may have committed. If he sued her for even one of her many, many offenses, that bed she had been so eager to kick him out of would belong to him. The house would belong to him. He could turn it into a museum dedicated to the life and death of infamous serial killer Henry "Galileo" Booth.

He banged against his ear with the palm of his hand, but it did little good. At least he didn't hear that god-awful chiming sound in it, as he had last night when he'd tried to go to sleep. He knew from one of his favorite poems what his condition was called: "tintinnabulation." He also knew that as soon as he returned to Florida, he was going to pay a visit to the highest-priced ENT specialist he could find, and send the bill care of Esme Stuart.

It just proved the well-known fact that one should never meet well-known people. They were always liable to be a disappointment.

Grover discreetly attempted to scratch his itchy balls with his right hand, but the agent who was driving almost immediately spotted him in the rearview. So Grover just sat there and stewed. By the time they pulled into the parking garage, he was ready to rip off his trousers, grab the nearest rake and scratch himself with that. The agents escorted Grover up to the requisite floor, and once again he was deposited in an interview room. No handcuffs this time, at least.

One-way mirror be damned, he used the corner of the table to go to work, running his crotch up and down the pointed-edge wood. This was what he was doing when the door opened and Tom Piper walked into the room.

"In some states, that's considered rape," said Tom.

Grover looked down. It indeed looked like he was humping the table. He returned to the chair.

"I got soap on my balls," he replied.

"Of course you did."

Tom had a series of nine snapshots in his hand. He spread them out on the table. Each picture depicted a decently dressed man or woman, posing as if for a work ID.

"Who are they?"

"These," answered Tom, "are your targets."

"My what?"

"Tomorrow afternoon, you're going to take an elevator to the roof of an office building in downtown Melville, across from the Long Island Resident Agency of the Federal Bureau of Investigation. Once there, you're going to remove an unassembled sniper rifle from its case, assemble it, load it, aim it and take out these nine agents."

"Take out?"

"Kill."

Grover blinked. "Excuse me?"

"I'm just kidding."

Grover relaxed.

Tom turned to the door. "Bring in the gun."

The door opened. A young woman brought in a long leather case. She placed it on the table, unfastened its clasps and lifted its top. Inside was an unassembled sniper rifle.

"This is an M107 .50 sniper rifle. Do you recognize it, Grover? It's the same make and model your hero Henry Booth used to murder over fifty men, women and children."

With expert precision, the young woman assembled the rifle, each piece locking with a soft, strong click.

"At 4:44 p.m., all nine of these agents will be in a conference room on the second floor of the Resident Agency for a briefing. That's when you're going to take your perch and fire off every one of these blanks at that window. They'll take care of the rest."

Then Grover understood.

"The Great Hunt."

Tom turned to the young woman. "Didn't I tell you he was a smart boy?"

She nodded, and handed the weapon to Grover.

"Go ahead," said Tom.

"I…"

"You what? Don't know if you can do this? Well, I'll tell you, Grover, here's the thing—you are going to do this. You're going to do this for three reasons. One, it'll be a service to your country. Two, it'll be a service to helping us catch a lot of really bad people. Three, you don't have a choice. See, the moment you started writing about all this, posting those amusing notes on those message boards, you became part of the story. This is how your part ends."

"Are people going to think I actually…killed these…?"

"Absolutely," Tom replied. "We're going to make sure everybody knows. We have to, for this to be believable. 'Galileo Writer Snaps, Copycats His Subject, Nine Dead.' Everyone in the country is going to know what you did. That's how we're going to get Cain. That's how you're going to help us get Cain. And then the truth will be revealed and you can go home to your Florida bungalow with a cleared reputation. Who knows? It may even help sell copies of your book. Now sit back and relax. Would you like a cup of coffee? Agent Ramirez here is going to show you how this rifle works."

22

Esme wasn't there for Grover's latest interview. She'd overslept.

Or rather, she hadn't slept—and when she finally was able to close her eyes and approach some weak imitation of slumber, it was almost 7:00 a.m. And so she hadn't heard the alarm, hadn't even needed to slap the snooze button. She just slept and slept and then, around 10:00 a.m., her eyes finally crusted open. The alarm had long since tossed its hands in the air and shut up, so for a moment, she thought she'd actually awoken early. She could take her time, enjoy a long, hot shower, maybe stop for a casual bite to eat on the way to the city...

And then her bleary vision cleared and she beheld the actual time and all thoughts of taking it slow went bye-bye. With a vociferous "Shit!" and an equally adamant "Fuck!" she bolted into the shower, nearly slipping on the bath mat and breaking her neck.

Wonderful. It was going to be one of those days.

One benefit of all her rushing about was that it helped to distract her mind off the fact that, less than twelve hours ago, she was essentially disowned by her husband and daughter. She had told them she wasn't going to cut and run. Rafe got angry, which made Sophie cry, and so Esme kissed her little girl goodbye, promised to visit tomorrow, walked to her own car and drove back to the house that Rafe melodramatically no longer called a home (despite all the warm years they'd spent under its ceiling). How he could let six months counterbalance all those years was beyond her comprehension.

Also beyond her comprehension: how she was going to explain her tardiness to Tom. But one thing at a time. First get dressed. She chose a sensible sweater-pants combination and matched them with a pair of soon-to-be-dead shoes (because the leaden sidewalks of New York City sapped the life out of even the most comfortable footwear). She grabbed a muffin from the fridge and almost made it out the door before bursting into tears.

Fuck. Fuck. Fuck.

She needed music. She needed pop music. She needed the Spice Girls.

She started up her Prius, checked her sob-smeared makeup in the rearview and on her iPod she dialed up *Spice,* the premiere album by the British purveyors of froth and "girl power." Too bad there wasn't a Doomed Spice. At that moment, she would have been Esme's soul mate.

Halfway to New York, she followed up the Spice Girls with pretty much the same group, the all-female quartet All Saints, and their self-titled debut album. Once she'd reached the George Washington Bridge, it was time for yet another album. Pop music evaporated so quickly. She cycled to the trio Sugababes and welcomed the next wave of studio-enhanced harmonies to buffer her from the twisting-down-the-drain realities of her life.

As she spotted the Federal Building, looming like the emotionless twenty-first-century skyscraper it was, part of her wanted to just keep driving, follow the traffic through the Holland Tunnel, and take the Jersey Turnpike down to Atlantic City. She had never been to Atlantic City. She heard the boardwalk was nice. It was at least valuable in Monopoly. Maybe if she resettled to Atlantic City, her life could become as simple as a board game. She'd get a job as a croupier, dealing out luck to eager tourists. At night she'd walk the old wooden planks by the Atlantic Ocean and— No, the Atlantic Ocean would just remind her of the lighthouse, and Rafe, and Sophie. *Go west, young woman.* Santa Fe or San Diego. Guam. Hong Kong. Dubai. Christ, had it been only ten days ago that she'd, tongue firmly in cheek, suggested during their session with Dr. Rosen that they move to Iceland?

Ten days. Six months. Seven years. Not to mention the 2,037 active members belonging to Cain42's website. She was drowning in a pool of mathematics.

She arrived on the FBI's high-altitude floor in time to run smack-dab into Grover Kirk, who was on his way out. He backed away, covering his left ear with a protective hand.

"You get away from me, you kung fu bitch!"

Esme looked to Tom, who was trailing behind the dickhead like a tall shadow. What was Grover doing here?

"Let's go, Grover," said Tom. "Remember, 4:00 p.m. tomorrow. The case will be on the roof exactly where I told you."

Grover nodded, glared at Esme and shuffled past her to the elevators.

"What's going on?" she asked Tom.

Tom motioned for her to follow him, and she did. He led her back to the conference room, still ornamented with all of those ghastly photographs. Almost three-quarters of them, though, now had victims identified, the locations highlighted and the murderers' user names labeled. Although it was, as she'd told Mineola, reactive rather than proactive, it remained a tremendous achievement. These poor men and women were close to receiving the justice for the lives that had been so brutally stolen.

Tom closed the door, giving them some privacy. It was a visual echo of her brief heart-to-heart with Karl Ziegler, and it left her feeling even more unsettled.

"What's going on?" she repeated.

Tom told her. It didn't take very long. She stood there, silently processing the information, nodding now and then, and out of respect to this man, whom she loved like a father, she waited until he was finished before she opened her mouth.

"Are you fucking nuts?"

"Excuse me?"

"You're giving that man a *rifle?*"

"This can't be done without him. You knew that yesterday."

But Esme couldn't shake the image of Grover, who had invaded Sophie's life at the museum, who had slimed into bed with her, holding a sniper rifle. It roused bile to gurgle up her esophagus. "There has to be a better way than this."

"This needs to be done this weekend. We had to have a plan in place and you—"

"This is bullshit," she replied, and began to pace.

"It's a good plan."

"It's lunacy."

Tom shrugged. "You can't be objective."

"Next you're going to tell me I should go home."

"Maybe you should."

Esme wheeled to face him, her face burning with a week's worth of fury. She wanted to take a swing at the man. Maybe she should go home? No matter what they had been through, he had never treated her as if she were expendable—until now. Maybe she should go home? And where, pray tell, was that, Tom, huh? Where was home? She wanted to punch him and kick him and take him down but she couldn't see him through her tears and she couldn't raise her arms because what little strength was left in her sleep-deprived, joy-deprived, love-deprived body seemed to vanish away and she was left with nothing. And that was the word that summed her up, that was her destination of all these weeks and months and years—*nothing, nothing, nothing.*

Sometime after, she realized Tom was hugging her to his chest and her tears were staining wet shadows across the shoulder of his chamois shirt. She heard sobbing and wondered what poor woman could be making those sounds, so reminiscent of…what? P. J. Hammond, after he'd murdered his son. That's where she'd last heard these sounds, and here they were again, in of all places this emotionless twenty-first-century skyscraper. How odd.

And now she was sitting in a chair, with a glass of water in front of her. When had that happened? Had she asked for some water? She was thirsty, actually, and sipped from the glass. Her hands were trembling. She watched them vibrate in the air. She thought about the fish in the moonlight. She thought about Sophie.

But she looked around the room, and Sophie wasn't there. Only Tom. Always Tom.

"Esmeralda," he said, "talk to me."

And she did.

* * *

A bruised and battered cloud formation hovered overhead, and left a dreary pall over Long Island. But that didn't change the fact that it was still Saturday, and so the playground at McCoy Park in Oyster Bay, Long Island, was bustling with the noise of hyperactive children sliding down the slides, swinging on the swings and Tarzan-ing across the jungle gyms. On the outskirts of the playground sat their vigilant parents and/or nannies. The Weather Channel meteorologists had predicted a cold rain by 4:00 p.m., and many of the adults were keeping one eye on their raucous offspring and the other on the time. It was now 4:06 p.m. Once the promised storm arrived, they'd be provided with the perfect excuse to go home, but for now, it was wait and watch and wait.

Esme wasn't with the other adults. Esme was with her daughter, and they were bouncing up and down on the seesaw.

Up, down. Up, down. Up, down.

"Is this like a catapult, Mommy? If you push harder enough, maybe you can send me up in the air!"

"Okay…" replied Esme, a twinkle in her eyes. "Let me try…"

Up, down. Up, down. Up, down.

The sky, Sophie's longed-for destination, groaned with growing darkness.

The rumbling above reminded Sophie of the ugly noises her stomach had made Thursday night, after they'd returned from the Italian restaurant. "It sounds like God needs Pepto!" She giggled.

Esme just smiled back at her daughter and replied, "Maybe."

"Mommy?"

"Yeah, sweetie?"

"Are you and Daddy getting divorced?" When she posed the question, there was no change in Sophie's facial expression. She'd asked it with exactly the same tone and curiosity she'd had about the fish. "Because I don't think that's a good idea."

"Who said anything about divorce, Sophie?"

"Grandpa Les."

Of course.

"Well, sweetie, sometimes Grandpa Les doesn't know what he's talking about."

"Sometimes he smells like old socks."

"And sometimes he smells like old socks," agreed Esme.

Another echo of thunder. The battered bruises up above were darkening ever further, as if color itself knew better than to stay outside today. The storm would be soon, and mighty.

"Sophie, I think it's time to go."

Esme expected a protest—they hadn't been out here very long—but her little girl just shrugged her shoulders okay and hopped off the seesaw once her feet touched the ground. They walked back to the Prius, parked alongside all the other cars. Other parents were escorting their children off the playground now, too. Esme offered a friendly wave to a few of the mothers she recognized. Only one waved back.

How lovely to be made a pariah for protecting your neighborhood.

They drove back to the lighthouse. Esme allowed her daughter to pick the music and, predictably, Sophie chose the Beatles. This was her little girl, after all. Sophie was especially fond of Paul McCartney's music hall contribution to *Abbey Road*: "Maxwell's Silver Hammer." Mother and daughter sang along with the bouncy chorus as they traveled north. The rain erupted in a cloudburst, providing wet percussive backbeats that echoed the "bang bang" of Maxwell's silver hammer in three-eight time.

Nolan Worth met them in the parking lot of the lighthouse, with an umbrella and a grin. Esme and Sophie scrunched underneath the vinyl octagon and, on the count of three, they all rushed, mud splashing at their feet, toward the warm, dry interior of the lighthouse. Rafe's car was gone. Tonight, he and Lester were elsewhere. That was the agreement. She didn't care where they were and hadn't even bothered to ask. If she needed to get ahold of her husband, she had his cell phone number. She didn't plan on getting ahold of her husband. This was her day with her daughter.

Not too far away, in an unmarked sedan outside the nondescript FBI substation in Melville, New York, Tom was also thinking about Esme's day with her daughter, among many other things. Esme's breakdown had hit him hard. Even though so much of it seemed to stem from the dissolution of her marriage, Tom couldn't help but shoulder some of the guilt himself. Here was his prodigal daughter, his beloved disciple and friend, of whom he was so proud, for whom he cared so much, and circumstances—which he had played a part in creating—had reduced her from a glacier, implacable and fearless, to an icicle being heated into nothingness. He longed for nothing more than to help her out and build her back up, but he couldn't. Her problems went beyond the scope of his prodigious abilities to solve. She wasn't a case to be concluded or a criminal to be profiled. She was his Esmeralda, and she was alone, and no amount of "It'll be okay" or "I'm here for you" counterbalanced the hot truth of that fact.

Meanwhile, there was the operation. Tom was supposed to be concentrating on the task at hand. Dozens of operatives were waiting for his go-ahead to abort the mission. The rain wasn't letting up, and this was a weather-dependent operation. Grover could still fire off all of his blanks, but what were the odds that an untrained marksman like himself would notch one kill, let alone nine, in this wind and with this rain? Galileo couldn't have even accomplished that feat. Credibility was vital here. So why wasn't Tom signaling the abort?

None of them could have known what was on the veteran special agent's mind, not even Grover Kirk, up there on the roof, no less wet than if he were underwater. For one, Grover was too busy trying to keep the soaked sniper rifle from sliding out of his hands.

As for the nine targeted agents in the conference room on the second floor, they were impatiently debating whether or not to contact Tom themselves. The operation called for radio silence (unless Tom were to breach it), but proceeding in this weather was ridiculous. Why wasn't he signaling the abort? They all recognized the important theatrical value that they played here, but they all also knew when enough was enough. It was time to call it a day. It was time to return home, cuddle up with a hot cup of coffee and watch some college football with their kids.

The operation was scheduled for 4:44 p.m. It was now 4:41 p.m.

From his vantage point at street level, Tom could see the tip of Grover's rifle and he could see the sheer surface of the conference room bay window. An hour ago he could have seen through the window and into the conference room itself, but the dark weather made that prohibitive. Could Grover even see his targets? Tom sighed. He was aware of how precarious the whole operation had become. But he was also aware of how absolutely essential it was that this operation succeed. This was their best opportunity to end Cain42 and his World Wide Web of violence. Perhaps they should have had a second operation on the back burner in case this one went FUBAR, but Tom had never been a fan of fallbacks. People with fallbacks tended not to commit as fully to their primary objective. People with fallbacks had a safety net.

Tom Piper worked best without a safety net.

And yet: 4:42 p.m.

He picked up his walkie-talkie. When he'd started his career, more than thirty years earlier, walkie-talkies had been these cumbersome pieces of machinery with long metal antennae that one had to extend to full length in order to send and receive a proper signal. The walkie-talkie in his hands was small and light, its wobbly antenna apparently made out of rubber. Technology was shrinking the world.

And the world at this moment was very, very wet.

Should he abort the operation?

Even a nearby bystander was wondering that very same question. He was a thin man in a ball cap who had taken shelter from the elements under the protective cover of a bus stop kiosk. Kid-friendly movie advertisements decorated the two interior walls of the kiosk. Thanksgiving was high time for children's entertainment. The thin man in the ball cap enjoyed movies and plays. After all, this was the primary reason he was there in downtown Melville—to watch theater unfold, if it was going to unfold, if the special agent in the unmarked sedan didn't call off the show. Cain42 so hoped he didn't call off the show.

Tailing Grover Kirk to this location had been a piece of cake, and once Cain42 saw the rifle and followed its barrel to the second-story window, the whole plan fell into place in his mind. He was tempted to climb up to the rooftop and keep his buddy Galileofan company. He was tempted to load live rounds into the rifle and watch the line between fantasy and reality blur. But no. Sometimes it was better just to wait and observe. He had something better in mind, anyway, his own bit of theater, for Monday afternoon, a kind of gift for the FBI for their efforts here on his behalf. Because surely all of this was being orchestrated for him, just as the Great Hunt was being orchestrated for them. He wanted Galileofan to win as badly as the FBI did.

He wondered how far they were going to take this charade. Would they be using stage blood on the "victims"? How were they going to mimic the rifle shots through the windowpane? Was there a second shooter somewhere about? No, that would be too dangerous. They probably had the window rigged from inside, precut and lined with fishing wire. Once the blanks fired, someone in the conference room would tug the fishing wire and the window would crash inward. How very Hollywood.

And all for his benefit.

He felt honored. He really hoped the operation wasn't aborted. If only this goddamn cloudburst would let up…

4:43 p.m.

What time were they scheduled to go? It had to be soon. Everyone was in place. The special agent had the walkie-talkie in his hand. One way or another, it had to be soon. Cain42 adjusted his ball cap. He was excited.

His gaze fixed on the sniper rifle, little more than a thin black line poking out from the rooftop of a midlevel high-rise. If he hadn't been following Grover's movements, he might not have seen it at all.

"Do it," he whispered. His voice came out in a wheeze. If he wasn't careful, he'd have to be put on a portable ventilator again. Goddamn asthma.

4:44 p.m.

Tom put the walkie-talkie down.

Grover Kirk pulled the wet trigger on the rifle. And pulled. And pulled.

The bay window on the second story fell inward.

Tom smiled, relieved.

Cain42 smiled, relieved.

The show had begun.

23

Lufthansa Flight 883, with nonstop service from Zurich, Switzerland, to Newark, New Jersey, was delayed six hours due to snow before finally taking off on Sunday evening, flying ten hours, thirty minutes, and eventually touching down stateside…on Sunday evening. Jefferson Harbinger countered any impatience, jet lag or all-around misery through the tried-and-true: constant intoxication. His cocktail of choice was two parts absinthe, one part champagne, and both were readily available in luscious Switzerland (absinthe being a Swiss invention and champagne being a popular import from neighboring France). The stewardesses in first class were reluctant to curb his binging for two reasons: one, he frightened them; and two, eventually he had to pass out.

What could Jefferson Harbinger have possibly done to frighten such seasoned Swiss stewardesses? It was simple, really. Shortly after takeoff, before he'd even mixed one drink, Jefferson had opened a sketch pad, which he'd rested on his lap, and with a sharpened HB pencil he began to draw a picture on a blank page. This, of course, attracted the curiosity of the other passengers, not to mention the flight crew. After all, this was first class. Perhaps the young man with the unruly red hair, pleasantly sketching away mere meters from where they sat, was a famous artist.

When the plane leveled off at thirty thousand feet, the stewardesses started walking the cabin, taking orders for drinks. It fell to Cerise, a tall, freckle-faced femme who happened to have a thing for artists, to ask Jefferson Harbinger what he wanted. The angle he held the pad made it nearly impossible for Cerise to sneak a glimpse—and she tried.

"Do you know how to make a Hemingway?" he asked, without raising his eyes from his work. His voice was high and reedy, and his long red curls bounced about his forehead as he sketched. "If you do, that'd be lovely. If you don't, I'll instruct you."

"I don't," replied Cerise.

"Two parts absinthe, one part champagne."

"Yes, sir."

She mixed the drink and handed it to him. He took it with his right hand and with his left, he moved on to shading, adding shadows and depth. Surely he was almost finished with his sketch. Surely it wouldn't be rude of her to ask for a peek. He sipped his cocktail and a small grin percolated below his long flat nose.

Anna, the senior flight attendant, signaled for Cerise to keep moving. Reluctantly, the tall, freckle-faced femme nodded. Her curiosity would have to remain unsatisfied. But as Cerise stepped to the next row—

"Miss?"

The redheaded young man touched her wrist.

"Yes, sir?" She saw his glass was already empty. Even the ice was gone. "I'll refill your drink in a moment. I just need to tend to the other passengers."

"Oh, I know. But I thought I'd give you a reward for mixing my drink so well."

A reward? Could it be…?

Yes, it could! He tore the finished drawing out of his sketch pad and handed it to her, that small grin of his showing very little teeth. But his green eyes betrayed his sense of anticipation. The pupils were huge. He watched the stewardess's face beam as she took his gift, and then her focus went from him to it.

It was a full body portrait of Cerise. Rather than outfitted in her snug Lufthansa uniform, though, Jefferson had drawn on a pair of lederhosen and what appeared to be a black nylon bra. The rest of her figure, including her privates, was well-outlined and nude. But that wasn't what caused Cerise to freak out. She was a liberated woman. What caused Cerise to freak out were the fishing hooks.

Ten fishing hooks were embedded in her throat, five on each side of her concave thyroid. And these hooks were pulling the flesh of her neck open as if each skin flap were the leaf of a book and the book was being held open for all to see, its contents viscous tissue, veins and muscle, drooling blood all the way down to her nylon cleavage.

Ten similar hooks were embedded in her vagina.

To her credit, she didn't scream. She did freak out, though, and quickly passed down the aisle to Anna, who was in the fore kitchen.

"Ich… Wir…hat…"

Anna raised an eyebrow and replied in perfectly enunciated Queen's English, "Stop babbling, child, and tell me what's wrong."

Cerise showed her the sketch and pointed to the red-headed young man.

Disgusted, Anna snatched the sheet of paper and stomped in high heels toward Jefferson Harbinger, who'd commenced another sketch.

"Sir…"

He didn't look up at her. "Another Hemingway, if you please."

"Sir…"

"If you don't know how to make it, ask the girl with the freckles."

He still didn't look up. His arm, fast at work, blocked Anna from spying the subject of his latest piece, but she lacked Cerise's curiosity, especially having had the misfortune to behold the subject of his first piece.

"Sir, I'm going to have to ask you to stop."

Now he looked up. "Is my art interfering with the cockpit?"

"You know very well the effect your 'art' has had."

"Actually, I don't," he replied. "I have hopes and desires like every other man, but that's all. I want to believe that all my work has a profound effect on someone. Take my latest piece, for example."

And he showed Anna his latest piece.

And she began to gag.

"Now if you would be so kind, ma'am, please get me another Hemingway. Two parts absinthe, one part champagne. And be quick about it. Unless, that is, you want to try to take away my pencils. I might like to see you try."

His thick tongue slimed its way across his thin lips.

She got him another drink, and told the other flight attendants to leave him alone. She watched him down cocktail after cocktail, hoping and desiring that this would be the one to slow him down and knock him out.

But he remained conscious, sipping and, when the muse struck him, drawing.

He completed eleven more pieces.

By the time they began their approach to Newark International, Anna—always the stalwart rock among her crew—was a trembling wreck. She'd already informed the captain, Adam Ludvorg, of the situation, and he'd notified airport security; apparently, a team of policemen was already waiting at the gate to take Jefferson Harbinger into custody. Anna was gratified. On the basis of the drawings, airport security could have maybe roughed him up a bit, but he hadn't broken any law, and he knew he hadn't broken any law.

Except apparently he *had* broken a law or the team of policemen wouldn't be already waiting at the gate. Anna could just imagine what obscene crime he had committed. She didn't want to imagine, but she couldn't help herself. The drawings had unleashed a flood of darkness into her brain and she couldn't empty it out.

The plane touched down on the rain-swept tarmac at Newark International. Its journey of ten hours and change was almost complete. Anna, who had the drawings secured in an issue of *Le Monde,* took note of how relieved poor Cerise appeared. That girl would be heading straight to the airport bar. Good. Maybe Anna would join her. They'd order something hard to blast away their demons.

Like absinthe and champagne.

Anna had to swallow to keep from vomiting.

As they taxied to the gate, Jefferson removed his PDA from the inside pocket of his parka and sent off a quick email to Cain42, informing him that the favor he'd requested had been completed. Jefferson then brought up the website itself. With four hours left until Monday, he was curious to see who was winning the Great Hunt. Galileofan, eh? Tip of the hat to the newbie. Jefferson tried to enlarge the thumbnail photograph that Galileofan had taken of his nine kills, but his PDA's touch screen refused to respond. The only reason he held on to the piece of crap was to please his aunt Carolyn. She'd given it to him for his birthday. Family meant a lot to Jefferson Harbinger.

They came to a stop at the gate.

When the cabin door finally opened and the small army of well-armed Kevlar-vested SWAT officers poured into the airplane, Anna immediately rose to her feet and handed the magazine to the last one in. She then strolled to the kitchen and threw up in the sink.

The SWAT officers formed a semicircle around Jefferson. Their pistols were at the ready. Their safeties were off.

"Evening, officers," he said. "What seems to be the problem?"

At Tom's request, Briggs and Vitucci had placed Jefferson Harbinger in the filthiest interview room they had. As Tom had guessed, the redheaded young man did not take well to filth, even going so far as to try to scrub the mildew off his own chair with one of his manacles.

To Vitucci, the whole thing smacked of irony.

He and Special Agent Piper were observing the suspect from behind the one-way glass. Mercifully, Briggs was off somewhere else in the building, probably gabbing with the SWAT boys.

Vitucci turned to Tom, whose attention was absolutely focused on the deviant on the other side of the glass. "We appreciate it, by the way. Letting us collar him, take him here rather than into federal custody."

"It's your case, Detective."

"But you think he's part of this fucked-up website?"

"He's part of it."

"He smells like a distillery. So what's the game plan, chief?"

Tom told him.

They entered the room.

As per Tom's game plan, Vitucci led the charge.

"Hey, there, chuckles. Hope you're comfortable. You're going to be here awhile."

Jefferson let out a long, bored sigh.

"Just so we're clear, I'm still Detective Vitucci. In case you've forgotten, this is Special Agent Piper, and you're the scumbag up shit creek."

The scumbag up shit creek shifted his gaze to Tom, who was leaning against the wall with his arms crossed and who appeared…embarrassed?

"So now that we're all acquainted, scumbag, why don't you start by telling us about the three dead girls?"

"Which three dead girls did you have in mind, Detective?" Harbinger's voice took on a nasal patrician tone. "History has provided us with so many."

"You know who I'm talking about."

"Detective, I just deplaned a trans-Atlantic flight. I don't even know what time it is."

"Eight-fifty," said Tom.

"Thank you," replied Harbinger.

Vitucci leaned in to him. "We found the bodies."

"Were they hiding?"

"They were exactly where you left them, buddy. In the basement underneath the store." The cop flashed a canary-eating grin. "Funny neither you nor your aunt mentioned there even being a basement when we first interviewed you. I guess you two must have forgotten.

But see, the doors in the alleyway didn't add up. Six doors. Five stores. What was the sixth door for? So we opened it and would you look at that? A staircase leading belowground. Inside the basement, besides the cobwebs and the mold, were all these extra rolls of carpeting, not to mention blood and three garment bags stuffed with mothballs—and the headless bodies of the innocent girls you murdered, their breasts mutilated!"

Harbinger watched Tom shift his position on the wall. The G-man looked uneasy, as if…

"Maybe it's the long flight I was on—maybe my ears are still clogged from the air pressure—but, Detective, you sound a little full of shit."

Vitucci's face reddened. Harbinger watched him puff out his chest: classic Neanderthal reaction.

"You think we don't have you dead to rights, you smug son of a bitch?"

"I think if you did, I'd be in a jail cell right now and you wouldn't be in here rambling. I think if you did, the FBI over there wouldn't look perturbed at your performance. Why are you here, Special Agent Piper?"

Tom took a deep breath and, with bated reluctance, answered, "Your family has expressed concern over the way this investigation was being handled by the local authorities. And I can't say that I blame them."

Vitucci wheeled on him. "Excuse me?"

"Oh, come on. Even your so-called suspect knows it. You're grasping at straws."

The detective looked as if he was going to take a swing at the special agent. To his credit, the special agent didn't even wince. Vitucci backed away, fuming.

"The truth is," continued Tom, "I found the bodies. But the Newark P.D. doesn't want to be shown up, so they dragged you in here in one last-ditch effort to make a case based on absolutely nothing."

"He's the only one who had opportunity!" Vitucci bellowed. "He had a key to the basement!"

"Mmm-hmm. Except keys can get copied. Or didn't you know that?"

"This is bullshit!"

Vitucci stormed out of the room.

"I'm sorry about this," said Tom, offering Harbinger another sympathetic look. "Just sit tight. I'm going to get you released ASAP. Just know, Mr. Harbinger, that in case you or your family wishes to pursue any type of legal retribution, the Bureau had absolutely nothing to do with this unfortunate screwup."

"Oh, I know where the fault lies. Thank you. And I'll remember your name to my uncle."

Tom nodded his appreciation and left the room. Vitucci stood there with a cup of coffee in his hand. He appeared calmer, although not by much.

"I hate playing the bad cop," he said.

"Because you're a good cop," Tom replied. He glanced through the one-way at Harbinger. The unease that had been so visible on the man before was gone. Jefferson Harbinger was now the epitome of serenity, patience and hubris. This was the man in control, as he so needed to be. This was the man those three girls had encountered the night of October 30.

Now they needed to wait.

Tom found a quiet corner of the station house and dialed Penelope Sue. She was in the hotel room, painting her toenails.

"Lime-green," she told him. "And I've got some polish left if you want me to do your nails when you get back."

"Not a chance," he replied.

"I wouldn't be so sure, Tom Piper. You've got to sleep sometime."

Tom let a small smile penetrate his lips and he almost forgot about the monster in the other room. "I'm going to be here a little longer."

"I figured."

"I'm sorry. I know you didn't come up to New York to be alone."

"I came to be here for my man. And when he's done saving the world, I'll be here in his bed, keeping it warm."

"How did you get to be so amazing?"

Penelope Sue chuckled. "Don't you want to know."

They exchanged tender, sweet nothings, but eventually had to say goodbye.

Briggs had returned from his gabfest with the SWAT boys and stood beside Vitucci by the one-way. Tom reached for the doorknob to the interview room.

"If this works," said Briggs, "it's still our collar, right, Dixie?"

Tom shrugged him off and entered the room.

"They just have to file the paperwork," he told Harbinger, "and you'll be all set."

"Thank you again."

"This whole thing is really unfortunate." Tom returned to his leaning place on the wall. "Oh, by the way, how was Switzerland?"

"It was resplendent. You should go."

"Not on my salary."

Harbinger responded with a universal "whatcha gonna do" shrug.

"It must be nice, being rich."

"I could complain, but I'd be lying."

"Your parents…they died, right? When you were a baby? That's why your uncle and aunt raised you? I'm the product of a broken home myself."

"Of course you are."

Tom smiled. "You think I'm playing you."

"Yes. I do."

"Can't fault a man for trying, right?"

Harbinger smiled back at him. "I wouldn't expect anything less."

"I'm going to go check on that paperwork. Do you want anything to drink?"

"Two parts absinthe, one part champagne."

"How about a cup of coffee?"

Harbinger shrugged (as best he could in shackles). "I suppose."

Tom ambled out of the room.

"So much for that idea," grumbled Briggs.

"Patience," Tom replied, and he took out his cell phone.

Mineola picked up on the first ring. "Yo."

"Don't you ever sleep?"

"I'll sleep when I'm married. What do you need?"

"Can you run a location check on Cain42's server?"

"Sure thing. Give me a minute."

He gave her a minute.

"Huh," she said.

"It's moved, right?"

"Still in Switzerland, but no longer where it once was. How did you know?"

"Get the State Department to run a trace on Jefferson Harbinger's movements in Switzerland over the past few days."

Tom hung up and stared through the one-way at the smug redheaded young man. All Tom had to do was crack the bastard, and they'd have the server and, with it, the names of every member of the website.

24

Grover Kirk won the Great Hunt. The results were posted at 12:01 a.m. on Monday morning and Grover's nine-victim tally trounced the competition (mainly because the FBI's massive national dragnet, orchestrated by one Assistant Director in Charge Karl Ziegler, had snagged, over the two-day weekend, twenty-nine of the competitors before they'd had a chance to shed a drop of blood). As per Tom's urging, the arrests of the twenty-nine would-be killers were kept on the down low, so as to keep from spooking Cain. In the end, only three website members were able to carry through with their actions, and those were the photographs that currently occupied Karl's desk. Three photographs equaled four new victims. But didn't the twenty-nine victims who had been saved balance out the four who had been lost?

Not in the slightest.

Grover Kirk was declared the winner at 12:01 a.m., and at 12:05 a.m. Grover's email account received a message from Cain42 himself, congratulating him on his laudable achievements and then informing him of the time and location for the prize delivery. Predictably, Cain42 had selected a public place. Less predictably, the public place he had selected was the end car on the uptown A-train as it departed from Washington Square between 4:01 and 4:16 p.m. Which day? This day, of course. Monday, November 22. No time like the present.

The entire New York office of the Federal Bureau of Investigation dedicated that morning to strategizing the best way to infiltrate the meet-up and the safest method of taking down Cain42. It was decided that the passengers on the end car would all be undercover operatives. Other undercovers would be stationed in and around Canal Street to (subtly) keep civilians from boarding it.

They took a break at 10:00 a.m. and Karl returned to his office. The photographs were still on his desk. He rubbed his tired eyes. He knew he had a minute, maybe two, before he had to call Washington and update them on the status of the operation. Everyone wanted a hand in this pie, including the director himself. This case would indeed make his career—if he didn't first have a stroke.

"I want in," said Esme Stuart.

Karl glanced up at her. When had she even entered his office?

"This is me saying no," he replied. "Go away. And please close my door."

She closed the door, with her on the wrong side of it. Great.

"I'm not saying I need to be on the end car," she continued. "But I deserve to be there on-site when he gets taken down."

"Mrs. Stuart, didn't we have this discussion? You're no longer a field agent. For me to authorize your presence in what could potentially be the line of fire would be a decision of gross incompetence. Go home. Your contributions to this case are greatly appreciated and very much complete. And besides…"

"Besides?"

"Grover Kirk has filed a restraining order against you."

"Oh, for the love of God."

Ziegler plopped down in his leather chair. "There you go. You know, prayer works. Prayer is welcome. Far as I know, nobody's ever filed a restraining order against God. Hey, listen, with all the variables at play right now in this monster of a case, you really want to help us out, Mrs. Stuart? Pray. Because it's when you see the end zone that you usually get tackled."

"And yet you're willing to turn away a seasoned field agent—"

"Ex-field agent."

"Karl, I need this." She stared him straight in the eye. "You don't know what's going on in my life right now and you don't have to know, but it's bad and I can't take another door slamming in my face. I just can't."

He drummed his fingers on his desk, inches from the victim photographs. "Are you sure?"

"Yes."

He paused, let out a long sigh, opened the middle drawer of his desk, removed a form and handed it to her.

"Read and sign," he said.

"What is it?"

"Read," he repeated, "and sign."

She read. She gasped. These were reinstatement papers, addressed to her, already signed by him.

"I…"

Ziegler's eyes smiled at her. "Read the contract rider."

She flipped to the back and read the contract rider. It declared that should she terminate this contract, she would be forbidden from working for the federal government in any capacity, be it full-time, part-time or even as a volunteer.

"You come back to the Bureau," he said, "and, this time, you don't quit. This time, we own you. Now, are you sure this is something you want, Mrs. Stuart?"

She thought about Sophie. The first time she rolled over by herself (at two months old, very precocious). The first word she spoke (which was *rain*). Her first day of school (not so long ago now). Esme had been present at each and every one of those milestones because she'd had the luxury of free time. If she signed these documents, she signed away the likelihood that she would witness any more milestones. If she was in the field, working a case, the case had to take precedence. Lives would depend on it. Lives would depend on her.

Many field agents had children at home. Maybe Esme would learn how they did it. Maybe Esme could do it, too. But what if she couldn't? She'd done a piss-poor job so far at balancing work and family.

"Mrs. Stuart, if this is a choice you're going to make, make it. Or go home. Either way, decide quick. I have a lot of people far more important than you that I need to call."

As Esme literally held her future in her hands, Tom held in his a foam coffee cup that had been filled and refilled more times than he could count, although to be fair at that moment he had trouble even adding two plus two. He had been awake for…well, a long time. To be aware of how long would have required using those pesky numbers, and that part of his brain shut down around dawn.

Jefferson Harbinger still hadn't cracked.

Tom had been correct before. The evidence they had against him, while overwhelming, was overwhelmingly circumstantial. Yes, Harbinger had opportunity, but as Tom himself had said, keys got copied all the time. Yes, there were those ghastly drawings, but if making bad art were a crime, half of Hollywood would be behind bars. Was Harbinger's DNA on the bodies? Probably—they were still waiting for the lab results from the sample Tom had snagged off a can of soda Harbinger had sipped around 4:00 a.m. But so what if it was? His lawyer would just argue that Harbinger found the dead bodies and was too shocked to go to the police.

Speaking of lawyers, Harbinger still hadn't asked for one. That was how confident he was that the charges against him wouldn't stick. And with a skittish D.A. arriving any minute, he could be proven right.

Tom's back was against the wall. He had to make him talk. But how? Again, he reviewed the drawings. To understand a madman, one must understand his work. What did this work say? That Harbinger was a misogynistic sadist? Yes. And? That he needed an outlet for his rage. Okay. So? Why hooks? Why—

Then Tom saw it, in the corner of one of the drawings, and was reminded of something Vitucci had noticed when Harbinger was first brought into custody, what seemed like eons ago.

It was time to play a hunch.

First, though, he ran an errand. It didn't take long. What he needed was right across the street. He returned with his purchases, catching some attention from the day shift. Briggs had gone home. Vitucci was napping in the locker room.

Tom went into the room alone.

"Hello, Jefferson."

He placed the whisky glass on the table, just out of reach from Harbinger's grasp, and removed the two bottles from the brown paper bag. What he was doing was visible to anyone in the squad room watching the CCTV. If they had any objections, they could stop him. If the D.A. showed up, she probably *would* stop him.

He opened each of the bottles.

"Two parts absinthe, one part champagne, right?"

"Special Agent Piper, are you assuming that if you become my bartender, I'll open up to you and share sad stories of my childhood?" Harbinger let slip a sly grin. "Now that's amusing."

Tom poured the drink, and then placed the bottles on the floor.

The whisky glass remained just beyond Harbinger's fingertips.

"You like to be in control, don't you, Jefferson? Prove it to me." Tom moved the glass within Harbinger's reach. "Don't drink."

"Excuse me?"

"I don't think you can do it. Just like I don't think you had any choice when you drew those sketches. I think you want to be in control, but the truth is, you're not in control at all."

"You're full of shit."

Tom moved the glass an inch closer, dragging it along the wooden surface of the tabletop. "Prove me wrong."

Harbinger stared at that glass, then at Tom.

"You know, Jefferson, I asked myself, why was a rich, smart boy like you working retail? Is it because that was the only job you could keep? Is it because your compulsive behavior alienates everyone around you? Is that why your aunt had to replace three clerks over the summer? Did you frighten them off?"

"If I drink this, it proves nothing. It proves I'm thirsty. I've been in here for twelve hours!"

"Would you prefer a Fresca?"

Harbinger glared at him. "So, what, every alcoholic is a psychopath? Is that your theory, hotshot?"

"No," replied Tom, calmly. "But every alcoholic has an addictive personality. It's a mental illness. They want to be normal, but they physically can't help themselves. Know what I mean, Jefferson?"

"You can't do this. I have rights. You think this bullshit will stand up in a court of law?"

"You're probably right."

Tom grabbed the glass and pulled it away.

"How old were you when you realized you weren't like the other boys? Eleven? Twelve? I'll bet you ran to the bottle to help you deal with your demons then, just like you do now—and I'll bet it even helps…for a little while. It must be awful. You're either a sober madman or a drunk asshole. Were you trying to go cold turkey back in October? Is that why you lost control and killed those girls?"

"I'm in control.…"

"When you cut off their heads and put them on display, I thought it was the signature of a boastful killer, but I was wrong, wasn't I? You were ashamed, and you wanted the world to see how ugly you were. I'll even bet when you joined Cain's little website, you thought you'd learn how to control your urges. Serial Killers Anonymous! Do you really want them to stop, Jefferson? Do you? Will you let me help you?"

Jefferson Harbinger had closed his eyes. His face was scrunched tight, as if it were ready to implode.

Tom had cracked the poor son of a bitch.

When Grover was informed that the FBI would be keeping him company in the subway car, he felt a modicum of relief, but that's all. The past week had not endeared him to the ways and means of the federal government. But he had been assured that the involvement of Esme Stuart (heretofore known as That Bitch) had come to an end, and that bit of news did provide him with peace of mind.

Also, and this he kept very much to himself, part of him was looking forward to meeting Cain42. The man intrigued Grover, in much the same way that Galileo had intrigued him so many months ago. What drove someone to kill? Was it simply a chemical imbalance or did that urge draw on something primal within us all? Could he, Grover Kirk, kill?

Not to mention the fact that Cain42 had quite an intellect and charisma. His actions were deplorable, yes, but his accomplishments were undeniable. Even the staunchest pacifist had to admire the achievements of Caesar and Napoleon. And he, Grover Kirk, was on speaking terms—in a twenty-first century, online context—with a modern-day cult personality.

It had the makings of another book, a personal narrative this time: *Cain & Me*.

Hmm. Well, he'd come up with a better title later.

And speaking of books, Cain42 had asked Grover to send him a copy of the manuscript for *Galileo's Aim!* Grover had hoped that one of the folks he'd encountered over these past few months would show an interest in his work, but he'd never expected Cain42 himself to want to read the book, offer pointers, etc. Imagine how huge it would be to get a jacket blurb from a serial killer!

This was what had Grover, for much of Monday morning, starry-eyed. No matter how the meet went down, in a few hours it would happen. He would be face-to-face with a bona fide human monster. As any American in the nineteenth century would have been excited to sit down with Billy the Kid or Jesse James, so, too, was Grover at the prospect of spending time with the modern age's answer to the Wild West outlaw. Because that was the analogy. The American fascination with serial killers wasn't birthed in the early 1960s with Alfred Hitchcock's *Psycho*. And was it so coincidental that a country which based its very founding on violent revolution should be so enamored with the gunslinger and the rogue sniper?

It was all there in *Galileo's Aim*.

Cain42 might even bring his printed copy with him to the A-train to have it signed by the author himself.

Grover made sure to tuck his brass-plated Cross pen into one of his blazer's inner pockets. He'd bought the pen months earlier, specifically for the purpose of signing copies of his book, and although he hadn't expected to make use of it for a while, he carried it around with him as a visual reminder of his future obligations. And now the future was today, wasn't it?

Maybe he could self-publish.

It wasn't unheard of. How was it any different from opening up one's own business? He could call all the shots (no pun intended) and reap all the benefits. He wouldn't have to be at the beck and call of some slow-to-respond New York publisher or at the mercy of their art department when it came to his book cover or at the mercy of their publicity department when it came to his title. He would be an American entrepreneur. He could eventually publish other true-crime books by like-minded authors. He had certainly met his share of crime aficionados over the past few months. Yes, the major publishing houses produced true-crime books, but they just took so damn long to respond! He would promise to respond to all queries with expediency.

Perhaps he could even get Cain42 himself to write a memoir. *I, Killer.* After all, one cannot appreciate the lightness in the world without first experiencing the dark.

His family would come to appreciate him, too. And that, he knew, would be the sweetest prize of all. No more disappointed looks. No more what-are-you-going-to-do-with-your-life lectures. He was a late bloomer, true, but what colors he was going to show....

It was time to go catch a train.

He took one last look in the hotel bathroom mirror and assessed his appearance. His blue blazer fit nicely around his shoulders. He loved his shoulders. They were the shoulders of a linebacker, and he hadn't even ever played sports. Even his baldness made him look tough, rugged. He adjusted his mustard-colored tie (which was nearly the same shade as his socks), gave himself a firm tug in the crotch for good measure and headed out the door. It was 2:00 p.m.

He drove west toward New York City, aware that the FBI were keeping a watchful, "protective" eye on his movements. One or more of the cars behind him had to be government-issue. Every time he thought he'd nailed his suspect, though, that car seemed to be the one to take the next exit. Ah, well. None of it mattered. From his perspective, their role in this was secondary.

Today was about Grover Kirk and Cain42.

Grover speculated on the nickname the man had

selected. The Biblical allusion was obvious, but why 42? Was it some kind of Douglas Adams reference? What was his real name? It probably was something especially bland. Certainly Grover was never too fond of his own name (and the *Sesame Street* teasing it had inspired in elementary school). Names held so much power. Would he have been so fascinated with the Galileo murders had the killer called himself Cookie Monster? Uh, probably not.

The Washington Square Station was not located in Washington Square. Washington Square was the grassy hub of Greenwich Village, populated by street performers and NYU students. With a touch of reluctance, Grover left his Studebaker in an exorbitantly overpriced parking garage (the expense of which he would most definitely bill to the FBI) and hoofed his way west across the park—which was more sidewalk than grass—to the corner of Fourth Street and Seventh Avenue, where he located what he was looking for: a staircase with a green globe above it, indicating this entrance was open. Beside the subway entrance was a pizzeria. Grover smelled it before he saw it, and his stomach nudged him toward the steaming decadence of cheese and tomato, just waiting for him to…

No, no. It was almost 4:00 p.m. The task at hand took precedence. Grover felt a pit of anticipation in his belly and descended the stairs into the underground world of the New York City subway system. Appropriately, the walls were tiled with colorful Asian mosaics. Grover followed the signs to the uptown ACE line and waited among the masses of bundled-up Gothamites (many of whom had to be undercover agents) for his train of destiny to arrive.

25

His train of destiny was running late. Signs were pasted against many of the iron pillars indicating that "due to track work at Thirty-fourth Street, service along the ACE line is running behind schedule." The *A, C* and *E* letters in the title were circled and blue, as if captured in a sniper scope. Grover smiled. Around him, the bystanders (if they were, in fact, bystanders) milled and mulled. Some were plugged into their music players. Some were engrossed in the late edition of the *Daily News*. Some were engrossed in the latest issue of *People*. Some talked with their friends. One or two talked with themselves. Old folks, tiny folks, dark-skinned folks, pasty-skinned folks, locals, tourists, tourists trying to be locals, giddy people, somber people, people in sunglasses, people in strappy shoes—all united as one impatient mass of humanity underneath Canal Street, awaiting the arrival of the uptown A-train.

Was Cain42 here? Grover scanned the faces, not quite sure what features he was exactly looking for. Serial killers didn't quite fit a physical type. Many fit a general profile—white, thirties to forties, larger-than-average in size—but those parameters were so damn wide and encapsulated so many people just here in the train station…heck, those parameters included Grover himself!

Then he felt the wind blow, here in this sunless world of cement. Down here, the wind always came first, followed by the train, as if the trains themselves were nothing but chariots yoked to zephyrs. The wind blew and the iron rails down below, the iron rails along the track, vibrated with anticipation. They weren't the only ones. Grover took a breath to steady his excitement. It would be very soon now.

Gentlemen tucked newspapers under their arms. Ladies stepped forward to the station platform's yellow line, but no closer. Mind the gap, whatever large city you were in. Mind the gap or lose a limb. Grover remained on the station platform and let the brisk breezes dance across his eyes, watering them. He almost looked as if he was about to weep.

Now came the train, the mighty A, halfway through its meandering journey from Brooklyn to Queens. It rumbled into the station, not a spot of graffiti on its sleek exterior. The image of the spray-painted, woebegone NYC subway car belonged to a long-past era. No, this was the revitalized New York here, set into motion in the 1980s and '90s, cleansed and purified and defanged. As the train squealed to a braking halt, Grover sauntered down the platform to the last car.

The doors opened with a hiss.

Grover stepped inside.

The car was already half-full, mostly with bright-clothed tourists from every part of the globe. Grover settled in the middle of one of the long rows of orange plastic seats and waited for Cain42 to enter. "I'll be the one in the mask," he had written. But what kind of mask would it be? As always, mystery. But any second now a man would step into the car and…

No one stepped into the car.

Grover frowned, craned his head forward. Where was Cain42? For that matter, where were the FBI undercover agents? He looked around at the tourists, with their cameras and their guidebooks. Of course. These were the undercover FBI agents. Naturally, they had boarded the train at an earlier stop, so as to secure the scene.

At least, he hoped these were the undercover FBI agents. At least That Bitch wasn't here.

The doors chimed, signaling their readiness to close.

And still no Cain42.

A harried Goth teenager bolted toward the last car, her loaded backpack hopping up and down with every bound the lanky girl took. One of the tourists spotted her approach, calmly rose, blocked the doorway she was angling toward and flashed something in his hand that Grover couldn't see but had to be a badge. Her pale face paled even further, and she stepped back.

The doors closed. The train rocked, and then resumed its uptown trip.

Next stop: Fourteenth Street.

Still no Cain42.

Grover pondered approaching the "tourist" who had the badge and asking if, due to Cain42's absence, the operation was off. Maybe they'd already caught him and this—the train, them, him—had devolved into nothing more than a precautionary measure. If that were so, he really would have appreciated being informed, and, if that were so, he knew he wouldn't be because they didn't care what he thought. They only cared about his usefulness.

Goddamn FBI.

Grover, getting antsy, got up from his hard plastic seat and did indeed approach the "tourist." He had an Arabic complexion, appeared to be in his late thirties and was draped in an oversize Yankees jersey.

"Excuse me," said Grover.

The man glanced up at him. *"دصقت ام؟"*

"Right. Listen, Cain42 obviously didn't show, so… what's going on? Is this thing still on? Are we all getting off at Prince? I just want to be in the loop."

The man blinked at him.

Grover sighed. So it was going to be like that, was it? Goddamn FBI. Grover returned to his seat as the train careered into the Washington Square stop, slowing to a halt with all the nimbleness of a rhino. This station was far less crowded than Chinatown's Canal Street. The demographics here were also decidedly more native than tourist. After all, there was no reason for an outsider to be here. This was more of a collegiate neighborhood, catering to NYU and chic Greenwich Village. The train doors opened and Grover almost rose to leave when an infirm young man wearing a nondescript brown ball cap and toting a portable respirator showed up at one of the entrances to the car. The Arabic FBI agent stood and blocked his entry, but the infirm young man in the nondescript brown ball cap whispered something to him and the agent backed away. The new passenger meandered into the car, his silver oxygen tank secured in a small black dolly with one wobbly wheel. He wore a long brown coat, a bit worn around the edges, with gloves and boots in similar hue (and condition).

He plopped down next to Grover with a sigh.

"Hello," he said. His wheezing voice was muffled

behind his oxygen mask. "I hope you weren't waiting long for me, Galileofan."

Could this sickly fellow really be…him?

"Asthma," Cain42 explained.

The train doors closed with a hiss, the train car shook with a rumble and they were off. With the doors sealed, there was little chance of Cain42 escaping (especially in his weakened state). All around the train car, in a cacophony of clicks, the safeties of twenty-four Berettas were thumbed into their off positions.

Apparently, the time for pretense and subtlety was over.

Grover agreed. He got up from his seat and stood in front of Cain42, facing him—and thus obscuring the sightlines of two-thirds of the agents. Before the government boys and girls took Cain42 down, Grover wanted to have a chat with him.

"So, did you read my book?"

Cain42 took a deep breath from behind his oxygen mask, and then looked to the left and then to the right. Many of the undercovers had left their seats and a few even had their sidearms at the ready, although none was foolish enough to lean a finger anywhere near the triggers. This was still a moving train, after all, given to sudden stops and starts.

"Mr. Kirk," declared one of them, *"please step away from the subject."*

Grover peered down at Cain42 apologetically. But then the costumed madman said the strangest thing.

"It's okay. I forgive you."

"I…"

"You should do as they say, Grover," wheezed Cain42. "Your friends don't want us to chat."

"My friends can wait."

"Why do you value my opinion so much?"

Grover opened his mouth to answer, but no words came out. The heaviness of the situation was overloading his mental circuitry.

"Yes, Grover," said Cain42. "I read your book."

"Mr. Kirk, I insist you step away immediately!"

The train suddenly began to slow down. Ah, yes, track work at Thirty-fourth Street. According to the colorful map plastered to the wall behind Cain42's head, Penn Station was their next stop. Penn Station was located at Thirty-fourth Street. The train slowed and slowed and came to a stop right in the middle of the dark tunnel, waiting for its turn in the construction-induced traffic jam to begin its approach.

Had Cain42 known about the construction when he picked the A-train? He must have. But why would he want to be stuck in a train car that he knew would be swarming with agents?

Cain42 leaned forward and gazed up with those dark, dark eyes. "Your book was interesting." He donned a pair of sports goggles, which had been dangling from around his neck. "I like the font you chose."

The font he chose? What kind of a compliment was that? Grover opened his mouth to retort, but Cain42 continued, softer now, almost conspiratorially.

"Now, you might think I'm putting myself in grave danger, appearing here, surrounded by all these people and their guns, but risk is part of the equation. And that's what's missing from your profile of Galileo. The sense of danger he must have felt. That addictive surge of adrenaline. I'm feeling it right now. Can you feel it, Grover? Can you feel the danger? You see, I forgive you, but I still need to teach you a small lesson. What better way to do so than by emulating your hero and committing mass slaughter in a public forum?"

At that, Cain42 winked. The motherfucker actually winked. Then he twisted the valve on his oxygen tank, flooding the train car with smoky chlorobenzylidene malononitrile.

Tear gas.

Unbeknownst to Grover, That Bitch was, in fact, on the train. Esme stood by the back door of the second-to-last car, keeping out any curious or antsy passengers who felt the need to wander from car to car and thereby invade a potential crime scene. The first person she had to turn away was a three-toothed panhandler, who agreed to comply if she contributed to his fund. She contributed, in the process revealing her packed shoulder holster to a few of the onlookers.

"Relax," she said. "I'm FBI."

Christ, it felt good to say that again.

"Sure, you're FBI," replied a fussy-looking man seated nearby. "That's what they all say."

"Who?" she asked. "Who goes around saying they're FBI?"

But he just rolled his eyes at her and returned to his *Wall Street Journal*. Esme noticed that it was dated seven months ago.

Freak.

Esme glanced back through the dirty window in the door and through the dirty window in the last car's door at the placid sight of twenty-four undercover agents, one dickhead and no Cain42. The train had left Washington Square and was already pulling into Fourteenth Street. The chatter over her earpiece from HQ indicated they hold position and wait, but where was the target?

Ah. There he was…looking like he was on leave from a cancer ward? This was their mastermind? This was the man who claimed on his website to have killed all those couples? Bullshit.

Although it was possible.

But unlikely.

But possible.

His appearance actually reminded Esme of Tom Piper. Six months ago, as her mentor had begun his slow recovery from his gunshot wounds, he, too, had been hooked up to a portable oxygen tank. She even remembered a picture of Tom taken from his attendance at the victims' funerals, a picture that had appeared in several newspapers, usually accompanied by a sensational headline such as Head of Task Force Returns from Death's Door.

Had Cain42 seen the picture? Was this his way of mocking them?

No, Esme concluded. That was absurd. She was projecting her own closed world onto the mind of a man she hadn't even heard of a month ago. Still, something else was going on here. Her spider sense was tingling. A man like Cain42 just walks (well, limps) into a trap? She reached into her coat and withdrew her 9 mm (which had been bequeathed to her, along with a temporary badge, only hours ago). Technically, she wasn't allowed to carry until she retook her exams at the firing range, but these were not ideal circumstances. Karl Ziegler was extending himself for her and she knew it. She was grateful. And she hated being grateful to a toad like Karl Ziegler.

The doors of the train were closing. That was the cue for the agents to take down the suspect.

"Are you going to hijack the train?" asked Fussy.

"Shut up," she replied.

"I'll take that as a maybe."

But before the agents could begin their approach on
Cain42, Grover Kirk stood up, obscuring their line of
approach. Why? Did Cain42 have a weapon on him?
Through the two panes of smeared glass, it was difficult to tell. Regardless, the dickhead was about to get
tossed, either by the frail loon in the oxygen mask or by
the agents eager to get him out of the way.

Esme glanced behind to make sure her own car was
secure. By now most of the passengers (save a few scattered boys and girls ensconced in their own isolation)
were staring back at her, as eager as she for whatever
was about to happen.

The train came to a halt.

"Goddamn MTA," muttered one of the passengers.

Esme was leaning toward the window, almost press-
ing her face against the glass, when the tank of tear gas
was activated. She didn't even see Cain42 don his safety
goggles or twist the valve. One minute he was chatting
with Grover and then the next minute the last car of
the A-train was opaque with smoke. Then the gunshots
began.

"Shit," she concluded, and yanked open the sliding
door. On the platform between the two cars, she withdrew her firearm. Thunderous gunshots continued to
ring out—*Bang! Bang! Bang! Bang!* Her white earpiece repeated and intensified everything, including the
agents' coughing. She reached for the handle on the door
and that was when she heard the first scream. And then
another. And then another. The roars of the gunshots tapered off but the screams increased. People were dying
in there.

Taking into consideration that smoke rose, she
ducked down to a crouch and tugged at the door to the
last car. It was difficult to open from her position, but

not impossible. It slid wide and the smoke plumed out. As her eyeballs began to boil (or at least felt like they were) and every meal she'd ever eaten began to rise up into her throat, she knew immediately this wasn't just smoke. She remained on the platform, pulling the door shut before the tear gas could completely incapacitate her. Esme's few seconds of exposure had reduced her vision to vague shapes and blurry colors.

The twenty-four agents inside had been exposed now for almost a minute. By now they would be blind, disoriented and utterly at the whims of a serial murderer who was wearing a fucking gas mask. She tapped her tiny transmitter.

"This is Special Agent Stuart. The scene has been compromised. Repeat: the scene has been compromised. The suspect's teargassed the train car. All agents on-site appear incapacitated, and the train has stopped between Fourteenth and Thirty-fourth. How should I respond? Over."

She knew exactly how she should respond. She should open the door back up, crawl along the floor, pray the poisonous gasses had risen enough to allow her safe passage and take aim. And yet—

"Copy that, Special Agent Stuart," replied HQ. "Hold for instructions."

Hold for instructions? How long? Until all twenty-four agents (and Grover Kirk) were dead? That said, she wasn't superhuman. If she entered the train car now, even if she held her breath, the effects of the tear gas would be instantaneous and debilitating. She needed a way to peer through the smoke, spot Cain42 and take him down from outside the car. But how?

And what if he had noticed her opening the door moments ago? What if he already knew she was there and was waiting? The screams continued, but they were becoming less frequent. Fewer men and women left to scream. Men and women with spouses and children. Men and women that Cain42 was slaughtering.

She considered hopping off the platform and inching her way to the last car's rear door—Cain42 would not be expecting her to come from there—but at this door, she served as a defense to every other passenger on the A-train should Cain42 come this way. Every option presented a dead end. But there had to be a solution. There was *always* a solution.

"Still holding for instructions!" she yelled. "Over!"

Silence. Goddamn it!

Maybe if she fired a couple shots into the door's windowpane and shattered it, the tear gas would vent out quicker and then—

And then the train experienced a brief epileptic fit, rocking back and forth. Esme grabbed onto the last car's door handle for support. It was a good thing, too. The A-train lunged forward, recommencing its trek toward Penn Station, and had Esme not grabbed hold of something, she probably would have been thrown from the platform altogether. Just then, the door to the second-to-last car opened. The fussy-looking man stood there, reaching out toward her with his arms. She grabbed one of them and let him pull her back inside the safety of his car. The door slid shut behind them.

"Are we going to die?" asked another of the passengers.

"What can we do to help?" asked another.

Everyone must have heard the gunshots, or at least saw the smoke, or both. She recognized panic in their faces, yes, but also perseverance. These were New Yorkers. They were here to assist.

"Back away from the door," she replied.

They backed away from the door.

Ambient light poured into the car. They had entered Penn Station. Predictably, a sizable crowd, milling with impatience, had gathered on the subway platform to board the tardy uptown A-train.

Any moment now, the doors would open.

Some of the tear gas in the last car must have dissipated by now, but not all of it. And who knew what carnage lay inside?

The A-train came to a stop.

Esme took a deep breath. She held her Beretta at her side, both hands around the molded grip.

With a chiming, the subway doors opened.

Esme launched herself onto the platform in time to spot Cain42 scurry out of the last car and plunge himself into the crowd. He was heading for the turnstiles. He cut a swath through the human forest with a long, serrated hunting knife. He slashed indiscriminately. A few people tried to be heroes and stop him. They received the deepest cuts. By the time he'd climbed over the turnstiles, his dirty brown boots smacking against them with a resounding thump, seven pedestrians were on the floor, bleeding.

Esme wished she could have stopped and helped them out. She wished she could have stopped and helped out whoever was left in the last car. But she knew she couldn't. She had a priority. At that moment a psychopath was armed and on the loose in one of the most heavily populated train stations in the world, and goddamn it, she was going to catch him, or die trying.

26

Penn Station in the twenty-first century was less of a train depot, really, than an underground mall. It abounded with the shops, kiosks, eateries—all the popular franchises. What else was a commuter to do while waiting for his late train home to Westport or Ronkonkoma or, yes, Hoboken, but grab a hot dog at Nathan's, a mass-market paperback at Hudson News and a chocolate-chip sundae at Häagen-Dazs? And this was the start of rush hour—4:45 p.m., according to the main concourse's blue digital departure/arrival screens. Penn Station was wall-to-wall with would-be passengers. This was the sight which greeted Esme as she bounded up the cement staircase from the ACE subway platform.

She also arrived just in time to witness droves of MTA and NYPD officers pour into the depot from every entrance. Word of the massacre must have gotten out, and in the span of seventy-five seconds, the police coordinated a complete and total lockdown of Penn Station. Esme wondered who was in charge, or if the local chiefs of police, Homeland Security and FBI were jockeying for authority. The airwaves were probably full of chatter, but she could hear none of it. Her earpiece must have snagged on something, and she no longer had it.

The good news: with all of the exits sealed, Cain42 wasn't going anywhere. The bad news: now the concourse was even more crowded, and locating the man among the masses had suddenly become exponentially more difficult. He'd stopped cutting his way to freedom. He was blending in.

Esme focused on what she remembered of his attire: brown ball cap, brown coat, brown boots. Hardly a costume that stood out, but maybe if—

There it was.

In a pile by a trash bin.

Sigh.

As she approached the pile of clothes, a hand firmly clasped her left biceps. Heart pounding, she immediately spun around, Beretta at the ready—and faced off against two SWAT team members swathed in body armor and armed with submachine guns, their laser sights pointed squarely at her chest.

"Put down your weapon immediately," said one.

"I'm FBI," she replied.

Esme reached into her coat pocket for her temporary badge.

The men pawed at their triggers. Their crimson laser beams concentrated on her heart.

"Okay, okay," she said, and lowered her sidearm. This was the second time in ten minutes that her identity as an FBI agent had been called into question. Exasperating. One of the SWAT officers reached into her coat pocket and removed her badge. Examined it. Showed it to his partner.

"We need to call this in."

"Of course you do," she replied. "However, in the meantime, do you mind if I leave you gentlemen and continue my pursuit of, you know, the crazy man with the knife?"

They ignored her and commenced radio correspondence with their superiors. Sighing, Esme glanced back at Cain42's brown coat, hat and boots. He could have been wearing anything underneath. As she looked closer, she noticed the gas mask and goggles he'd worn among the discards. He must have thought he was one clever son of a bitch.

Then Esme noticed something else—a fresh stain on the left shoulder of the brown coat. She knelt down to take a closer look. The dark stain was still wet, and contained two holes, one larger than the other.

Bullet holes and a bloodstain.

One of the agents in the subway car must have shot him.

All she had to do now was locate, among all the thousands in here, the man with the matching wound.

Before entering the last car on the uptown A-train, the first responders sealed off the area. They actually sealed off two areas—one to contain the crime scene and another to corral the hundreds of witnesses, which included those on the platform when the train arrived and those in the second-to-last car who'd peered over Esme's shoulder as the carnage began. Ideally, the witnesses would be separated from one another to lessen the likelihood of memory-bleed (wherein the witnesses' chat with one another about what they saw and their collective memories coalesce into an unreliable amalgam), but this was far from an ideal situation. There was a third, smaller area being set up now by the paramedics. This was the triage center. Two of the people Cain42 had slashed during his escape were already dead.

The forensics teams, with their kits and swabs and

digital cameras, arrived shortly after the paramedics. Scouring the crime scene would prove to be problematic, though. There was just so much blood spatter on the floor and walls of the train car. The slightest misstep, the most accidental nudge, and the fluid pattern would be irrevocably altered. They needed to maintain the evidence, if only to tell the story of this massacre.

They all knew how the story ended.

The forensics photographer stood at the threshold of one of the doorways, carefully avoiding the scarlet footprints (size fourteen) left by Cain42 when he made his getaway. She prepped her camera and did a quick count of the bodies. Twenty-five. Most appeared to have had their throats slit. Very deep incisions, too. The slashed necks also explained the sheer quantity of spilled blood, which was splashed every which way, across ceiling, floor and walls. Even the plastic-plated advertisements, with their dentist-enhanced grins and exaggerations of pleasure, had been Jackson-Pollocked.

The bodies lay scattered throughout the car, some on the floor, some on the orange seats, some half on, half off. Some held guns. Some were as empty-handed as the day they were born. None were at peace.

The forensics photographer took note of the smell of the place. Bitter. Perhaps a remnant of the tear gas or of the gunfire. Or perhaps what she smelled was soullessness itself.

She turned away from the train car, took a deep breath to steady her lungs and then turned back to commence her photography. The memory card in her camera could hold countless images. Today it would get its fill.

Other amateur photographers had, of course, beaten her to the exclusive. By the time the police had arrived on the subway platform, every civilian who'd been on the train or waiting on the platform for the train had snapped off a dozen shots with their camera phones. The wireless signal strength down here was spotty at best, but not unheard of. Hundreds of low-resolution DIY images were already being texted and forwarded and reforwarded all across New York City, sharing the massacre with the masses.

The forensics photographer took a careful step into the train car. There was a body underneath an orange seat across the aisle. It was the body of a tall man. His back was to her. He appeared to be bald and—

The photographer staggered back, nearly dropping her camera. The man had rolled over and was facing her. His throat was untouched and his eyes were wide with terror.

Before running his MetroCard through the turnstile at the Fourteenth Street Station, Cain42 stopped across the street at a Duane Reade. He bought a bottle of water, a Milky Way candy bar and refilled his prescription for Ventolin, a short-term asthma preventative that would allow him to overexert himself physically over the next few hours with little fear of inducing an attack. The only side effect he ever noticed was an increased heart rate, but since he only took it before a kill, he never was completely sure that the increased heart rate was a result of the medication or a by-product of his pregame excitement.

He changed out his regular nebulizer for the Ventolin, activated it, pocketed the inhaler, fixed his oxygen mask to his mouth and, with his gas tank in tow, slowly made his way down, down, down and into the underbelly of Fourteenth Street. Halfway down the cement stairs, a young man offered to help carry his oxygen tank for him. No, thank you. Once at the platform, waiting for the A-train to arrive, he split his Milky Way in two and offered half to the young man, who politely said no to the delicious combination of nougat and milk chocolate. Cain42 washed the candy bar down with his water and tossed the empty wrapper and the empty bottle into a nearby receptacle. How he abhorred littering.

The killing was over now, but his heart was still galloping within his chest. Each staccato beat pumped more and more blood to his perforated left shoulder. No matter how much pressure he put on the wound, the bleeding just wouldn't stop. The sleeve of his left arm was drenched now, but he only knew that because he could see it. He couldn't feel it. The arm had gone numb.

He needed help, and he needed help fast.

There was the triage center down on the ACE platform, but so many of the people there had seen his face, if only for a moment. No, his only salvation lay outside Penn Station. So he moseyed toward the massive Seventh Street exit, which of course was under heavy guard by a team of SWAT officers. But he knew they'd lower their weapons as soon as they saw him. Because although Cain42 had borrowed the discarded clothes—the oversize brown boots and that ass-ugly brown coat—from a homeless man who'd been napping near the Manhattan Bridge, underneath them he wore the uniform of a transit cop, and this was the uniform they would see. They would lead him up the ascending stairs into daylight and freedom....

Except...wait. Who was that over there holding his coat, talking with those other two SWAT officers? She looked so familiar. Where had he recently seen her face...?

That was Esme Stuart. Galileo's Esme. Grover Kirk's Esme.

Timothy Hammond's Esme.

In the aftermath of the Galileo murders, Cain42 had

seen her photograph on TV, but he had also seen her photograph again as recently as last night, while perusing Grover's book. Esme Stuart.

And she had his coat. From which she could surmise that he'd been shot in the left shoulder. And, judging from the reactions of the two SWAT officers beside her, they were radioing in that vital piece of information to every other armed cop in Penn Station.

Esme frickin' Stuart.

Okay, so the daylight and the freedom would have to wait. No big deal. That just meant he had one more job to do. With as much casualness as he could muster (given that ten percent of his body was currently hanging wet and limp by his side), he made his way toward a nearby clothing store. Why someone would feel the need to buy jeans at a train station was beyond him, but more to the point, one of the two clerks currently in the store was a man in his thirties who might, in poor light, be mistaken for his cousin. The other clerk was a teenage girl. That made the man the manager. Good.

"I need you to come with me," said Cain42 to the manager.

The manager took one look at Cain42's uniform and didn't even hesitate. "Of course."

Cain42 led him toward the dressing rooms in the rear of the small shop. On the way, he grabbed two baggy coats—one black and one red—off a sales rack and tucked them under an armpit.

"Into a stall," Cain 42 instructed.

Now the manager hesitated. "A stall?"

Cain42 took out his .45 revolver (standard issue for MTA police) and shoved the barrel against the manager's right nostril. "Into a stall."

They went into a stall.

"Now turn around."

"Please don't kill me...."

"Trust me," replied Cain42. "If I wanted to kill you, I'd use something a lot more torturous than a gun. Now turn around or I'll demonstrate what I mean."

The manager, weeping now, obviously convinced he was about to meet his maker, turned around. Cain42 contemplated how best to proceed with just one usable hand and decided to let the two baggy coats fall to the floor. As the barrel of the revolver was no longer threatening the manager's right nostril, it was free to be used to pick the red coat back up and position its amorphous form against the manager's left shoulder. It wouldn't silence the gunshot as effectively as he might have wished, but desperate times called for desperate measures, etc.

And so: bang.

The manager fainted.

Cain42 tucked his revolver back into its holster and carefully slid the baggy black coat over his torso. He checked in the mirror, making sure it both covered his uniform and that his shoulder wound wasn't seeping through the material. Good and good. After hanging his gun belt on the stall's hook (because ordinary folks in baggy black coats regrettably weren't allowed to carry firearms in New York State), he returned to the front of the store, where the teenage clerk still stood, using the store computer's internet to Tweet her experiences with all eighty-three of her closest buds. He grabbed a wool hat off a rotating rack and waved goodbye. She didn't even notice.

The manager had a solid alibi and couldn't have been the same man who arrived only minutes earlier on the uptown A-train, but in a hunt, any amount of misdirection slowed the hunter down, and Cain42 very much did not enjoy his current role as prey. He spotted Esme again,

halfway across the concourse. More SWAT officers had
gathered around her now. It looked as if she was giving
them orders. She still held the brown coat in her right
hand. And in her left...

She had his hunting knife, sheath and all.

How had she gotten his hunting knife? Cain42
patted himself down. After climbing over the turnstile
and sheathing the knife, he must have tucked it into the
pocket of the coat. Such a stupid mistake! The gunshot wound must have rattled his nerves more than he
thought.

Such a stupid mistake because his fingerprints were
on the handle of that knife.

It was his fault. He'd broken one of his own cardinal
rules and used the same knife numerous times. It wasn't
an especially good knife. In fact, it cut unevenly. But
that was why he preferred it. When he buried that cheap
blade into flesh, he just knew it had to hurt.

Esme—and the coat, and the knife—trundled back
down the steps to the ACE platform, and Cain42 followed her into the lion's den of cops and witnesses. Daylight and freedom would have to wait even longer still.
He needed to retrieve that knife, and had to hope he
wasn't recognized. And if he was, well, he would just
have to get creative again.

Tom was so slumber-deep into REM that even his
dreams were dreaming. So it took more than the usual
prodding, poking and nudging for Penelope Sue to wake
him up. She had to resort to shoving. When Tom woke
up, he was on the carpet. He was disoriented—and to
make matters worse, Penelope Sue had the TV news
blasting and the male reporter's voice sounded as if it
was being shouted into his ears. What time was it? He'd

returned from Hoboken around noon, after handing Jefferson Harbinger off to a team of federal agents, who would be escorting the whacko back to Switzerland so he could hand over to them the server, and with it the keys to Cain42's website. But Tom's end of the operation was over. The case had been solved. It was time for a long-overdue nap.

And now Penelope Sue had interrupted his nap. Since the sun was still out, he couldn't have been asleep for very long.

"Are you awake?" she asked him. She was still on the bed and was staring down at him the same way a pet owner stares down at an unruly dog.

He was not amused.

Then she pointed to the TV. "Look."

"Penelope Sue…"

"Look, you fool!"

He looked.

The station was NY1. The broadcast was live. The story was the massacre at Penn Station.

Tom leaned on the bed for support and pulled himself erect. Two minutes later, he was out the door.

While the uptown A-train was resting comfortably beside its platform in Penn Station, the downtown C-train, expected to dock across the platform, was still stuck in a tunnel, impatiently awaiting clearance to continue its journey. The impatience was clearly shared by its passengers and by its conductor, a round man named Chester London who lived at Fifty-nine Gelston Avenue in Brooklyn, New York, and who suffered from serious attention deficit disorder. That was why he'd applied for the job at the MTA so many years ago. What better job for a person with ADD than the operation of a subway train? For him, the world was always go-go-go.

Except for right now.

He hopped up and down on his seat in his small compartment and fingered the levers in front of him. They were so close to Penn Station. Surely whatever was going down there had been taken care of by now, right? As a passenger he was at the mercy of the machine, but as a conductor, didn't he have the right—no, the duty—to get his people to their destination?

Chester London fidgeted in his seat. Would they actually fire him if he did his job? His was a union position, after all, and in his years at the MTA, he'd made a lot of pals. His passengers would be grateful. His ADD would be eternally grateful. The bosses might suspend him, but suspension was just an excuse to go on vacation. When was the last time he'd been to Atlantic City? It was before Velma died, that's for sure.

Fuck it.

He shifted the brake lever forward. Penn Station, here we come.

Confident that the SWAT officers had taken up her cause and were actively searching for a man with a shoulder wound, Esme had returned to the platform to check on the status of the wounded. So many more victims, but soon it would be over, right? Penn Station was in lockdown. Not even Cain42 could walk through walls.

In fact, she had proof of his tangibility in her hands. This coat had been part of his disguise. She hefted its weight in her hands. No, Cain42 was real. And that made him fallible. And today he would fail.

She took note of the detectives walking the A-train's last car. Soon she would head over there to give her statement. She knew she would be delivering her statement on today's events many, many times before this nightmare was truly over. She also would be turning over the coat, and the knife she'd uncovered in its deep pockets. The knife she knew would be especially valuable. Murder weapons always were.

The echoes of the Galileo case were unmistakable.

Had she made the right choice?

As Cain42 approached her from the shadows, the same question resonated through his mind. Creeping up to her like this was foolhardy. His risk of exposure was enormous. He neared her now. She didn't know he was there. His heart quickened. It felt good.

Tom noticed him, though. Tom was descending the stairs toward the platform and spotted Esme immediately. He always did. He saw Cain42 come at her from behind and he tried to quicken his pace, but the lack of sleep had left his body uncooperative. He opened his mouth to shout out a warning, but the headlights of the C-train were within view now, and as with lightning, the thunder quickly followed, rumbling itself into a monstrous angry bellow.

Cain42 reached out. But he didn't pull to retrieve the coat. No, with the onrush of the train, he had a better idea now.

He pushed.

And Tom Piper watched from afar as Esme and the coat went toppling down toward the train tracks and the impatient C, forty-four tons of stainless steel per car, roared home.

27

The C-train came to a stop at roughly the same position it always reached at this platform (at least when Chester London was at the brake). He had seen the woman on the tracks, but by then he had been reaching for the brake already. Trains took time to slow down. He knew he wouldn't be held accountable...unless, of course, the woman on the tracks had been the reason for the red light.

He left his compartment and rushed out to the platform. Everyone stared in silent shock at the spot on the tracks where Esme fell, which was now covered by the second-to-last car of the C-train. The tragedy had turned the hundreds of people into mute, gawking statues.

All but one, that is. Tom Piper approached the back of the train. Cain42 had scurried away when he'd realized everyone's attention was fixed on Esme, but even if the monster had remained there on the platform, Tom would still have bypassed him for her. The gray-haired special agent climbed down to the tracks. He refused to believe she was dead. He didn't know what he could do to help her, but God help him, he was going to try.

Chester, meanwhile, noticed ragged bits of the long

brown coat caught up in the front wheels. The woman had been holding that coat. Still, there wasn't any blood on the subway car. That had to indicate something, didn't it?

Tom was on his stomach now and peering into the dark underbelly of the C-train. He lay in the one-and-a-half foot ravine between the subway's two main rails, among potato chip wrappers and rat feces. He ignored it all.

"I need a flashlight!" he called out.

Two of the paramedics who'd been manning the triage center were already climbing down to the tracks. One had a flashlight and handed it to him. Tom shone the beam along the undercarriage.

The other paramedic had a body bag.

"It's Tom!" His voice cracked, like old leather. He needed water. *"Can you hear me?"*

He crawled farther, now half-underneath the subway car. If he could fit like this, perhaps she'd been able to. He peered forward. A pair of yellow eyes peered back at him. They belonged to a furry rat the size of a puppy. The plump rodent squeaked a curse at him and then scampered off.

Tom crawled another few feet forward. He was now completely under the aft of the last car. The flashlight beam extended to the last car's fore section, but no farther. He heard more squeaking, but no breathing. No Esme.

To make matters worse, the folks on the platform had recovered from their horror and had recommenced their chattering gossip. But at least they'd exhibited a few minutes of awe. At least they hadn't yet become too desensitized.

Not all of the folks on the platform had recovered. One

in particular was drowning ocean-deep in post-traumatic stress. The paramedics couldn't find anything wrong with Grover physically, aside from the typical aftereffects of prolonged tear gas (a mind-splitting headache, which they treated with Tylenol; and excess phlegm, which they treated with an empty plastic cup for him to spit into). No, the injuries he was suffering were invisible and thus all the more deadly.

For the past ten minutes, a veteran NYPD detective named Chuck Rowling had been attempting to get something, anything, out of the poor man that could help add order to the chaos in the last car. Rowling knew there was another FBI agent on the train, Esme Stuart, but his Herculean task was to wrangle some sense out of this witness who was so obviously still in shock.

Then the woman was pushed to the tracks, and Rowling's interview stopped. He saw the man who did it and, as the train braked to its screeching halt at the other end of the platform, watched the black-coated assailant casually make his way back to the turnstile. With one hand on his holstered sidearm, Chuck Rowling was in pursuit.

His other hand went for his radio.

"She's breathing!" shouted someone, and Rowling, by instinct, turned to look. The voice came from the subway train—no, below the subway train. The woman was alive? How was that even—

Rowling turned back to look for the man in the black coat, but he was gone.

How Esme survived her showdown with the C-train was not as miraculous as it was ironic: the knife saved her life.

It took her body two-point-three seconds to travel the

five feet from the platform to the tracks, and not once did Esme's neurons fire up the notion of survival. Or rather, they did, but in their own mischievous ways. To shield her psyche from what was about to be an inevitable violent end to its existence, her subconscious culled for her a pleasant memory from years ago, almost eight years ago to the day: a delightful episode from Sophie's first Thanksgiving.

Sophie's first Thanksgiving began with a wintry early-morning road trip from Oyster Bay up to Rafe's parents' house in Sullivan County. No, actually, Sophie's first Thanksgiving began at 4:34 a.m., when she awoke crying and Esme awoke yawning and mother and daughter sat on the sofa and watched *Home Alone*. When Rafe finally joined them at around six, sauntering into the living room like a brain-starved zombie, he at least had the good sense not to ask what she was doing up.

What had woken Sophie up was gas. For some reason, her metabolism wasn't tolerating any of the formula they bought. She was fine with (and eager for) breast milk, but the formula gave her an upset stomach and that meant lots of crying and spitting. And Sophie spat milk as if she were a faucet. One minute she could be playing with a toy and the next, the toy and much of the carpet would be both white and wet. Esme was convinced that the child spat out far more milk than she consumed, that somewhere a separate universe was supplying her with excess milk, but, ah, well. According to the books she read (and she read many), infants spat up about as regularly as they slapped themselves in the face with their tiny hands, which is to say often.

So they got in the car around seven and, on the way, Esme breast-fed her until Sophie napped, and then Esme napped, and then there they were in Sullivan County.

Lester and Eunice were there on the front stoop to greet them when they pulled into the driveway, next to his blue Cadillac.

Eunice Stuart was the type of woman who insulted you in French, all the while pretending to offer a lovely and sophisticated compliment. Esme spoke French. She was not amused when, five minutes into their first meeting, the woman called her, *au français,* "city trash." It was no wonder that Lester got along so famously with Halley Worth. She and his late wife were cut from the same *bourgeois* cloth. And Esme meant *bourgeois* in only the loveliest and most sophisticated way imaginable.

Eunice Stuart wore an auburn wig large enough to nest a pair of ostrich eggs, and on that cold Thanksgiving morning, the wind was bending the grass and flapping the lapels of their coats and Eunice Stuart's auburn wig lay conspicuously unaffected. Esme removed the convertible car seat, with Sophie asleep inside it, and carried it toward her in-laws. Rafe offered to help, but she shook her head. She wanted to show them what a good mother she was.

All this Esme's mind provided for her as she fell to her certain death toward the C-train's steel tracks. All this condensed into mere seconds, as well as what happened next on that cold Thanksgiving morning, the payoff of the story.

Esme brought Baby Sophie over to her grandparents. They hadn't seen her since her birth and beheld her now with the requisite responses of *aww*'s and *ooh*'s. Rafe beamed proudly. Look what he accomplished, Mom and Dad. Esme was happy for his happiness. It didn't even occur to her that she was a bit jealous, that perhaps she wished her parents were still around. All that occurred to her right then, really, was one, man, convertible car seats are heavy; and two, her mother-in-law's wig must have been made of plaster. Fortunately, at that moment, Eunice reached into the car seat, unfastened its complicated array of buckles and elevated her granddaughter into her arms.

"Hello! Hello, there! I'm your Grandma. Can you say *Grandma?* Grand-ma. Grand-ma."

Sophie simultaneously opened her eyes and her mouth. And Rafe and Esme knew what was about to happen about half a second before it did, but, much like Tom Piper on the subway platform stairs, could do nothing to warn or to prevent. Not that Esme would have warned or prevented her beautiful little girl from, with a giggle, hosing down Eunice's overrouged face with about a gallon of semidigested milk. The milk went everywhere—on Eunice's eyelashes, up her nose, in her mouth—but most significantly, it splashed into her wig.

The wig absorbed it like a sponge.

Eunice excused herself, went inside, and when she met them all a few minutes later in the parlor for tea, she was wearing a floppy beach hat. Indoors. On Thanksgiving.

It was memories like that which made the mind chuckle and snort. It even brought a short smile to Esme's lips, as her body collided with the first rail. The bottom half of her body had conveniently landed in the depression between the two rails, but the top half of her body was splayed over the first rail like a drunken sailor over a pub bar. But her mind was far, far away from the emergency at hand, and it didn't even register with her that she was about to be sawed in two by friction, torque and train.

That was when Cain42's knife saved her life, or rather,

the combined efforts of the knife and, well, gravity. The coat, naturally, came down with her and, in fact, landed before she did, and also partially on the first rail. So when her torso, which had fallen on a precarious angle to the rail, attempted to correct itself, it rolled in the direction of the fallen coat. The knife, although sheathed and pocketed, poked back at her torso. Reflexes did the rest. She flinched away from the poking and thus rolled in the other direction. Her torso joined the rest of her body in the filthy depression between the two tracks and there it lay as the first car of the train passed over her location.

Unfortunately, that was when Esme snapped from her memory-lane stupor. Her subconscious, no matter how strong, could not in a million years compete with the cacophonous fury unleashed by so many tons of steel traveling so many miles per hour less than twelve inches from her face. It was the sound of ten thousand sticks of chalk being dragged across ten thousand boards of slate, somehow emanating from the inside of a pizza oven and washing over Esme's entire body in a hot and screaming wave. The liquids in her eyes began to sear. All she saw was darkness, heavy monstrous darkness, and she couldn't escape it, she daren't even move; she had to sustain it without going mad, but, Jesus Christ, it wouldn't stop, it wouldn't stop, it wouldn't stop....

And even when it finally stopped, it didn't kindly stop for her. And so she didn't hear Tom calling out her name because all sound had become a choir of tonal ringing. As she lay there, underneath the second-to-last car of the train, as Tom finally spotted her with his flashlight, her subconscious resumed its fanciful associations, and she thought about the ear-swatting she'd performed just the other day on Grover Kirk. Was this fate reminding her of what comes around?

Then she felt a hand touch her right foot, and she opened her eyes and tried to lift her head to see if Grover was there in person, perhaps to drag her to hell, but that simple effort of raising her head an inch apparently tipped the scales of her sanity too far, and Esme passed out.

She woke up on Grover's cot.

Detective Rowling had transferred his witness to the station, in the hope that a different setting might ease the poor fellow's stress level and elucidate a coherent statement. In fact, it was when the paramedics shifted Esme to the now-vacant cot that Tom first learned Grover Kirk was still alive.

He learned a few other things, as well....

"Tom?" Esme's brown eyes shifted left to right, full of confusion. "What are you doing here?"

He sat down beside her. "How do you feel?"

"Like I got run over by a train."

"Mmm-hmm."

She tried to sit up, and that was when she noticed her left arm was in a sling.

"When you fell, you busted your shoulder."

"Fell?" Then she remembered. "Oh."

She noticed the rest of her body appeared intact. There were cuts and bruises every which way, and her outfit was in filth-stained tatters, but she spotted no broken bones or missing limbs. Her hearing, though, remained fuzzy, as if her ears were stuffed with seawater.

Tom went on to tell her about Grover, and that, according to the security tapes, a man fitting the description given by Detective Rowling of her assailant had nonchalantly walked out of Penn Station with everyone else and was long gone.

"Why did they lift the lockdown?" she asked. There were still people here on the platform, but she recognized most of them. These were her fellow passengers from the second-to-last car of the A-train. Everyone else had apparently been allowed to leave.

"The manager of one of the clothing stores upstairs was shot," replied Tom. "When one of the store's sales associates staggered into the crowd, screaming, it created a panic. So the bosses made a decision."

"And let Cain42 slip away."

"From their point of view, they lowered the temperature on a pot of boiling water."

"Yet another reason never to eat a meal prepared for you by a politician." Then she asked him about Hoboken, and he told her what had gone down with Jefferson Harbinger.

"You always get your man," she said.

He chuckled. "I don't know if you're implying I'm gay or a Mountie."

"A gay Mountie."

"Mmm-hmm."

She smiled up at him, this woman who was the closest thing he had in the world to a daughter, this woman who he'd almost lost only a few minutes ago, this extraordinary woman.

"There's a long line of detectives waiting to interview you," he said. "Not to mention Ziegler."

She released a stoic sigh and nodded. Duty called.

To which Tom added, "So what do you say we get the hell out of here?"

"But…"

"You're in no condition to argue. Or drive, come to think of it. Hand me your keys, young lady."

"But…"

"Listen to me." He looked her in the eye. "Every man, woman and child with a badge is out there right now looking for him. Two more sets of tired eyes won't make a damn bit of difference. We've done our bit for king and country today. And besides, they've invented these devices now called telephones. You think your statement would be any different if you were at One Police Plaza versus on your sofa at home?"

No more protests. She handed over her car keys. And that was that.

Next stop: Oyster Bay.

Grover Kirk had made peace with his own mortality. It wasn't that—when he realized what Cain42 was doing, he wanted to die. But he'd expected to. Once the tear gas filled the train car, and once the gunshots and the screams joined the tear gas, Grover had waited for death to arrive. Would it be heaven? Would it be hell? Would it be oblivion? He was about to enter the Undiscovered Country. So be it. His life had been one of constant battle, and finally he was to be at rest.

But Cain42 had spared him. He had taught him a lesson, and he had done so by forcing him to bear witness to a massacre. Now, surely, he would be able to treat the subject of serial murder with freshness and vigor.

No, thank you.

Not a chance.

Never again.

He had located his car in the overpriced lot. As soon as he returned to his room, he was going to load up all the research on his computer, all of the audio files and interview transcripts and the book—of course, the book—and he was going to delete it. Then he was going to delete the bookmarks from his web browser. Then he was going to find the nearest seminary and…what? Run away? Hide? That was surely an attractive option. Not for nothing had mankind honed a superior survival instinct. Would his family wonder about him? Would they worry about where he might have vanished to and why? No. And hiding away had the added advantage of hiding away from them. He booted up his car's GPS. He would ensconce himself in some ecumenical retreat and he would know peace and he would be able to wash away the mistakes and misconceptions of the past. *Retreat*— what a perfect word!

Retreat, yes, but what about responsibility?

Someone had tipped Cain42 off, and although it was probably someone inside the Bureau, probably someone Grover had never even met, there was the niggling possibility that it was someone he *had* met, someone not inside the Bureau at all, someone perhaps who had sat at that poker game in the strip club and learned about the ruse from Lester's unstoppable mouth. What were the odds? How unlucky would he, Grover, have to be?

But that was a self-answering question, wasn't it.

Grover envisioned the poker game in his mind. He could remember who played what hand, who flopped into the pot, who folded early, who bluffed, who won big. All his life, he had been attuned to the behavior of small groups. It had allowed him to ingratiate himself with the survivors of Galileo. It had allowed him to become one with the denizens of the message boards. So, during the game, what behavior, if anything, was out of the ordinary? This was a challenge. He had just met these gentlemen. Who was he to say what was ordinary and what was unusual?

He needed assistance, and certainly not from the authorities. Where was it that Lester said he was staying? At a lighthouse? Yes. Nolan Worth ran it as a B and B. If Lester couldn't help him, perhaps Nolan could.

Grover drove east through the wild birth pangs of a late-autumn rainstorm. The lighthouse, the storm— all the requisite Gothic ingredients for the end of his mystery.

28

"Mother of Christ," mumbled Nolan Worth. He'd just banged his thumbnail with his hammer. Again. He was attempting to hang a mural that Halley bought at a charity auction. She wanted it above the front desk. But that's where he had his genuine Saginaw M1 carbine rifle on display. He bought that rifle at a flea market when he was fourteen years old. He bought it with his own allowance money and he prized it above all his possessions.

Halley told him he could keep it under the desk, out of sight. If someone tried to rob the place, they would be in for a surprise. She said it with a wink and then returned to her sewing. She knew she didn't need to say any more. He would do what she wanted. In the end, he always did.

Standing on a stepladder he'd built himself, on the second floor of the lighthouse he'd renovated himself, he gripped that hammer in his hand so tightly that he was convinced the wooden handle would split open. These days, he was rarely without his hammer. He even snuck it under his pillow one night. Just as he'd drifted off to sleep, it fell behind the bed with a loud clunk. Halley slept right through it. He reached behind the mattress and picked it up. When Halley slept, her lips were curled in a perpetual frown. He imagined driving the claw end of the hammer down and shattering that frown into a million pieces.

He sucked on his throbbing thumb and took another look at the nail in the wall. He'd had to go to the hardware store and buy heavy-duty nails that would support his wife's mural (which must have been painted on some special canvas that was interwoven with steel). The nail's head was almost as wide, and nearly as dense, as the male end of his trusty hammer. And this was just the first nail. He had two more to put up to properly support a mural of this size and weight...not to mention ugliness. It was folk art, which to Nolan Worth was just some salesman's phrase for marketing childish doodles to rich wives. Halley's expensive mural, for example, was ostensibly an oil painting of a lighthouse by the sea, only the lighthouse curved like a ripe banana and the sea was the color of snot.

Oh, what improvements he could make to the painting with his hammer...but who was he kidding? He was never going to actually harm anyone or anything. He was just a geriatric Walter Mitty living in a world of pipe dreams. He would for the rest of his pathetic life be nothing but a—

Bzzzt!

That was the front door. Were they expecting guests?

"Are we expecting guests?" he called out to Halley. Lester Stuart and his granddaughter were upstairs in their rooms. Rafe Stuart already had a key. He was certain there were no reservations scheduled, not for this time of year. That had been one of the reasons he and Halley had been so eager to take Rafe and Sophie in.

They enjoyed the company. "Halley, are you expecting anyone?"

Bzzzt!

With a sigh, Nolan dismounted the stepladder and descended the spiral staircase to the ground floor. The *ratatatat* of raindrops echoed and abounded throughout the stairwell. Millions of watery nails, mused Nolan, shooting down from the sky. He put on his innkeeper face and opened the front door.

The man who stood there at the threshold was sopping wet and pale. His puffy black coat appeared to be at least two sizes too big for his slim frame, but maybe that was the fashion these days. Nolan never understood fashion. The man was in his late thirties, maybe, but possessed such alertness and wisdom in his eyes that Nolan felt immediately laid open and dissected.

"They say once you're wet, you can't get wetter," the man told him. "That's not true."

Nolan stepped aside and allowed him entry. "Of course. I'm sorry." He closed the door. It locked automatically. "How can I help you?"

The man wandered the round room, nodding at the historical artwork on the walls. "Ever since we first spoke, I've wanted to come here. How often does one find a fellow connoisseur in one unusual hobby, let alone two? I've wanted to meet you for a while now. I just wish it were under better circumstances."

Yes. This *was* him. Nolan knew it. He was tempted to fall on one knee and pledge his life to his liege. Instead, he offered his hand in greeting and asked, "Better circumstances?"

Cain42 shook off his coat. His shoulder wound no longer ached. This wasn't good news. "I appear to be leaking," he said. "Can you fix me up?"

* * *

Penelope Sue insisted on tagging along. What an ideal opportunity, after all, for her to finally meet the famous Esme Stuart! And besides, as poor condition as Esme was in, Tom, with his two hours of sleep, wasn't much better off. Begrudgingly, Tom acquiesced, and occupied the backseat while the two women sat up front and chatted. His mind desperately wanted to nap, but his ears wouldn't let him.

The conversation began idly, as most introductory conversations did. They compared childhoods, somehow finding equivalences between Esme's urban upbringing in Boston and Penelope Sue's rustic early days on a Kentucky farm. What really hit it off between them, though, was their common guilty pleasure: Ringo Starr.

Tom did his level best not to groan.

Esme and Penelope Sue rooted for the session man, the humble professional. They spoke on and on about Ringo's underrated skills as a drummer and his place in history, and Tom, humble professional that he was, had no idea they could easily have been justifying their affection for him.

As they merged onto the L.I.E., Esme scrolled through her iPod and played Ringo's "Don't Pass Me By." By the time they'd moved on to "Octopus's Garden," they'd entered the rainstorm. Dark clouds were massed like fat vultures over much of Long Island. According to Penelope Sue, the meteorologists on NY1 expected it to freeze over by morning, and were warning commuters about black ice—a phrase she had never heard before in her life.

"Don't get much frost down in Kentucky, huh?"

"Oh, we get frost," she replied. "We just shoo it away before it gets comfortable."

"You must miss it."

"Miss it?"

"Well, I mean, how long have you been up here now? A week? And I know Tom's been too busy to properly show you around New York, not that he'd be the best tour guide. He hates the city."

"I love it." Penelope Sue smiled at her. "I do. I love that the weather's different and the people are different and the shops are certainly different. We've got a Macy's at the Red Fork Mall down near where I live. As soon as I fly back, I'm marching straight into that store and I'm going to ask them to change their name. That store at the Red Fork Mall may call itself a Macy's, but I've been to Macy's, the real Macy's! Please. In fact, I'm hoping me and Tom can attend the Macy's Thanksgiving Day Parade. I've seen it on TV but to be there in person, to see a fifty-foot-tall inflatable Spider-Man floating over Fifth Avenue? I love my home. I do. And I do miss it. But I am very, very happy to be here. With my man. Isn't that right?"

She glanced in the rearview at Tom.

"Hmm?" he replied.

"Exactly."

Now Esme checked the rearview. The scowl on her mentor's face was priceless.

"Does Sophie like the parade?"

"She's never been," said Esme. "We almost took her last year but she had a sore throat and with the weather being this cold…"

"So take her this year! I know me and Tom would love the company. Then afterward we can go to the ice rink at Rockefeller Center. Because if you're going to be a tourist, you might as well be a tourist, right? What do you say, Tom Piper? Think we can get you into a pair of ice skates?"

Tom grumbled something in response, but neither Esme nor Penelope Sue heard him. They were too busy giggling at the image in their minds of their latter-day John Wayne in ankle-high laces.

Once they reached the turnoff for Oyster Bay, Esme directed Penelope Sue first toward the house. She was desperate to see her little girl, but she wasn't so desperate that she would let Sophie see her like this. Her clothes and face remained an utter catastrophe. She let them into the house and told them to help themselves while she hopped into the shower. Before she left, though, Penelope Sue stopped her and asked discreetly, "Where's his crotch rocket?"

Esme blinked. "Beg pardon?"

"You know. The motorcycle."

"Ah. In the garage. Aren't Harleys called cruisers?"

"Take your time in the shower, dear," said Penelope Sue. "We'll be in the garage."

The older woman waggled her eyebrows and let Tom lead her. They looked like two spin-the-bottle teens on their way to a dark private closet. Esme watched them go, and then mounted the stairs to her bedroom.

Halley did not like her husband's friend, not one bit.

"And how did you get a hole in your shoulder?" she asked him.

"Will my answer determine whether or not you sew me up?"

"That's for me to decide, isn't it?"

He was sitting on the edge of Nolan and Halley's bed. Or rather, he was sitting on a brown towel that Halley insisted be placed on the bed before he even entered the room. This strange man was not going to bleed on her silk sheets.

Halley had her sewing scissors in one hand and a spool of black thread in the other. "Are you going to tell me or am I going to have to put this away and call the police?"

Nolan reappeared with the bottle of rubbing alcohol he'd left to get.

"What are you waiting for?" he asked Halley.

"I'm waiting for a logical explanation," she replied.

"I told you. He's a friend from *B and B USA*."

She cocked a mascara eyebrow. "Do you think I'm a moron?"

"Of course not…"

"And why are you still carrying that goddamn hammer? Is it your security blanket, Nolan? Is that what it is?"

Nolan glanced down at the hammer. He hadn't even realized he was still holding it. He handed the rubbing alcohol to his wife. She didn't take it. "For Christ's sake, Halley, you're always going on about your charity work and what a humanitarian you are. Well, are you, or aren't you?"

She glared at him, but took the bottle. Cleaning the wound was a simple matter. Halley had cleaned enough cuts when her rambunctious children were growing up. Certainly none of them ended up pierced straight through, though. With every application of rubbing alcohol, he winced as if being jabbed by a cattle prod.

Nolan watched from the corner of the room. Nervous. The hammer in his hands. A security blanket? Might as well be for all the good it was to him.

Now came the sewing. Halley unfortunately had to

sit beside Cain42 to properly stitch him up. The stench of the rubbing alcohol irritated her nostrils. "If you're just going to stand there," she barked at Nolan, "at least make some coffee."

He left them alone.

She dipped the needle in the alcohol, threaded it, leaned in and began her work.

It was far from painless.

"Are you his lover?" she asked.

The wounded man let out a chuckle. "No."

"Someone he served with in the war?"

"What war?"

Halley shrugged. She continued to sew. Then: "The person who did this to you, are they still out there? Are they looking to do it again?"

"I would imagine so."

"You're about as informative as a goddamn Magic 8 Ball."

He smiled, and then grimaced as her needle once again tugged on his open flesh, forcing it shut.

Nolan returned with the coffee. He placed it on her desk, beside her sewing machine. On the mug was printed a brief uplifting anecdote from *Chicken Soup for the Soul*.

"Almost done," she said.

"Thank you," replied her husband.

"Thank you," replied the stranger. "But I need another favor."

Halley ground her teeth. He needed another favor, did he? Of course he did. She tied off the stitches, stood and sipped down her coffee. Its smell alone was comforting, but not so comforting that she still didn't want to jab her sewing scissors into the man's shoulder wound, which she was more and more convinced resulted from a bullet. What holy hell had her husband brought into their home?

"What is it?" Nolan asked him. "What do you need?"

Halley eyed her husband. There was the hammer, yet again, in his hand. Why was he so deferential toward this man? Was there some kind of blackmail going on? She knew he spent some of his days at that godforsaken strip club with all those other retired buddies of his. Had they gotten themselves involved in something nefarious? No. The very thought almost made her snicker. He was Mr. Reliable, Mr. Middle-of-the-Road. He'd never even cheated on his taxes, and they would have been even wealthier if he had. They would have been able to afford that wintertime beachfront property down in Cozumel, rather than stuck here, impotent, in snowbound New York. She could hear the rain coming down even now, driving in icy sheets against the old walls of the lighthouse. She took another sip from her coffee, this time for warmth.

"What do you need?" Nolan asked again.

"A syringe, for starters."

"Oh, Christ, he's a druggie."

"I've lost a lot of blood," he explained. "I need a transfusion."

Enough was enough. Halley rested her coffee down on the desk beside her sewing scissors and approached him. "What do we look like? *General Hospital?* Look, I stitched you up as good as I can. If you want us to call you a cab, we'll call you a cab. There's an E.R. not far from here. I'm sure they've got all the blood you need."

He ignored her and focused his attention on Nolan.

"I'm AB positive, so it doesn't matter who contributes. I'd say a pint should do it."

"Oh, a pint is what you want?" Halley shook her head in disgust. "There's a pub across the street from the E.R. Knock yourself out."

"Halley…"

"Nolan, you get this man out of my house or I'm calling the cops."

She narrowed her eyes and stared at her husband. It might take him a few seconds, but he'd comply. He always did.

But he appeared frozen with indecision. So Halley leaned in toward her husband and whispered, "Need I remind you, Nolan, that there is a little girl upstairs. Do you really think it wise to have him here in the same place as her?"

"Don't let me down, Nolan," said the man on the bed.

"You know I'm right, Nolan," said the woman by his side.

And it all crystallized for him. Yes, of course. His wife was right. The little girl was in danger.

His cock stirred.

And he struck his wife in the right temple with the blunt end of his hammer, as hard as he had struck one of those goddamn nails she'd forced him to purchase for that goddamn mural. Halley staggered back, more confused than anything else, and brought a hand to her head. She glanced down at the hand. Why was it covered with blood? Had there been an accident? Someone really should call the police. Nolan, call the police. Nolan? I'm having trouble standing. Help me, Nolan. Please. Help me.

Her legs gave way from underneath her, and she

crumpled. Blood emptied out of her head like syrup, passing through the flap of scalp and brain the hammer had unhinged. It pooled beside her onto the carpet floor.

Nolan hurried into the kitchen to get a measuring cup. One pint, coming up.

Rafe emerged from the car umbrella-first. He didn't especially mind the rain, but he wasn't keen on getting the papers in his valise wet. He considered leaving his valise altogether on the passenger seat and retrieving it when the storm dried up, but he had no way of knowing how soon that would be, and he really wanted to grade these essays and be done with it. They were a collection of reader-response papers from his senior seminar on Semiotics and American Subcultures, and while they undoubtedly contained glimmers of insight, he just wasn't in the mood. The news reports about the incident in Penn Station had left him uneasy. He had no evidence that anyone he knew was involved, and yet his first call had been to Esme, and she still hadn't called him back.

Curious, he mused, as he slid his keycard through the card reader beside the lighthouse's front door. Worrying so much about his soon-to-be ex-wife—hardly the feelings a man bent on divorce should have. The lock clicked open and he yanked on the handle. This was one heavy door.

Rafe was on the first step on the circular staircase when he heard the footfalls behind him. He turned around, half expecting to see Esme there, that unmistakable look of love in her eyes, but instead he saw Grover Kirk. Grover caught the door before it shut and managed his way inside. He was as sopping as a fresh-caught fish and well out of breath.

"Leave, or I'll call the police." Rafe stood his ground. "I mean it."

"Your wife… It was a trap… Penn Station…"

"What do you mean 'your wife'?"

Grover paused to catch his breath, and then gazed up with eyes afire. "He knew about our plan! Don't you see? Someone tipped him off!"

"What happened to Esme? What are you talking about?"

With the frenzied energy of a madman, Grover approached. Rafe backed away, slowly climbing up the metal stairs.

"It might have been someone who was at the table!" the writer explained, spit flying every which way from his lips. "Your father would know. Or Nolan Worth."

"What table? What happened to Esme?"

Now it was Grover who was on the first step. Rafe stood on the third. Mere inches separated the two men.

"I'll explain everything upstairs. First, we need to talk to them."

Grover shoved past him and continued up the stairs. Rafe quickly followed him, clutching his valise close to his chest. By the time he'd reached the second floor, Grover was already at the front desk.

"Nolan!" he called. "It's Grover Kirk."

Rafe's patience had all but evaporated. He placed his valise on the floor and opened his mouth to speak, but then the door to the Worths' living quarters swung open, and Nolan Worth emerged, a hammer in his hand. Rafe noticed the tip of the hammer was wet and…hairy?

"Welcome, gentlemen," said Nolan, and he swung his hammer wide. He took down Grover first with a blow to the side of his head, and then struck Rafe, who, to his credit, was reaching for the rifle on top of the front desk when the iron struck him flat in the face.

Nolan smiled at his handiwork. What a man he was! His erection throbbed with joy as he walked over their limp bodies and began his ascent of the stairs, two flights up, to pay Lester and his lovely, lovely granddaughter a visit.

29

Her shower finished, Esme climbed into a nice pair of blue slacks. Her shoulder injury precluded any top she had to don by lifting her arms, so she instead selected a white blouse and very slowly slid her arms into its sleeves. Her coat and holster lay on the bed, where she'd put them before undressing.

She left them there, opting instead for her old red jacket she'd bought years back from L.L. Bean. There was no reason Sophie needed to see her with a gun, certainly not yet. Esme did still need her sling, though, and made sure to put it on under her coat.

Downstairs, Tom and Penelope Sue were snuggling on the couch. Apparently, they had finished their business in the garage with the "crotch rocket." So much the better. Esme didn't want to think about what they might have been doing in there on his motorcycle, which made it impossible for her not to think about what they might be doing in there on his motorcycle.

Then she noticed that, in addition to snuggling, they had a scrapbook on their laps, currently open to a photograph of Esme, nine months pregnant, in an orange muumuu.

"Hey, excuse me," she said.

"You still have that outfit?" asked Tom.

"I think she turned it into curtains," replied Penelope Sue.

Tom gave the windows a once-over. "Then what did she do with the rest of the material?"

"Are you two just about finished?"

They were. Penelope Sue attempted to sneak the scrapbook under her coat, but Esme caught her and demanded she return it to its proper place on the shelf. She grabbed an umbrella from the closet and the three of them rushed through the rain to her Prius. Penelope Sue still insisted on driving, so Esme hopped into the passenger seat and, once again, Tom Piper folded his lanky body into the back.

The streets had become rivers, so Penelope Sue drove slowly. Not an overcautious person usually, she'd experienced more than her fair share of flooding, and so she took no chances. She even pumped the brakes every minute or so just to keep them unclogged. It made for a jerking trip, but a safe one, and they arrived at the lighthouse without having once lost traction with the road.

Esme spotted Rafe's car in the gravel lot, parked beside Lester's blue Cadillac and...wait, was that Grover Kirk's Studebaker? What the hell was he doing here? Anxiety pumped through her circulatory system in the form of adrenaline, and left her light-headed and on edge. She searched her pockets for her cell phone, but must have left it at home in her other coat.

They parked in the lot, and chivalric Tom stepped out first, braving the torrents, so he could open the umbrella. He maneuvered to the driver's door and canopied Penelope Sue, and then they both hustled to the passenger door to protect Esme. They made their way across the muddy gravel to the front door and Esme pressed the buzzer. Her hands were trembling, and not from the cold. Why was Grover here? She pressed the buzzer again, and waited.

In their stateroom on the fourth floor, Lester was teaching his granddaughter how to cheat at cards. They were sitting cross-legged on the floor; rather, Sophie was sitting cross-legged, her limbs apparently made out of licorice, while Lester had his ass on a cushion and his legs stretched out and he still felt uncomfortable.

"The first trick is in the shuffling. Remember what I taught you about shuffling?"

"Uh-huh…"

"Show me."

He handed her the deck of cards. She took them, split the deck in half, placed the halves side by side on the carpet, lifted the halves' corners with her thumbs and jabbed her tongue into her right cheek. Rafe used to do the same thing with his tongue when he was her age. What had been an annoying habit for a boy was, Lester decided, adorable for a girl. With her tongue firmly in place, she let the corners of the halves riffle into one another. The cards mixed. The shuffling was a success.

"You've been practicing," said Lester.

Sophie blushed. "A little."

"That's nothing to be ashamed of. You think I became a captain of industry overnight? It took me years to learn the vending machine business."

"I like vending machines that have gummy bears."

"Nice profit margin on those." He nodded at her. "Now that you're a captain of shuffling—"

"*Princess* of shuffling!"

"My apologies. Now that you're a *princess* of

shuffling, let me show you how you can make sure you always get the cards you want."

He picked up the deck and fanned the cards out, faceup.

"Okay, so, let's say you want four aces in your hand. You see where the aces are right now? Point them out."

She pointed them out: "Clubs, diamonds, hearts, spades."

"Very good. Now that you know where they are, you can—"

Knock, knock, knock.

They both simultaneously glanced over at the door. Then: "Daddy!"

Sophie hopped to her feet, her licorice limbs magically bouncing into place, and she scrambled for the door. But why would Rafe be knocking at the door? Lester put down the cards and, using his granddaughter's bed for leverage, pulled himself to his feet. His joints sounded off like fireworks: pop, pop, pop, pop, pop.

Sophie opened the door, ready to embrace her father, but this was not her father. This was Mr. Worth, and he had dots of red paint all over him, and especially on his hammer.

"Hi, Mr. Worth," she said. "I thought you were my daddy."

"Do you want me to be your daddy?"

Sophie's brow furrowed. What did he mean by that?

Lester was now standing beside her. "Mr. Worth and I need to have a chat. We'll just be a second. Okay, Sophie?"

Lester joined Nolan out in the hall, closing the door behind him.

"What's wrong?" he asked. "Did something happen?"

"Like what?"

"We both know that's not paint. Has there been an accident?"

"Oh, no. It all happened on purpose."

He drove the hammer into the old man's chest. Ribs cracked like potato chips, and Lester fell to one knee. He tried to breathe, tried to scream and warn Sophie, tell her to lock the door, something, anything, but the blow had knocked the wind straight out of his body. He held up his hands and blocked the second swing, although the air filled with the crackle of more shattering bones. Rather than finish him off, though, Nolan just kicked him aside as if he were a troublesome pup and reached for the doorknob.

Grover watched it all unfold from the second floor, where he lay spread-eagled on his back. He was as helpless as Lester, though, and could only stare up the stairwell as Nolan opened the door to Sophie's room. Then he disappeared from view, and Grover shut his eyes.

This was his fault. He should have swallowed his pride and come here with the police or the FBI. What had he been thinking? He hadn't been. He was so eager to find out the truth that he hadn't bothered pondering the consequences. But wasn't that the story of his life? If someone were ever to write a book about these murders, the chapter on him would be brief. Grover Kirk: victim of his own frustrated ambitions. He shook his head. It was almost comical. And was someone pushing the buzzer for the front door?

Three or four feet to his right lay Rafe Stuart, facedown, the rifle by his side. If he'd only been a little quicker…but that was just passing the blame, wasn't it? No. This was Grover's mess. The least he could do was man up and accept responsibility for it. This wasn't self-pity. This was acceptance. Too little too late, maybe, but—

Two floors up, the little girl screamed. Grover's blurry field of vision returned to the stairwell, and he saw Sophie scamper past Nolan Worth—go, girl, go!— but she didn't flee down the stairs. She went up. In her haste, she, too, hadn't thought out the consequences of her actions. She went up, and Nolan followed her, and soon they reached the roof, and there was no escape from there.

Damn it, Sophie. Grover glanced back at her father, still unconscious. He tried to reach out to him, wake him up, tell him. Someone had to save that little girl. He nudged Rafe with his foot, and then with his hand. No response. Nolan had clocked him good, and one half of Rafe's face was so purple and swollen the skin had split right open.

Grover sat up. His head felt funny and his hair was wet. He tasted copper. His vision didn't clear, but at least he had his equilibrium again.

"Rafe," he whispered. That was all he could muster… a whisper. "Rafe."

Nothing.

His fingers found the rifle before his mind made the decision to pick it up. He used it to lever himself up-right. For a moment, he thought his head was going to roll clean off his shoulders, but it didn't, and he was still conscious, and he had the rifle in his hands, and he knew what he had to do, what was his responsibility to do.

The lighthouse stood ten stories, with a lantern room as its crown. Grover had eight stories to climb. He got moving, winding up the spiral staircase that functioned as the building's spine. He was ascending its spine. No, not spine. Helix. Double helix. DNA. What a thought. Third floor. Keep moving.

He pulled himself up with his right hand on the railing. The rifle in his left hand gained ten pounds with every step he took. His brain fluttered from the image of the staircase to the sight of his feet—one, two; one, two; one, two—and then he was on the fourth floor, and there was Lester, and he was as unconscious and batter-bruised as his boy Rafe but also still breathing, somehow, after the beating he took, still breathing. Good old Lester. Grover liked him. He patted the old man on his scalp and continued up, up, up, to rescue the maiden in the tower.

Esme thumbed the buzzer again and again. Only the rain responded, the never-ending autumnal rain. Meanwhile, Penelope Sue sifted through her cell phone applications and Googled the phone number for the Worths' B and B. Somewhere inside the lighthouse, a landline was ringing. And no one was answering it.

Tom took out his Glock, made sure they were all at a safe distance from the door and aimed his weapon at the door lock. He nailed it in one. The lock popped off and the three of them entered the ground floor of the lighthouse.

Esme took the lead. "Nolan? Halley?"

She wound her way up the stairs, and halfway to the second floor, she saw a hand and knew that wedding ring and rushed the rest of the way and knelt beside her husband. His pulse was weak but steady. *Rafe.*

To her credit, Penelope Sue didn't freak out. She didn't gawk at the scarlet spatter on the walls and ceiling or tremble at the gory smear of blood and pus that used to be Rafe's right cheek. She took out her cell phone and dialed 9-1-1.

"Grover did this?" asked Tom.

Esme wanted to say yes, but as much as she loathed the dickhead, was he capable of this? Sure, he'd experienced tremendous emotional trauma and perhaps… perhaps…was experiencing a psychotic break, but this? This was just—

Sophie.

"Sophie!" she cried out. "Sophie!"

No response. No sound. Esme peered up through the stairwell and that was when she spotted her father-in-law's twisted, purpling form.

"Give me your gun," she said to Tom.

"Esme…"

She held out her free hand. "Now."

He gave her his Glock.

She bounded up the stairs, peeked into her daughter's quarters, hopeful, hopeful, but knew they would be empty, as empty as the pit deepening in her heart.

She checked Lester's heartbeat. He was alive. And he had defensive wounds. At least there was that.

Still no sign of Grover. Or Nolan and Halley Worth, for that matter.

She continued up the stairs, closer and closer to the hatch at the top, and the rain, and the lantern room, and answers she was terrified of learning.

The lantern room occupied the middle third of the lighthouse's roof, and the middle third of the lantern room was occupied by a first-order Fresnel lens, almost twelve feet in height and rotating at a horizontal arc of two hundred and eighty degrees. The mightiness of the beam momentarily blinded Grover, and he stumbled back against one of the lantern room's thick glass storm panels. He felt so faint. How much blood had he lost? How much blood was there in the human body? How easy it would be to just sit down for a spell and just nap. *No. Think about the girl.* Grover rubbed at his eyes and his vision cleared, somewhat, and he looked away from the light at the rest of the roof, which was little more than a bare terrace, perfect on a clear day for sightseeing or on a clear night for stargazing, but tonight was just a wet platform, towering above sea level, and with Nolan Worth standing by the narrow railing beside seven-year-old Sophie Stuart.

One hand was snaked around the little girl's arm.

The other had the hammer raised.

Grover pushed open the lantern room door and raised the rifle and shouted, "Stop!" and despite the roar of the raindrops Nolan heard him, and faced him, and smiled.

"I'm glad you're alive, Grover! You can write another book! How do you like this pose for the cover?"

He twisted the hammer around so the claw end now faced down toward Sophie's soft blue eyes, which were only an arm's reach away.

Grover thumbed the hammer on the rifle. The rudimentary training the FBI had given him for Saturday's mock-execution kicked in. He held the edge of the barrel level with the target. Even with his diminished vision and unsteady equilibrium, at this range, he couldn't miss.

"Go ahead, Grover. I finally became a man tonight. Can you do the same?"

Grover could. He had Nolan Worth's chest in his sights. He pulled the trigger.

Click.

What?

Grover tugged again at the trigger.

Click.

Nolan replied with another smile. "You don't think I'd leave a loaded gun around, do you? This is a family establishment! My grandson comes here!" Then he returned his focus to Sophie, who was struggling to break free. "I'm going to make you so lovely."

Grover didn't lower his rifle, but he didn't move, either. Perhaps it was his concussion. Or perhaps his heart simply chose that moment to surrender. He didn't lower his rifle, and he didn't move, but he also didn't look away.

Once again, Nolan brought the hammer back.

Then…a bass drum thump of thunder: *bam!* But not thunder, not on a night like this. Nolan looked to the dark sopping skies. Where had that…?

But that question of his went unanswered, because the bullet Esme had shot, the bullet which had penetrated Nolan Worth's heart, at that moment snapped off the blood to his brain, and he fell face-first to the wooden floor. The hammer clanged free from his hand and lay beside him, a small metal corpse in the rain.

Grover watched Esme pass him and run to her daughter. She collected Sophie in her free arm and held her so very tightly. It was a lovely sight, he decided. He placed the rifle down on the floor, not far from the hammer, and sat with his back against the storm wall of the lantern room. It was time now for that nap. Yes. His head had been cracked like an egg. Ha, ha. That needed to be written down. He took one final look at the mother and her child. A lovely sight indeed. He thought about his mother. He thought about many things in that half second before his eyelids finally fluttered shut forever.

* * *

Tom watched Esme disappear up into the lantern room, and then returned his attention to Penelope Sue.

"They'll be here as soon as they can," she said.

He nodded. Still, there had to be something they could do to help Rafe, perhaps ease his bleeding.

She must have read his mind. "They've got to have a first-aid kit," she said, and the love of his life, headstrong and gung ho, went toward the open doorway of the Worths' living quarters but never made it all the way there because Cain42, pale, brown hair a mess, leaped out at her and slashed her carotid artery with Halley Worth's sewing scissors. Habit drove Tom to reach for his gun, but it was gone, it was upstairs, and Cain42 stared him down, and the ever-perceptive sadist inside of Cain42 concluded from the look of sudden utter despair on this man's face that leaving him alive would be far crueler than cutting him down. Tom tried to stop the madman's rush for the stairs, but overwhelming emotions dulled his tactics, and Cain42 easily evaded, descending down the lighthouse's spine and out the front door, into night light and freedom.

30

"I told you two weeks," said Dr. Rosen. She had a cold, and each of her throaty coughing fits was now punctuated by a ten-second concerto of snotty sniffles. "But given recent events, perhaps we should table that deadline."

"No," replied Rafe. He was the one in the hospital bed. His cheek was thickly bandaged. The painkillers kept him from screaming. Screaming would have ripped open his stitches.

Beside him, Esme sat in a folding metal chair. Her left arm was no longer in a sling, but her fall to the tracks still left a constellation of slowly healing cuts and bruises on her face. "No," she echoed.

Dr. Rosen, all four feet eight of her, was standing awkwardly by the far wall (so as not to spread her germs to her injured clients). Decisions made in crisis were seldom positive, and she wanted to tell them that, but didn't. The truth was, with what they'd just been through, any advice that popped into her mind seemed in contrast flimsy and inadequate. So she remained silent, and waited to hear the verdict they'd reached on the matter of their marriage.

"It was about security," Rafe began. "But that's what it's always about, isn't it? The maintenance of a pleasant and safe status quo. The white picket fence, etc. We achieved it, and then, six months ago, we lost it. Esme had compromised the security of our family. That is what I believed."

Esme pursed her lips and looked away

"I blamed my wife. I blamed the FBI. I even blamed our house for not shielding us from the outside world. That was its job. This is what we're told. I relocated myself and my daughter to a different home. I retreated."

"Fight or flight," muttered Esme.

Rafe glanced at her and nodded. "Yes. Live to fight another day. I was only thinking about the best interests of my family. It's something, isn't it? How selfish we can be when we're trying to do what's best for other people… how naive we can be when we're trying to be mature. What's the psychoanalytical catchphrase for that? I'm sorry. I don't mean to be hostile. I've had a rough two weeks."

He took a break and reached for the flimsy plastic cup of water on his small mobile table. Since he couldn't open his mouth very wide, he had to drink it from a straw. When Sophie had been in earlier, she'd asked the nurse if they had any bendy straws to give him, because bendy straws were more fun. She even had a red bendy straw that went around and around and around like an upside-down roller coaster. Rafe thought about Sophie and had to close his eyes for a moment.

Feeling a little better, he let the straw drop from his lips and watched it bounce a bit in the water. He returned the cup to the table and looked their marriage counselor in the eye.

"Do you believe in security, Dr. Rosen?"

"Do I believe it's important?"

"No," he replied. "Do you believe it exists?"

Now Esme looked her in the eye, as well. She opened her mouth to answer, but once again censored her knee-jerk reductionist response. These two people deserved better than that.

"I'm not sure," she said. "I like to think so. Otherwise, what's the alternative?"

Esme replied, "Living in fear."

And there it was. That was the alternative.

"You're not getting divorced," said Dr. Rosen.

"No. We're not. We're going to live our lives in our house and if tomorrow the sky comes crashing down, that's where we'll be when it happens."

"Fight or flight," Esme repeated, and intertwined her fingers in Rafe's.

"That still doesn't resolve the issue you had with your wife returning to her job."

He shrugged. "We'll figure out a way to make it work."

"That doesn't sound very definitive."

"Show us a marriage that is."

Their session lasted another ten minutes, and then Dr. Rosen said goodbye and left to return to her own home. She couldn't wait to crawl into her own bed and let two tablespoons of NyQuil cast their narcotic spell. They all agreed to have another session in two weeks, but Dr. Rosen had a feeling that would be their last. For better or worse, her clients had reached their own solution.

Esme chatted with Rafe another half hour before he, too, was ready for sleep. Given the level of painkillers being pumped through his IV, she was impressed he'd lasted this long. She kissed him good-night, smile to smile.

As she went to leave, he gently touched her wrist. "Check on my dad before you go, okay?"

Lester was on the fourth floor, in ICU. The doctors had done their best to repair his shattered ribs, but his lungs had also suffered significant concussive damage, and at his age... But he would recover. She knew he would. If anyone was a fighter, it was Lester Stuart. No, he would recover if only so he could continue to make her life as agonizing as possible. She watched his frail body through the glass. He would be fine.

She hoped he would be fine.

It was nearly 8:00 p.m. Monday's rain had tapered off sometime mid-Tuesday, but now the Doppler radar geniuses were predicting overnight snow showers. Apparently, it was going to be a white Thanksgiving. Esme buttoned up her coat and took the elevator to the parking deck. Her cell phone rang as soon as she started her car engine.

"We've cracked the pass codes on the servers."

"Hello, Karl."

"As of an hour ago, Mineola Wu became the new owner of Cain42's web page and, as such, has access to the names and addresses of every single one of the members. The list will be distributed nationwide in the morning. By tomorrow afternoon, I imagine we'll have at least half of them in custody pending further investigation."

"Are we sending them to a gulag in Siberia, Karl?"

"Excuse me?"

She shifted into Reverse and pulled out of her spot. "Never mind."

"I thought you'd be happy."

"I'm ecstatic."

"Funny. That's not the word that I was thinking of."

"English is a flexible language."

"Have you finished the paperwork yet?"

Sigh. "No, Karl."

"It's not optional."

"I'm aware."

"There are the health forms, the insurance forms, the tax forms," he said, "not to mention the AAR justifying your use of lethal force in the field."

"If anyone wants to question my shooting of Nolan Worth, let me send them a picture of my daughter. If they still aren't convinced, send me their pictures so I can show them in explicit detail how they can go fuck themselves."

This time Karl sighed. Oh, how she enjoyed that deflating sound.

She paid her five dollars at the gate and made it fifty whole feet before braking for a red light. Wasn't that always the way.

"Karl, you said you got all the members' names and addresses?"

"Yes."

"Even Cain42's?"

Pause.

"No."

"God knows how much it cost him to maintain a server in Switzerland. There has to be a money trail."

"We're looking into it."

But it would be another dead end. She was sure of it.

The light turned green. She accelerated, made it two blocks and then promptly braked again for another red light. Goddamn it.

"Anyway, please fill out the paperwork. I wouldn't want to have to hold your paycheck."

To her left was a bookstore.

"Karl…"

"Yes?"

"Don't forget to send flowers to Grover's family."

Silence. Then: "Anything else, Special Agent Stuart?"

He emphasized her title. She wasn't sure if he was offering respect, mockery or both. She didn't care. The light turned green and she told her boss good-night and she drove home, where Tom was babysitting Sophie, and vice versa.

For Sophie, the events of Monday evening were a blur. She remembered coming home from school. She remembered playing cards with Grandpa Les. But everything after that was mercifully locked away in some closet of her mind. Someday, though, that closet door would open.

When Esme returned from the hospital, she found Tom and her daughter at the kitchen table, playing Go Fish. The little girl was wiping the floor with the old man.

Half a pizza pie lay in an open box on the counter. Esme grabbed a lukewarm slice and joined them in the next hand. Ten minutes later, Sophie was wiping the floor with her mother and the old man.

"Had enough?" she asked them.

"Little girl," Tom grumbled, "I've been playing cards since before your mother was even born."

"Then how come you're so bad at it?"

Sophie grinned at him.

"Deal the cards."

"I think maybe it's time for Sophie to go to bed..." said Esme.

"After this hand," replied Tom.

Esme shrugged, snatched another slice and watched the two of them go at it one more time. Tom dealt: seven cards each, same as everywhere in the world. By the time Esme finished her slice, Sophie had all of the twos, sevens and queens laid out in front of her, and was arranging them into a little house, which ticked off Tom even more.

Oh, how she loved her little girl.

But eventually it was time for bed, and Sophie hugged Tom good-night, and Esme escorted her to her room. They talked about this and they talked about that and mother and daughter exchanged I-love-yous, and then it was time for eyes to close, and for sleep.

Tom was still at the kitchen table, shuffling the cards.

Esme put on a pot of coffee.

"Did you let her win?" she asked.

"You know me better than that," he answered.

"I do. I just wanted to hear you say it."

"You Stuart women are ruthless."

"Damn straight."

She sat down at the table and shared with him the news about the case, and Cain42. Through it all, Tom listened without speaking. When she was finished, he just nodded his thanks and returned to the cards, shuffling them back and forth in his weathered hands.

She filled them each a mug of coffee.

"I spoke with Penelope Sue's brother," he said. "The body got there okay."

"Good."

"He wanted to know if I was going to speak at the funeral on Friday."

"Are you?"

Tom glanced up at her, quick, then back to the cards. And that was the only answer he gave.

She sipped her coffee. Then: "So I was thinking about tomorrow morning."

"Tomorrow morning," he echoed.

"It's Thanksgiving."

"Want me to teach you how to deep-fry a turkey?"

"Sure, why not. Since we're spending the afternoon at the hospital, anyway..."

A smile flickered across his lips.

Esme mustered her courage and continued. This was not going to be easy. "I want to take Sophie into the city. For the Macy's Day Parade. I want you to come with us."

He stopped shuffling.

"Tom, I think it's what she would have wanted. Isn't it?"

He stared intently at the cards, as if he were anatomizing them for dissection.

"Tom?"

He put the cards down and found her with his eyes. "You are something else. You know that?"

"I think it will be cathartic."

"Is that so?"

"What's the alternative, Tom?"

"When I have my gun pressed up against that bastard's face and he begs me for mercy, mercy only I can give to him, and in that moment I make a choice...that will be when I get closure."

"So, what, you're going to isolate yourself from the rest of the world and go hunt down your white whale?"

"I don't have to do it alone," he said.

"That's right," she replied. "You don't. And that's why you're going to come with us tomorrow to the parade."

He chuckled and drank his coffee.

"What's so funny?" asked Esme.

"I was wrong about your husband," he answered. "That man is a saint."

She punched him in the arm.

He drank some more of his coffee through a wide, wide smirk.

Shaking her head, she rose from the table and wandered over to the stereo. It was time for music. She sifted through her CDs. Each album conjured different memories. Collectively, they formed the soundtrack of her life with Rafe, and with Sophie, a life that had almost ended, a life that had only begun.

Tom's voice called out to her from the kitchen. "So are you going to stand there all night or are we going to play some cards? We've got an early day tomorrow."

She smiled, chose a CD from their collection and pressed Play. It didn't matter which album it was. The music was theirs, and that made it good.

* * * * *

Acknowledgments

The following people, in alphabetical order, were instrumental in keeping the author from running through the streets naked.

Steve Bennett, Carla Buckley, Pam Callow, Rebecca Cantrell, Alan Corin, Heather Corin, Kelly Corin, Michele Corin, Noah Corin, Seth Corin, Sharon Corin, Shiela Corin, David Cromer, J.T. Ellison, Heather Foy, Kristy Hamer, Amber Hutchison, Miranda Indrigo, Alan Jackson, Jud Laghi, Mariya Marvakova, Rebecca Maizel, Meghan McAsey, Linda McFall, Nicolette Rose, John Russo, Brooke Tarnoff, Ted Wadley, Jordan White.

For their patience alone, they deserve sainthood.

Debut author

Joshua Corin

IF THERE WERE A GOD, HE WOULD HAVE STOPPED ME

That's the message discovered across the street from the murder site of fourteen innocent men and women in Atlanta. The sniper Galileo is on the loose.

Where others see puzzles, Esme Stuart sees patterns, a skill that made her one of the FBI's top field operatives. But she turned her back on the bureau eight years ago to start a family and live a normal life.

Now her old boss needs his former protégée's help. But is Esme willing to jeopardize her new family?

And what will happen when Galileo aims his scope at them?

WHILE GALILEO PREYS

Available wherever books are sold.

MIRA®

www.MIRABooks.com

MJC2811

REQUEST YOUR FREE BOOKS!

2 FREE NOVELS
FROM THE SUSPENSE COLLECTION
PLUS 2 FREE GIFTS!

YES! Please send me 2 FREE novels from the Suspense Collection and my 2 FREE gifts (gifts are worth about $10). After receiving them, if I don't wish to receive any more books, I can return the shipping statement marked "cancel." If I don't cancel, I will receive 4 brand-new novels every month and be billed just $5.74 per book in the U.S. or $6.24 per book in Canada. That's a saving of at least 28% off the cover price. It's quite a bargain! Shipping and handling is just 50¢ per book in the U.S. and 75¢ per book in Canada.* I understand that accepting the 2 free books and gifts places me under no obligation to buy anything. I can always return a shipment and cancel at any time. Even if I never buy another book, the two free books and gifts are mine to keep forever.

191/391 MDN FDDH

Name	(PLEASE PRINT)

Address	Apt. #

City	State/Prov.	Zip/Postal Code

Signature (if under 18, a parent or guardian must sign)

Mail to the **Reader Service:**
IN U.S.A.: P.O. Box 1867, Buffalo, NY 14240-1867
IN CANADA: P.O. Box 609, Fort Erie, Ontario L2A 5X3

Not valid for current subscribers to the Suspense Collection
or the Romance/Suspense Collection.

Want to try two free books from another line?
Call 1-800-873-8635 or visit www.ReaderService.com.

* Terms and prices subject to change without notice. Prices do not include applicable taxes. Sales tax applicable in N.Y. Canadian residents will be charged applicable taxes. Offer not valid in Quebec. This offer is limited to one order per household. All orders subject to credit approval. Credit or debit balances in a customer's account(s) may be offset by any other outstanding balance owed by or to the customer. Please allow 4 to 6 weeks for delivery. Offer available while quantities last.

Your Privacy—The Reader Service is committed to protecting your privacy. Our Privacy Policy is available online at www.ReaderService.com or upon request from the Reader Service.

We make a portion of our mailing list available to reputable third parties that offer products we believe may interest you. If you prefer that we not exchange your name with third parties, or if you wish to clarify or modify your communication preferences, please visit us at www.ReaderService.com/consumerschoice or write to us at Reader Service Preference Service, P.O. Box 9062, Buffalo, NY 14269. Include your complete name and address.

MSUS11